OUR RECKLESS HOPE

MUTED HOPELESSNESS
BOOK 3

LOVE BELVIN

MKT PUBLISHING, LLC

Our RECKLESS hope

book 3 of the Muted Hoplessness series

For Cousin Connie & Lynda, my "Diva."
Soar.
You're at home now.

ISBN: 978-1-950014-48-4 (Paperback)
ISBN: 978-1-950014-46-0 (eBook)

MKT Publishing, LLC
First print edition 2020 in U.S.A.

Cover design by **Visual Luxe**

CHAPTER ONE

-Now-

August

12 YEARS AFTER BSU

Ashton

We landed in *Kamigu* at an airport which was nothing more than an open field with a single, modest sized-building. Then we were quickly transferred into jeeps; our luggage following in a van. The ride turned out being nearly thirty minutes. Thirty minutes of my restlessness, wondering if this trip was the right decision. I could have interviewed Tori on U.S. soil and skipped her training for this fight. But no. The curious journalist in me had to gain a keener insight into this undisputed and awfully bizarre marvel.

The twenty-two hour flight was tense. I didn't want to run into Tori, and it was clear she didn't want to see me either. We managed just fine as I stayed at the front of the jet, using the same restroom as the pilots. Antsy Keyonna meandered toward the back a few times, just to stretch her legs. Other than swearing to having tempered eyes on her by a few in Tori's entourage, she didn't complain much about the energy. That was to be expected, I knew. So I didn't trip.

Finally, we passed through opening gates. Armed guards were near large, black SUVs. Soon, a village-like setting with small homes came into view. They were huts of varying styles and colors. A few residents could be seen in their yards, some even grilling. There were two children walking a dog on my right, and an older woman airing out an area rug. Most waved, friendly and inviting as the sun set beautifully ahead. After another half a mile, the terrain turned into a resort-like setting.

The jeeps split with mine going right and a couple going left. We stopped in front of luxury bungalows.

"Mr. Spencer," Taja, the driver, called out in a thick accent. "You and Ms. Lee are staying in this two-bedroom unit. Natalia there will show you around your quarters. Your luggage will be delivered to you momentarily."

As I assisted Keyonna off the jeep, I nodded. "Thanks, Taja."

"My pleasure, sir. Enjoy your stay!"

As he took off, having others to escort to their bungalows, a rhythmic sound hitting the sanded floor caught my attention. Just before taking off for the entrance of the villa, a lean, feminine body sprinted past us. Tori wore a hat with her hair in a ponytail, bouncing in the air. She was in full running gear with her face low and attention internal.

"We just got off a twenty-two hour flight, and she has the energy to run?" Keyonna trilled.

Before I could answer, someone else yelped, "That's right, champ!" A short, Hispanic man I'd seen on the jet called behind her while scrabbling with a small camera and a phone. His stride was broken, telling of his unpreparedness. "Straight off the $G550$ and into warrior's mode!" He tottered behind her.

Then there was a chocolate, short woman, heaving with a tight face after them. She stopped almost in front of the bungalow. Her hands slapped her kneecaps and clutched for dear life.

"Fuck that, man! After that long ass flight, I can't fuck with Tori's moody ass," she swore, out of breath.

Then her eyes met Keyonna and me as we stood confused by this whole fiasco.

"Damn," the woman hissed. "Y'all act like you 'on't know what we came all the way out here for."

Keyonna looked at me and I her. Then, as though of one mind, we both turned for the villa. A gorgeous woman with olive skin, long silky hair down her back, and chiseled cheeks awaited us at the door. There was a twinkle of wicked lust in her eyes when our appreciative regards met.

"Welcome, Mr. Spencer and Ms. Lee." She beamed while giving a slight curtsy. "My name is Natalia. Welcome to my home. I'd love to show you around your villa. It will be your home while you're here."

Keyonna gave her back to the stunning hostess and warned, "Peep the wedding band and act accordingly."

I growled at her, pretending to attempt a bite of her index finger in my face. "Ms. Natalia," I called out while peering into Keyonna's tired eyes. "*Please*. Show away."

"Just calling to check in before I get my day started."

3

I glanced around, observing the calm sky's orange, yellow, and purple hues, remembering we were twelve hours ahead of him. My heart rate had just stabilized after a long run on the peaceful beach of *Kamigu*.

"How's New York?" I countered.

Thomas sighed deeply. "Nothing terribly exciting here. I have Lucinda with me, and she's biting at the bit to get back home."

"I guess that's something we have in common."

"What do you mean?"

I scratched my head, feeling guilt when gazing out at the setting sun dancing on the rippling water. This place was too majestic for me to feel so peeved.

"What I mean is I should not have come out here. I could have easily done the piece from home. I believe Tori lives on the East Coast like me. I should have worked around her schedule instead of opting to fly out to *Kamigu*."

"You're in *Kamigu*. I've flown in for a day to attend a birthday celebration there. How could you not be in your glory, son?"

I stopped, eyes closing to reel my temper in. "It's been three days since we arrived and I haven't been able to get one word in with her."

"Is she refusing to cooperate?"

I nodded with too much enthusiasm. "*I* would think so." Then I took a deep breath. "Listen. Apparently, I made a mistake. I shouldn't have taken this project on knowing the history I have with Tori."

"I patently disagree, sir. I believe you'd be the one to have Tori McNabb reveal a degree of honesty most cannot."

"When? On the plane ride home?"

Oh. I forgot. I'm not allowed outside of the first quarter of the cabin!

"No. When you harness the professional mien you have and demand to be respected as a journalist, I'm sure you'll get what you need."

As I approached my bungalow, a feminine figure sat on the step of the entryway.

"Yeah," I sighed when seeing the woman wasn't my Keyonna. "I'll try that on for size and see how it works. I'll be sure to keep you posted."

"I look forward to it, Spencer." There was a counsel in his tone.

I dropped the phone and gaped at the woman, my head to the side. She lazily smoked a cigarette, dark hair in her face, and lips a natural dark shade as she peered back at me. The rolls in her abdomen were thick and pronounced from her lazy posture. Her hair was voluminous and wild, almost as long as what I remembered Tori to have.

"You don't remember me, do you?"

"I'm sorry to say I do not." The only recollection I had of this woman was her heaving when trying to catch up with Tori's manic run the first day we'd arrived on the island. "How would I?"

"'Cause you came to my momma's trailer to pick up Tori on Thanksgiving night back in the day."

That stunned me. I'd forgotten all about that. Didn't know how I could. It was my first time in a trailer park. I thought it was a euphemism for a low class of white people. Imagine my surprise to learn it was where the tomboy I'd been obsessing over had been born and raised.

"You're..." I thought for a second or two. "Remada?"

She shook her head, holding a pocket of nicotine smoke inside her mouth. I waited until it pushed from her nostrils and lips. "You mean Renata." *Oh, yeah. That could be the name.* "That's my sister. She back at home. I'm Treesha."

Oh...

"And you were there that night I picked Tori up?"

"Like a pussy fiend." She plucked her ashes into the bushes next to her.

My head swung to the other side, brows knitted. "I hadn't fucked Tori."

"Well..." She tossed her head in a shrug. "We all know that even-

5

tually changed." She placed the cigarette to her mouth again. "Right?"

"I'll let her fill you in on those details. In the meantime, you can tell me why you're here."

She snorted, cigarette hanging conversantly from her lips. "You was fine as fuck then, but you's a sexy ass muthafucka now. You still rich?"

"Who's asking?"

Treesha scoffed. "My nosy ass. But not like that; you off limits, bro. It's just..." She pulled from the cigarette, eyes plunging toward the ground. "I've always wondered about you."

I switched weight on my legs. "Why?"

She didn't speak at first or for a while. "Because that uppity Black school changed Tori."

Blakewood?

"Positively, I hope."

She shrugged again. "Mostly. But it fucked her up, too."

That gave me pause, my response rolling out slowly. "What's fucked up about Tori McNabb?"

Treesha flicked her cigarette onto the ground, stood, and squashed it with her flip flop. "I said too much. I ain't the one being interviewed here." The muscles in my face relaxed. "I only came to tell you tomorrow's your day to ask her whatever shit you wanna ask her."

"When?" I asked as she turned away.

"She's up at a quarter to five to start her training. You can slip in the gym around one. She's gonna cut her day short for you."

Tori's cousin didn't wait for a response before ambling off.

As I ascended the steps of the dimly lit dining area, immediately,

I noticed how sparsely filled the place was. That was but for the copper toned feminine stature in the far left corner. She sat stock-still, wonderfully postured at a table topped with a small floral arrangement, tea-light candles, and a tumbler one-third filled. Her impassive attention was locked onto me.

"A one-on-one with the champ without her handlers," I muttered. "This trip may be salvageable yet."

Her eyes followed mine, sweeping against the *Mauve* again. "Your little girlfriend arranged it after your controlling hissy fit earlier at the gym."

My brows raised, begging her pardon. When Tori's hard gaze didn't relent, I pulled out the chair and took a seat.

"My little girlfriend. Predictable," I scoffed, nodding. "Regarding my assertion earlier during your training session, that was not what most would consider a hissy fit so much as it was a demand of professionalism. I came to Indonesia to do a job, too."

Her head shook softly as she peered me deeply in the eyes. "Nothing trumps my training."

"But this trip was scheduled for Tyler Thomas," I argued. "Foolishly, I haven't changed the itinerary. Thomas would have never begun his work with you in between you sparring with a man who looks to have just completed a fifteen-year bid in a state penitentiary. I value my work, just as he does."

Earlier today, when I was told I was scheduled to finally speak to Ms. McNabb, it was not the early ending of her daily training session as Treesha described. It was actually a break in between, where she sat down with me in the corner of the makeshift boxing gym the resort put together for her. Tori was sweating and out of breath, sitting across from me while hydrating. I was told we had twenty minutes before her workout resumed.

Offended, I stood from the table and refused the conversation. Tori watched mutedly as I spoke to one of her handlers about rescheduling a dignified time when we could speak without distraction. Tori didn't utter a word, and after a few pleas from her on-duty public relations person, I walked out. An hour later, Keyonna came out onto the deck of our villa to tell me Tori and I would be sitting down here, in the main cafeteria, to begin the interview. I didn't envision us being alone.

I pulled the recorder from my pocket and placed it on the table. Using my eyes, I guided her attention to it. "I'm sure you've been made aware of the method by which all of our exchanges will be noted."

Tori's arm swept up from beneath the table, revealing her own tape recorder. "Oh, absolutely." Her tone was firm, though soft.

I nodded.

Touché...

Tori didn't trust me, and I honestly didn't give a shit. I'd been in investigative and feature writing journalism for a few years now. I can't say that all of my subjects were thrilled to share with me. So, I tapped my recorder and issued a nod to Tori, inviting her to do the same. Without wasting much thought measuring her energy, I decided to get started. The questions I would lead with were meant to flatter and disarm. Icebreakers were paramount.

"From the first day of your training, I saw the kids from the island were in the gym. I was told you were explicit in your demand to allow them free access to the facility."

Blinking successively, Tori's eyes fell to the table, telling of her lack of preparation. She was jarred, but visibly struggled to regain the control of her steed.

"Yeah. I'm a visitor in their home. I've come here for the beauty and isolation of it; why shouldn't they have access to the benefit of me being here?"

Nodding, I loaded my follow-up question. "So, why are you here? You can train virtually anywhere on the planet. Why come to Southeast Asia to prepare for a fight?"

Tori nodded, ready to answer. "Well, this is a special fight to me. Monica and I have been circling each other for years, examining and flexing. She's a heavyweight, and not a priority to reset my regimen for. Aside from that, I've had a few opponents I felt I needed to defeat before manipulating my weight to engage her. Gaining weight while conditioning can be a challenge. Monica's fast and a smart boxer. I needed a place where I could wake up to stable conditions and the people project positive energy.

"A trusted spiritual advisor recommended *Kamigu*. It's..." She rubbed her hands together then gestured to the caressing mild winds, the applauding palm leaves from countless branches, and the brilliant celestial bodies winking down over the resort. "... heaven here on earth. I was told it was sanctified and consecrated. This is where I need to be to prepare for the biggest fight of my career..."

My brows met when her intonation changed. I'd taken a sip of my drink, warming into what had begun to transition into an amenable exchange. Tori's attention was on my mouth. I realized I'd licked my lips and quickly hoped I wasn't loud with swallowing, not that I could imagine how she'd hear such a distinct sound from across the table. There was no music playing in the dining room, but the collective sounds of the ocean and general village around us created an audible backdrop. Rolling her eyes away, she shook off her thoughts.

"Words—at least not mine—can articulate the power beneath soil that bubbles over the island and water, encapsulating harmony." She nodded, biting and pulling on her bottom lip.

Immediately, I was tossed into a trance of yesteryear where that single act was the most revealing—unknowing—communication of hers. Casually, I attempted another sip of my *Mauve*.

"So, this spiritual advisor was correct."

Affirmatively, she gave a single nod. "Clearly."

"Is this your first time in Indonesia?"

"I've been to Bali two or three times. Last year, I was at a wedding on Gili Air island. It's beautiful." I nodded myself, appreciating that fact. "Some of the best fresh seafood cooked over hot coals. Have you been?"

"I've not. No. A business associate—partner, actually—goes regularly and has been imploring me to give it a shot."

Tori shrugged, but not in the empty sense I once knew of her. She was simply expressing indifference. "Not my ideal vacation spot, but it's certainly beautiful."

"What *is* the ideal getaway destination for a Tori McNabb?" Then I thought to amend. "For the purpose of understanding your appreciation of *Kamigu*, of course."

"My ideal place is for personal mental escape," she made clear. "My appreciation of *this* island is for professional retreat. They're two very different things." Tori was prefacing her answer. "I'm more of a cold climate retreater."

Not thinking much of it, I moved on. The last thing I wanted to do was prolong this session.

"At thirty-one years old, you're taking on an opponent six years your junior. For many, that can be detrimental. Is that why you say this fight is so important to your career—or special was the term you used."

"My opponent could be ten years younger than me, and not stand a chance. I'm the undefeated champion, full stop, not just for all the women my age. I will fight O'Connor and win the way I've always defeated boxers coming my way. Let's make that clear first. So, as to your question of that being the reason why this fight is so special, you can see the answer is no." Tori didn't flinch at one syllable. She sat stiffly, giving me her full, emotionless attention. "This fight being special to me is for personal reasons only." She finally gave a nod again, adding a gesture to her cocksure words. "It's special because it will be my last."

The tumbler held unmoving at my lips as I processed the shocking, unexpected piece of information a guarded Tori fed to me without probing.

The water felt good pushing against the crown of my head, my back, and arms. Thoughts flowing more fluid than my body.

Employee support and approval.

The concept hit me out of nowhere. That was it. That was where *B-Way Burger* needed to focus a significant portion of its efforts ASAP. It's where a few highly successful companies strengthened their brands. Increasing minimum wage, offering stronger benefit packages, and implementing incentive programs to incite confidence and a family-like environment company-wide, spur on acts of loyalty, and create a healthy workplace, decreasing turnover. When I reached the end of the pool, I pulled up from the ledge for air.

We need to focus on our biggest constituents. Our staff...

"She doesn't like you."

I cleared the streaming water from my face and peered over at Keyonna, who sat at a table working. She turned away from her laptop and my recorder to face me with buds plugged inside her ears, her expression loaded with curiosity.

"What did you say?"

"Tori McNabb. Either you pissed her the hell off royally when you met with her a few weeks back to introduce yourself or you've fucked her." I sighed, trying to switch mental gears. Keyonna had been transcribing the first sit down I'd had with Tori a couple of hours ago. It was something I, as the journalist, would do then turn over to the publisher for them to go over and make needed corrections when editing. Keyonna handled those duties for me, which allowed for me to work on other pertinent details of my layered world. "So," she asked aggressively. "Which one is it?"

"What makes you come to that stunning conclusion?" I swiped my itching nose. "Let's start there."

She shifted to face me fully, pulling the earbuds out. "Several

11

reasons. For one, I know you. Your questions were very surfaced. I've researched other interviews McNabb has given *and* what's already out there about her. You asked nothing that would reveal more information. Secondly, she shared about this being her last fight, but doesn't want you to include it. Why share it with you, a practical stranger? Third: your voice was flat, uneasy, which is so unlike you. With each female subject you've taken on, you're viewed as captivating. You're the king of finessing, which leads to my next point." She used her fingers. "Fourthly, McNabb PR'd the fuck out of your questions. Like your questions, her answers were shallow and pre-made. So was her tone with you. She was neither comfortable nor revealing. That was proven with your one question about the amount of time she's been fighting."

I squeezed excess water from my beard. "What do you mean?"

"Your words, and I quote: *I know you began boxing at twelve, which means your career has spanned over nineteen years. Nineteen years is an astounding track to have been fighting consistently...* Then she cut you off to correct you saying, *I never said I've been fighting for nineteen consecutive years. Yes, I've been fighting since twelve, but I haven't been competing consistently. Where is that printed?* Then fumbling, you add, *that fact was gained by way of a credible conversation.* Then *she* countered with, *a credible conversation that fits this context. I've not been competing since I started as a kid. I took a couple of years off.* That's when your ass fumbled with silence before apologizing."

"Okay. And what does that mean?"

"It means I can sense an established chemistry."

Shaking my head softly, I mumbled, "I think you're reaching here, cupcake."

"Okay. Then who was the correspondent of this credible conversation?"

I tossed my fingers. "It was so long ago..."

"Listen, all I'm saying is this doesn't sound good. And if it doesn't sound good, it won't read well. Get in her ass. Find the meat in her story. Okay. So she was adamant about you excluding the bit about her early retirement, something you didn't even press her on. Whoop-tie-woo. No one reading this will know that critical piece of info. You've always said meat isn't synonymous with salacious, but it can be just as captivating and entertaining." She pointed back to her makeshift workstation. "This shit is a fluff piece at best. I've supported your journalism career, but even *I* know it's more of a passion than a bill-payer for you. You have more pressing matters to be concerned with than to be flying across the globe for this weak sauce."

I scoffed, entertained by her scolding. Keyonna was adorable when annoyed with me. "Like what?"

"Huhn?"

"What are more pressing matters than my journalism?"

Her head dropped to the side. "Like where y'all gonna be living permanently. You've been in that apartment forever now. It was only supposed to be until you bought a house."

"Are we not looking for a house?"

She shook her head. "Jaquana, your New Jersey real estate agent, is looking for houses. She sent over another six this morning. The real estate agent we let go in Texas was looking. Hell, even I look from time to time and you shoot down each suggestion. *You're* the only person not looking, sir."

"Forward those six from Jaquana and I'll look into them as soon as I figure out how to be less shallow in my questions to McNabb." Smiling, I pushed away from the wall of the pool and commenced to backstroking to the other side.

Tori

"Hey!" I answered the scheduled video call.

"Hello, champ," Elle replied, her professional hat evident at the very start. She reached for something on her desk that appeared to be behind the device she used to call me. "You look good; nice and bronzed, and your face is amazingly clear."

My free hand went to my face, unaware of having blemished skin in the first place. But I had to remember who the compliment came from. Elle was an observant diva: beauty could be found in a multitude of places by her eye.

"Thanks," I mumbled, reclined in a chair, having my feet massaged.

I ran four miles on a beach floor in hot conditions a couple of hours ago. My feet had swelled and I needed to redistribute the water in my body after a hot bath earlier.

"Ed had Sam send over footage. Your new shoulder roll technique, deflecting right hand jabs, left hooks, and body-shots is smooth. *The Banger* may have another signature move!" she expressed with more excitement. Her smile then faded. "Your speed has improved in just days, from what I hear. And endurance is being added to your regimen beginning today."

"Swelled my feet like a mutha," I replied, exhausted by today's run.

"How's the meal plan going?"

I shrugged. "It's going...or coming. However you want to say it."

"Another shipment of your supplements arrived there yesterday. The chef confirmed he received it. Do you like them?"

"Everything healthy is bland to me, but I endure for the end goal."

"And how're the *S.I.* talks coming along—*or going?*" she dropped an octave.

Sports Illustrated...

I couldn't help my eye-roll. "Just as pleasant as a thorn in my side. I don't know why I agreed to it while training."

"But you did." That remark was a snippy one, causing me to snap into a more mentally acute headspace rather than the drained one my workout put me into.

"And I'm here, taking his stupid questions."

"Questions about your artform aren't stupid. They're golden. This isn't a back alley publication. It's *Sport Illustrated.* They're taking seriously a Black woman who has broken more records than any in the history of boxing. I think you should take them as seriously as they're taking you."

Bingo!

I knew she was on her bullshit with this call. This was Elle, my regulator here. Niceties and casual chatting were out the window when this part of her persona exuded.

"I'm paying for his trip to friggin' *Kamigu* instead of charging the magazine. I think that counts as taking this seriously."

"Getting the job done defines it. Let him do his job. It's why he's there. Put aside whatever history you have with him and show this guy why his publication believes your talent possesses the validity to engage with you."

My eyes rolled again. "I've talked to him already. It's not like I'm ignoring him, Elle."

"All I'm requesting is your professionalism here. Please consider the strenuous efforts on behalf of the *L.I.A.* family to make this feature happen. You're not just representing you, Tori. We're all in this together." She lifted a perfect brow.

I felt the bite in that scolding. It would have been easy for me to make clear she worked for me, and if I didn't have my mind cleared to train out here, there would be no champ to be covered by any publication. I could have reminded her how getting these opportunities was her job and what I'd been doing out here was mine. But I didn't. The worst part about being yelled at, at this point in my career, was Elle was right. I needed to remain professional.

"You're right."

"I know I am," she shot right back at me. "And keep this in mind: No matter what the details are of your history with Mr. Spencer, if he shitted on you, making the relationship go south, here's where he eats the consequences of his actions. The best form of revenge in any relationship is the ability to move on. You avoiding the inevitable time needed to get this done can be demonstrating a lack of maturity, not the tough exterior you're trying to project."

"Elle."

Her head fell to the side. "What?"

"Point proven. I gotta go."

"Go with grace, dear." Her sarcastic wit twisted the knife of her chiding.

Elle disconnected before I did.

And that pissed me off, too.

After the fourth ring, the call, once again, went to voicemail. Again.

I exhaled and tried to set my focus on the sparkling pool two feet ahead. I knew we were twelve hours ahead back at home, so where could he be at close to noon that he couldn't simply answer his phone? I shook my head, reminding myself I would never be one of those women insecure in their relationship.

"I know you're a Sag, but what's Deon, T?" Treesha asked from behind me.

She sat at the patio table with a laptop, burning cigarette, and a bottle of beer—her fourth in the hour, I noted.

I glanced over my shoulder. "Why?"

She shrugged. "Doesn't matter." Pointing toward the sky, she advised, "That's a full moon. And this full moon ain't a new one: it's active." I rolled my eyes. The second rehab program I put Treesha in had her come out deep in astrology. Oddly enough, one of the patients in there was into it heavily and had put Treesha on. I didn't mind her head being on something other than getting high. But it got annoying at times. Tonight, it was more of an inconvenience. I needed alone time. Traveling with my team could be draining at times. They were overwhelming humans, choking me with questions and/or orders. "That means there's a lot of shit shifting for you right now. The shifting could happen real fast, putting your ass on a journey you ain't got no idea of."

With my back to her, I rolled my eyes and sighed, "Oh, really?"

"Yup!" I could hear her clicking away on her laptop; the second one I'd bought her because she'd sold the first a couple of years ago. "Peep this bomb ass craziness. Mercury makes this sparking connection with Saturn-Neptune," she mumbled. Then her head whipped to face me. "You feeling triggered by life, Tori? Overwhelmed? 'Cause it could be one of those breakthrough moments." I gave her a blank look for an answer.

She rolled her eyes and continued, "Anyways! You need to depend on your Higher Power and what your heart feels is real and right for you. If you're feeling like you're getting beat up by confusion, it could mean I'm right, and you'll soon be on the right path of your truth."

"Well, right about now, what I'm feeling is the restless need to be alone." I stood from my crossed-legged position at the pool. "I'm going for a walk."

As I took off, she yelled, "You want me to come, Tori? It's late."

"This island is secure. I'm good. Don't wait up." I rolled my eyes again.

I loved Treesha like a sister—lately, more like a child—but I needed regular breaks, too. The flip side to it was her fragile sobriety.

I didn't fully understand her triggers but knew they existed, per the expensive ass therapist I'd been paying for her.

I hated this headspace I'd been in. Coming to Indonesia was supposed to be the best location for peace of mind. Emptying my mind to focus on this fight had been the priority. Instead, I'd been feeling cagey, not wanting to roam around alone. The island gave me claustrophobic vibes. And I was hungry; had been for hours, thanks to staying awake past my bedtime. Meditation down the shoreline would cure my foul mood.

An annoyed human.

Me.

CHAPTER TWO

Ashton

"Hopefully the backend is user-friendly as well," I noted. "At least, for us to explore so we can decide on it."

"Yes. Because that last program from *Syntax* was hell to play with."

"Yeah," I sighed, eyes straining at the screen of my laptop. "Simplicity is our friend."

"This is a great idea, by the way," the head of technology commented. "When I worked at *RBI*, I pushed for employee approval measures, but they viewed it as an expense without profit. As you obviously know, that's simply not true."

RBI owned *Burger King, Popeyes*, and other restaurants. Our marketing team had finessed Tim, the head of technology for *B-Way Burger*, from the competition with a package he couldn't refuse. The guy was innovative with endless knowledge. I'd pitched the idea of employee satisfaction to the board yesterday. It was met with a medi-ocre unanimous approval. Last night, which was morning Eastern Standard Time, I contacted Tim to set up a time to chat. Here we were, twenty-four hours later and he'd had three potential app devel-opers' programs for me to test out. Once selected, the app would be used by all restaurant-level employees to give us feedback on their experience.

"It isn't. Consumers love predictability, and that can simply be seeing familiar faces. Retention happens when employees are adequately paid and overall satisfied."

"It's what *Starbucks* has done, and it's been proven to be prof-itable, especially with an intimate product such as your regular morning java..."

My attention fled to the back of the restaurant, near the kitchen."

"You okay, dude?" Tim asked, watching me via a company's videotelephony application.

"I better be." My eyes dashed all around. "Let me hit you back."

"Okay, man. Be safe—and use those guns if need be." He discon-nected after that.

I was too preoccupied to reply in humor. Suspiciously, I wandered into the kitchen. At nearly midnight, I couldn't think of who'd be in this building. The supervisor gave me explicit shutdown instructions. Was he back?

Pushing through the flap door, my gaze swept the dimly lit commercial kitchen. I saw nothing, but distinct sounds of chewing drew my attention and steps to the right, towards the refrigerator. She didn't even hear me coming against the sound of her unraveling parchment paper to ravish another piece of cheese.

"Oh, my," I murmured. "I've never seen a rodent of your size before. You must be exclusive to this region."

Before I could finish my last sentence, Tori's full body was in the air as she yelped. The cheese had fallen to the floor, cubes rolling underneath the counters. As she grabbed her chest and struggled to chew the food in her mouth, I stood with my hand on either side of my waist, waiting.

"What are you doing here?" she asked, struggling to catch her breath.

My eyes rolled around in their sockets as I considered my answer. I didn't want to be rude.

"Working. Now, I'm seeing if I had an intruder."

"An intruder? Why are you in the restaurant at this time of the night?"

My head swung back. "I'll let you answer first."

Tori's eyes rolled slightly before she caught herself. "I was out for a walk and got hungry."

"At this hour? Aren't you way off your training schedule?"

"It's the same hour you claim to be working in." Tori's eyes narrowed and she rested all her weight on one hip. "What're you working on?" Her tone was laced with suspicion.

"I work around the clock, *KaTori*—" This time, my eyes rolled at that unexpected reference.

I hadn't spoken that name in years before seeing her a few weeks ago at the restaurant. It damn sure wasn't a fondness I'd once known. Tori was her professional moniker and the only one I'd use ever again.

She cleared her throat, markedly just as uncomfortable as I felt. "That doesn't answer my question."

"I had calls set up with my team."

"What team? There are more of you than what you brought out here on my dime?"

Snorting, I brushed the tip of my nose with my thumb. "*Royal Foods.*" Her chin dipped, claiming confusion. "The owner of *B-Way Burger?*"

Her lashes clapped, recognizing the name, possibly recalling my professional lineage. "I forgot."

My forehead stretched. "Forgot what?"

She shook her head. "You still haven't answered my question."

Tori was lying her ass off, but I didn't wish to argue about it. "I'm a partner and have responsibilities to the company. That part of my life never gets cut off. Then—speaking of who I brought out here on your dime—Keyonna listened to our conversation yesterday as she transcribed it and believes our entire exchange is surface. There are no reveals. Nothing you gave me hasn't been shared before."

"So?"

"So, I'm not doing my job." I found myself scratching the back of my head. "I'm allowing our past to interfere with the work I'm trying to do here."

"That's not my fault," Tori claimed with sass.

I gave her a pointed stare before turning for one of the freezers where I'd transferred a few bottles of *Corona* from the bar earlier.

"Can you have that beer?" she asked when I pulled one out.

I snapped the lid off with a bottle opener. "Sure can." Bringing the cold bottle to my lips, I took a generous quaff. "All on your dime."

Then I turned for the wood brick oven, hoping my pizza hadn't overcooked. Using the wooden peel, I captured the pie and pulled it out, sliding it onto a waiting platter. I sectioned it with a cutter, then gathered it along with my beer and headed for the door.

"Where are you going?"

"To eat and work some more."

"You're going to eat all of that alone? I paid for that!"

I stopped to pay her a glance. "I'll share a slice *if* you're open to sharing more about yourself. The real you outside of the ring and off-camera."

I watched her chew her lips, her eyes swinging back and forth below. "And a slice of pizza. I paid for it."

Unable to help myself, I shook my head. "It's my favorite pizza, and only dinner. I had calls earlier I couldn't miss—"

"I'm starving and it's *my* favor—" Tori's eyes fell in embarrassment.

Remembering my slip-up earlier, I showed her grace. "C'mon. It's getting cold." After walking off, I amended, "And only *one* slice! *And only* because I know Dr. Shaquana Wilson's nutritional plan has you trying to gain weight for this fight."

Her resounding gasp ripped through the air. "How do you know who my nutritionist is?"

"It's my job to know all the nuances of your professional life right now."

"Patti LaBelle, Young Lord, Viola Davis, Dave Chapelle, Jordan Johnson and Trent Bailey—before your involvement with Deon Johnson—, Stenton Rogers, the Carters, Bill Clinton, and the likes attend your fights, paying premium prices for seats closest to the ring. Does this inspire you during a time like now when you're training?"

I bit into my second slice of Margherita pizza. *My neglected taste-buds!* How could something made at the hands of flaky Ashton Spencer taste so good? It was still hot, a great distraction from what my senses had been disturbingly picking up from this guy.

I chewed and answered, even licking my lips. "No. At this point in my career, it's safe for me to admit, high-profiled people were invited to my fights and they came on the strength of relationships they'd already established with my sports agency."

Ashton's head swung back. "They were paid to come?" His voice dropped a few octaves.

I covered my mouth while laughing, hoping food wouldn't fly out. "God, no!" Jackson and Elle were going to kill me for my honesty.

"No. It was one of those things in entertainment when you urge your friends in Hollywood to come check out your talent. Someone you truly believe in. My people are tenured and know lots of the right people. The most amazing thing was, they were all invited once—and not all at the same time—and most returned of their own volition. No one was asked to attend again. Jackson Hunter explained that trick of the trade to me. He said, 'When it comes to family, friends, and Hollywood associates, you don't sell knives to people who don't need cutlery. You only pitch to those you know have an interest. This way, they'll come back for more.' And lucky for me, they came back, and some brought others."

I shrugged. "So, no. I don't think about who's coming when I train or when I show up. I don't care if no one's there but me and my opponent. I came to do a job, and the job always gets done."

Ashton nodded. "I've researched images of your ring corner and the reserved sections at your fights over the past seven years since your talent met celebrity status. The inarguably artistically endowed Ragee is often seen. How has he grown to be one of your most consistent supporters?"

I mentally stumbled at that as he bit into his slice of pizza. Ashton knew Ragee and I were friends before the world knew him. Then I had to quickly remind myself how Ashton had to be neutral, which was great because I preferred it.

"I've known Ragee McKinnon since I was kid—he was basically a child himself. I guess most don't know his father trained the both of us. Uppercut Michaels was my first official trainer. I met Raj at the gym Cut—I mean, Uppercut—ran in New Brunswick, New Jersey."

"And what about Brielle? She's seated close regularly." That made me laugh. "What's so funny?"

I squinted, playing coy. "I'm pretty sure everyone under the sun who knows my name at this point knows Brielle is my best friend."

His face fell. "Brielle, Brielle? *The* Brielle?"

I laughed again before biting into my pizza. "Either you're playing games or you've honestly not followed my career at all."

24

I could sense his mental head shake. "I've never been much of a liar in my life."

That struck me as interesting. Foolishly, I challenged that claim in my mind. Had Ashton ever lied to me back at *BSU?* Quickly, I switched thoughts. I hated thinking about *Blakewood State*, and rarely did since leaving. Though that was extremely hard after being scared out of my mind by a half-naked giant of an Ashton Spencer. He may have no longer been a star football player of a Division I school, but his cut chest, bulging arms, and rolling abs down to the plumpness in his oblique muscles together told stories of his former athletic discipline.

No, I was not interested in Ashton. I would never stupidly consider him in that respect again. It was that his body was hard to ignore when so much of his skin was exposed. Before sitting down with him for pizza and questions, I had to request he put a shirt on. Without a complaint, Spencer complied. That made this conversation bearable.

"We met my earlier days at *Love is Action*."

Ashton's eyebrows lifted as though surprised. "Oh, yeah?"

I nodded. "I ran into her at a few functions." A random thought crept in and I sputtered a laugh, quickly covering my mouth.

"What?"

I rolled my eyes, feeling silly about the memory. "Nothing. It's that, the last thing Bree was looking for at those events was a friend. She was never checking for me, exactly."

After a few seconds, understanding blossomed in his eyes. "Oh. Like, since you were up for grabs when Bailey wasn't?"

I gasped. "You knew about them?"

The general public didn't...until that stupid blog, *Spilling That Hot Tea*, reported on it with receipts. I was in disbelief about them having proof of their affair, although it had taken them years to discover it and by then, Trent and Brielle had been done and over.

"*Spilling That Hot Tea* can be useful in my line of work," he murmured, sporting a cheap grin.

I tossed my head back. "Ugh! You give those people views?"

He shrugged. "They're hard to ignore, man. But now I know. I had no clue you two were good friends."

I used my tongue to swipe food from my gums as I nodded. "How could you—if you weren't paying attention, I mean."

I believed him now. Ashton, like me, had been actively blind to my world.

He wiped his mouth, eyes not on me. I watched him toss the napkin before he asked, "Your support—and I don't mean your love life—who is your core support team? I've not seen your mother."

A rush of air vacuumed into my nostrils. "No. You haven't, but I have my cousins: Renata and Treesha. Ragee and I are still tight. He's married now and we both have hectic schedules, but we make sure to check in." Bizarrely, it felt strange to feel uncomfortable to share, "I *do* have my fiancé." I nodded, behaving like a weird human. Why was this so hard to speak? This was my life. "And oddly enough, I have my father."

Ashton's eyes burst wild. "Your father? As in biological."

I hummed, "I only have one of those."

"How did that happen?"

I flicked my brows, not really wanting to get into that story. But I knew I had to give something. This is what Ashton was demanding, and I got it.

Shrugging, I answered, "Got a call one day, saying my father wanted to meet with me—"

"*You* got the call or..."

I rolled my eyes, feeling silly for my obvious lifestyle. "My agency's reception service received the call, and it was pushed up to the top because of the father claim. My father has never been evident to the public, so I guess that's why they at least passed it up. My assistant got the call from my agent." I rotated my pursed lips around in the air. "I was on the phone with him a couple of weeks later."

"What was that conversation like?"

My brows pinched as I thought about it. "Strange." Ashton

laughed, spurring my own humor. "Very strange," I suppled while giggling.

"You wanna be more specific?"

"The man called after twenty-seven years. That's strange in and of itself."

"For what?" Ashton asked, sitting up in his seat. "Why did he call you?"

What was left of the Margherita pizza was old news at this point. Cold.

I pulled in a deep breath through my nostrils, lengthening my spine. "Apparently, his daughter was an up and coming fighter—"

"Really?" Ashton gasped, clearly into this story.

"Mmmhmmm." My head sprang up and down. "She was a huge 'The Banger' fan and wanted to meet me. The kicker is..." I did a table-drumroll with my hands. "Her father was a trained fighter, too."

At my melodramatic recount of this pathetic story, Ashton blinked hard and successively. "No shit..."

With closed eyes, I shook my head. "Yeah. So, he found out how to get in touch with Cut, up in North Jersey. Cut must have told him he no longer trained me, and sent him to my agency—of course, in Cut's customary 'fuck off' manner."

Ashton still appeared stunned. "So, he was able to perform some type of research to find you?"

I nodded, going for my water. "For his daughter. Yes."

"Then what happened?"

"Well, I spoke to him and heard him out. I was so shocked, I didn't react. I told him I'd think about it and call back."

"How long did you think about it before telling him to kiss your ass?"

I couldn't look him in the eyes when I mumbled, "That was my intent, but it didn't come to fruition."

"Because?"

I swallowed hard. "Because I spoke about it to my therapist—well, a few of my friends and family first. Elle softly suggested I should speak to Trent Bailey. I learned when I did that he'd had a similar experience with his own father. The difference was TB's father wanted money for his other child. My father wanted to make his daughter's dream come true."

"What did he ask, specifically?"

My senses kicked in. "Is this off the record?" I tossed my chin to his fancy recorder.

"I would hope you'd let me keep some of it."

"I'll think about that, and if so, what." I was already committed to sharing the story since I'd done as much as I had. "He wanted me to train with her a few times. Maybe give her a few pointers."

Ashton whispered breathlessly, "Tell me you didn't." His eyes were shooting bullets.

I shook my head. "Not at first. Instead of giving into my feelings and giving him the finger, I called my therapist. I'd been seeing her for years and learned a lot about myself...my shortcomings and insecurities...trauma." My eyes blinked away. Okay, now this was a weird conversation to be having with Ashton Spencer. Honestly, I still couldn't believe he was here—in my peripheral. I never thought I'd see him again. Never wanted to. "I had the opportunity at his attention and wanted to gain a better understanding of his side of the story."

"Have you gotten it?"

"Maybe." I shrugged dismissively. "Maybe I have and I'm in denial. He's been in my life for four years, and I feel neither satisfied nor regretful."

When I braved my eyes on Ashton, his were squinted and locked on me, chin dipped. "What does your mother have to say about this random connection?"

I cleared my throat, mouth suddenly dry as I reached for my water. "Nothing. She's dead."

"Oh." That one word reply packed lots of emotion.

"You're doing it."

This time, Ashton blinked successively. "What?"

"Acting like you know me." I took a sip while applying a fake smile.

Professional. I had to remain professional, per Elle, even when I wanted to ask Ashton to disappear.

"I never said that."

"It's in your performance, minus what you're not saying."

He raised his hands defensively over the table. "Tori, listen. I'll admit: it's wild running into you again after all these years, but it's not ideal for me anymore than it is for you."

My face tightened. "Why? Is it still hard for you to take me seriously? Because I'm not your type?"

"What?" His face heated with disdain. "You don't know me. You have no idea what my type is."

My eyes burst wide and I palmed my face. "I didn't mean... romantically. I meant as a random, interesting individual." When he didn't answer, my aggression slipped. I was ready to go in for the kill. Who did he think he was—who did Ashton think *I* was? The same nobody Tori from his little school? I didn't think so.

"By the looks of what you brought out here with you to 'work' in *Kamigu*, I see your type. At least one of them—"

"Why is this fight special to you? And don't give me the generic, 'it will be my last' bullshit."

I couldn't help my snicker. What I wasn't willing to reveal a couple of days ago during our first sit down, I could easily share now.

"Because behind this victory is me building my family. You know: marriage and kids with someone whose type I am. Someone who values me, respects me—that type of thing."

Maybe I was harsh, or maybe I'd given off too much energy because Ashton's only response was a subtle head-nod that could have meant many things.

Enigmatic annoying human...

Ashton

Some things about Tori McNabb may have changed in terms of her personality. She was better spoken, paced with her words, and exact with negative emotions. Sitting with her last night had been a test of my patience, and hers toward the end. When I thought we'd eased into a mutually comfortable space of dialogue, something triggered her anger. And as much as I fought to stay focused, her anger triggered my own by the end of our conversation.

Nonetheless, as I observed her this afternoon in the gym, one thing about her that evidently hadn't changed was her athleticism. Today was my third time observing the flow of her training. I'd been amazed by her focus and strength back at *BSU*, but seeing it had only improved at age thirty-one awakened my athletic competitiveness. While I was still fit and worked out regularly, I hadn't competed in anything since my *Blakewood* days. Sitting here watching her practice her head movements to set up several counter-jabs while sparing reminded me of what that fire when practicing or conditioning felt like.

Tori was great at conditioning. A few days ago, her team had her do cardio and focused on her hand speed and footwork, sometimes using weights. The last session I sat in on, Tori performed ten circuits consisting of pushups, mountain climbers, shadow boxing, bicycle kicks, and punch hops. Just as in *Blakewood*, Tori was obedient, laser focused, and with an impassive expression. Rarely did she show signs of fatigue or pain. That fact compelled me to wonder how her ability to maintain a mask translated to the way she handled stress.

That thought led me to recall her past childhood traumas and how they affected her today. I hadn't been able to find any articles that addressed her being sexually assaulted as a child. I now struggled with if I wanted to be the one to introduce it, or ask Tori if it was okay if I did. I didn't have to make her story appealing. Tori's skills and rise to the top was a compelling story in and of itself. But for my own personal curiosity, I wanted to know if that trauma had been one taken on by the therapist she shared she had.

Admittedly, I thought of Tori often over the years. This was something I kept to myself until a therapist I'd been seeing after my assault at *BSU* had chilled me emotionally, though I'd healed physically. The talented professional was able to pull the betrayal by this "tomboy" out of me to get me to understand how impactful her short time in my world was. I'd only voiced my thoughts and memories of Tori to two therapists, in fact. Yes, I'd been seeing professionals after having my *League* dreams cut short. Life was cold and gray for me for years after that day.

But since seeing her in the restaurant with her sports agent a couple of weeks ago, I'd reawakened an acuteness to her presence I hadn't experienced in over ten years. It had been thirteen years since I met Tori, and twelve since I'd last seen her. Her hard-wearing aura was just as magnetic as it had been back in college. I had no desire to ever see or reconnect with Tori in life, but this reawakening was a symptom of taking on this job for Thomas. I had to take her in. *All* of her. Tori was no longer a little girl who hated to be seen outside of the ring. She was now the woman who employed, in some fashion, all of the dozen or more people in this makeshift gym the resort created for her. Tori couldn't hide. It was no longer possible.

She hadn't looked at me the entire three hours since she began today. I didn't know if that meant she was still upset by the end of our short chat last night or she was super focused on getting through her training. It could have been the latter: Tori never acknowledged me

31

in here. Again, how much of her past contributed to her focus for boxing?

"Hey." I felt Keyonna's heavy hand on my shoulder before I heard her voice. "Just got done exploring the two apps Tim sent over first thing this morning. Then I got an email about the trends of the third quarter earnings."

"Why the hell is Tucker running those fuckin' numbers before the fourth quarter?"

She rolled her eyes, taking the seat across from me in the corner of the room. "Being the impossible asshole he is. *But...*" She smacked her lips, emphasizing the word. "The good thing is he isn't happy about some of the numbers, which could work in favor of your employee support initiative."

"How's that?"

"Some of the categories like retention, suspension, poor evaluations. All of these categories directly relate to your current 'baby.' And speaking of which, the *Syntax* app sucks ass. It's a good thing Tim snuck in the *LennoxTech* one at the last minute. It's hella user-friendly, and looking over the specs, their troubleshooting, repairs, and updates package is more generous than all of the other prospects."

"Length-wise or pricing?"

"Both!" Her head bounced back and eyes flashed wide. "*Lennox-Tech* is a new firm out of Atlanta. They're trying to build a portfolio right now. A partnership with *B-Way Burger* is just what they need to plant their feet in this industry."

I nodded, attention back on Tori, who had just stopped for her towel and water. Her face was strained and posture lazy, finally giving a hint of exhaustion. Where was she mentally? Her trainer, Ed Schott, spiritedly voiced his feedback as she gulped down cold water. She gave him minimal eye-contact, but nodded her acknowledgements. Seconds later, she was back at it with the sparring partner, a fully built man. He had to have been north of two hundred-fifty pounds.

"You want more tea?" Keyonna asked as she stood and grabbed my room temperature, half full mug.

I shrugged with my head, indifferent. Keyonna took that as a yes and turned for the food table. Just as she took off, I noticed stocky figures creeping into the tent. Most held phones, balloons, and flowers in the air following behind one who looked familiar.

Deon Johnson...

Within seconds, I realized this was a popup visit. Deon, dressed in a tank, shorts, and boat shoes, held his index finger to his mouth, shushing those noticing his presence. People seemed to have caught on quickly, their faces broadening into pleasant smiles. Ed Schott was the first person Deon spoke to. His assistant had to gain his attention first. Ed didn't seem as pleasantly surprised as everyone else, but he received Deon's greeting. Then Deon whispered into Ed's ear and he, too, caught on quickly to the plan.

He's surprising her...

But how? Deon Johnson, a *League* veteran of four years, had been signed to the *Connecticut Kings* as a backup running back for the past two seasons. He began his career with the *Green Bay Packers*, but was released after his second season when they signed a free agent rookie who'd made Johnson look like the rookie in training camp that particular season. The *Packers* did what they had to do, based on the cap space and roster availability. Many were surprised when the *Kings* picked Johnson up, locking him into a three-year free agent deal. He wasn't a franchise player, so not a lot of information about him had been available. I'd read Johnson, not a big celebrity player, was likeable amongst his teammates, yet arrogant. That purported claim was made obvious by his presence here in Southeast Asia in mid-August. Johnson should have been between training season and practicing for the upcoming *League* pre-season.

I watched as Ed motioned for the attention of the guy Tori was practicing the block-jab maneuver with. Deon crept into the ring, then received the bouquet of flowers from one of the guys who'd come in with him. The guy sparring with Tori threw a few more jab routines before he backed away a few feet, ending their cadence. When his attention went over Tori's shoulder, she automatically followed his line of sight. That was when the zone she had been habitually cast into was broken. Tori squealed as she leaped into the air. After landing, she charged Johnson, crashing into him without caution.

The flowers had almost fallen to the floor of the ring. Cameras snapped and videos rolled as several people cheered for them. *Or her.* Tori's feminine and girlish yelps went on for seconds long before she pushed into Deon, crashing her mouth into his. When his eyes closed and free hand went intuitively to cup her ass, my dick lurched in my pants.

The fuck?

I scanned the room, ashamed at my private reaction to seeing Tori intimate with a man. Is that what she looked like in the arms of her lovers? *Did she curl into my frame with seductive lithe?* I'd never seen her from the other side. It was always me receiving her.

Quickly, my attention flitted over to Keyonna, and I caught her festive smile wane as she looked my way. *Fuck.* I didn't want to create an awkward moment here, neither did I want her off kilter from thinking I had a problem. In the past five days, I'd managed to keep my knowing Tori before taking on this piece under wraps. And the last thing I wanted Keyonna thinking was I had former dealings with Tori. I wanted nothing to do with that woman outside of this S.I. piece, and then we could chuck the deuces and go back to our lives.

Thinking on my toes, I motioned for her to remember the lemon. That was so damn unnecessary. Keyonna knew my preferences better than most. Her assistance in my world had made my need of a wife clear. The problem with that was I no longer had an interest in marriage. Now, almost midway into my thirties, the idea of being locked to anyone legally yielded zero desire for me.

Needing to escape this bizarre state I found myself in, I decided to narrow my attention on my laptop where I'd been taking observation notes of Tori's training. Not only that, I needed distraction from my visceral reaction to Johnson's intimate touch on Tori. That shit was deviant as hell. Maybe I should have flown Nadera out here for a few days. I wasn't particularly in need of pussy. I could go another few days before the craving kicked in, and I'd certainly make it until next week when I'd return to the U.S. So that quick reaction was quite strange. This shit had never happened to me.

I tried editing a few lines I'd written earlier, describing Tori's focus. Some of these observations would be included in the final draft, most wouldn't, but all details were significant at this point. After a couple of minutes of focus, voices grew louder near me. It was Deon Johnson and his crew. He'd left Tori in the ring to continue her work. That led my curious thoughts to Tori's mental training. Historically, boxers created rules about limiting and/or abstaining from sex and physical gratification.

She never implemented such a rule with me...

I rubbed my dry eyes. Tori likely had never developed restrictions for sex because she hadn't had any before me. A volt of electricity cannonaded from my groin, up my spine, forcing me to sit up straight in the chair. My pulse hiked, beating viciously in my neck. Tori and I were kids then, just going through the motions. I understood that, now, in my thirties. But another very reactive part of me wasn't present back at *BSU* and recounting our history felt new. A known aphorism of *you can lie to many of men and be believed, but you're the one man you cannot tell the same lie to* was a painful truth right now. Not many had known about Tori and me twelve-thirteen years ago, but I did. She did. And as great of a job as I'd done to suppress those memories, erasing them was impossible.

Breaking from my reverie, I glanced up from the screen. My attention mindlessly traveled over to the food table across the room. Johnson and a couple from his entourage were there near Keyonna. She was squeezing juice from a fresh lemon into a mug.

Between his lip movements and the slight volume, I could make out, "You sure you doing that right? I bet you ain't a better squeezer than me."

His suggestive words close to Keyonna's ear, priapic slanted eyes, and the posture he assumed, keeping his back to the ring—

Tori...

My regard traveled there, wondering if she'd gone back to sparring. Nope. Tori's gaze was on her fiancé. And her body language expressed her unease about his proximity to Keyonna. Then Tori's gaze shifted to me. When she found me looking her way, her regard faltered as she bit her lip, then moved to engage her sparring partner waiting on her to resume.

Shit.

She'd caught her man slipping. From what I'd learned over the past few weeks, Johnson had a penchant for gaining the attention of the ladies. It was a discovery I could have thrown in Tori's face last night when she proclaimed having a man who valued and respected her. That would have been a classic move for me. But I decided, since accepting this story, to err on the side of caution with Tori.

Keyonna made her way to me. She placed the mug in front of me then cupped my shoulder with her palm, forcing intimacy. Johnson had grossed her out, this sidling up under me revealed that.

"You good?"

Keyonna cleared her throat. "Yup. I'll live...if you tell me McNabb didn't catch that."

I sighed, closing my laptop. I was done for the day. "Wish I could lie."

"Shit," she swore under her breath.

I grabbed my computer and, at this point, useless tea, then took her at the shoulder. "C'mon. Time for me to fill you in on some shit."

Keyonna gasped. "You've got a random ass baby on the way like Alton Alston?"

Her dry sense of humor tickled me. "Silly ass."

CHAPTER THREE

Tori

"**D**id you ask Elle about a planner?"

I turned from the calming rhythmic ripples of the ocean rushing the sanded floor. "What planner?"

Deon snorted. "The wedding planner, lady."

"Oh!" I blinked hard and took a breath. My mind had been miles away from wedding planning. "No," I kind of lied.

Over a month ago, Elle mentioned knowing wedding planners while having dinner with Deon and me. She said to let her know if we needed suggestions. What Deon didn't know was Elle had passively passed one my way, weeks ago when she pitched the karaoke stimulator proposal. I didn't want to explore the subject because my focus now was on *The Banger*, not Tori. That was until Deon popped up here in *Kamigu*.

"Is it the prenup thing?" My face lifted to peer at him again. "My lawyer told me yours hasn't sent back over the contract."

"It's not a contract. It's a draft of responsible planning of our assets," I countered. "You were insistent on beginning the negotiations with your list of what you feel is a reasonable arrangement. Now give me time to absorb it and respond."

"It's been a month and a half, though, T!" he droned like a child.

"I've been preparing for a fight for two months."

Deon stopped his paced stroll and shifted in front of me. He leaned over to reach my eye-level. "Hey, everything okay? We good?" His voice small and tender.

I didn't know how to be honest without being rude. "I'm training."

He stood straight, exhaling his frustration. "I know, but..."

"You're an athlete, too. You should be focused on the season."

"I missed you, T, and thought this would be a nice way of letting you see it."

I grabbed him by the cheeks, fighting the crushing guilt, and pulled him down to me. "It is a romantic gesture, but not a sensible one. You know what's riding on this fight for me. Right?"

"Yes. Us settling down and starting a family."

"That *and* what this season means to you."

Deon rolled his eyes, though he didn't remove his handsome face from my palms. "I'm gonna kill this season. This is just a break for me from a tough ass training season, T."

"You being here is bigger than that. It tells your team and bosses you don't want to be seen by them. I'm sure they felt some kind of way when those videos went viral yesterday."

This was the third day of me ending my training days early out here. The first was to begin Ashton's interview; the second was yesterday. No matter how many times Deon insisted that I forget he was on this island, I couldn't. It threw me off my game. When I'd taken a break from sparring yesterday, Treesha came into the gym, showing me all the posts on social media. The *Kings'* fans slaughtered us. Honestly, they had every right to: Deon should have been back in Connecticut.

"Look, T," he tried pleading with me, voice pitchy. "I'm going to perform my ass off out there."

"But you also want to be seen as a position player, and not just a good special teams' player," I kept my tone even. Firm.

"And I'm going to! I'm going to bring home the bag, T. I'm going to get the big contract this time."

This time.

I had never been the type of girl or woman who needed a man with lots of money. I'd been blessed to have my own, but even without it, I felt me being a good, hardworking, and faithful human should qualify me for marriage. Wealth wasn't necessary to make me happy. Neither would I treat a man who didn't have as much as me as less than a respectable partner. But drive and wisdom were hard limits for me.

I'd heard a lot about the *Kings'* front office over the years, including their owner, who was involved in the management of the organization, which was unusual in the *League*. I'd met the man on several occasions before and since meeting Deon nearly two years ago. Eli Richardson was a shrewd businessman. If Deon wanted more money and respect from the *Kings*, he had to work for it.

"What do Dawn Taylor and her PR team have to say about this tactic of leaving Connecticut weeks before your first game of the pre-season?"

Deon's face was contorted as he asked, "What the hell is that?"

He was requesting a five-year extension, which included three million dollars a year as a base salary along with an eight to ten million dollar signing bonus. Getting that would make his contract with the team worth twenty-three to twenty-five million with the guarantee that he would get the eight to ten million dollar signing bonus up front after signing the contract. How could he demand a lengthier and more robust relationship with his team when he was popping up out here practically when the pre-season was due to begin?

In the middle of eye-warring with him, I turned into the direction of the loud audio. Leaving him near the shore, I sauntered a few yards behind the umbrella leaf palm trees where the sound grew greater in volume and familiar. It was a fight. Ashton was watching an old fight of mine on a huge projection screen. It was the resort's cinema, based on the screen and oversized chairs arranged movie theater style. Ashton sat with his laptop, a writing pad, pen, and a champagne flute in his hand. He was captivated, shirtless, and focused.

Who was this guy? He certainly wasn't the bossy, arrogant human I knew him to be at *Blakewood*. There was a peace and new level of confidence to Ashton's aura. I didn't trust him and even hated seeing him around, but couldn't ignore his strong presence.

"Who the fuck is that guy,"—I leaped on my toes, startled to find Deon over my shoulder—"and why he always observing and watching shit?"

Enduring a racing pulse, I licked my lips, trying to calm myself. "He's a..." I swallowed. "A reporter—journalist."

"Which one?" he asked impatiently.

"I guess both. He's doing an interview for *Sport Illustrated*."

"On you?"

I snorted, finding that question foolish. "Who else?"

Ignoring me, but keeping a distrusting gape on Ashton, Deon nodded. "Oh, that's why I been seeing him around, always writing. I thought he was fuckin' with ol' girl."

"Who?"

He shrugged nonchalantly. "That young girl."

I couldn't help it. "The one you walked up on yesterday when you surprised me?"

Deon's neck snapped, his face tightened, and eyes narrowed on me. "What you talking about, T?"

I backed away from the trees, needing to be at a distance from Ashton. The last thing I needed was him hearing this conversation.

Humiliation couldn't begin to explain what I'd been feeling since yesterday, but I hadn't addressed it with him until now.

"We need to talk," I told him once he followed me back to the shoreline. "I totally understand you were single for a long while before meeting me. And, although I'm not a man, I'm guessing you may need an adjustment period? But what you did yesterday with that young girl didn't seem appropriate at all."

"Young girl?" He snorted. "She's an adult."

But she was young to you just a minute ago…

"Oh, she's most definitely an adult: that's not up for debate. What's also not up for debate is my respect and dignity."

Deon rolled his eyes. "Ah, man, T. We ain't on this again. Are we?"

My forehead narrowed. "I guess we are. See," I folded my arms beneath my breasts. "when you crowd a woman's space and speak lowly so only she can hear you, it's inappropriate and grist for the rumor mill. It's what those bloggers are reporting on."

"You know we don't care about what they got to say. They're just social weirdos playing tough behind a keyboard."

"I care about what energy is out there about me when I can control it." I rested my weight on one hip. "Do you want to get married, Deon?"

He licked his lips and angled his head. "I'm the one reminding you to get in touch with the planner, T."

"You didn't remind me. I never forgot. What I need to be sure of is whether or not you want to be tied down to one woman. It's a question I'll continue to ask before we get married until I'm confident in your answer."

Deon scoffed, directing his attention out into the far distance as though affronted. "I flew all the way out here on a damn near twenty-four hour flight—on my dime"—*oh, thank God!*—"and you're questioning my loyalty to you?"

Coolly, I countered, "I'm concerned about your respect for me as it plays out in your conduct."

"What conduct?"

"For an example, yesterday with that young girl."

Deon dramatically bounded to the sand in front of me, going down on one knee. "KaToria McNabb, there is no other woman for me. I would be a fool to fuck up a good thing with a bomb ass, beautiful, smart, and tough queen. You've introduced me to Jesus Christ, got me into therapy to figure my shit out. Ain't no way in the world, I'm gonna compromise my paradise."

love belvin

Ashton

The water in *Kamigu* was remarkable. One of the island's best features was the dual energies of waters. With one end of the island having wavy water, it was ideal for surfing and boating. The other side of the property, and surrounding less than half of its ovular contour, was calmer and appropriate for swimming. This evening, a long swim was in order for me and the water felt like silk against my skin.

After the evening I'd had with Tori's team, her fiancé, and his crew, this trip quickly became one of a fruitless pursuit for me. It was Johnson's second day here, and the atmosphere had shifted palpably. Tori had become tense since he'd arrived, and so did her entire team. It had been evident to me since day one out here in Indonesia, that *The Banger's* camp was cohesive and immeasurably competent.

Earlier today, training was cut short again, due to Johnson's presence. Yes, Tori could have continued on then moonlighted with her fiancé tonight, but I had a strong suspicion she had specific reasons to keep an eye on him. Apparently, Deon Johnson was a ladies man who had been finding it difficult to settle down with one woman. Keyonna had to catch me up on the *Kings'* running back after his shitty ass attempt at flirting with her in the gym. I knew some because he'd been in the media for his philandering ways a time or two, but not how wild his reputation was. Keyonna, however, believed many of the accusations were untrue, and that he'd slowed down since being linked to Tori. Nonetheless, we learned yesterday, on his arrival, that Deon liked ass, and ass unattached to the woman he'd asked to marry. And his crew ran with the same energy. They flirted with the women in Tori's crew as well as the staff as though it was *MTV's Spring Break* in the nineties. I was all for fun in the sun, but this wasn't it.

I'd become a loner over the years, preferring my time with just the handful of people I was accountable to. Coming out here was no vacation, no matter how majestic the setting. Earlier, at dinner, Johnson's friends became rowdy at the main restaurant being loud, blasting music, and dancing suggestively. Not wanting any parts of that energy, as soon as Keyonna and I were done eating, I escorted her out of there.

What confused the hell out of me was Tori's tolerance of that shit. She didn't seem like the type of woman who could become pliant for a man. She sure as shit never yielded to me, even when I needed it all those years ago. Perhaps it was that epiphany that had me so restless since dinner earlier. I left Keyonna with research and travel accommodation work to do as I came out for a swim. Thirty minutes stretched into two hours, according to the last time I checked my wrist watch.

Surfacing from beneath the cool water, I thought to check for the time again. But the first thing to catch my attention was I was far away from my villa. Initially, I didn't recognize my surroundings. Gazing all over my peripheral, a small image gained my attention. It was a figure up on a balcony. I swiped the dripping water from my eyes as I waded to the dry sand. She watched me unrepentantly, and

I could perceive her view. I was stark ass naked after dark, which made my escape from reality while swimming so irresponsible. My trunks weren't around. Noting that, I trekked back into the water, but with my attention on her as she leaned over the railing of the balcony with her elbows perched, watching me.

Deon moseyed outside grabbing her from behind. "Come fuck me," I was able to make out.

She tried to wrestle from his hold. All I could make out was her adamantly declaring, "No!"

I leaped into the water, throwing my arms into a breaststroke until I could fully swim.

Why the hell is he trying to fuck her while she's training for a fight?

Goofy ass bitch.

The air smelled fresh, like morning, although it was still dark out. I sat with crossed legs on the beach. There was a pleasant chill in the air, declaring the beauty of *Kamigu*. Things had been hectic here, but soft reminders of the resplendent nature of the island had been making themselves clear since the night I arrived. Quiet, open air, me, and no other human in sight had been the ideal remedy this morning for my restless mind. The one and only thing keeping this moment from being perfect was my bikini top. I wished I could sit out here with my breasts hanging free of restraint.

That thought was followed by a soothing whimper leaving my lungs as I untied the knot at the base of my neck. My breasts were immediately released, but not enough. They were still covered in cotton. I decided to let it be. I didn't want Treesha coming out looking for me and finding my headlights on full display for the ocean. I exhaled at the sight of the tip of the orange sun ascending on the other side of the reflective body of water.

"Good morning," a velvety warm timbre startled me.

"Shit!" I grunted, palm flying to my heart. That's when I realized my bikini had shifted and my right boob was exposed. "*Shit!*" I gasped harder.

Once my hand secured my breast, oddly I braved a glance over to Ashton who stood unmoving, eyes going between my face and breasts unapologetically with proprietary. His legs were mountainously long from my vantage point, thighs spaced apart, chin to his chest, and dark eyes with a brilliant gleam.

"Like what you see, Spence?" Rolling my eyes, I arranged my breasts into my top under his intentional gaze, securing a knotted tie at the base of my neck.

"I've never been indifferent to your anatomy."

My eyelids exploded wide and head shot up to face him. "You're flirting...and inappropriately."

He chuckled, a coat of arrogance further layering his enigma. "What's appropriate flirting?"

I swung my eyes toward the rising sun, low key finding humor in him playing coy. Maybe it was because after putting Deon on a redeye flight last night, I could use a break from my frustrated state. Possibly, it was Elle's words of tough wisdom about moving on emotionally. Perhaps it was because being stressed out had been a lonely place for me, and there was something familiar and safe about Ashton's aggressive persona I hadn't experienced in over a decade. The safety was in the fact that he couldn't hurt me anymore. I had no expectations of him being anything he wasn't now.

With playful sass, I answered, "The type of appropriateness that applies to women who aren't engaged."

His brows rose and so did a wide grin on his hairy face as his head bobbed. "Okay. Touché. I forgot about that small, yet significant detail."

I rolled my eyes away from him again, a pang of embarrassment twisting in my belly. "I deserve that." Licking my lips, my head bounced. "*We* deserve that. I apologize for making your friend feel uncomfortable. Deon can be unwittingly socially aggressive."

Are these words of apology for my grown ass fiancé really spilling from my lips—and to Ashton Spencer regarding his girlfriend? Yup. I couldn't admit how embarrassed I was about whatever transpired between Deon and the girl in the gym the day he arrived.

When I peered back up at Ashton, his attention was on the sun now mounted over the water. I was confident he thought my apology was as pathetic as I had.

"I'm leaving."

My face tightened, head pushed back. "When?"

Ashton's regard found me again. "This morning."

"Are we done?" That would have been great for me.

"Not exactly." His gaze lingered over me. "But I've gotten enough to no longer impose on your training retreat."

"So that's it? No more probing questions for me and my team?"

Last night, after a private dinner with Deon, we strolled past the main cafeteria. I saw Ashton at the table with my trainer, Ed, taking notes with one hand while cupping a glass of brown juice in the other. He had spoken with a couple of people in my camp since we'd arrived, from what I'd been told.

He shrugged. "I have a few more, but nothing imminent. We can resume after your fight."

My face fell. "You mean to tell me I have to be in touch with you for the next couple of months?"

Ashton chuckled coolly again. "To some degree, yes. I know it's not been the most pleasant experience for you—"

"I mean, how has it been for you?"

His honesty was delayed. "It's been..." His mouth twisted as it was clear Ashton held his breath while thinking. "...quite the task." A sputter of laughter cut through my lips and my torso swayed to one side. Even with my eyes closed, I could hear Ashton's teeter. "Nah, but seriously. You're almost done, and need to focus. I can understand how intrusive my presence here is. We can wrap this up after your fight."

"Are all your arrangements made? Do I need to sign off on anything for your flight?"

His smile was ghosted behind his thick beard, but loud at the same time. "No. I've taken care of my own transportation."

My eyes closed when it hit me. The Ashton Spencer I knew back then was wealthy. I didn't know if that was still the case, but it felt damn good to not have to pay for someone attached to me in some form.

"Duly noted." My head bounced up and down. "Please give my kind regards to your associate, Keyon—"

"Oh." He snapped his finger as though struck with a thought. "About that." Ashton pulled his phone from the pocket of his chino shorts. "A few days ago, I called back to Jersey to have a search done for an old photograph." I didn't speak while he swiped the face of his phone continuously, but was crazy intrigued. "She almost didn't retrieve it, but as fate would have it, Precious, also known as Karen, sent it last night."

Ashton leaned down until he fell on his haunches and angled his phone toward me. On the face was a screenshot of a printed picture. It wasn't the best quality, I was sure from a personal camera. But it was me. I was in a big room with rich, lofty trimmings. The wooden furniture with intricately embroidered coverings, vibrant wall paintings, and even a portion of a colorful, festive Christmas tree caught in the shot all felt familiar.

My mouth fell open as the memories began flooding in. "That's me...at your father's place." Ashton nodded when my eyes met him.

He didn't move the phone and I was grateful. I wanted more time with the young me. Then I noticed the little girl whose little hand was in mine as I laughed. "I remember her. She was cute, so funny, and—oh, my god—so smart!" I thought for a minute. "KeKe. Kema?" I tried.

His eyes brightened with a smile his face didn't correspond with. Then just as quickly, his face darkened. "Keyonna."

"Right!" I gasped. "Her father. Your cousin—best friend..."

"Keyonna, to my dismay, thinks she's my personal assistant."

My face tightened. "*That* baby? How old is she now—" I couldn't speak and think at the same time.

Suddenly, I was speechless. Dumbfounded! The child in the picture was the adult young lady he'd brought to *Kamigu*? *No way!*

Sensing my revelation, Ashton answered, "My baby girl's nineteen. She won't be twenty until January."

My thumb flew over my shoulder, referencing the mahogany beauty with long, dark hair and the legs and eyelashes to match. "She looks twenty-five, at least."

Ashton's eyes closed and his head swayed left to right. "Perhaps twenty-three tops, but not a quarter of a century. You're killing me, Tori." Ashton sounded wounded.

Out of nowhere, I giggled. "You sound like a dad."

Ashton nodded with a sober expression. "Because I am."

This was too much for me.

"You've taken care of her all this time?"

"I'm a man of my word."

"You were a kid."

"She's my blood," he argued. "*He* was my blood."

My open palm met my face. "I feel like shit." Not only had Treesha and a few of my female crew traveling with me picked her apart as a gold digger, my fiancé may have been too friendly with her. That was gross.

"I'm embarrassed. I need to talk to her." I turned to scan the beach behind me.

"It's cool. I've talked to her already."

"When?"

"A couple of days ago, after Johnson popped up."

I cringed. "So she didn't know who I was all this time, and I'd been..."

"Giving off nasty vibes?" His smirk was crooked. "Yeah."

"You're an ass."

"She says the same all the time. It's all good, though." He stood to his feet, pocketing his phone. "For the record, I can bag young adult-females if I wanted. I just have no interest in fuckin' them. They're not my vibe."

Then what's your vibe?

Did I really think that? I did. This parting meeting was getting out of hand.

And Keyonna...

"Does she think I'm a bitch?" I had a brand to protect, and especially an obligation to young Black girls. This was unacceptable.

"She was on the incline after dinner last night when Treesha bumped her at the buffet table."

I gulped in a heap of air. "No!" My head swung back. "I'm going to kill her."

"No worries. Keyonna's a balanced girl. She's used to being targeted for some reason or another. She's also accustomed to being around a broad range of people, class-wise." His brows narrowed. "That may have costed me a *Louis Vuitton* bag and *Asé Garb* sneakers, but I'll live." He pursed his lips as he shrugged.

In spite of myself, a snicker pushed from my throat. I covered my mouth with my hands as I giggled. Why did this hurt so bad and feel good at the same time?

"I'll cover the bag and sneakers. No sweat, I promise."

Ashton's neck snapped back. "And steal my thunder? *Neeever!*" he emphasized, keeping his volume low.

Fighting off a harder laugh, I pushed. "I've got to do something. I can't not take responsibility for the energy she's endured here."

"Wow, Tori. Look at you. That's very...accountable of you."

"Years of therapy should have yielded something other than a dent in my bank account."

With his regard locked onto me, Ashton's face relaxed. "Let's make a deal."

I couldn't believe I was having a civil conversation with Ashton Spencer again. Maybe it was because I was grateful for him leaving? I didn't know, but here we were.

"Shoot."

"This fight with Monica O'Connor; fight her with your skill set only."

My forehead tightened and head angled. "What else would I fight her with? A chair? A gun?"

Ashton shook his head softly. "Your anger."

"What anger?"

He shrugged mildly. "Whatever has you stressed. Whoever's upset you or put an obstacle in your way leading up to 'D-day.'"

My blood began to boil. It was the insecurity from the judgment I sensed. "Who puts obstacles in the way of *The Banger*?"

"Whoever has you out here on the beach before sunrise. Maybe it's the person you just put on a plane back to the States." His pitch heightened, trying to explain. "That's for you to answer. But whoever or whatever it is, don't take that in the ring with you. Don't let 'that' earn another victory for you."

"You don't know me, Ashton. You have no idea what I take into the ring with me. I don't need anything but my body, mind, and heart."

"And I think you rely on your bruised heart to win fights." His tone was calm, even. Patient. "I've watched your fights over the past five years and aligned them with the headlines reported from your personal life. Leaving Cut's camp pushed you in many matches and helped you snatch several belts. I can't help but guess there was some correlation...for years after."

I was offended. Who in the hell did he think he was? Forget that. Who did Ashton Spencer think *I* was?

"You're crossing a thin line with me right now, Spencer. One that will have your ass laid out here across this sand."

Ashton scoffed. "That isn't even a blinking concern of mine, no matter how much I believe in your talent. Let's put the threats aside and be objective here. It's not my intent to insult or critique you. This is simply an observation made by a cat who's pored over your videos, interviews, and headlines as well as talked to people you've intersected with in the past six years of your career. Also, as much as we, equally, want to stow this inconvenient fact, I am someone who knew you way back when."

I was silently heaving at this point. *The audacity.* Shaking my head, I made clear, "Hardly two semesters. What could you have really known about me?"

Ashton's preoccupied regard went to the water and he scratched the back of his head before returning his gaze to me. "That fight you took with the Rodriguez girl right after Thanksgiving at *BSU*, you gave her the advantage—"

"What? That was thirteen years ago!"

"Let me finish. Your victories—all of them, I'm strongly shouldering here—have been motivated. You use anger, disappointment, and abandonment to fuel you in the ring."

"That was one fight? You sound ridiculous, Ashton."

"Do I? When have you ever fought when you were...happy, carefree? That night, right after Thanksgiving, at *BSU*, you'd just had your first orgasm by a guy you trusted—hell, the first 'human' you trusted sexually." *He remembers my quirky language.* And he made me remember sex with him. I was beyond annoyed at this point. "You didn't carry that cadre of pain into the ring with Rodriguez. Yeah, you had the skill set to defeat her, but you didn't have the savage you call *The Banger* to demolish her without prompting."

"And what's your fucking point, Spencer?"

"My point is, maybe you should try to let go of the 'anger' comfort blanket for once. Try life without pain, mistrust, betrayal, and unhappiness. Why don't you choose happiness for once? Passion is what should be carried into the battle, but anger is like popping a Molly before sex. Why the need for performance enhancers? Where is your faith and confidence in your skills?"

A barrage of arrows pierced each inch of my body and wouldn't stop. In my ten years of professional fighting, I'd been critiqued a lot and by many. But never had I been criticized about what's happening internally when I fight. It wasn't something I'd ever considered. I wouldn't allow Ashton Spencer of all people to get in my head and make me doubt my God-given skill, but the need to be alone out here again was beginning to suffocate me.

"You and Keyonna have a nice flight, Spencer," I bade. After a few seconds of passing silence, I added, "And if you change your mind about the bag and sneakers for Keyonna, contact my assistant at either *Love is Action* or *Bobby's Hope* and they'll get the request to me."

With thick furrowed brows, sparkling ebony irises, and a final neck bow, Ashton turned to walk away. Cursorily, I returned my gaze to the water, expelling all the air in my lungs. I was, by no means, an insecure woman, but for a moment there, I was the unsure, unknowing, and uncultured eighteen/nineteen year old colliding with the unimaginably forceful Ashton Spencer. Those days were gone. And thankfully, so would Ashton be from this island, and eventually my life. Again.

"Tori..." he called from behind me, causing me to twist my upper body to see him. "I'm proud of you." A peculiar sense of neediness washed over me. My fingers combed violently into the sand, burying themselves. Ashton's head swung left and right, expressing discomfort, but fortitude. "I know it sounds patriarchic as hell, but learning about the empire you've amassed in the past six years or so is vastly impressive to a man who knows where you've come from. I always knew you were especially skilled and even smarter than you gave yourself credit for, but now I know that radiant star not even you saw back in school wasn't a figment of my imagination. You've done well. I hope all works out for your ambitions beyond this fight."

Again, we locked gazes mutedly. So many thoughts, possibly emotions—ugly and true—yet no words for them.

"Thanks," was the rudimentary reply compelled from my overwhelmed mind. "Good luck with the article. I'm sure you'll do well."

Again. Two muted, hopeless stares.

"Tori..."

"Yeah."

"If I'm right about your rage-enhanced victories, whether you consciously fight without it this time or you've never had, and you win with just your skills, we'll have dinner for our next sit down. On me."

"You think you can afford feeding me?"

"I'll do you one better. I'll cook." And as though he knew my rejection was coming, Ashton smoothly turned to finally walk away.

love belwin

September

I'm hungry...

My gaze was locked onto myself in the vanity mirror as Gia, my makeup artist, finished my face. Today had been a long one, starting at dawn with a rigorous workout with my trainers. Gia was able to conceal the bags beneath my eyes for this photo-op I was about to shoot for my foundation.

Renata bolted through the small room with her phone to her ear. My heart dropped.

"You heard from her?" she asked me.

I lifted my phone from my thigh and softly shook my head. "This NeNe on the phone. She said she spoke to Toya who said Treesha was down by the gas station in Bridgeton, off of East Broad last night. She asked her if she was going to the fight tomorrow and Treesha ain't answer."

I didn't respond. Treesha had to contact me for her ticket to the fight. I set it up so that she couldn't go through anyone else. This was getting exhausting. And this time was rude as hell right before my fight.

"I'mma beat her ass!" Renata swore, looking at me in the mirror for a response.

My cousin knew me better than most. I couldn't yield my emotions to Treesha's selfishness right now. I had money to get; a legacy to continue.

When she got the hint, Renata returned to her call with NeNe. "Yeah. She ain't call Tori yet either. Y'all keep looking. She could be in that trap house." She listened to NeNe. "No. The pill house." After a beat, she continued, "All this because Tori cut into her ass about how she was acting out there in *Kamigu!* You see what happens when you try to be nice and take her ass out of the country? She's selfish!" Renata was out of the room again.

"You good, Tori?" Gia asked cautiously as I fingered my edges around the braids I had put in two days ago. "I hate that Treesha's on the run again right before a fight."

"Yeah." I exhaled. "I'm good. Just ready for this Irish victory." She laughed as I air boxed in the chair. "You know."

"I know that's right, *Banger!*" Gia gassed me up. I allowed it, deflecting. Deflecting was okay in this instance. I needed to preserve my focus for tomorrow night. "And just wait: after tomorrow, you gone be free to do whatever the hell you wanna do. It's gonna be your time, T." Only a few in my camp knew I was stepping away from boxing after this fight. I'd been keeping it under wraps to not steal away from the victory I would earn tomorrow. Gia moved on to my lips. "Then you and D can go and get married. Y'all can have babies if you want."

My belly fluttered at the mention of her one word. I clenched my fists to keep from ascending into a euphoric mental place.

"Mmhmm." I thought to respond.

"Does that mean you want kids, Tori?"

As though on cue, my phone vibrated.

DeJo: *I luv u T baby*

I murmured while she lined my lips. "You spoke him up."

Then I typed back an obligatory response.

Me: Love you too.

"Really?" Gia gasped. "See! That's what I'm talking about. You got more to look forward to than you do things to stress over. Treesha gone finally get her shit together. Plus, when you finally get married, she's gonna see what she could have if she get her shit together."

When Gia stepped back to observe my whole face, she attempted a convincing smile.

I pulled in a sharp breath. "Yup."

"Too bad this beatness is only for twenty minutes."

"What time is it?" Today was one of those "every moment mattered" days.

"You got two minutes."

"Hope that's enough time to pee, 'cause I gotta go." I hopped out of the chair for the door.

"You got time."

As soon as I made it to the door, Renata came bustling through again. "You ready?"

"Can I pee first?"

"You got ninety seconds."

As Gia snickered behind me, I rolled my eyes and jetted out into the hallway.

CHAPTER FOUR

Tori

The cameras' flashes were blinding and their sounds deafening. Although I should have been used to this, I was not. My silver lining was the cause. As I shook hands with Shenedrea, owner of *The Sewing Heir*, the photographers didn't cease fire right away, making our withdrawal from one another odd.

"Whew!" I sighed. "I don't know about you, but my heart is full from partnering with you, but my face hurts."

She laughed. "Thanks again for this opportunity," the cedar-toned woman from Chicago husked. "I thought this was going to play out in a way to show me you're like other short-tempered celebrities."

I was momentarily taken aback by her honesty. Being labeled a celebrity was still difficult for me. "You've met lots of famous people?"

She was a slender woman, just a couple of inches beneath me.

Her red stained lips pursed as her head bobbed over her thin shoulders. It made her meticulous peacock-styled pixie cut bounce on top of her head. "I'm from Chicago, we birth celebrities like nobody's business." She swung her neck with sass.

"Well, I hope you had a good experience with me. I'm confident my team treated you with the dignity and appreciation of you I feel. Your design for the fight is amazing."

I decided to go with Shenedrea's entry for my shorts for the fight. With a few specifications to add to her design, I was more than happy with my attire for tomorrow. The idea to select an independent designer was mine for my nonprofit. Its mission was to bring attention to Black women and children with entrepreneurial pursuits.

Shenedrea's lashes smacked behind her eyeglasses and she offered a dramatic neck bow. "You all did." Behind her, my assistant, Lidia, was in the doorway, waving me on. I forced my attention back to Shenedrea in front of me. "I know you've got to go, but can I say something weird to you?"

Mentally, I rolled my eyes. I've come across strange birds in my career. So long as they didn't get physical, I could deal.

"Have at it." I granted her.

"This morning, a vision woke me up—a dream. It was you, running through a field of lilies under a dark blue sky." She studied my reaction.

"Hmmm!" I hummed on a deep breath. Confused, but I wouldn't share that.

"Sounds forbidding, but it wasn't. The sky was mostly blue, but the clouds were a pattern of blue mixed with orange and white. They were billowy and trancing. Dark but colorful, warm, and comforting. You were in a field of lilies, overlooking beautifully manicured valleys. Peaks and valleys, peaks and valleys," she whispered in a particular cadence. Her eyes closed and head swung as she smiled. "You danced; arms in the air, body twirling. And your smile... My God, it was permanent." Shenedrea's eyes opened again. "You were home, Tori. Even under the cloudy sky, you were happily at home."

My eyes burst wide. "Like dead?"

"No!" she gasped. "Not at all. Very much alive. Just out loud with it. No more muteness—"

"That's it, Tor!" Renata called. "We've got to get that makeup off and changed so we can hit the road."

When my regretful regard landed on Shenedrea, I didn't have to explain.

She nodded. "You go. Get ready to win this last battle. The ones after will be rough, but I think you'll enjoy them." Shenedrea smiled slyly with confidence as she backed away, dismissing me.

"Tori, really," Lidia warned, her eyes closing dramatically. "Elle's setup ground zero at the house."

That's when I knew something was wrong.

Of course, before fight day...

And this had to be "big" wrong because I paid people to predict, prevent, and eliminate problems before they escalated to my knowledge.

On the way up to my room, no one whispered a clue of what the emergency was. The only sounds from my camp were my two body-guards, communicating with others in the vicinity via their two-way devices. Honestly, I wasn't in the mood to push. I didn't even have my phone; Lidia did. My mental and physical downtime was due to begin as soon as the weigh-in ended. However, I'd just take it as it came.

When we stepped off the elevators, I noticed several people in the halls. They were mostly more security, considering so many were in Atlantic City for the fight tomorrow. The big event was happening at the *KAHRI Resort and Casino*, a newer property for the community. My team booked out the penthouse in one of the hotel's wings. Monica and her people were in another.

We sauntered down the hall, a few faces coming into view I recognized. They were Deon's friends. They eyed me warily; prefixing their verbal greetings were nods of the heads.

"What up, Tori."

"Hey, Maine."

"What it do, *Banger*," Lee offered before a dab.

With the mood I was in, I went for it, returning the manly hug. "You already know."

One of the doors to the suite was opened for me. "This way, Tori." I was ordered and followed Lidia into the massive living room overlooking the Atlantic Ocean.

Right away, Elle, Dawn Taylor, an Asian woman suited with heels, and Deon came into view. My heart fell from my chest. Deon did not approach or greet me. The man gave off child-like vibes, unable to look me in my face.

Casually, I sidled up to Elle's side as she stood to mirror my posture. She wore a lilac hued track suit with metallic lock and key *Tom Ford* stilettos. The informality of the track suit along with the off-white *The Banger* baseball cap made it clear, Elle Hunter was a fixer this afternoon.

"Well, you know I don't believe in prevaricating when a crisis has arisen, so here we go. Tori, you know Dawn Taylor from *Taylored Communications*—formally *DT-PR*—"

"Let's play nice, Elle," Dawn warned with a hint of a smile. "We're both pretty in heels today. We can leave the brawling for *The Banger* tomorrow night."

Pulling in a deep breath, Elle's hazels sparkled. "I can arrange for two victories, Dawn, but one won't be necessary if you allow me to fill my client in without disruption. Thanks." Elle cleared her throat and continued. "But whom you don't know is Kim Rivera. Rivera is Deon's legal representation at *Taylored Communications*."

"Ooh," I singsonged as I took to the seat Elle had just vacated.

She was on one. I could let her do all the posturing while I figured out what in the world was going on here. "Lawyers and salivating public relation representatives. Are we talking divorce before the prenup *and* marriage, Johnson?"

Deon's eyes rolled into the air as he shook his head. "You got my text earlier. Right?"

I nodded.

"I don't think this is a moment for jeering, Tori," Dawn advised.

"Ms. McNabb, Ms. Taylor," Elle requested. "Let's show some decorum here."

Dawn's permanent grin didn't fade. I didn't think it ever did. It was Elle who suggested Dawn when Deon asked to sign with *Love is Action* six months after we began dating. Elle declined taking him on and recommended several firms in lieu of her rejection. Dawn's reputation had to be up to par if Elle passed her name. Talented and all, she was no Elle Hunter.

"Okay." Dawn sighed. "Elle, I'll allow you to do the honors."

"Great. I believe that's best anyway." Elle turned to me. "There's a young woman—twenty-six years old—out of National City, which is a small town next door to San Diego, who claims to be five months pregnant by Deon."

My eyes shot over to him, a wave of nausea hitting me, but I wouldn't fold.

"Come on, T, baby," he lamented. "You know me. You know the bullshit that follows me."

"Then what's this gathering about if it's just a rumor?"

"She's demanding fifty thousand dollars or she's going to the bloggers," Dawn explained.

I shrugged. "Why not let her go."

"Because we can't," Dawn informed passionately.

My attention went to Elle before I asked, "Why not?"

Elle took a deep breath. "Because neither one of you need the bad press right now. The young lady, Miranda Caldwell, gave a deadline for payment which is in an hour—something I was just told less than an hour ago. The story will break just before you hit the ring, overshadowing the real main event. There will be a media circus while you're in combat."

"How do we know she's going to do it?" I asked. "She could be calling his bluff."

"I knew Ragee knows the *Spilling That Hot Tea* admins. He checked in with them and, luckily, got a rapid response twenty minutes ago. The girl has been in touch with them about Deon cheating and, just as she's told Deon, she hasn't dropped the pregnancy jewel yet."

Ragee.

My friends know...

Dawn shifted closer to me. "What we need to do is decide on our response."

"Our response has been decided," Elle stated firmly. "Ms. Caldwell will be paid."

Dawn regarded me with arched brows. "Tori, are you sure you want to do this?"

"*Ms. McNabb*," Elle corrected. "will not be the sponsor of this blunder." She turned her admonishing gaze to Deon. "Mr. Johnson will be. In fact, a comprehensive agreement between Mr. Johnson and Ms. Caldwell is being drawn as I speak on behalf of *Taylored Communications*. Ms. McNabb's name or image will not be included in any communication with her, neither will *Love Is Action*. You will have—" She paid a cursory glance to her wrist watch. "—just a few minutes to copy and paste it onto your own letterhead."

Dawn's head popped back with incredulity. "But what if the terms are not reasonable?"

"That's what Ms. Rivera's here for," Elle answered as the door opened and a visitor was announced from the entrance of the suite. "That's our legal representation there. Let's get to work, shall we?" Her tight beam was beautiful and cunning all together.

This was the Elle, who was deceptively calm and dangerous.

Dawn, an undeniable beauty herself—a warm syrupy hue with a

natural wild mane of gorgeous patterns and a soft touch of makeup—
switched weight on her hips. "Deon and Tori are engaged. I believe
it's their dilemma equally, a matter they should pursue together."

Elle's chin dropped and eyes narrowed just slightly. "*Ms.
McNabb* is preparing to fulfill a seventy-million dollar contractual
agreement in that ring downstairs on tomorrow. Even now, before her
payout, standing before you is a woman worth over three-hundred
million dollars: there's no equity in this shakedown. No fifty-fifty
payment option once Ms. Caldwell's demands pass the one hundred
thousand dollar mark."

Ouch...

My eyes fluttered closed as I tried maintaining my poker face. It
was no secret that Deon wasn't a franchise player. He made the *Pro
Bowl* as the top special teams' player, holding out for a contract extension and raise since going into his final year of the contract with the
Kings. They offered Deon the new contract, but he was upset,
wanting more guaranteed money. The *Kings* were trying to put more
money into the contract, but less guaranteed money. And guaranteed
money is gold for a *League* player.

After dating Deon, I pitched him to Elle and Jackson to be signed
as a client. He was in need of media representation to increase his
visibility, and still, no other firm had been able to increase the popularity of an athlete the way *Love is Action*, aka, *L.I.A*, could.
However, Elle rejected the notion. She told me Deon's portfolio
wasn't the right fit for *L.I.A*. He was disappointed, but I was alerted
to her wisdom. Months later, while having drinks at a gathering at
Young Lord's home in Malibu, her inebriated mouth shared it wasn't
attractive doing a deal with the "new guy" Tori was dating. Deon was
on the outside and not proven to be profitable on his own merit. If he
had, she would have gone with him. That was one of the many times
Elle Hunter proved to me her mastery in public relations.

"You gonna just let her talk shit about me like that in my face—
your face?" Deon challenged, chewing his thumb, still seated.

As one of the attorneys from *L.I.A.* crossed the room for the coffee table to open his briefcase, I had no words appropriate for Deon right now. If I wasn't careful, I'd be on the precipice of a dangerous physical and emotional spiral the day before I fought.

"I ummm..." My regard met Elle's. "I'm going to get ready for weigh-in. I'll leave this to you."

Deon's muffled grumbles tried following me into my bedroom.

Ashton

I stood from the conference table to meet palms with my partner, the other original founder of *B-Way Burger*.

"Congratulations, sir," Briggs offered.

Meeting him in a firm shake, I returned, "I appreciate your faith in my vision once again."

"Well." He aired out his suit jacket, then buttoned it. "It's the way it's supposed to be. You're doing alright, man."

Lawrence Briggs, my father, and another gentleman by the name of Barry Wick opened up a hole in the wall burger joint on the west end of Paterson, New Jersey. They slaved for years just to stay afloat in a predominantly poor neighborhood. That was until my father finally got the balls to share his plans of expansion with Briggs and Wick. Briggs, being the beta male he still exhibited, was amenable and all in. Wick expressed his unease about taking such high risks but went along with it.

That was until having *B-Way Burger* locations all over the state turned into a vision of becoming a national chain. Wick couldn't stomach the gamble and asked his team to slow down. My father wrote him a check, telling him to have a nice life. Years later, my father was able to see the fruits of his dreams. He and Briggs continued their quest to become burger chain kings. Today, with nearly three-thousand restaurants in forty-eight states in the U.S., my father's dreams were my reality.

I officially joined the helm of *B-Way Burger* a few years after graduating from *Blakewood University*. It had seemed to be my inevitable destination after losing my football career. But it, along with journalism, helped keep my sanity when life grew stale then rocky. It had kept me challenged mentally while writing and investigating did the same for me, but physically, too.

"You going out to fuck up that fairway?"

Briggs made a golf swing motion with his arms. "You know me well, young man." He chortled, headed for the door of the room.

"Mr. Spencer, a moment of your time, please?" Mary, the head of our charity department, came charging into the room.

"Ms. Mary," I greeted her dramatically as I packed up my things from the table. "It's great to see you today."

She stopped and scratched her head. "I saw you this morning in Jim's office."

I knew that, but enjoyed fucking with her. "Oh. I forgot."

She shook her head, segueing into her purpose of bursting into the conference room instead of waiting until I returned to my office.

"Do you have any plans tomorrow night?" She immediately expressed her nervousness by exposing all her teeth.

I froze. "May I ask why?"

Mary let go of a deep breath, sighing dramatically. "Because one of our partners is having a recognition dinner, which my department knew and processed regularly without expedience. That's because we didn't know they billed *B-Way Burger* as the top recipient."

"And?"

"And we need a face there—a recognizable one," her volume hiked.

Again, I asked, "And?"

The apologetic lines in her face deepened as her shoulders dropped. "Mr. Briggs is going out of town for the weekend."

"And?"

"And I was hoping you could attend." Her lips still stretched wide, exposing most of her teeth.

Going to an unexpected boring charity dinner on a Saturday night? Had my life eddied to this pathetic social level of zero? My plan was to sleep as late as my house would allow, then slowly freestyle an itinerary. This would be my first free weekend since returning from *Kamigu.*

Just as I was about to speak, Tamia, my assistant, was at my side with a rapid response. "Actually, Mr. Spencer isn't available and has professional duties to pursue."

My eyes damn near jumped out of my head. "What?"

Tamia nodded. I believed her heeding. She held the pen to my master planner, which meant all of my appointments went through her. Anytime I searched the calendar on my phone, the events were either loaded by her or I'd have to fit in my own around what she put there.

"Ut—okay," Mary forfeited, shoulders still low. "I guess I'll have to see if Brown or Tucker's available. If not, they'll have to settle for a representative."

"Sorry about that, Mary," I spoke to her back as she took off for the door.

After gathering up my things, I left, too, with Tamia on my heels. "How could I not know about a Saturday obligation?"

"Because I didn't put it on your schedule," she answered from behind me as we threaded the busy hallway.

"Then how did it get there?"

"I put it there this morning."

"A last-minute entry?" I made the tsk-tsk sound.

"Yes, actually. Apparently, you had an invitation sent here that got held up in the mailing room."

"How does that happen?" We stepped onto the elevator.

"When the recipient doesn't know how to send things here and address it properly."

My forehead stretched in confusion. "Why would we adhere to any invitation sent by an entity who doesn't know how to send it to my desk?"

Tamia was the first to leave the elevator when the doors opened. "Your other job."

Flummoxed, I proceeded to my office without another word. I dropped my files from the conference room meeting on a coffee table. There, at my desk, was a black box. I threw my gaze over to Tamia who leaned into the doorjamb with crossed arms. Tamia had the box open. The first thing I noticed was a large bottle of limited edition *Mauve*. The stained glass had silver and gold plates with intricately engraved designs and script.

"Shit," I murmured, impressed by the gesture.

A *McNabb vs. O'Connor* detailed logo was printed on the tissue paper and envelope inside the box. I opened the thick stationery with unfounded anticipation. It was clear what this package was about. Inside were floor tickets to the fight. There was no formal invitation but for a one-line, hand-written note.

Know-it-all human.
-The Banger

A smile opened in my chest but didn't ascend to my face as I peered over to my assistant.

"Now do you know who sent that here via snail mail, because I sure as heck don't." Tamia awaited an answer.

I sat down in my seat, dazed, and murmured, "Atlantic City... tomorrow night?"

"That's the hottest damn ticket in the country right now! The woman who wants to take you doesn't have the finesse factor, I see."

"This isn't that." My gaze was lost to the sky view of my window.

"Really?" Her tone dropped an octave.

Was I interested in going to a celebrity-studded affair right now? *Hell no!* But Tori invited me personally, and it felt like a challenge. The decision was made when she invited me.

Growling, I sat up and snatched the receiver from my desk phone.

In my periphery, Tamia's face fell toward the floor. *"You're stressed about having to find a last minute date?*

"Nah. I know who my arm-candy will be?"

"Who?"

A half a ring later, she answered the phone. "Yeah."

"Ms. Wanda..." Finally, I smiled.

Tightening the strap on my robe while pacing from the bedroom, I met him in the living room of my suite. His face was with a mask of hard muscles.

"You good?" he asked with tight lips.

I chuckled. "Of course, I'm fine, boy."

"No, you ain't."

"Raj—"

He looked me up and down, taking in my silk robe, the only thing cladding my skin. He gave me no notice of his visit. My security called me, saying he was on his way in.

"He here?"

I blinked. "Deon? No."

"Good. You don't need that nigga's low vibrations."

I noticed his fists balled at his sides.

"Raj, I'm good."

"You're going to win," he stated with conviction.

Taking a deep breath, I toed over to the sofa and sat on my leg. I made clear, "I know." while nodding my head. "What all did you hear?"

His deep pecan eyes swept the room. "I'm not killing your vibe with that. But here." He pulled out a keychain with two dangle keys. "Wynter thought between your drama with Treesha and now Johnson, and with you looking for a new place, you may need a cut spot after the fight to land."

He handed me the keys. Studying them with confusion, I asked, "Where's this 'cut' spot?"

"My place in Jersey City."

"Don't y'all live there part-time?"

He shook his head, face still tight. "The boys'll be moving in next week full-time now. We don't want them living in two homes like that. Not yet, at least."

Ragee and his wife, Wynter, were adopting three boys Raj had pretty much been sponsoring for years by way of a modern-day orphanage. They'd been working, taking steps to mentally, emotionally, and spiritually prepare to be parents.

"Wow," I exhaled. "It's finally going down? What if you both change your minds about having your own kids?"

Raj shook his head adamantly. "Ain't gone happen."

"Does Wynter agree?"

"Probably more than I do. But this is good for us. We're excited. God is expanding us through these boys. Benji, Mathew, and Devon are our increase."

I nodded, eyes falling. "I agree. I'm happy for you."

"Matt wanted to come down this weekend."

I snorted. "Tell buddy he has a few more years before he's ready for Atlantic City."

Raj's brows lifted. "Tell me about it."

After a spell, I asked, "Were you coming here to molly-wap my fiancé?"

"Nah." His fists flexed. "Why would I do that?"

I angled my head, challenging him. "Why didn't you bring Wynter?"

"Because I knew you were in your solitary zone. You looked good at weigh-in, by the way. Your back and triceps are cut, man."

"Raj."

"Hmmm..."

"Your ass is lying."

"Whoa!" His head swung back. "The language."

"How can you expect me to get better at it if you bullshit me?"

"Tori, there's no way I'd fight ya man the night before a fight—your fight."

"Then why are you here in my suite flexing?"

"Because you're hurting—"

"I'm not—"

"You are, man," he declared dismissively. "I know you."

I shook my head, chewing on my thumbnail. The thought reminded me of Ashton thinking he knew me, too. Why did humans think I was knowable?

I took a deep breath, gazed fixed into the upholstery of the sofa. "I'm trying not to be."

"Why?"

"Because," I rolled my eyes into the air, deciding to be honest. "I've been told I win fights because I fight angry."

Raj shrugged. "What's wrong with that?"

Rolling my eyes closed, I fought back unexpected tears. "Only the fact that I've been angry all my life—"

Raj was at my side on the couch in a millisecond. "That's not true! Can't be." His thick arms encased me. "Wait. You think it's true?"

That made me giggle. "That would be fucked up. Right?"

"It would be. That ain't something I'd say about you—you always being angry—but it's something only you can answer. Have you been angry all your life?"

I swiped my wet nose while sniffling, grateful to have escaped the tears. "I don't know. I do know I'm a better human now. These past few years, I've gotten healthier as a person. I feel strong. I have faith in God. I know He's got my back, but..."

"You can say you're angry now, Tori. You have every right to be."

I turned in his bear hug. "I know, right! This nigga got me in some ghetto ish, knowing damn well I'm ready to ghost the 'famous' life and finally..."

Raj nodded, his long lashes meeting when he blinked slowly. "Finally start a family of your own." I, too, nodded, this time, unable to stop an escaping tear. "Listen, the Bible says in Jeremiah twenty-nine verse eleven, '*For I know the plans I have for you, declares the Lord, plans for welfare and not for evil, to give you a future and a hope.*'" *Hope?* "The people of Israel spent seventy years in oppression—enslaved—but the Lord waited for them; had plans to prosper them. He'd already had a set agenda for the people, although they saw no reason to hope. To me, in the case of your life, that means no matter how long your heart has been longing for a family of your own—whatever that represents in your mind—the plan for your welfare, your future, and even hope is already in His will."

My eyes closed again. It was official: I was emotional and, of course, it would be Raj to bring them to the surface. I loved him. God, I loved my brother.

"Take it from someone who held the keys to their own mental and emotional prison and sat there decade after decade, not releasing myself: Your day of hope will come. Your day of peace is not only possible, but nigh. *I know.*"

I rolled my eyes at him, feeling silly for being so emotional. Playing it off, I joked, "That church talk bangs. I don't know if you get it from Ezra or Grandmother McKinnon, but you're good, son-son!" I smacked his hard shoulder.

Adorably, Raj rolled his eyes. "Don't get stupid when I'm ministering, man." Laughing, I covered my mouth. "I'm just saying, being in the wilderness isn't an uncommon place for believers in Christ. We have an advantage, though, which is Emmanuel."

"Okay, preacher man!"

"Tori! I'm not playing."

My shoulders fell, and I sighed. "I know. I know, and I need it."

"Okay. Now, let's go to our Redeemer in prayer." Raj didn't leave room for a rebuttal. He grabbed my hands, closed his eyes, and bowed his head. "God, we give you glory…"

This was my Ragee McKinnon. To the world, he may have been a sexy, burly, heart-throbbing peculiar R&B crooner Ragee. But to me and those who knew him intimately, Raj was a passionate church boy.

Back in the darkness of my room, lit with glowing candles and filled with soft sounds of old school jazz music, I felt a bit pensive. My belly was full, body felt amazing after a long bath and oil rub down, and yet this sucked. I was supposed to be relaxing, mentally preparing for tomorrow. But I was far from relaxed; I was ready. If I could fight Monica now, I would. The pent up energy was near an explosive degree.

Trying to occupy the buzzing feeling, I picked up my cell to call my assistant. Lidia's room was down the hall in my suite. She answered within three rings.

"What do you need, *Banger?*"

"Just checking on the RSVPs. Are they all in?"

"Ummmm..." I could hear her tapping away. "Most, yeah."

My lips twisted as my gaze brushed the shadowy walls contemplatively. "Who hasn't?"

"Uhhhh... Let's see." I listened to her hum away. "Well, Treesha...in the front row. And...pretty much the whole second row—"

"Second row?" I breathed out as soft as a whisper. *Wow!* "Uh—okay. I'm out for the night."

"See you charged and ready to go in the morning," she bade.

I didn't reply before hanging up; I'd decided.

Fuck Treesha.

Fuck Deon.

Fuck Monica "Four Leaf Clover" O'Connor.

And fuck not being angry. I closed my eyes, telling myself it was time to rest. Twisting and turning, I couldn't get my mind to slow. Finally, I grabbed my phone again and tapped my way into my contacts. The phone rang too many times for my insecure heart to take.

Just as I was about to disconnect, the line clicked and a deep rasp sounded, "Hello, KaToria. Is everything okay?"

Overcome with emotions, I couldn't speak. Tears poured down my face and from my nose so suddenly, my only answer was a sniffle.

"Christ!" he whispered forcefully. "Hang on." Then I heard him speaking to someone near. *"Beloved, can you finish this? I'm going to need a moment."*

CHAPTER FIVE

Ashton

Me: **We'll discuss it in the morning.**

I glanced out of the large window into the dark air over the Atlantic Ocean. The waters were troubled, clashing tempestuous waves were violent. I wondered if it was a presage for what would happen tonight, inside the ring.

My vibrating phone brought my attention back down to my hand.

Maggie: *That's what you said last night.*

My head bounced back and eyes blinked.

Me: I did say that. And guess what? I'm saying it again. Goodnight.

Not wanting to continue that conversation, I tucked my phone into the pocket of my blazer and made my way over to the bar. My life consisted of constantly answering and catering to women. Tonight was *technically* supposed to be a night off from it.

It took no time for me to catch eyes with the bartender. I greeted him with a nod. "*Mauve*, clean. And *Corona* in a glass, please."

"Right away, sir." He turned to prepare my order.

"Hey, you." I glanced down to the beckoning feminine voice and found a pleasant surprise.

"Mrs. Jacobs," I greeted while meeting her in a physical embrace. "Why do you seem so perturbed?"

"Oh, you can tell, huhn?" She motioned another bartender for service. "It's because a particular seasoned woman is across the room flirting with my husband, and I can't do anything about it."

My attention brushed the cocktail room of about forty people, or so. "What old ass woman got you running away from her instead of running in her mou—" When my eyes landed on my mother, grinning in Azmir's face, my words halted. "That damn Ms. Wanda." I pursed my lips playfully.

Rayna ordered a glass of water in a champagne glass before commenting, "Ahn-huhn. Now, what were you saying about that seasoned Brick City woman?"

I cracked the fuck up. Rayna Jacobs, the wife of business tycoon, Azmir Jacobs. I met her when she was dating Azmir, a friend of my father, who I'd known since I was a kid. In fact, it was Jacobs who introduced me to my mentor. Rayna here was a New Jersey native and we'd always found common ground and conversation from that topic alone. "If it makes you feel any better, she dallies with StenRo, too."

"Listen, my name is Rayna Brimm-Jacobs, not Zoey Barrett-Rogers." She issued a pointed expression with her meticulously painted smoky eyes as I howled.

"Yo, I'm so out of the game now. Is that the thing? Hyphenating?"

Rayna shrugged. "Just some of us stubborn women. How have you been?" I could see the twinkle of concern in her eyes and hear it in her inflection.

"I'm good." My drinks were placed next to my arm. "Can't complain."

"I'm not used to seeing you at sporting events. You're not working, are you?"

I cocked my head to the side as my face went taut with wonder. "That's a very good question, Lady Jacobs. I don't know what the hell I'm doing here. But I do know I'm with Ms. Wanda—" My regard skirted over to my mother, still beaming at Azmir. "—and there's no way I can bring that cougar behavior to work."

Rayna snickered in good nature. As she sipped on what appeared to be water with lime, a thought occurred.

"How's this pregnancy coming along?"

"So different from the last. People, including my OB, think it's supposed to be easier because it's just one baby, but the five-year gap is making me feel like this one's giving me the same energy as the one with the twins."

"You look amazing either way." I leaned to the side, trying to gain a view of her shoes. "Those must be what...? Four and a half inches?"

"Your shoe game sucks, Ashton. Try four point one."

Rayna pushed out her foot, showing off. Snickering, I nodded while eyeing them now from a better view. "I don't think I'm too bad. I do know those are *Giuseppe*'s Odile. Let me guess, Mr. Jacobs' choice."

Sipping her water, Rayna hummed while shrugging I was right. "Just don't bring it up to him. He's unnecessarily fixated on me in heels while pregnant."

"Are you over here flirting with my bone, man?" I heard the strong New Yorker intonation in his tenor, something he couldn't shake, no matter how long he'd been on the West Coast. "You got her leg hanging the fuck out and shit. I expect that from many, but not my people."

Pretending to ignore him, I returned my gaze to Rayna's black suede sandal with the chiffon bow at the heel. "Not at all, sir. Her majesty here is accusing me of having garbage ass shoe game, and instead, I'm wondering why not go with *Saint Laurent*'s Talitha Feather leather sandal."

"Those are so...twenty eighteen'ish. I don't think they're available anymore."

"They would be to Mrs. J here if they were purchased when available." I gave him a duh expression using my head and hands. "It's a sexier shoe with the same feather look, only the *YSL*s would have added ornaments to her incredible dancer-calf muscles. They're about the same size in heels. So if you're okay with the *GZ*s here, I'm sure you wouldn't have objected to—"

"Is this Ms. Wanda's?" Rayna asked over me while going for the glass of *Corona*. "I'm sure it is. It seems very...Newark'ish. I'll take it to her while you two very wealthy, women's shoe idée fixe, six-foot plus men continue to squabble in this discussion."

As she strutted off, I taunted, "Idée fixe. Nice, but you're back in Jersey now, expat." I turned back to her husband. "Ms. Wanda got her fucked up, man." Azmir's head shot back as he laughed his ass off. "Like for real. You know Rayna loves me. Tonight, my moms killed that."

"Yup." He agreed, and I couldn't help but laugh with him. "She'll be fine. TB's here. She was his biggest fan before Jade."

"Yeah. And Jade doesn't hyphenate." I sipped my drink, watching his brows slowly furrow.

"Okay. And who does?"

"Mrs. Brimm-Jacobs."

"I've never met a Brimm-Jacobs in my life."

This time, my face fell. I searched for Rayna until I found her with my mother, arm in arm, cracking the hell up. "Did she just play me?"

Azmir chuckled silently. "Indeed." He sipped his drink. "There are many things I've relented to when making her mine, nonetheless I've branded and marked her."

I shrugged with my mouth. "Talk that shit, player." Then I moved in for a dab. There weren't many I'd believe so easily as I did Azmir

Jacobs. I also knew his claim wasn't limited to his last name. "I also like your new spot." To gesture the posh resort, I swept the room with my eyes and head.

If I didn't know Azmir as well as I did, I would've missed his truth before his poker face settled in. "I'm not sure what you're speaking of."

After gulping back golden water, I replied, "And that's because you forget with whom you're speaking." As he always did when calculating, Azmir read my body language under the guise of allowing me the opportunity to share more. I took the bait. "An associate of mine out of the Midwest is doing a piece on the gaming industry in the U.S. and is touching on the revival of Atlantic City. He sent me the paperwork with *ADJ Enterprise* billed as the diversified conglomerate holding company for *KAHRI Resort and Casino.* He thought it was strange that the Cotton family—a white ass Puritan family—would change their name at the time of your bailout. Did I mention the name Kahri means kingly in Swahili and, to some, is considered Arabic? Either way, the name has *a black man backing* it all over it. Only kings do king shit like that." I raised my near-empty glass in the air.

After a long, decided stare down, Azmir met my tumbler on a clink. "Indeed."

"Whaddup, Divine," someone called out from behind Azmir.

When Azmir turned, he gave me view of Ragee. "Aye, what up, Raj." I watched as they dapped it up. Then Ragee's attention landed on me, but his smile dwindled. Azmir turned fully toward the woman hand in hand with Ragee. "Mrs. McKinnon, what a pleasure."

As I swallowed back the last of my drink, Ragee took a couple of steps toward me, breaking hands with who I now assumed was his wife.

"Does she know you're here?"

I didn't like his tone or audacity, and almost went the asshole route of asking who *she* was. Quickly, I decided against it. I'd never formally met Ragee when Tori and I were friends at *BSU*. I'd heard some things about him from her and vaguely recalled him coming to Brick's funeral, but this was as close as I'd been with him in a room.

"I'm not sure." I placed my empty tumbler on the bar.

"Are you here for work?"

"I'm not sure about that either, but I'm sure I'll gain inspiration to add to what I'm doing."

"Did you tell her you were coming?"

"No." I shook my head, exasperated with all the questions already. "I was sent tickets and decided to use them."

"Do you two know each other?" Azmir rejoined the conversation.

Ragee's eyes bounced between the two of us. "I see you two know each other."

Azmir chuckled, scratching just above his mouth while read-justing his stance and widening his legs. "Yes. For a very long time." And he waited.

And I understood that wait.

Diffusing whatever the fuck the energy was misting between us, I extended my hand. "I wouldn't insult you with a lie by saying I don't know who you are. But I am Ashton Spencer. And while I'm many things, what brings me here tonight is solely the article I'm writing up on your friend for *Sports Illustrated*."

It didn't take Ragee long to reciprocate the shake. "I've heard about your work. Good to officially meet you."

This shit was instantly weird. Now, dude was acting like he didn't want anyone around to know the strange ass bravado he let off my way. And Ragee was a big nigga. Although my height, he had to have been at least thirty pounds heavier. Throwing around an authoritative energy could give off antagonizing vibes, and I was not the type to cower to it.

"Well, if it isn't my favorite three men," my mother purred, gliding to my side with the slip of her arm beneath mine. "Ashton, I was just coming to tell you I met Ragee, and here he is!" I caught when the muscles around Ragee's eyes loosened. She asked him, "Do you know my son? He's the CEO of *B-Way Burger*, you know?" Her attention returned to me. "He said he's not singing as Tori's doing her walkout tonight."

I couldn't return my mother's innocent banter. The realization of Ragee's sonnin' me had begun burgeoning in my mind. It didn't matter that he'd moved on and, now, appeared shocked about my mother being at my side.

That was until it dawned on me. Unless my mother was flirting with him, too, Ragee could have been processing whatever Tori may have mentioned to him about my mother. She wasn't so kind to Tori back then. *Neither did she ride her like she had other women I dated.* Tori and I didn't last very long for my mother to see her enough. Also, my mother didn't know much about Tori and me.

Suddenly, the room was disrupted in energy. After listening, it was clear the time had come for us to finally take our seats if we wanted to see the main event.

"Come on, baby," Rayna was at Jacobs' side. "I know Ashton doesn't care about missing the undercards. Ms. Wanda told me he doesn't like sports."

Azmir tossed me a glance with humor dancing in his eyes. Rayna was clowning me again. This time, my wit was tied around my neck choking me, thanks to Tori's aggressive ass peoples. Ragee, still looking tight, took his wife at the hand and ambled off.

"Touché, Mrs. Jacobs in high heels."

Rayna stumbled a bit when swinging her head back to look at me with her mouth agape. I tossed her a wink. Smoothly, Azmir leaned down and whispered something to her as they sauntered toward the door.

"What you messing with that woman for?" my mother scolded lowly.

I glanced down at her glass of beer. It was almost empty. "Are you done with that?"

"No!" Her head bobbled. Chuckling, I pinched my brows as her arm tightened around mine. "I'm grown tonight. Shit, I'm kidless and single, Ashton! Now, let's go." She nudged me on our way to the door.

love ∞ *belvin*

Tori

As we waited behind the closed doors for the cue, I bounced on my toes, shook out my arms, and rolled my head over my shoulders. My focus was on my body, feeling connected with each inch, which meant my toes had to align with my back and nose. That was the level of cohesion I attempted to achieve each fight. For this one, it was much more imperative that I stayed aggregated so I could think more.

Taking full breaths, I felt light as a bird as I mentally chanted, *"And You did just what You said…"*

"That's us!" I heard shouted over my large group of bodyguards, trainers, ring team, and Brielle, who stood a few feet in front. "We're ready back here," the little guy with headphones and a clipboard spoke into a wireless microphone.

Someone else near the door gave the countdown, specifically to Brielle, and before I knew it, she was belting the first of the lyrics. Then the doors opened to a thunderous burst of applause and cheers. My head dropped as I bounced on my toes and wiggled my shoulders. The energy was here, and what I needed.

"Come Through the Fire" was the song she sang. It held so many truths for me and spoke to the plight of female boxers trying to legitimize our talent alongside men. I'd done it. I came from nothing and turned my pain into a skill. My skill took me places before my heart

and mind were ready to go. I later learned that God had my path laid before I was born. The success I'd amassed in such a short time was beyond my intention. It came fast and unexpectedly, breaking all records set in women's boxing. Now, I was preparing to reach an even more fulfilling plateau, and the only thing standing in the way of my destiny was Monica "Four Leaf Clover" O'Connor.

Time to finish her...

We began to move forward, into the arena. I'd seen the setup with the music and my name and silhouette of my likeness in big, bright lights yesterday. Brielle and I had rehearsed this twice with the sound people, which was great because I was now in my zone and couldn't open up my mind to much other than the job before me in the ring.

I threw air jabs as she sang, giving the short walk a long journey. Brielle's talent was like none other. She represented the same level of greatness I attempted. And she wouldn't be the dynamic performer she was known to be without choreography. The walkout wasn't long, neither was it a Brielle concert, but I allowed her to add her zing into it someway.

The number she performed was from her latest album. I cameoed in the highly-anticipated video, a woman's anthem that had gone platinum in sales and excelled in streams in just days. So, just as in the video, once the intense intro transitioned dramatically into an up-tempo bridge, due to the need of a shortened version, Brielle and I stopped, and I threw rhythmic air jabs to the strong bass as I peered directly into a camera. The crowd replied with deafening applause, and I knew my job was done for this condensed performance.

We made our way to the ring, where an opening of the ropes was created for me. And I felt at home. This was my dominion, my playground. It hadn't settled in my mind this would be the last time of this sort, but it had been in my heart. The ring was packed with O'Connor's people, mine, the federation's admin staff, the referee, and cameramen. The dynamism couldn't be any better for the occasion. I took a quick sweep of the arena. It was packed and frenetic with barbaric anticipation.

With my fists in the air engaging the crowd, I turned until I found Lidia and motioned her over.

"Everything okay?" She had to nearly shout in my ear.

"How's my section?" To be more specific, I amended, "How many no-shows?"

She shook her head, going into her tablet. "Zero. Everyone's checked in—except for Treesha, as you know."

A surprising spread of warmth blossomed in my chest. Quickly, my face fell to the floor of the ring. It was game time. After the final pre-fight words and reiterations from my team, I met O'Connor in the middle of the ring with the referee. He ran down the rules of the fight as I gazed deeply into her green eyes. She was afraid, but prepared to survive as many rounds as she could. Monica knew, just as I did, she was not my level of talent. She didn't have the aggression, swag, or boxing intelligence. But she had heart, and that accounted for something.

"Are we clear?" the ref ended his list of rules.

I nodded my understanding, then O'Connor followed.

"I'm gonna eat your weak ass heart tonight," I declared with a slick grin while shaking my legs out. Then I flashed my tongue wide and sensually, throwing her off her game while extending my gloves to her.

Monica lifted her fists and whacked my gloves hard with harsh impact. Her face turned red as she snatched herself away from me.

Ashton

By the middle of the fourth round, I was unable to sit down. My mother next to me was constantly slapping or yanking my pant leg. Tori kept me on edge. From my research of her career, Tori was known for throwing fight-ending haymakers. It was something she had been criticized for by many. Haymakers were also what I remembered of Tori from *BSU*. In her home fight with the girl from California, Luke had to remind Tori to pace herself and not knock her out too soon. That night, the fighter had Tori cornered until the command from Luke.

Tonight, it was clear to me from her going beyond three rounds, Tori and her team had a new game plan that included high endurance. And Tori had been ahead of O'Connor for jabs landed for all of the rounds. Tori was fighting with focus and a plan. Sweat sprouted from her toned, bronzed skin as she executed laser focus, throwing successfully from a distance she created and maintained.

"Damn, Ashton!" my mother hissed from beneath my right side. "You can tell you don't go to fights often!"

I heard a few snickers behind us, likely Rut Amare and his crew. They were in the row behind us as well as Trent Bailey's and Jordan Johnson's. This fight was star-studded, which was common for Tori McNabb's matches. She brought with her talent A-list fanfare, which equaled high viewership. She was the first female boxer in history to demand ten million-denomination payouts from the networks. And being here, watching her live and in action, I could see how. Tonight, since Monica O'Connor smacked Tori's gloves violently, I'd been on edge, barely able to sit through an entire round.

Monica, apparently, had the stamina for Tori's endurance. That was until she wasn't and threw an obvious blow of frustration into Tori's groin. The impact winded Tori for a minute. The angry roar from the crowd distracted a red-faced O'Connor, giving the referee time to recover. He called a timeout, allowing Tori's team to come in and examine her. It was clear Tori didn't want the intermission. She kept nodding, indicating she was fine.

"*Four Leaf Clover* mad *The Banger* still making her ass earn them one-point-five Ms!" Rut shouted from behind me, causing the entire section to go up in laughter.

As funny as his comment was, I was on a different plane of attentiveness to this fight. Tori wasn't fighting angrily. It seemed to me, she was using her skill set and not emotion. O'Connor's sucker jab may have ruined that professional focus for Tori. After about a minute and a half of inspection and the referee warning the O'Connor corner about malicious conduct, I assumed, he gave motion to resume the fight.

Then the bell tolled and the two women were making their way to the center of the ring. Monica threw the first jab and Tori was able to block it, throwing her own. It landed on Monica's chin, snapping her head back just a little. Then the two began with a series of blows mostly landing. It went on for a while, stirring the audience. We assumed someone would be affected soon. It didn't happen as quickly as one may have thought. After a few back and forth punches, two things were clear. Monica was growing exhausted, and Tori was alone in the room with just her opponent.

She was doing it, largely to my surprise. Tori was fighting with something other than rage. She slowed her throws, giving O'Connor more leeway. Twisting and dodging most of them, Tori's agility and acuity were on full display. It was actually O'Connor fighting emotionally when she fell for Tori's trap that eventually cost her the fight. Tori blinded O'Connor with the left, flushing her with a powerful right, and knocking her on her ass. The referee rushed to O'Connor examining her. The poor girl was dazed long enough for the ref to call the fight in her loss.

Winded by it all, my legs finally weakened from being strained for what seemed like forever. My mother and everyone around jumped to their feet, shouting Tori's victory. As people all around cheered, hooted, and hollered, expressing their excitement, I laughed quietly at myself, holding my face in my palm as I shook my head.

"Yo, my nigga! Yo, my nigga!" I heard shouted continuously from behind me in a tenor not belonging to Rut, the loudest in my section of ringside.

"She did it! G.O.A.T. for sure, my nigga!" *That*, for sure, was Rut Amare. "Where that victory party gonna be at again?"

"Ah, man! I lost that venue. I got my people looking for another place as we speak, my nigga! My baby deserves the best. You feel me?"

"Oh, word? What about Raj's spot, *Checkerboard*?"

"Too small. This victory party finna be epic for baby girl, you heard me?"

I didn't need to turn around to confirm it was Deon Johnson near. As he continued in conversation with his teammates behind me and my mother spoke over people to Rayna and Ragee's wife, I pulled out my phone to send a text to Keyonna.

Me: Have Louis reach out "randomly" to Deon Johnson's people for a package deal he can't refuse.

Slipping my phone back into my pocket, I gave no concerns to my request being honored. I just hoped it worked.

"Asia's getting so big," I murmured from my balcony overlooking the beach on *Marye Island* in the Florida Keys. "She's finally potty trained?" I glanced over to my father.

He nodded, the biggest beam on his face as he, too, watched his grandchildren play on the beach below. "Nessa said she hasn't had an accident in almost two weeks now." I nodded, my attention going back to the kids. Vanessa, Asia's mother, took pictures of the kids as they laughed, chasing each other along the shoreline. "She's going to be starting school soon, you know?"

"Oh..." I hummed half-heartedly.

I couldn't recall if Vanessa had mentioned that to me. I hadn't really spoken to her since before I began training.

"Yeah. Nessa wants to get her into a private school in Mullica Hill." I nodded again, attention now on Julia, his oldest daughter, who was two years younger than me. She was lost in her phone, likely on social media. That was her life. Her diary. It annoyed me like crazy. "Did you hear me?"

I turned to my father. At now fifty-two, he was still slim with all his hair, though salt and pepper. He wore glasses, loved boat shoes, and was pretty laid back. That was until it came to his family. Timothy Jameson was very involved in the worlds of his children and grandchildren. He and his wife, Patty, lived and breathed their family. Together, they had three children: Julia, Timothy Junior, and Vanessa. The Jamesons also had seven grandchildren. But my father still looked good and was cool.

"School in Mullica Hill, yeah. She's moving out that way?"

"She wants to. She needs a job first."

I would have thought so. Vanessa couldn't keep a job to save her life. She'd been to a few trade schools for hair, administrative assistance, and HVAC—heck, I'd even paid for her to get her real estate license a few years ago and it never materialized to anything. Vanessa even took up boxing, which led to my father contacting me for the first time.

"What she thinking about?"

"Remember when I asked you about your need for a personal assistant when the fight was over?"

"Yeah."

"Patty and I think it's a great idea if Nessa signs on."

I couldn't help the contortion of my face. "Why?"

"Because you won't have Lidia anymore now that you're retired." His smile hid the incredulity he believed my question held.

"Because my lifestyle will be changing, not because there's a problem with Lidia, Timothy."

He blinked hard and reclined away from me a few inches. "You know I don't like when you call me that."

I did it when he didn't feel like a father or felt like more of one to his children with Patty. Nonetheless, I didn't feel like expressing that.

"I won't have a need for Lidia after this week. I've transitioned duties to Renata."

"But Nessa's your sister."

I steeled in my seat. *Did he really just go there?* This was supposed to be my healing retreat from the fight in the sun and warm weather. I took more punches from Monica than I was accustomed to, to make the fight last longer and to prove a stupid point to someone who didn't matter to me in life. Someone I may have had to see once or twice more until I'd be relieved of him again. The last thing I needed from anyone, including my father, was an attack on my real family; my day ones. It was enough that I still had Deon's drama to deal with. My trip to Florida was supposed to be peaceful and away from demands.

As I gazed into my father's eyes, willing the right words, Lidia stepped out onto the balcony, handing me an *iPad* where Renata was *FaceTime*'ing. "Treesha said Elle rerouted a floral delivery from L.I.A. to the apartment."

"Who's it from?"

I watched as, I assumed, Renata stood on something to give me a view of the massive amount of bouquets in the foyer. They were black roses surrounding brown ones. The brown roses were arranged in various letters. "They spell out something." I could hear her, but not see her.

Treesha was arranging them. She had the word *CHAMP* together. My eyes raced over the letters Treesha had separated from that group. I saw the *M*, *A*, and *N*. After a few seconds of concentration, my brain subconsciously searched for an *H* and *U*.

"Human," I murmured, feeling my father's curious gaze on me.

"Oh," Renata chirped.

"Really?" Treesha began gathering the bouquets to spell *human*.

Faintly, I whispered my revelation, "Champion. Champion human."

My pulse began to race and I felt myself slipping into a trance of wooziness I hadn't experienced in years. *What the...* Why would he do this? He showed to my fight. Yes, I invited him, but he actually came when it wasn't necessary for his article. If it was, the publication would have requested tickets for him. Who did he bring? What was up with the internal explosion of adrenaline as my ankles bounced from the balls of my feet? Why did my tummy flip over and over and over?

"This sounds like you," Renata accurately noted. "That's somebody tryna be funny, Tor?"

I shook my head, trying not to reveal the hike in my breathing. "Open the card that came with the delivery and screenshot it to me in a text."

"Okay. Give me a minute," Renata replied before I disconnected the call.

My attention went beyond my father's family, out into the water.

"Wow! Your cousins are on top of things back home," my father remarked. "I was surprised they didn't come down here."

I could have explained they understood I liked to be alone after fights, but since he asked if we could celebrate his grandson's birthday while I was here, that shattered my plans of solidarity. I could have said a lot of things, but didn't.

"They've always been there for me." I took a deep breath, my attention going to his family below. "I'll try to find something for Vanessa. Something that makes sense for both of us." Then I turned to him. "Sound fair?"

He stood and sauntered over to me for a gentle kiss on the forehead. Just as he left the balcony, my phone vibrated on the table next to my latte. Renata sent two screenshots with a scrawl I recognized.

Congrats, champ. Clean fight. As a man of my word, dinner's on me. Now that you have my direct contact info, holla at me. A. Spencer

The second image was his telephone number. Impulsively, I recorded it and tapped out of the text app to call him. My pulse wouldn't slow as the phone rang.

"Hello?" A woman answered. My first thought was to hang up. Then I remembered Keyonna. "Hello?"

I licked my lips. "Hi, I'm looking for Ashton Spencer."

I thought this was his cell number. Did he hit me with the personal assistant line? It was something I did often.

"Sure," her tone still perky as it was when I called. "Who should I tell him is calling?"

My head bounced back. "KaToria."

"Okay. Hang on KaToria." Then I heard nothing.

Hang up. Forget him...

But I didn't. Foolishly, I was doing yet another thing to extend this guy's time in my life. I rolled my eyes toward the sun.

"Tori." His voice was smoky and clear. "You finally responded?"

"I'm finally getting the flowers. Thanks. What's up with the *now that I have your direct info* line? Sounds like a jab." My words shot out harsher than I intended.

I was uncomfortable being connected to Ashton now, and I hated it.

"Just addressing the fact that we weren't properly connected."

"You showed to the fight."

"Narrowly."

"How so?"

Damn! I'm snappy...

"The tickets went to our central mailing location instead of to my office. It was a miracle that it made it to me at all. Usually, those things are trashed or snailed up to corporate."

"Oh." My face fell. "I didn't know."

"I knew you didn't. But it worked out. I was even able to snag a date."

"Good for you."

"Not really. Ms. Wanda flirted with too many of your associates."

"Your mother?"

"Yup." *Wow! She came!* "Anyway, I presume you're calling about my invitation?"

"I am. And *I* presumed this was your personal cell."

Tone it down, Tori!

"You were correct. I give it to my assistants if I'm in an important meeting."

"Holy shit," I murmured. "Is that where you are now?"

"I thought you no longer used profanity," his voice now low and...intimate.

That annoyed me a little. "I told you I'm trying."

"You didn't, but you've also not said yes to dinner either."

I rolled my eyes, then somehow turned my attention to my father below, gathering both Vanessa and Julia in his arms. They smiled brightly as Patty took a picture of them. This had been my life: servicing and pleasing others and accepting their lack of reciprocity.

"How soon are you talking?"

"I can clear my schedule for you this week."

My belly fluttered. Fighting against it, I shook my head. "I'm away." It had been less than two days since the fight with Monica. My face was slightly bruised and body achy. "Won't be back until next weekend."

"Saturday?"

I hesitated. What was I doing? I didn't want to spend time with Ashton Spencer, but I was curious about him. His aura seemed to be different from what I remembered.

"Text me the time."

"Any allergies."

Other than you? "No."

CHAPTER SIX

October

Tori

The tendons in my knees trembled as I rang the doorbell. I was caught in a trance of *BSU* déjà vu, likely from the first time I visited his apartment on campus. That was such a daunting experience for me. I was out-cultured by Ashton on every level then.

Not anymore...

Clearing my throat, I whipped my neck to push my hair over my shoulder. I was ready. Within seconds, the door opened. There was no old school music being played for a tank filled with fish that I could hear. But what I saw was unfair. Ashton's lengthy frame was robust in a deep salmon dress shirt with the first few buttons undone and rolled up his lower arms. The shirt was tucked inside a pair of slim-cut, penny-hued dress pants. How could he appear so masculine in fitted clothing?

"Welcome, champ." Louder than his volume was the mystifying gleam in his eye. I could have confused it for lust or genuine happiness to see me, but was sure it was general hospitality.

The scent of garlic and herbs wafted to my brain via my nostrils instantly while I took in as much of his foyer as I could. Immediately, views of the nighttime Hudson River beamed into floor-to-ceiling windows. It was everywhere—water views—making me feel like I was floating in the air. I didn't feel this way in my apartment. It could have been because my place wasn't this big.

"I'm still trippin' off you living in *Hudson in the City, and* having the penthouse suite."

When he sent his address, my mouth fell open.

"Really?" He reached down for an arm hug and kissed my cheek. The hairs of his thick beard tickled the side of my contoured face, and his scent floated through my nose and shot straight down to my groin. "Why?" he asked when he pulled back.

I played it off as best as I could with a breathy giggle. "Because when I was shopping for a place to live a few years ago, this was the property my real estate agent ran to but was told it wasn't available."

"Not my fault. It's not my deed. I'm subleasing from a friend of mine until I can find a home." He gestured down the hall. "Please tell me you don't need to remove your shoes."

I glanced down at my feet. They were brand new strappy *YSL Opyum* sandals. "No. Why?"

"Good. You look incredible in them." he managed to keep the sleaze out of the comment by maintaining a formal tone. "Let's go into the kitchen. I'll be serving dinner in there."

I followed him, narrowing my focus to the marble floor rather than his toned ass—an ass I could only assume was toned considering his other body parts. "So, you're in the market for a home? What kind?"

"Ahhhh..." He hesitated. "Something traditional and lowkey."

"For you? Really?"

Ashton peered at me from over his shoulders. "Should I be offended by your many assumptions of who I am as a grown man?"

Ignoring him, my eyes perused the cool gray walls with sporadic artwork. The place gave off clean and chic vibes. Either this was Ashton's bachelor expression, or the place was a rental.

"Not at all."

"Good." He turned a corner that gave way to a gigantic chef's grade kitchen; I knew right away from the black stainless steel seven-burner stove. It was a double convection oven, and I had a little thing for kitchens and stoves. There was a long peninsula, brown marble countertops throughout, smart door stainless steel refrigerator, and a large table with tufted high wingback chairs.

"Whoa," I breathed. "This is lush."

Ashton scoffed, "Lush?" His brows met for a mixture of confusion and humor.

I nodded. "Yeah. Did the furniture come with the place?"

"Not much."

I moved to place my purse on the back of one of the chairs. "I'm looking for a place myself. Who's your designer?"

Ashton began soaping his hands at the sink. "Ms. Wanda Lee."

That name brought a thunder to my chest. "How is she?"

"Around. Well..." I watched him cross the room with conversant comfort. Ashton stirred a pot then grabbed wine glasses from the cabinet. "She enjoyed the fight."

"Does she remember me?" The question felt awkward the moment it left my mouth.

He returned to the peninsula with tall and wide-bowl glasses and a bottle of wine. "I would offer you *Limited Edition Mauve*, but I'm saving it for a special occasion." He winked lasciviously when mentioning the bottle of brandy I had sent along with the tickets to my fight—but not for me, which was weirdly disappointing. "Please tell me a dry red blend tickles your fancy."

"How can anything else?"

His brows lifted as he angled his head. "I don't know. *Limited Edition Mauve* may give you new wings." I found that funny. "And to answer your question: no, Ms. Wanda doesn't recall you, which is awfully anticlimactic for me." He handed me the glass.

I scoffed, expressing my concern without shame. "How so?"

"Because I once knew and was friends with *the* Tori McNabb... brought her to my home...around my family, and no one remembers?"

"I wasn't 'Tori McNabb' back then."

"You were always Tori McNabb." He gave a neck bow, matter-of-factly.

Ashton swirled the glass by the stem and raised the wine to his nose for a sniff. I followed suit, enjoying the fruit and woodsy aroma. It tasted even better when I tossed the small taste-testing portion he poured me. Then he motioned, asking if it had my approval, to which I nodded.

As he poured a more generous amount into my glass, I moved the conversation along. "Speaking of your homes, you had two. What happened to your mom and dad's places?"

"She still has her apartment in Newark. Wanda Lee is a Brick City chick down to the socks." I laughed as he shook his head. "The house in West Orange is still there, but vacant."

I almost choked on my wine. Quickly swallowing what was in my mouth, I coughed up the little that crept down the wrong pipe.

"Excuse me," I grunted with tears in my eyes from choking.

"You okay?" Ashton turned for the counter behind him, ripping off a piece of paper towel. "I can get you something softer if you'd like."

I shook my head. "It's all good." Blotting my eyes, I attempted dramatic humor. "Whew!"

"You got a thing about empty homes?"

"How's Jimmy?" my voice barely carried, and I didn't want to prolong my burning question.

Ashton's eyes flashed wide and that smirk disappeared from his face. "You remember him?"

"Of course, I do." My regard fell and I dabbed the corners of my eyes again, unable to look at him. "How could I not?"

"I don't know. How could you? I couldn't remember Treesha's name back in *Kamigu*; I wouldn't be terribly disappointed if you didn't recall my father's..." He raised the glass to his mouth.

I assumed Ashton was being evasive.

"Widower? Your dad's widower."

Ashton shrugged, placing his glass down, then paced over to the stove. "If that's how you remember him, sure." He went into a second pot this time, sniffing from afar then stirring.

My stomach grumbled.

"But you didn't answer my question."

He peered over his shoulder. "About the house?"

"No. About Jimmy. How is he?"

"The last I heard, he was merrily adjusted in his world."

"So he's alive?" I exhaled those words with relief.

Ashton turned to me with his head first. He laughed then fully faced me, laying the serving spoon on a metal reservoir. "Alive? What the hell, Tori? Why would the man be dead? He enjoys being a pain in my ass. He lives for it."

"Really? How is he?"

"He's fine," he scoffed. "I told you that."

"Where? You said the house was empty."

Ashton's neck jerked back and he slowly blinked deeply as though dazed. "Dawg, the first casual conversation I have alone with you, feeling successful at getting you to lower your guard, your first expression of sentiment is for lil' old Jimmy, the innkeeper."

I rolled my eyes. "He's no such thing if the house is empty."

Ashton really seemed offended, but I didn't care. I'd always felt horrible about not keeping in touch with Jimmy. It had been years since we'd last exchanged letters. I'd left him hanging three times before he finally gave up.

"James Porter is an especially content resident of a luxury assisted living facility that's costing me nearly as much as my rent here. He's well-adjusted in a corner wing with all the accoutrements of lavishness, including friends whom he interacts with when his royal highness pleases. Is that satisfactorily enough of an answer for you?" His forehead squeezed and eyes narrowed with contempt. "You *were* soft for that guy, weren't you."

I swept my hair over my shoulder. "He was nice to me. Treated me like a human being." *Unlike many of your people...* "Why did he leave the house?"

Ashton grabbed leafy vegetables and a knife, bringing them over to a waiting cutting board. "He's aged." He shrugged, cutting the leaves with the technique of a chef. My brows shot up. "He was diagnosed with COPD about eight years ago, making it hard for him to get around the place. Plus, no one was there but him and the grounds people."

A memory hit me.

"What happened to the housekeeper? She was sweet. I'm sorry I can't remember her name."

"Muriel had a stroke and retired—no. I had to make her retire. I offered her a package she couldn't refuse."

My palm met my chest. "That's sad."

"It's life." His attention remained on the task of cutting. "She died eight months later."

That palming turned into a tight clutch of my blouse. "Oh, no, Ashton!" I whispered, pained by the knowledge of that sweet woman leaving behind her family.

"It's all good. Anyway... Jimmy's time was up there, so we got him into a place he'd been plotting on for some time, but couldn't afford."

"That's very generous of you."

Things went silent, affording me time to enjoy the wine. It was delicious, rich, and in dope stemware. But I wouldn't have expected anything less from Ashton Spencer. It was clear to me he was still wealthy. I just didn't know how much for sure.

After a few beats, he asked, "So, where are you looking to move to?"

"Out of the metropolis. I'm over the city life."

"Oh, right: You're going to start a family."

I nodded, going for another sip. "That's the plan."

"Where are you two looking specifically? Any desires of going back to SoJo?"

I seesawed my head. "Not really. I just want the cut life; suburbia, but with a diverse community."

"There are loads of towns in the 'cut' in those southern counties."

"But I can't raise Black kids in most of them, though."

Are we really having this conversation?

Ashton nodded, considering my stance. "Ready to eat?"

"Starving."

"Good. I'm ready to wow you. There's a powder room in the hall, to your right. You can get washed up in there while I set the table."

I swallowed the wine I had in my mouth, taken by how in charge this guy still was. "Okay."

Moving swiftly, I left the kitchen, following his instructions.

"Is discussing your mother on the table for the piece?" My eyes rose from my plate. Ashton was across the table, holding his wine glass as his tongue cleaned debris from his front teeth behind his closed mouth. I shrugged, sitting up to wipe my face. Sauce had splattered beneath my lip line. His eyes sparkled when he smirked. "How is it?"

I glanced down at my plate. "You didn't use too much lemon and your sauce isn't dry. Mine is better, though." I winked.

Ashton laughed. "My Italian repertoire is up, girl! But I'll let you have your foolish hyper-confidence."

"I make my own pasta, too."

His head bounced back. "Really?"

With a nod, I confirmed, "Oh, yeah. It's been therapeutic; the patience, specific process...the anticipation of the outcome."

Ashton angled his head. "You're trained?"

"For about four years now."

When he broke out in laughter again, I straightened my spine. "What's so funny, Spencer?"

"Was this that therapy you mentioned."

"A part of it, yeah." I waited for him to explain what he found funny.

Ashton nodded, eyes bouncing all around the table. "I trained, too—a while ago, though."

"Cooking?" He nodded. "By who?"

"Boucher."

"The French guy?"

"You've heard of him?"

"Yeah. They tried to get him for me, but he wasn't available." Then I began to laugh, and that left him hanging. "I guess I'm still not on your level socio-economically. First the apartment building, now the world-class chef."

"Who did you train with?"

"Lefebvre."

His eyes widened. "Gabriel Lefebvre, the Black French chef?" I nodded. "You went to his school in Bordeaux?"

I shook my head. "I didn't have the time. We flew him in for twelve sessions. But he gave me almost double that when our schedules permitted." I went back to eating.

His voice dropped. "That had to cost you at least a *M*."

"It was costly, but it helped. I really got into it. I'm surprised you gave business to a non-Black owner." Over the years, I made strong efforts to support Black businesses and communities, and had always believed the allegiance came from my few days at *Blakewood State University*. Ashton was a huge influence back then. "Did you fly out to Paris for Boucher?"

"No," he scoffed, gesturing his arms to the room. "but he didn't come out to my place to give me lessons here. That factor alone makes us even on the privilege scale."

I shrugged. "Like I said; it helped and still helps."

For a moment, silence hushed the table and we both ate.

Though I was eating, my mind was going. I hadn't forgotten about his question earlier. "A heart attack."

Ashton stilled, fork midway to his mouth. "Huhn?"

I chewed and swallowed my food. "My mother died of a heart attack."

"Is that what was wrong with her that spring semester?" Ashton's eyes fell, giving away a moment of his vulnerability. "I only remember you mentioning multiple sclerosis—"

My forehead stretched. "You remember that?"

With his eyes bulleted into me, Ashton shook his head. "Why wouldn't I?"

This time, my attention fell to my plate. "I don't know. There was lots going on around that time."

"Lots," he agreed. "When did she pass?"

I thought for a minute before I answered. My mind was compart-mentalized in a strange way around trauma. I'd had them back to back for a little more than a year beginning when I left *BSU*. "About ten months after leaving school."

Silverware crashing into china had my head snap up. Ashton's face was tight when he murmured, "I'm so sorry to hear that, Tori."

I shook my head, shamefully with nonchalance. "It's okay. I got through it." I tried forking through my salad. Ashton's homemade dressing was pretty good.

"I know you two were estranged. What was that like; going back home and losing her?"

I sat up and wiped my mouth again. It was easy to forget just how much of a connection Ashton and I had. It was likely because, for so long after leaving school, I believed it was one-sided. Then eventually, I suppressed all the emotions and memories of them into a compartment deep in my mind.

"We actually were pretty cool when I got home. The timing must have been perfect. Raj loves quoting the Bible. He likes to remind me of the scripture, '*All things work together for the good of those who love God and are called according to His purpose.*' I guess it's true in my case. When I got back, she made it clear she needed me."

"Did you two reconcile your differences? Did you speak to a professional...get therapy?"

I shook my head. "We didn't have time to get help. Honestly, I don't think we needed to—well, because she was going to leave the earth when she did. I feel like God knew to supernaturally release my heart of all the anger, hurt, and animosity. Because the moment I stepped foot in her trailer, all that was gone. We became partners instantaneously. Like..." My head bounced. "...literally."

"Shit," he snorted. "And that was before therapy?"

"Way before therapy. I needed her and she needed me at the same time."

"Margaret Maureen wasn't there to make it happen," he whispered like he understood.

In fact, Ashton's gaze on me was blank and unmoving as though in a trance. For a stretch of time that could have only been for a few seconds, I felt it. The warm, luring, impatient need of love I used to feel, but couldn't express at eighteen/nineteen years old lurked eerily over me at the table. The sensation lasted a spell, and a small—teeny weeny—part of me wondered if he felt it in that moment, too.

Needing to end the trance, I cleared my throat and forced myself to finish the last of my food. "You remember her, too."

Seconds later, Ashton began to move again, going for his wine glass. "Why are you surprised I gave business to a non-Black company?" he revived my comment from earlier.

I shrugged with my head while chewing. "Because what I

remember of you back then was *'all Black everything.'*" I did a shimmy in my seat as an ode to an old Jay Z track.

Ashton chuckled, but this time dryly. "It's still my practice to uplift Black enterprises and people by way of businesses, but I wanted the best. And like you, cooking is therapeutic for me. I didn't know that when I sought it out, but I learned eventually. There aren't many Black, internationally trained top chefs around. He met a need at a desperate time, and..." The wings of his back opened when his open palms slowly swung into the air. I nodded, appreciating his honesty. "Anyway, your parent-organization, *Bobby's Hope*, offers a myriad of services like counseling for young Black, underprivileged girls. Is therapy a passion for you?"

"Emotional health is." I blotted my mouth—with the cloth napkin that didn't surprise me this time because I now used them—trying not to disturb my lipstick beyond what eating had. Sitting up in my seat, I explained, "I know it sounds like the same thing, and maybe it is, but the term therapy is now so pop culture. Everybody's talking about it, but therapy can cover so much. I try to focus on emotional health. That's important to me. It's what I've struggled with since my child-hood. So, that's what I raise money for and invest in professionals and outreach workers who can facilitate my vision of reaching girls without means to assist them in becoming emotionally balanced."

"What does emotional balance look like for Tori McNabb?" Ashton was good at sounding like a reporter.

"It means *feeling* my interactions with people. It means me mini-mizing my judgment of people who have social and emotional strengths I don't, or didn't have. It means gaining confidence so I can participate in healthy relationships with people beyond my two cousins and Ragee." I shrugged, thinking. "It means appreciating and loving KaToria enough to allow her to feel safe giving and receiving in all relationships. I've learned and am still learning to love myself, and not just protect myself."

"There was a period in your life where you felt you had to protect yourself from people?"

"Everybody," I confirmed.

"Do you still feel that way?"

My eyes squinted and circled the walls around us. "If I had to scale it, I'm about eighty percent better. Maybe eighty-three. And I don't cuss no more." I gave him a cheesy smile.

It successfully broke the sharp line in his forehead, and Ashton snorted a laugh. "Cute." His head shook softly, then he pushed back from the table. "Hope you left room for dessert."

"I'm retired. I now own my diet. Bring it!"

The magic in his true smile, the sincere one, relaxed me. "Cool. Let me clean this up right quick and then start on it."

"I'm going to use the little girls' room again," I joked while standing, but not before catching the flash of shock on Ashton's face. "Your powder room again. Is that okay?"

The muscles in his face relaxed and he scoffed, "Of course. You know where it is."

Nodding, I ignored the weirdness and left for the hallway. The powder room was just as regal as what I'd seen of the apartment. Top tier fixtures: tree mural fixed in the tiles of one wall, fresh floor plants in two corners, marble vessel sink resembling a big rock with a smooth finishing of a hole on top. This place was nice and so "Ashton" that I could see how he lived here, but found it perplexing that he didn't own it. After drying my hands, I shrugged off the thought, remembering I didn't own my apartment either. What was supposed to be a temporary leasing agreement for a year or so turned into over four.

When I returned to the kitchen, he was moving about, cleaning the countertops. "That's your phone vibrating," Ashton advised, gesturing my purse on the empty barstool. I followed his line of sight without making a move. "Why do you look like you wanna cuss me the hell out?"

That was because I was annoyed, but not by his gesture or heads up. My nerves were irked by the call interrupting me this evening.

I narrowed my eyes playfully, but was sincere when I shared, "I told you I don't curse anymore."

As I ambled for my purse, he chuckled. "Why do I find that hard to believe?"

I threw a hard gaze at him over my shoulder. "Because you don't know me. Remember? That's why I'm here."

I pulled the phone from the back pocket of my purse just as it stopped vibrating. As I held it in my hand to see who'd called, a text came through and my stomach leaped.

DeJo: *Where you at t? I need to kick it with you about our plans.*

I dropped the phone to my pelvic line, my mouth twisting as I processed my irritation.

"He checkin' on you?" thick cords inquired from across the room.

When I turned his way, Ashton's gaze dropped and he shifted toward the stove.

My lips twisted contemplatively even more.

"Not exactly." I surprised myself by answering. "He's trying to secure time on my schedule."

"Oh?" was the one word he used to further his inquiry.

Nosy human...

"Yeah." I rubbed the tip of my nose. "I no longer have anyone handling my schedule. That's the beauty of retirement: I control my time. Whereas just a few weeks ago, if he was planning a surprise for me, he could easily do it by contacting my assistant. Now, he has to attempt mind-trickery to be sure I'm where he needs me to be for the surprise."

"And what's the surprise?" I peered up from my phone to find Ashton facing me again, his expression blanket. "Is it for the win against O'Connor?"

My forehead wrinkled. "You need this information for the article?"

His brows flickered. "This is actually a congratulatory gourmet meal for you. I'd also like to think of it as a hybrid gathering amongst two once familiar souls."

That comment dazed me for a moment.

Is that what we were?

Mentally shaking myself into the here and now, I answered, "A party. Yeah. For the fight." I glanced down at Deon's message. "He's spoken to my assistants, trying to find a location for it. The place he booked fell through—I'm not supposed to know. He must've found a new location."

"A club flaked on a party for Tori McNabb?" His tone was incredulous.

"I doubt Deon mentioned the name to keep it out of the media. Hey... You mind if I just..." I pointed to my phone.

Ashton's lips pushed out with the bottom one more noticeable because it was heavier. Suddenly, I recalled how beautifully uneven they were. "Take your time," he muttered before turning away.

I turned myself, thinking of how to respond before typing away.

"I thought I smelled food when I got off the elevator," a feminine tenor chirped.

I didn't turn to see who it was, wanting to finish up my message to Deon.

"Oh, hey," Ashton greeted without any particular welcome in his tone.

"Hey. I was coming to pick up a textbook I left a couple of days ago. The place is so quiet. Where's everyone?"

Me: Meeting for a Sports Illustrated interview. Are you coming by tonight?

I was horny. God, was I suddenly and indescribably horny.

"Oh!" the woman trilled, causing me to look up from my phone. "You've got company."

I couldn't see her. From where we both stood, a tall vase with fresh tall flowers on the counter blocked our immediate view, and I didn't know if we were supposed to see each other.

Ashton chuckled quietly, scratching his forehead as though slightly embarrassed. "I do."

"Oh. I can go grab my book and—"

"No. It's alright, Lori. You're not busting up my killer playboy vibes, or nothing like that. I'm celebrating an old friend, is all."

Friend?

In spite of not wanting to meet anyone, I took a few steps to the left of the vase and waved with a tight smile, keeping my head low. "Hi, Lori." I remembered her name.

Her thin frame in a simple white tee under an apricot cardigan ranged inside a little more to meet my greeting.

"Oh, my god. I've never seen him with a woman, so I'm a little weirded right now." She giggled innocently.

"Lori's one of my assistants around here. She's a student at NYU."

"Oh. Nice. What are you studying?" I rested my elbows on the countertop.

"Kinetic—" She sucked in a breath. "Holy shit," she murmured. "Anyone ever tell you, you look like—" Her head swung over to Ashton, and I watched her eyes rove over him from head to toe, as though mentally processing, then her shocked regard returned to me. "Dude, you've got Tori McNabb in your kitchen?"

The poor girl turned pale white.

Ashton's face tightened, a hint of a smile beneath his beard. "Have you been drinking, Lori?"

"Ummmm..." she squealed, eyes lashing between Ashton and me. "Maybe." A hard snort broke through my nose and I covered my face. "*But...!*" Her index finger shot into the air. "I'm not on the clock. I'm out with my friends before a full day of studying tomorrow!" Lori shook her head. "We're getting off track right now. Tori fucking McNabb is in my boss' kitchen right now! This is insane."

Ashton's head dropped forward, then his adorable embarrassed gaze found its way to me. I couldn't help my giggling fit.

"Lori, there're plenty of leftovers. I can fix you something," he offered on a deep exhale.

She shook her head, visibly swallowing while gaping at me. "I'm not going straight home. I can come by in the morning to pick it up, though," she returned to him. "You know," her attention, and now words, were directed toward me now. "I now see you're so beautiful in real life. I thought it was just a professional makeup artist, but you're not even as bulky in person."

My eyes followed hers down my frame—what she could see of it. Then I noticed Ashton paying the same trail of observation, only he had the perfect view. He could see all of me. A shiver ran from the base of my neck down my spine. Nervously, I went for my glass of wine.

"Lori," Ashton began.

"I'm gonna go," she croaked, clearly in shock. "I know I signed a NDA, but can I wait till tomorrow to tell my friends I met Tori McNabb?" Ashton gazed my way for an answer. My brows hiked, communicating it was his call. "I mean, this isn't anything private. It's work." There was a slight pause before she trilled again, "Right?"

Ashton scoffed, scratching his nose. "Yeah. It's just that Tori and I went to school together."

"Which school?"

"*Blakewood.*"

She sucked in a breath. "I don't think I knew you went to *Blakewood.*" Her face fell. "You do look like a *Blakewood* dude."

I laughed again. Ashton *did* give off pretentious *BSU* vibes. Lori's face lifted in a smile when she noticed me cracking up.

"Lori, I think you've had enough to drink tonight." He pushed off the counter to walk her out. "I have no qualms with you sharing you met McNabb, but please leave out all the details of it."

"Oh, I will!" she called out to me from over her shoulder as he guided her hurriedly out of the kitchen. "I'll even tell them how goddamn fine you are." They were out in the hall when she shouted, "Can I come to your wedding?"

I lost it, laughing hard at that point. As though timely, my phone vibrated in my left hand.

DeJo: *OK We can talk but soon. U want me to come over?*

I knew it was a strange request. Deon hadn't touched me the way he wanted to in over a month.

I took time to think about it. I didn't want Deon tonight.

But still...

Me: only if you're in town.

I needed my sudden urge satisfied. It felt like forever since I felt this...needy physically. Since finding out about this alleged baby, I hadn't wanted Deon that way. My guard was way up with him and I hated it—

"Can I pour you more wine?" My nipples pebbled at the sound of his timbre.

Ashton had come back into the kitchen, grabbing the bottle of wine. He held it in the air, reading the label. "This *Château Blevin* shit is a'ight."

"It is." I turned toward him while tucking my phone in the back pocket of my *Classic* bag. "Just a little. Please." I handed over my glass. "Is it a reserve?"

"Nineteen seventy-nine," he muttered, affirming. "So, where did we leave off with questions?"

"I don't know, but let's flip the microphone for a bit."

"What do you mean?" he asked, pouring the wine like a trained sommelier.

"Let me ask you some questions."

There was that innocent smirk with furrowed brows again. It was cute on adult Ashton, I'd decided. "Questions for me? I'm afraid."

"I don't believe you."

"Try me." I followed him to the table and took a sip of wine after we sat in our seats. Ashton gave me another shy expression, the top half of his face taut and the bottom broadened. "Is this off the record?"

"I didn't come with a recorder." My brows lifted. "So!" I exhaled. "Are you a serial dater?" Ashton laughed. Hard and for a while. "What's so funny?"

His head tossed back and he grabbed his stomach. I playfully slammed my elbows on the table, pretending to attempt his attention. Though smiling, I was feeling a bit insecure.

"My bad." He tried to breathe. "It's just that no matter how sophisti—" He cackled again. "Sophisticated you are now, and how cultured and boss ass, you still suck at punctuation." His chest heaved as he tried to mirror my straight face when what he really wanted to do was laugh.

I blinked hard, pulse taking off. "You know, I still don't know if I understand what that means."

He lifted an index finger. "Hang on a bit. I need to serve dessert." I waited as he crossed the kitchen and pulled open a door looking similar to a bread box, but larger. "Before things go left with inquiries on my life, I wanna give you a moment to flex. This was the agreement, after all."

He carried a large porcelain platter over. The smell traveled faster than his feet. It wasn't until he set it on the table that I could see the arrangement of macarons. There was an assortment of colors and flavors, but in the center of the platter were chocolate ones with white letters frosted over them spelling out *CHAMPION HUMAN*, similar to the roses he sent me.

My head swung up to face him. Instead of addressing my trademark term, Ashton took to his seat.

"Serial dater? No." His lips pouted in sober contemplation. "I honestly don't have the time. You were lucky to get off the market when you did."

Ashton

I opened the front door for her and fought like hell not to check out her ass in those black leggings. Instead, I tried to focus on the small brown paper shopping bag she carried macarons inside of. It was a difficult, but possible feat for me. Once crossing into the hallway, she turned to face me. I leaned into the doorjamb.

"How many more times must we meet to finish this?"

That question threw me askew no matter how reasonable it was. "Maybe none. My deadline is right around the corner." I answered honestly. "I actually have a lot of material and my outline completed, and can email you with any questions I may have."

To my surprise, Tori pouted and angled her head. "That's too bad. I was looking forward to showing off my culinary skills."

My smile wasn't intentional. "Competitive much?"

"Nah. Just confident with *my* skills."

A stretch of silence fell upon us, eyes locked to each other. Tonight had been revealing for me. Tori answered all of my questions and even had a few for me regarding my personal life that I wasn't expecting. Yet not once did Tori show any signs of reflection of the friendship I once thought we'd had at *Blakewood*. Through all her mentions of therapy and self-evolution, none of that seemed to have rendered a reference to that time. I had so much to process, but still no connection to this worldly woman before me other than the hobby of cooking.

Lifting her bag in the air, Tori, murmured, "Thanks for this, Ashton."

After my neck bow, she flounced off. And this time, I did ogle her ass. Bad decision.

Oh, damn...

"You sure I can't walk you out?"

"Why?" she asked, still moving ahead. "Who's going to attack me on the way to the garage?"

"Touché." She had a point.

Tori didn't have to wait long for the elevator. My unit had its own and would take her directly down to the parking garage, which was guarded by armed security twenty-four/seven. Those were our last words. She didn't even look back before stepping into the car.

Once I heard the doors close, I sauntered back into my apartment. The living room was dark, entire place eerily and unusually quiet. I had it all to myself, which was a rarity, and felt restless. I dumped myself onto the sofa, landing on an *American Girl* doll. Scoffing, I kissed its forehead then tossed it aside and lay back, stretching my arms and legs out.

What the fuck just happened?

Who is this...woman?

As my mind turned over with so many questions and realizations, playing back her visit, my phone vibrated in my pocket.

"Hello?" I didn't think to look at the ID.

Not answering this evening wasn't an option.

"Are we still getting together?"

"Shit," I breathed, pulling the phone from my face for the time.

I'd forgotten all about her.

"Are you still in a meeting?"

I hesitated, then lied. "Yeah. I'm sorry, Patrice." She groaned her frustration. "I swear I'll make it up to you."

"You better." I could hear the pout in her tenor. "I've been looking forward to this for almost two weeks now. I've been needing a release in a major way—more like three or four."

My face constricted. "We're not exclusive, Trice. You could have had three or four in the past two weeks."

"Yeah, but not in the same night with the same guy. And for sure as hell not with your flavor."

My eyes rolled into the back of my head. Patrice was fun. I met her at a 10K run out in Philly a few months ago. Good girl who'd been very straight forward about her sexuality. That was a delight for a man like me, but she wasn't an anomaly. I'd come across countless women since my teen years who enjoyed fucking with little limitations. "I'll make it up to you."

"Soon." Patrice was quick with her response.

"Bet."

"Bye." The call disconnected.

Looks like it's going to be a "me and a fresh bottle of that Château Blevin until I fall out" kind of night for me...

"*Shit...*" I swore out into the dark air. "The life."

CHAPTER SEVEN

Tori

I knew when I came bustling through my doors everyone would likely be there, including Deon because he'd been in the dog house since the eve of the fight. But I didn't expect the energy when I had a set agenda, which didn't include my cousins in any form.

So from the moment the door slammed, when Treesha rushed into the foyer looking goofy and apologetic, still, after her no show to the fight, I wasn't in the mood.

"Tori, NeNe called earlier and said her car is making noise under the hood and the treads on two of her tires are crazy low. She said her apartment is a mess, too. I told her I could come down and help her out for a couple of days, but I gotta get some money..."

Her voice trailed off as I stopped and swung my head her way. At the same time, Deon turned the corner and peered into the foyer.

Next, Renata, came barreling through with her tablet, glasses over her eyes, and tapping away.

"Tori, we need to talk about your fitting for the shoot next week. And you haven't signed off on that write-up for the upcoming charity boxing event with Raj. Please don't forget about the video conference you have with the realtor in the morning. You've been canceling—" Renata stopped when she peered up from her Penny from *Inspector Gadget*'s tablet.

I took a deep breath, closing my eyes to prepare my words. Then I began unfastening the buckle of my right sandal. "Treesha, I spoke to NeNe before the fight about her car. She's going to cover whichever is the cheaper tab between the tires and what's going on under the hood when she gets paid next week—"

"But what if something goes wrong before payday and her car don't make it?" Her eyes were big and expressive. "I don't understand why she don't have a brand new car. It ain't gotta be a *Benz* or a damn *Beamer*."

"Because college students don't typically have the money for new cars. Their parents may, though." I rolled my neck, daring for a rebuttal. When she visibly swallowed back her words, I continued. "Now, to answer your *other* question: NeNe and I have a clear understanding of her being as self-sufficient as possible for her age. And I like to think she's doing it. She has far more resources than I did in college: her own place and a car so she can work to pay for her needs. She doesn't have to worry about how school or books are being paid for. So I think a college student shouldn't need help cleaning a studio-sized apartment." I cocked my head to the side, daring her again.

NeNe had been through an assortment of changes coming up. When I left for North Jersey to return to boxing, Treesha's life had begun to spiral out of control, and NeNe's father had been in and out of prison that same year. She went between my aunt Sonya's, Treesha's friends, and her father's family in Philly until Renata retired from the military. That's when NeNe had a primary home. Then when I began to make money, I helped with each check I got.

We had no idea for years, NeNe was developmentally delayed. The girl didn't speak fluently for years, and she was a bit underweight, which was why we treated her like a baby for so long. She only ate a limited number of foods. It wasn't until settling in with Renata that Treesha got the heads up from the school. I was able to come home and sit in on some of her *Early Intervention Program* meetings. As my career grew, I was able to afford more services for her. We enrolled her into several therapy programs that, thankfully, worked.

But I didn't stop when NeNe began to speak and fill out in weight when finally able to eat an array of foods. NeNe was classified in the state because of her *E.I.P.* status, but she had no learning disabilities in my mind. She was smart, but grossly behind her peers. So, I made it my mission to catch her up. I bought a house in Millville. It was small with three bedrooms for my cousins and NeNe, and with a little back yard. It was nothing fancy, but away from the riffraff of our old trailer park. It was so modest, I slept in the living room when I visited because there was no space for me. The goal was to give NeNe stability, which her therapists pushed for.

Within months and lots of money, we noticed significant changes in her social skills. By the next school year, NeNe was bringing home awards for improvement, then eventually honor roll, and, finally, the principal's list. She continued that momentum into high school. That's when most of her therapies had expired because she no longer had any need for them. I pushed for her to get into a social club and into a sport. She didn't do well with sports, although she tried them all. By the time she graduated earlier this year, the only sport she stuck with was track, finishing up with mediocre rankings. I didn't care. I was proud of her. She'd survived developmental delays, her mother's addiction, and father's absence; NeNe didn't need to be an athlete.

Her mother, on the other hand, wanted to pick and choose when she would be a parent—and on my dime. I paid for everything: NeNe's clothes, food, housing, resources, and now college. I had been grooming my little cousin for adulthood since I could remember. We'd planned for her college years and, so far, NeNe held up her end of the bargain. I'd paid for furniture and had bought her a hooptie when she first got her license. All she had to do was work to pay for her food and personal needs. I opened a bank account to share with her. She could never let it go past a specific limit without me questioning her. We had our emergency plans worked out. Treesha didn't know because Treesha checked out too often.

"I was only tryna help," Treesha finally replied. "Y'all always saying I ain't doing my part with her." She turned on her heel with an eye-roll and stank-walked to the back of the apartment.

Before Renata could speak, I addressed her points. "I must have forgotten to send you and Lidia a text saying let's do the fitting on Monday afternoon. I'll take a look at the write-up before I go to bed tonight." *If I can ever get there.* My eyes skirted over to Deon. "I'll plug in my laptop to be ready for the video conference in the morning. Please tell me that is all." I hung my head.

"I'll charge your laptop now and set it up at the nook. And I'll hit Lidia up now about the fitting." Her head fell to the side. "Anything else from you?"

Dramatically, I took Deon by his folded lower arm and pulled him behind me down the hall. Seconds into it, I stopped. A thought occurred and I turned back for Renata, who was tapping away again.

"I'm gonna be doing lots of cooking tomorrow after the call with the realtor. I'm thinking croissants, maybe shrimp and veggie spring rolls..." I thought for a minute. "A couple of quiches—meat and veggie —and maybe beef on a stick? Enough for about thirty people." I thought some more. "You know... Maybe I can get some help there from the community college like before?"

"You having a party I don't know about?" Deon asked.

Turning to him, I murmured, "No. But *we're* about to have some fun."

I pulled Deon all the way to my bedroom for an agenda I was sure even he wasn't expecting.

Damn good looking, controlling, always cool and in control, cooking ass human...

love belvin

Ashton

"Only twenty-three percent?" I asked the conference room table, peering up from a spreadsheet. "All the money we've dumped—and expeditiously so—into employee quality assurance and only less than a quarter of our beta-sites have participated?

Billy nodded with pursed lips. "I'm afraid so, Mr. Spencer."

I began flipping through the pages of the report binder. "Who and why?"

"Well, it seems the managers have been the most compliant parties. The next group reporting even lower numbers are the cooks. I can only assume it's because they're vying for managerial roles."

I sat back in my chair, hands reaching for the crown of my head as I considered it all. This was my first meeting of the morning, too early for news of failure. In the past two weeks, we'd spent well over two million dollars purchasing and customizing an app for our employees to engage in for the betterment of their workplace experience. It was obviously an investment to reduce high turnover and ensure better customer service for all *B-Way Burger* locations across the country. We rolled it out to just five carefully selected locations in hopes of testing it out, and only twenty-three percent of the employees across five restaurants engaged the app. This was a fucking disappointment for momentum. I expected participation in the neighborhood of fifty-five percent, but twenty-fucking-three?

It was clear. "They don't trust the effort," I thought out loud to the room of twelve of my staffers assigned to this endeavor. I shook my head with pouted lips. "Our fuckin' staff doesn't believe we give a damn." My attention landed on Shericka, the assigned lead of this venture. "Ms. Lops, what do you propose we do to tackle this?"

The bright *Princeton* mind shot back immediately, "Start our upper-level staff on a campaign tour to each region of the country, targeting our larger locations." Her head swayed, eyes to the table as she enunciated and ruminated at the same time. "We, obviously, don't 'touch' each restaurant, but we can hit the largest ones and include a few smaller in between, and invite others to our targeted locations. We look them in the eye, professing appreciation and support, then implore them to participate in this—"

She was cut off by a loud rap at the door followed by, "Sorry, Mr. Spencer, but a food delivery is being made, and Tamia insists it be brought in here now."

I dropped my chin, deeply disturbed by my meeting being interrupted. "Who ordered food?"

The general receptionist's eyes fell to her shoes, expressing embarrassment. "No one, sir. I believe it's being delivered to you. Tamia said the note explained it should be shared with your...laden staff."

"Laden?"

She shrugged as my assistant, Tamia, rounded her, pulling in a tray covered with platters. "I think it's tongue-in-cheek," she offered, less timidly than the receptionist.

"I'm sorry. What's going on here?"

As the receptionist worked to remove plastic coverings from the food, Tamia tossed a card in front of me.

From my competent kitchen to the bellies of your laden staff.
-KaToria
Shit...

She cooked food for my staff?

Competitive much?

Or have I made an impression on her?

Why in the hell did I occupy thoughts of what she thought of me? The shit was confounding.

"What is that?" Billy sniffled into the air.

"Looks like fresh croissants," someone else guessed from the conference table, peering over to where the food was being set up."

"Yup," Tamia confirmed. "And quiches. Looks to be different kinds. I think these two are vegetable."

There was protocol to this. What if someone fell ill because of the food? Who held the liability?

"You mind, sir?" Shericka asked, gesturing to the food.

There were even utensils included.

I reclined in my seat, sighing.

Me. I'd be liable, and definitely if the food was especially good. Croissants? I didn't have to ask to know they were fresh. Tori was trying to one-up me for dinner at my place a couple of nights ago.

Nice play, McNabb. Nice play...

"A chief information officer?" I murmured the question rhetorically as I sauntered over to the floor-to-ceiling window in my office. "Lance Bridges as the chief information officer."

I then turned to my guests consisting of my partner, Lawrence Briggs, the CFO, Louis Brown, Julio Hernandez, who was an operations executive, Tom Caldwell and Billy Tucker, who were two other executives at the helm of *B-Way Burger*. Julio didn't belong here, but I'd been exposing him to more decision-making events for the purpose of training. It was something I could do in my position.

They all peered my way, awaiting my feedback on Billy's recommendation for the vacant position.

"So, you're telling me you want a seventy-four year old man in charge of our technology?" When I posed the question, Julio snickered immaturely. "Can you tell me if I'm the only one in the room who feels that's an unrealistic—unfeasible—feat?"

"Ashton," Billy attempted to argue. "Lance has an impeccable tenure in fast foods. Look at what he did for *KFC* with their rebranding."

"That was in the early nineties, Billy," I argued.

"Yes, I understand, but let's keep in mind his track record with his time at *Pizza Hut* and *Hardees*. He's even been instrumental at *Mercedes Benz*."

"All true." I nodded. "But you're referencing a forty—fifty-year—resume. However, Lance wasn't the damn CIO in charge of global technologies for any of those companies. Do you see the huge discrepancy, Tucker?"

Briggs sat up in his chair, expressing discomfort of Billy's insistence, and Caldwell cleared his throat.

"I can understand you wanting to look out for a family-friend, Billy," Caldwell went the nurturing route. "But as you can see, Spencer here is taking us in a direction where we're rolling out a major undertaking which requires considerable technology."

"This isn't a cold chair-position we can afford for him to warm in just title alone, as you can see," Briggs tried.

We all knew the deal. Fast food, like any other industry, was small once you'd planted your feet in it. It was common knowledge that old man Bridges had squandered his money in brothels and bad investments over the years. The man should have been a millionaire a few times over at his age and breadth of experience. Right now, he was looking to go anywhere just to afford his medical bills. *B-Way Burger* wasn't into harboring for the good old boys' club. Had the roles been reversed years ago in Bridges' prime and my father, Briggs or Wick had been in need, he'd have never considered them.

Billy's face heated up behind his spectacles. It was laughable, his audacity. Bridges and Billy's father had been roadies since before Billy and I were born. Billy was here trying to look out for him. It was unprofessional.

"Technology is a young man's game, Billy," I came in for the benedict. "At best, I'm looking for a person in their fifties, whose brain is constantly evolving and adapting to the fast pace of technology. There's this woman..." I snapped my fingers. "Figueroa is her last name..."

"I know who you're referring to," Julio chimed in, seemingly struggling to recall her first name, too. "Beautiful Latina—"

The door was pushed open and Tamia rolled in a cart of food again. I felt my face tighten in confusion.

"Lunchtime, sir," she announced, clearly amused by another abrupt delivery of food being made. "I'll set it up over there, Mr. Spencer. There's more that I had sent into the cafeteria. An email is going out about it. It appears we've finished all the quiche and croissants before eleven this morning." Her smile was too bright.

She thought I was fucking Tori. *Yup*. She did, and it was all Tori's fault. Tamia hadn't forgotten about the tickets to her fight and how they were directly from the champ herself. And today, Tori was feeding my staff. My dating life wasn't something I discussed with my subordinates, but I was a young, fit, and single CEO. And between assignments for flower deliveries and restaurant reservations for two, Tamia was very aware of my status.

"Holy shit," Caldwell breathed. "Are those spring rolls? My wife loves those things."

"Beef on a stick with a special teriyaki sauce, too, according to her menu," Tamia shared.

It was two in the afternoon, and I hoped this would be the last of Tori's stunting. At this rate, I wouldn't be able to keep my staff focused on shit.

Ashton: Well played.

Tori: *I'm sorry. You talking to me? LMAO*

Ashton: Hahaha. My staff collectively thanks you. Your culinary skills were the talk of the day around the entire building.

Tori: *And what about the bo$$?*

Ashton: Well...other than not being able to hold the attention of everyone in two crucial meetings today, I was feeling the rolls...the beef (although I would have gone with a cilantro and chimichurri sauce in addition to the teriyaki).

Tori: *What about the croissants? I worked hard on them.*

Ashton: The croissants were buttery with a nice flake quality, but by the time I got to one it was cooler than I prefer.

Tori: *No microwave?*

Ashton: I prefer mine straight from your oven in the morning.

Tori: *I thought you'd say yours, but I guess you know better. Your croissants could never!*

Ashton: I don't make them, but I could serve you the best buttermilk biscuits from my oven.

Tori: Biscuits? *That's so middle school home-ec! Are you serious?*

Ashton: Very.

Tori: *My bad. I thought I had a real contender in you.*

Ashton: It must be so lonely for you over there in Delusional World.

Ashton: I gotta go. Just wanted to express my thanks and give you your little props. Take care, champ.

love ∞ *belvin*

Tori

"See! That's the shit Coach Brooks' been saying not to do," Rut shouted excitedly while pointing to the tablet Trent held in his hand at the other end of the table where most of the guys were huddled. "That nigga be leaving his feet when it's unnecessary!"

"Yeah." Jordan Johnson, standing behind Trent, watching footage from practice, shook his head. "We've been working on this since training camp. Not only jumping unnecessarily, though. He just got better at catching it at his hip." He demonstrated receiving a ball.

"Yeah, but we gotta stop putting so much pressure on these cats coming in," Deon argued. He sat in the huddle, watching the plays, too. "The *Kings* got this reputation of—"

"Excellence?" Trent's head turned to Deon, his tone affable.

Trent's presentation may have been gentle, but his question was rhetorical. It was obvious by the expectant gaze he and Johnson issued Deon. They were still salty with him about that spontaneous trip to *Kamigu* during my training. I couldn't blame them. It was very irresponsible and selfish of Deon to do that during the pre-season. Then to add insult to injury, Deon and his boys took pictures while there, driving the media reports beyond social media blogs. He'd accomplished exactly what he wanted to. It was a slap in the face of the organization.

"You know what else Coach Brooks been doing since we've had the interim head coach?" Levi, an offensive guard with the sweetest personality, interjected.

As he continued, my mind drifted off. The guys were all engrossed in football talk. I couldn't blame them. They were playing a home game tomorrow against *Tampa Bay*. We were unusually gathered in a private room at a restaurant in Connecticut, having just finished up on dinner. There were a little more than a dozen of us. A linebacker, Ryan Wilson's, new fiancée was in town, which was rare because of where she lived. They were a young couple from Missouri. Wilson was drafted out of *Kansas State*. Trent took a liking to him immediately, which meant Jade embraced his fiancée. When the Baileys and Johnsons liked you in *Kings* Nation, you were in, in.

Wilson's fiancée, Simone, had a bridal shower last month given by her family, back at home in Kansas. Naturally, the *Kings* family was unable to support her in person. No one visited there, and the *Kings* weren't due to play the *Chiefs* for a while. Even when they did, none of the wives and girlfriends would attend. So, Jade gathered us tonight at this restaurant for a cute impromptu shower. She was sure not to make the biggest of deals of it, even opted to not have the private room decorated, as to not step on Simone's family's toes. Besides, Melody Richardson, the wife of the owner of the *Connecticut Kings,* sent a package of gifts to Simone's official shower.

"Awwwww! The *B-Rocka Collection*—bae!" Simone called down to Wilson. She held a package of candles, lotion, soap, and oil in the air. "Parker got me the *B-Rocka Collection*! I'm so geeked!" she squealed.

B-Rocka was one of Parker's scent lines for her fragrance company. She was amazingly talented and generous with her creativity. From what Elle shared with me a few months ago, B-Rocka was Rut, Parker's husband's, cousin and best friend, killed in Rut's hometown. Something related to gang violence.

Hmmmm...

"No, ma'am!" Wilson shouted, traversing the room from the guys to the women. It snapped me out of my thoughts. "That would be for me, sweetie." When he made it to her, he lifted the ivory lace lingerie number from the first box she'd opened from Parker. "Don't you think I don't have eyes behind my head. I saw this little number. This is her gift to you. *That's* her gift to me."

As the girls tittered, Simone pouted.

"Awwwww, baby," he sang. "I'll let you rub me down with the oil and lotion." He planted a sweet kiss on her pouted lips.

Then, predictably, the women aww'd the couple.

"You guys are absolutely adorable!" Maria sang.

"How long have you been together?" Jade asked.

"Since freshman year in college." Wilson flashed a million-dollar smile.

Simone coughed out, "What?" Even I had to laugh at that. "Don't get at work and try to make a fairy out of this tale, boo."

"What?" Wilson's exaggerated expression told it all. "This lace made out of cotton?" He lifted a piece of her lingerie into the air, playing coy to change the conversation.

"Oh, he lyin', lyin'!" Maria charged.

Simone nodded, eyes sparkling each time they landed on her man. "The truth is *I* fell in love my freshman year, something I had no plans on doing. Even gave him his first sniff of cootie kat—" The room lit up from both sides, even the guys heard that. I held my belly, laughing my head off. "Yup. It's no secret. I was crazy over this boy and gave him my everything, all for him to tell me after the first year was up that '*things were moving too fast*'," she playfully boo-hoo'd. "He had the nerve to say he needed to focus on football and growing up!"

Wilson stood with his hands clasped at his pelvis, wearing a cheap grin as he stared at her. It was hilarious! No matter how personal this story and topic was, these two seemed absolutely secure in sharing it.

"Awwwwww!" Jennifer cried. "And you broke up?"

"She left me!" Wilson pretended to sob, amp'ing up our raucous laughter. "She didn't come back that fall. The girl transferred schools!"

"Oh, no!" Parker yelped.

Simone's face was still lit and eyes filled with love when she chirped in her country twang, "What was I 'posed to do?"

"Wait for me to grow up!" Wilson continued with his toddler roleplay. It was cute. "You know it takes men longer to do. I was coming back around for you. You knew we had something special."

"How?" she begged. "It was all about football and you growin' up. Right, Ry?"

"No, man!"

"Yes, sir. I gave you my all and you break up with me? *Tuh!* You don't deserve the right to see me every day. New school, new life, honey!"

Most of the women in the room cheered her on. I, on the other hand, felt myself warping back into the mind of a nineteen-year-old freshman in college.

"She kinda has a point there." Jade turned to me and argued.

That woke me out of my thoughts.

"What made you come around, Wilson?" Marie asked.

"She ain't know, but I knew I was gonna get her back." Wilson's declaration was loud and clear. "I had to. Because I wasn't finna wake up ten years later and live with her being with some goofball. She was mine back then. I just needed time to mature up to her level."

That admission made my abs jump.

"He had to grow up." Simone agreed. "And to be honest: me jumping up and transferring schools possibly cost us some of our college days. I was a hothead. I only saw things one way. When we started talking again, the guy had really grown up—and did it on his own. There was no work required of me. It was a big lesson in my short life."

Wilson sidled up to her, leaned over, and kissed her again. I couldn't believe the actions of two virtual strangers affected me. It forced me into self-reflection. What if I had waited? What if I'd just finished the semester at *Blakewood* and took whatever Aivery and her minions threw at me? What if I let Ashton tell me he didn't want to be cool anymore before being hurt and running? What if we *were* more than friends?

An even bigger question crossed my mind. Why didn't I consider Ashton my friend after all he'd done for me at *BSU*?

"You've made me see beauty in shit I never paid attention to. You help me look deeper into people—or at least you—to understand I don't know shit about life. You make me look for beauty and hope in everything I see. That's what I wish for you and hope you learned this semester."

"What?" I was so confused.

"To hope. Life's quite miserable when you're hopeless. When you have zero expectations of it. What do you wake up and look to do? What's the purpose of your life, your creation? Why did God allow you to pass into the earth?"

"To box, I think."

"That's the gift He gave you—possibly a means to making a living, if you're smart with it. But there's so much more to your purpose than fighting. There are so many things to hope for."

"I don't know how to hope."

"You don't truly know how to live."

"I do. I'm breathing."

"You're existing, not thriving. Not trusting, not exploring."

"I don't like to be seen. Sue me."

I remember his warm lips on my forehead. *"You're existing mutedly. It's your thing. I wish I had another semester to help you find your voice. Your hope."*

What if I had seen his maturation happen before my eyes but was too immature myself to understand it? And now, we were in an awkward space because of my anger and lack of maturity to possibly see Ashton as a grown man and not the kid who hurt me beyond recognition. I'd been to his home. He cooked for me. The man had told me several times over the weeks how proud he was of me.

But here I was, stuck, twelve years later, wondering about his life in my absence. I found myself curious about his dating life. Ashton was generous back then. How did he woo women now? As the CEO of *B-Way Burger*?

How did he fuck now—

"Tori!" my name was shouted, making my eyes circle wildly around the room to find by whom. It was Simone. "This is from you and Deon. Right?"

She was holding custom his and her *Asè Garb* robes. I was able to get *Mr. Wilson and Mrs. Wilson* embroidered on the backs of them.

"*Ye*—yeah." I blinked hard, laughing at myself. "That's *me*—from us, I mean."

"Well, thank you!" she sang.

"That's what's up, playboy!" Wilson called down to Deon, who was lost in his phone, now totally detached from the room.

I smiled at Wilson when his regard returned to me as I waved off his teammate. Then I thought of something and went into my purse for my phone. I'd had it on silent to not be rude to the room. Ignoring the gazillion notifications, I made my way to the messages app.

Me: Hey. This is going to be crazy but you don't have to respond. I apologize for my coldness toward you. It's been immature. It's actually been hard as hell on my side. One minute I regret being connected. The next I'm curious about who you are and if you're different. Sorry about asking about your dating life. It was none of my business.

And with that, I put my phone away, and just in time. Deon leaned over, kissing me on the cheek before resuming his seat.

Tori: *Hey! Just wanted to say my agency sent me the article. Great job on making me look good.*

Ashton: **It wasn't hard at all. Again, you're an astounding business woman and hella fucking skilled. I'm honored to have documented it. Proud of you, champ.**

Tori: *Yeah. Me too. Proud human.*

love belvin

Ashton

"Mr. *Spence*—I mean, Ashton, I can't say thank you enough for this." The muscles around her eyes tightened just enough for me to catch the priapic gleam. "It feels good to know my daughter's going to be safe and living in luxury while away at college."

Her husband next to her nodded in agreement. "And that we ain't gotta take out that big ass loan for housing again, man."

"Dad!" their daughter, Terra, cried, feigning annoyance.

She stood with her arm wrapped around Keyonna's as we stood in the living room of Keyonna's apartment in Princeton, not too far from campus. Like Terra, Keyonna wasn't feeling the dorm life. She'd always been an astounding student, so when I challenged her for dean's list her first year in college in exchange for me to consider getting her an apartment, she rose to the challenge with a fifteen credit course load. That meant me keeping my word. I learned of a condominium development going up over the summer and quickly purchased two units: first and second floor.

I figured I'd teach Keyonna how to be a landlord when she explained her friend from freshman year, Terra, not wanting to stay on campus either. The problem was this unit Keyonna moved into in August was just a one-bedroom. Terra was from Dallas. Her parents, Ryan and Cynthia here, were a middle-class family with the salaries of a firefighter and college professor respectively, per their credit reports. Like my niece, Terra was an exceptional student and earned her way to *Princeton University*. The tuition and fees were steep, so not having to pay for housing was a huge relief to the family.

I challenged Keyonna, as the pseudo-owner of this property, to charge her friend something affordable, yet a fee that would cover some of Keyonna's expenses. It was somewhat of a joke because I paid all of my niece's expenses. But like I said, I was teaching her how to be a property owner. She was able to come up with a number for the rent that satisfied my requirements and was affordable for Terra.

"Well, it was my pleasure. I'm glad we were able to work out something in both the girls' favor."

"Hell, yeah!" Ryan agreed. "I think it's great how Keyonna was able to buy this place. It's smart that she has a tenant now."

"I hope Terra's rent is helping out with the mortgage," Cynthia low key chided Keyonna.

I wanted to laugh. Mortgage my ass. The place was paid for. I was sure my niece knew that although I hadn't discussed it with her in great detail. At best, Terra's rent would pay for Keyonna's utilities. And that was something I wanted to look over before I left.

"Well, again. It was nice meeting you," I shared my final bade.

Standing at the front door, they were about to leave themselves. And to kill the eye-fucking Cynthia was performing my way, I turned to walk off, giving a final wave.

"And *B-Way Burger!*" Ryan shrilled with excitement. "I can't believe I know the owner of my favorite burger restaurant. Wait till I tell the guys at the house."

"Daddy," Terra whined again, this time, apparently serious.

"That's enough. You guys need to rest up so you can catch your flight in the morning. You've got a shift starting tomorrow night."

I didn't hear much past that before heading for the kitchen, but I did catch longing in Cynthia's eyes. That was something I was sure Keyonna caught, too. If I knew her, no matter how much discipline Cynthia thought she was exercising, Keyonna hated it. It was best I kept my interactions to a minimum.

On my way to the kitchen where Keyonna's laptop was set up for me, my phone chirped. It was a text message from Tori.

Champ: *Which one?*

There were two pictures of herself, modeling two pairs of footwear. What was captivating was her ensemble. A short jersey of sorts, exposing her long, toned, pecan-hued legs. Tori had been texting me lately. The first was the cryptic apology about being guarded against me and curious at the same time. I didn't reply, because she'd just turned our already awkward situation to hella complicated.

Tori still found me attractive. That was clear in *Kamigu* with the long, appreciative stares. Then at my place, she asked about my dating life. Nah. I'd had enough experience with women to know the crux of Tori's curiosity was about my sex life. What she really wanted to know was my status on fucking. And that only meant one thing: Tori wanted to fuck—or she'd be willing if the opportunity presented itself. I stowed that fact in the back of my brain, dissimilarly to what I would do to any other woman I found attractive. I couldn't go there with Tori for sundry reasons. *That* wasn't what this was about with her. I'd done my job. It was now over.

I took a seat at the breakfast bar and impulsively typed back.

Me: I think I can better decide if you put on the entire outfit.

I went to the laptop, already disturbed by the disorganization of the spreadsheet I'd set up for Keyonna's finances. At nineteen, she knew how to budget and even the tools to do it. I'd sent her to business conferences and summer programs since she was twelve years old. Some were appropriate for children her age and some were not. But they were all useful because Keyonna could grasp onto complex topics easily, she was that brilliant. So now, looking at how fucked up the electronic spreadsheet was that I'd created for her to use, I was disappointed. It was what I'd used myself since my first year at *Blakewood*, and what I'd taught her years ago.

"It took everything I had inside to not call Cynthia out," Keyonna appeared at my side, nudging my head with her own. "She was being a weirdo."

"Well, it's a good thing you were raised right."

"I'm still being raised, in case you didn't know," she sassed.

"By the looks of this *Neiman's* bill, you damn sure grown, grown."

"Ughhhh!" she grumbled behind me. "You're the one who told me to charge the *Asè Garb* shoes and the *Louis* bag to my account instead of you just buying them."

"Oh!" I heard a third voice behind me, realizing Terra must have returned from walking her parents out. "Have you shown those to me yet?"

Champ: *Oh shit! Those were meant for my stylist! I'm sorry. I guess you were the last person I texted.*

That was yesterday when she thanked me for the *Sports Illustrated* article. I snickered while typing back.

Me: You ain't got to lie, Craig.

"I don't think so, I've had them for a while now."

"Though, they're on your current bill," I interjected.

Champ: *LMAO I'm serious!*

Me: How do you have me programmed in your phone?

"Oh," Keyonna tweeted. "I guess it took me a while to act on your apology gift because I had to get acclimated to the semester."

My eyes rolled up; thankfully, my back was to them.

Champ: *Ashton Spencer duuuh!*

Me: And what's the name of your stylist?

"Apology gift?" Terra asked.

"Yup." Keyonna slapped me on my shoulder cavalierly. "My guy here has taught me a language very beneficial to my closet."

"Oh, my god! What did you do, Mr. Ashton?"

My neck whipped as I turned to Terra. "Ashton. Just Ashton, sweetheart. I'm younger than your father."

"Only by four years." Keyonna rolled her eyes. "Anyway. Did I tell you my uncle is a journalist, too?" Terra's eyes ballooned as she visibly sucked in air. "Yup. He travels the world, reporting on shit that would otherwise be boring without his spin." That was so not true. "The only thing he doesn't report on is sports. He watches everything, but never writes about that one topic. That was until his mentor asked him to cover a sports figure because he couldn't do it even though he signed on."

For as many girls as I had, girlie chatter still annoyed the hell out of me.

"Who was it?" the poor girl asked, sounding a bit lost in this unnecessarily drawn out story.

"Tori McNabb, girl!" Keyonna finally said.

"*The Banger?*" Terra trilled.

"Hell, yeah. *The Banger*, girl! We traveled to Indonesia where she did her training a couple of weeks before the fight."

Champ: *Andrea. See! It starts with an A too!*

Me: Why are you asking her which shoes? Do you pay her for that type of consultation?

"Holy shit—my bad, *Mr.*—I mean, Ashton!" I glanced over my shoulder and saw Terra covering her mouth.

"You're good. He's the coolest ever." Keyonna never failed to melt my iciness with her sweet words. She taught that trickery to my girls. "Anyway. He wrote the *Sports Illustrated* piece people are quoting the fuck out of all over social media. It got like the most tweeted shares in like five years, or something, for the magazine."

"Oh! I've seen those. I can't go nowhere on social media without pictures or quotes from that interview!"

"Yup. And it was dope as fuck out there where she trained. The only problem was her people were throwing me fucked up vibrations—"

"Okay! Can we kill the profanity until I leave?" I barked.

Ignoring me, Keyonna continued. "They thought I was my uncle's girlfriend or fuck buddy or something."

"So they harass you for it? It's the lack of feminine power for me."

"That's what I said!" Keyonna cried. "Then big head over here finally tells me he and Tori McNabb had a history."

I dropped my head to my palm.

Champ: *Sorta*

Me: So are you gonna send her the rest of your ensemble?

Terra inhaled sharply again. "For real? How?"

"They went to *BSU* together, girl!" Terra sucked in air again, foolishly captivated. "And, apparently, didn't get along."

"Ah, damn!" Terra commented.

Champ: *This IS my whole ensemble! LMAO I just needed to decide on the boots for the party I'm sure you know about.*

I decided to play coy.

Me: Party? I'm still stuck on what's underneath that big ass jersey you're wearing.

I tried to include the worried face emoji to not come off as thirsty.

"Yeah. So because he withheld that pertinent information from me, he had to pay up."

"Sounds like Tori holds grudges. Did she try to fight you back at *Blakewood*, Mr.—I mean, Ashton?"

Champ: *I guess you'll see when you pull up tonight.*

The zany face emoji had my face opening in shock. Was she flirting with me?

Does Tori even know how to flirt?

"Did you hear her?" Keyonna sidled up next to me, laughing.

"What?" Their conversation was now lost upon me.

"She asked if Tori tried fighting you back at *BSU*."

The first thing coming to mind was our play fights. Damn. I used to love seeing her big ass tits bouncing around in a flimsy shirt when we did. Her sports bras had to be durable, because Tori's breasts were midget MMA fighters, even now.

"She was a tough one back then," I shared, though my mind was reeling at the invitation Tori had just pushed on me.

I had not been invited tonight. Deon Johnson had fallen hook, line, and sinker for the steal of an offer I sent his way via Keyonna's uncle, Louis, on her mother's side who'd opened a nightclub earlier this year. I'd helped him out with financing, being proud of him stepping out and becoming an entrepreneur beyond promoting parties in the New York Tristate area. But for this bone of business I'd just thrown him, I had to write a check.

"Un-bully-able, I bet!" Terra laughed, high-fiving Keyonna.

"Aye," I stood from the bar, closing the laptop. "I'll finish going over this next week. I gotta be somewhere."

"Where?" Keyonna asked behind me. "Ain't the girls in Texas with the Coopers for the weekend?"

"Yup. And after a long week with them, daddy needs some adult time. I'll hit you later and give your ass time to clean that damn spreadsheet."

"Okaaaay!" she breathed out in a grunt just before I shut the door behind me.

CHAPTER EIGHT

Tori

"**D**amn!" Paulie D shouted into the mic once I made it on stage. "I feel like we should be singing Happy Birthday or some shit!"

His sidekick, Ruby Voodoo, added, "We don't get invited to birthday parties. *The Banger* is part of the cool kids club."

I laughed along with the audience on that as I stood between the two of them, joining Deon, who had been up on stage already. There was a big cake and sculpture of hanging purple and gold boxing gloves. It was an amazing design. The party had been great, filled with so many of my loved ones. Friends and family who had been with me since I decided to take my talent serious and pursue boxing again. Raj even managed to get Cut's cantankerous ass here. It had been a celebratory night. This place was a great pick, I had to give it to Deon.

Even now, standing under his arm, I could almost ignore the fact that the pregnant girl from San Diego asked for seventy-five thousand dollars this morning and gave a deadline for tomorrow morning at eight AM, Eastern Standard Time. This was humiliating, becoming real to me. Deon had cheated on me. Little did he know, I was meeting with my public relations team in the morning to figure out how to dissolve this relationship publicly because I had it in the bag privately. I was done with Deon's lying ass.

"Well, Tori," Ruby Voodoo began. "someone here would like to pay tribute to you tonight." Then she laughed. "Damn! Why this feel like a proposal setup? Like this nigga gone get on one knee and we're hoping Tori ain't too drunk and say hell no!"

The place exploded in laughter.

"Shit!" Deon, scoffed. "With what I'm paying y'all to host this party, she better not say no!"

I performed the phoniest smile I could, considering how tipsy I was. I didn't want to say anything to add to the façade of love between Deon and me. So I smiled, unable to look him in the eye.

"I just want to say, baby girl, how I'm so fucking proud of you— we all're proud of you here. You've done shit no other woman in the history of boxing has—just read what *Sports Illustrated* told the world about you! And I'm lucky to call your fine ass, boss ass, crazy-fucking-smart ass mine." And that's when he grabbed me: by the ass.

When he tried going for a kiss, I leaned away and he captured my neck instead. Everyone was so taken by his open affection, the slight wasn't obvious or awkward. While enjoying those who supported me, I counted down till this shindig was over. I was grateful for Deon's gesture of celebrating my last win, so I fought to play nice. Always being the responsible one was truly exhausting.

Paulie D handed me his mic, signaling it was time for me to reply. With great restraint, I did. I waited for the audience to quiet down enough for me to hear myself. The stage gave me a vantage point I didn't have anywhere else in the club. I'd been all over, greeting as many as I could since they yelled *"Surprise!"* when I walked in hand-in-hand with Deon.

I noticed a small balcony almost directly across from the stage. It would have been an odd place for a VIP section because of the ceiling lamps blocking the view. But I could see two men's hands as they gripped the ledge.

Snapping myself into the task at hand, I lifted the mic. "Thanks, Deon. Thanks to my team who assisted. Thanks to all of you here with me." I gestured to the *New York Power 105.1* radio personalities. "Thanks everyone for helping me celebrate and monument this milestone in my life and career. I'm excited about the next chapter, and looking forward to seeing many of you there. Cheers!" I lifted my glass in the air, trying not to be blinded by all the flashes from cameras. Then I crept off the stage.

The place was packed with guests and staff like waiters and cameramen. Deon made a statement with this celebration. I hoped it was one he could afford because I couldn't afford for my reputation to be lost to his sloppiness and immaturity. I was emotionally tired and felt alone in a building filled with people who supported me. If it wasn't trying to keep up with Treesha and NeNe, or being on top of Renata about her self-care, it was business and my image. Reaching my goals was a lonely feat when that meant the pressure of maintaining others' livelihood.

"Aye!" Brielle shouted, gassing me up to dance. She'd been on ten the whole night, something very common for her when Trent and Jade were around, or their friends. "Get it, bitch! Be my *whooooore!*" she singsonged.

And me, being the queen of bottling my emotions I was, I dropped down eagle-style, covering my crotch and giving her and her dancers a show. Brielle was in New York, shooting a movie, so it worked out for her to be here tonight. What didn't work was Trent and Jade being on the other side of the club. I'd just been with them before hitting the stage for Deon's tribute. Jade looked amazing and had been fighting through their loss. The last thing I needed was to bring any more drama to her world during this time of grieving. It had only been a couple of months.

"Aye!" Brielle's dancers chanted around while some twerked with me. "Be my *whooooore!*"

That was a line from Ragee's latest album. In the last seconds of the track, he riffed, "Be my whore!" It was something he threw in there, landing the song, and it was genius. Everyone everywhere was talking about the last line of the song before the outro music played and faded out. Young Lord, being the pop culture forward thinker he was, had uploaded a video on *Instagram* where he remixed the one line to a fast-paced track. It had been a hit, coining the phrase. And everyone ran with it, including Brielle.

As I twerked and laughed with them, my phone vibrated in my palm against my knee. I nearly lost my balance when I saw his name.

Ashton: *I showed up like you asked and you've still not answered my question.*

I stood straight, lengthening my legs.

Me: Where RU?

"You okay?" Brandi, Brielle's head dancer, asked, I guessed seeing the change in my demeanor.

As I swung my neck around, looking everywhere I could, Brielle shouted, "Take a shot with us, Tor!"

Paying a final gaze behind me, I took a few steps over to the booth and received a shot.

Ashton: *Here still wondering what are you wearing underneath that shirt.*

I downed the nasty ass shot, then my eyes immediately fell to my legs. Was he flirting with me? Maybe my custom made hockey jersey dress did look like no more than an oversized shirt. But it was a gift from *Asè Garb* as they were moving into apparel and the pieces were hella exclusive. My name, *The Banger*, was embroidered on the back. I slammed the glass down on the table and texted back.

Me: Tell me where you are and I'll tell you.

The second I tapped to send the message, a memory flashed and I turned and lifted my gaze to the balcony, where I saw Ashton's lengthy frame. My pulse beat audibly in my neck. I could hear the blood rushing in my head all of a sudden. He was gaping my way, unmoving.

Me: I'm coming up

For seconds, I couldn't move, the room swaying slowly along with the music. It wasn't from intoxication either. I wasn't drunk—at least, not from alcohol. I glanced back at the table and saw the girls were in their own zone, dancing after their shots. If I were to slip away, they likely wouldn't notice. After all, I'd been doing it all night with all of my guests.

Ashton: *Don't come if you're not willing to let me see.*

That's it...

I took off, passing greeting guests with empty smiles and arm clutches. Initially, I didn't know how to get up there. I also knew I couldn't ask, not wanting to announce my destination. When I made it to a door in the back I'd hoped led to a staircase to the second floor, a beefy guard stood in the middle of it with crossed arms. Remembering I was the guest of honor, I lifted my phone.

"I need to make a call. Is there a quiet place upstairs?"

Recognition washed over his face as my knees trembled. "Oh! Yeah. Right up those stairs. Ain't nobody coming to bother you in there!"

I tried for a smile as I rounded his thick frame. Thankfully, there was no door leading to outside the club in this vestibule, which could have worked in my favor. It was dark for the first few steps until light broke through near the landing. I had no idea where I was going, but the pounding in my chest guided my curiosity. Down a hall resembling a balcony without chairs, I could see below into the busy club. Trying to stay near the wall to not be seen, I made my way to an open door down on the right.

Ashton was there waiting on me when I peered inside the room. He sat against a rectangular table with his long legs crossed and a tumbler nestled in his cupped hands. Nervously, I gaited toward him like floating on a conveyor belt. I couldn't feel anything but the magnetic pull to him. Couldn't hear anything other than the blood rushing in my head. I stopped mere inches away, our eyes locked onto each other's. The moment I could claim his cologne-mixed fragrance, I was teleported back into a ki that once caused me immeasurable pain. And I leaned into it.

Willingly.

Wholly.

And eagerly.

His regard fell to my legs and Ashton stood, partially circling me for a full view. I heard the door close behind me. Then he studied my face, his eyes tight from either drinking or passion. My lips parted when he stopped toe-to-toe in front of me, his head nearing my own, making my forehead stretch at his brazenness. We were practically nose to nose when his advancing stopped. Our muted deliberation was piercingly loud.

Then he asked, "You ready to show me?"

Suddenly feeling weak beyond the nostalgia of being a green eighteen-year-old, my eyes closed and I nodded. That quickly, I'd transformed into the reckless web Ashton and I seemed to weave all those years ago. Or was it that tonight, I'd made it to a place emotion-ally where I was tired of being the responsible party. Maybe I wanted to be reckless, no matter the danger. Because that was the state of recklessness. Right? Throwing caution to the wind and submitting to what felt good.

Like his long fingers trailing from my calves, slowly up to my inner thighs as they trembled. My neck didn't hold tight and my head wobbled over my shoulders. I bit my lips when a few of his fingers rubbed against the bed of my panties. I was hot and wet. What made me feel twisted was my lack of embarrassment. If seeing what I wore beneath the jersey was what he wanted, I'd let him satisfy his curiosity.

Then Ashton put the glass on the table and took me at the waist, his big hands swallowing my hips as he glided behind me. He urged me to the table, and like I knew what his internal command was, I placed my palms on it, my phone beneath my right one.

Cool air rushed up to my lower back as the material was gently lifted. My lids collapsed, head rolled to the side. I was subdued. But when his hot hands found the elastic band of my lace boyshorts, my eyes bulged wide. I felt heat course through my sex. Feeling like his cheap conquest, I let Ashton pull my panties down and from under my shoes. My eyes dilated at the view ahead, the floor of the club. I closed them, hoping my focus would return soon.

What was I doing? How far would I let Ashton go?

When I felt his lips at the back of my thigh, I couldn't think to decide. No matter how slow and seductive he moved, it all seemed to be happening too fast and not quickly enough for me. His tongue caressed the back of both my legs and when he arrived at my mound, he bit my right cheek. It hurt, causing me to arch my back and spread my legs. His tongue traced the crease of my ass and my head gave out, almost meeting the table.

Then his face was in my ass, tongue swiping deep to my front lips. I pushed my hips into his face, rocking into his cadence. It was warm and slithery and strong. I had never had a man behind me like this, not even Ashton. Deon's head game was trash. I never had the heart to tell him but believed he knew, which was why he rarely tried after the first few months of us being intimate.

But this...

My core vibrated uncontrollably, and I wanted so badly to moan my pleasure. Ashton felt amazing behind and beneath me. Too good. When my spine began to quake and palms misted beneath me, I suddenly wondered if the table could hold my rocking frame. After a while, it didn't matter. My groin exploded and I rocked back into him with an urgency that should have embarrassed me. My head swung back as I came so hard, the table jerked.

Ashton licked and licked, then retreated. He used both big hands to slap both cheeks, enhancing the aftershocks of my orgasm. Soft kisses rained on the back of my thighs again soothed my galloping heartbeat. Below, I could see Paulie and Voodoo dancing on stage, reminding me of my callousness up here. I soon realized I was still swollen and melting. My nipples were hard pebbles, and I felt abandoned by his lack of touch.

As though he sensed me, Ashton returned, pushing his thick tongue into my dripping pussy again. His licks were measured and thorough as he made his way to my clit again. They were patient when he beat against my swollen pearl, commanding another orgasm. It didn't come as fast as the first, but my body trembles wouldn't stop. Then a sudden slap on my ass set my next orgasm into motion and I was cumming on his tongue again, arching into him with squeezed eyes and a trembling spine.

He slowed when I did. Licks turned into kisses as I vibrated on all fours.

When did I climb on top of the table?

Again, too fast for my impatient needs. A course sensation swiped inner thighs and sensitive *oasis*. It was my panties. Ashton was using them to wipe me down. Then my phone vibrated next to me with two missed calls and four text messages. How? When?

Taking me at the waist, Ashton lifted me off the table and pulled my dress down. He ambled over to a sink from a small bar and rinsed his face. My phone vibrated again. I watched his broad, clearly muscular back in a tan, V-neck cashmere sweater as he brushed down his face. Before I knew it, he was drying it off with paper towels from a dispenser over the sink.

Ashton turned to me. "You good?" I closed my mouth and nodded, even though I had no idea how I felt. I could only focus on the bulge in his pants leading to his thigh. Then he ambled over to the door, opening it. "Take your time and get back to your guests, champ."

Then Ashton was gone. And I was alone, feeling the weight of my recklessness.

Ashton

I made a right at the door for the hall leading to the stairway where the rear exit was. My dick was rock hard and chest uncomfortably tight, making me vulnerable as hell. I needed to get the hell out of here.

The moment I made it to the stairs, Louis and one of his partners were coming up.

"Oh, there you are." He stopped as I trunked down past them, refusing to be in close proximity. "Your receipt is up on my desk." His thumb pointed behind him. "You see it?"

"Nah. Email it. I got a call from the girls. I'll hit you!" I shouted on my way toward the private rear exit.

"A'ight, man!"

The cool air of the night momentarily erased her musk from my lips. Feeling the sodden lace material in my pocket, I knew my reckless ass wasn't quite done with it yet.

Tori

At well into the eight o'clock hour in the morning, I felt like hell. Last night was a blur of drunken emotion, celebration, and passion. My head was fuzzy and my heart muddy. So far, retirement sucked, and so soon. The truth in the sententia *"life can change in the snap of the finger"* was evident in my world right now.

"Did you get that, Tor?" Elle asked.

The shimmer in her hazel irises was brilliant, even after just a few hours of sleep. She was one of the last to leave last night, making sure Deon's vision landed as well as it soared.

I did and didn't hear the last of Dawn's pleading on Deon's behalf. I understood she had a job to do, but I didn't have to make this quandary more of my problem than it had to be. My relationship with him had quickly turned into a liability. The dilemma was the money on the table because of our pending union.

I turned away from the window, secretly wondering where I was in relation to the *Hudson in the City*. "How can he not have the money to pay her?"

"After cutting the check for the party last night and the repairs he's paying on his parents' home, his money is pretty much accounted for until January," Dawn tried to explain into the camera as she was projected onto the screen in *Love is Action*'s conference room.

I nodded, chewing on my lip. My attention to Elle. "I'll cut him a check for fifty. He'll have to come up with the rest on his own. I don't want to be linked to the money. Have his fingerprints on it for all I care. And I want my money back—by June of next year, the latest." Elle nodded, typing away. "Have you spoken to Deon about how to deal with the split, Ms. Taylor?"

"Briefly." Dawn's expression was regretful. "As you can imagine, it's not what he wants at all. My suggestion is to give this time. We can make this go away with the girl. We don't even know if it's his baby."

"He believes it can be, and that's enough for me. I'll make my feelings and plans crystal clear to him and have his things sent to his place in Connecticut."

When I left the party last night, Deon asked if he could stay at my place so we could speak this morning before this meeting. I told him no and that we needed to seriously talk about our future. I was still so dazed from my time with Ashton earlier in the night that I couldn't deal with my own fiancé.

"Tori, keep in mind the magazine cover shoots and features we've agreed to. We still have charity events on the books into next year—"

"Something she's very aware of, Ms. Taylor," Elle made clear, tone uncompromising. "But we also understand matters of her personal life are not a ploy for media attention. Ms. McNabb will make this call on her own, under the advisement of her team here at *Love is Action*."

I couldn't take it anymore. Having more pressing matters to address, I stood from the table and grabbed my purse.

"I couldn't have said it better myself. And on that note, I'll leave the rest of the deets to my competent team to tie into a nice bow. Good day."

I left the conference room, on my way to the general reception to have my car called.

"Tori..." Elle's body hung from the door before she began my way. I waited for her, anxiety peeking from my need to go. "Just in case I haven't made it clear, as a friend, I'm sorry this is happening to you. Since I've known you, you've been selective with the men you've dated, taking almost none public. The one time you decided to share your life with one, all this happens. Professionally and personally, we're going to get through this."

I took a deep breath. "I know. And we're not friends, Elle. Remember?" I walked off.

Behind me, I could hear her exhale, "Oh. Right."

Ashton

"These are all bullshit!" I tossed the portfolio of tentative policies on the desk.

"They're not that bad," Julio argued. "I looked over them myself —extensively—last night and thought they were air-tight, minus a few I had them take out."

I sat back, massaging my eyes. It was almost nine in the morning and I was preparing for my third meeting. I'd just closed the last with the tech company regarding updates on the software we purchased from them last month. This next one was with my operations team and our legal band for the revisions of our employee manual. It was now my vision to execute a complete overhaul of our relationship with local team members. I wanted to build communities and not just restaurants.

And this morning, I had to start with me. I had to be graceful— although I'd delegated this responsibility to Julio weeks ago—no matter how much I wanted to throw the report in the fucking trash. My guy, Julio, the same guy who wanted more responsibilities—"an enriched role" was what he'd said. My mind was fogged from flash-backs of eating pussy from behind and talking myself out of analingus, because it would have been nice with her sweet ass.

"These are not community-based policies. They don't make any sense." I reclined in my desk chair. "And now, we're less than twenty minutes away from a call regarding it."

"Okay, Ash-man." Julio's arms shot into the air, then he palmed his waist. "What should I have done?"

Julio Hernandez was a childhood family friend. He started his career pursuits in biology at *Kean University* over ten years ago. Then he switched over to business, something he felt better fit his natural interests. Before coming aboard to my birthright at *B-Way Burger*, I'd gotten him a job here as a cashier while he was still studying in under-grad. He worked his way up in management before I got him an administrative position here at corporate. Technically, Julio had been employed here longer than I had. Lately, he'd been vying for corporate incline, something I had no problem with, but now, as chief executive officer of the company, I had to be sure he had the talent for it.

Julio, a ladies' man, likely didn't take this delegation seriously and didn't prepare for today's meeting with the attorneys. Attorneys' time meant money, none of which I cared to waste on mediocrity. Because he was with his peers, I couldn't rip into his ass the way I would in private, so instead, I had to curb my tongue and play clean-up. There were three others in my office awaiting the call, and we were unprepared.

"You should have gleaned toward the parameters I gave you when assigning this task. Keep in mind our corporate goal...lax on the whip and heavier on the partnership."

My cell phone rang and when I saw Tori's name, my fucking stomach dropped.

"Spencer," I answered.

"We need to talk," her thick tenor shaky. "Now!"

My regard swung over to the windows as I reclined slightly in my chair. "Is everything okay?"

"I'm hoping it will be. I just left a meeting at my agency's office, crossing over into Jersey now. I can meet you at your place."

I rubbed the back of my head, processing the frigidness in her tone. "I'm not at home. I'm at the office and can't leave until late this afternoon."

"I don't want to come there. I don't need the fanfare."

I nodded understanding. "I'll have my car pick you up from home. Is that okay?" Why did I suddenly feel scared as shit? "I can promise you discretion."

"I'm not coming inside *B-Way Burger* headquarters, Ashton. Not for this conversation."

"You don't have to. Let me call my driver now. He can pick you up from in front of your building."

After waiting for her response, I heard the line disconnect.

I pushed open the back doors to my office building, stepping out without my suit jacket. The walk to the tinted out limo felt like the one to the proverbial principal's office. I knocked on the window twice and when the clicking sounded from the locks, I let myself into the back of the car. From the moment I lowered myself inside, I could smell her alluring scent. It was different from what she wore last night, but the same as when she came to my apartment for dinner a week ago.

"Ms. McNabb," I greeted, knowing this wasn't a friendly meeting. "you look great."

She did in a cropped leather jacket, fuchsia blouse, dark jeans, and strappy sandals. Her hair was back in a ponytail and makeup mildly done compared to last night.

"What the hell was that, Ashton?"

I sat back, exhaling. The day had been long already. The last thing I wanted to do was face the consequences of my rash decision last night.

"I'm sorry." I opened my eyes, turning to face her again. "I really am."

She blinked hard. "Sorry. Just sorry? Is that all you have to say, Ashton? Someone could have seen us—probably did!" she shouted, panicky.

Taking a deep breath, my eyes fell away. "Calvin, give us a minute here."

"Shit!" she swore, dropping her hand into her palm.

The divider was down, and he was in full earshot of her fury. For a while, muted passion swelled the air around us.

"Did you plan that?"

"No." I didn't. But when I got to the club last night and had a couple of drinks while watching her, I couldn't help myself. "It was just a celebratory gesture. That's it."

Her head snapped back. "So, you're in the habit of eating women's asses as a way of congratulating them?"

That was a low blow and insulting. But I deserved it. When I woke up this morning and recounted my thoughts in bed, I cringed and groaned out loud.

"Look. The last thing I ever wanted was to be in this place with you again, but let's not hit below the belt, champ."

Her eyes ballooned. "In this place with me again?" She sucked in air. "I am engaged, Ashton; not a single and very clueless and naïve eighteen year old on a college campus! Engaged!"

Internally, I recoiled at the mention of that arrangement. "You're right. Again, I'm sorry, Tori."

"I can't believe that's all you have to say."

"What more do you want me to say? What can I do to demonstrate my regret?" I turned to Tori, who was gazing out of the window on her side of the car, shaking her head. She bit her lip, not disguising her disdain. "I can see I made the wrong call. You said you wanted to be done with the interview so we can go back to our opposite ends of the earth. The article has been published. I swear, I'll abide your wishes and won't contact you again."

Tori scoffed, an empty smile playing on her cheeks.

What the hell is that for?

For seconds long, she didn't speak, only gave me a beautiful view of her profile. And I had to go. My call would be coming through in just a few minutes. I still needed to brief my team.

I exhaled deeply. Trying to be empathetic, I reached for her hand resting on the center console. Tori's head turned, eyes landing on our physical connection. It felt horribly inappropriate. Like a line had been crossed, making me a perpetrator. Is that how this read?

"Putting the genie back in the bottle," she murmured, her eyes slowly raking up my arm until they bore into my face. "Isn't that what you said to me all those years ago at *Blakewood*?"

"Oh," I snorted. "So, are we ready to go there? Can we acknowledge we have a past?"

Tori shook her head, eyes low. "I'm not ready for that right now."

"Then what do you want, Tori?"

"Not another complication to add to my life. I'm not that girl anymore."

Understanding her sentiment right away, I nodded. A pang hit my chest—or ego—and I was prepared to leave. It was one thing for her to tell me I was out of line for my aggressiveness last night. It was a different matter to feel her rejection again. That fucking pain, as distant a memory, was still palpable.

I turned to open the door. Stepping out, I was resigned to being a fucked up individual for my miscalculation last night. I was also late for a meeting. "Be well, Tori."

I closed the door behind me and motioned for Calvin. There was no doubt in my mind Tori had some place to be. Her life was one in great demand.

"Ashton!" I heard called from behind me just as I'd made eye contact with the driver.

I turned to find Tori hanging out of the limo. How would I explain I didn't have more time to be berated? Quietly, I reversed my steps.

Opening the ajar door, I leaned inside. "Yeah—"

She grabbed my tie, pulling me deeper inside the limo, slamming her face into mine. My heart slammed against the wall of my chest and pounded. One hand slipped from the grip I had inside the door, and my other struggled to find an anchor for balance. Her lips were soft. So fucking soft as she exhaled wildly in my face. Her tongue was warm with the faint taste of mint, possibly from gum or candy. But more than the texture or scent of it, I tasted the hunger in aggression. I knew a hungry woman from a farther distance than Tori and I were. Her movements were insistent and unrestrained.

Out of breath and with a racing pulse, I wanted to drag her deeper into the limo and fuck her into a coma. The switch in vibrations made me wild and disoriented. And I couldn't stop kissing her, tasting her needs.

She pulled back, panting hard as my feet had just begun to heat. "Ashton..." she cried forcefully into my lips.

"Tell me where to go."

She shook her head, trying to swallow. "I don't. I can't believe we're still dangerous to each other." Her gaze remained on my mouth as she heaved loudly. "Just tell me you're not married." I shook my head. "Engaged." I never stopped. "Exclusive."

"No." I dated very little, but fucked when my schedule would allow. "What more would you like to know?"

Was I consenting to this shit?

I felt desperate for an unnamed saga.

"You're at work." She was right. And if I could leave with her right now, I'd crawl behind her ass, on my knees, to wherever she led me.

"Tell me something, KaToria!" I growled.

Tori slipped onto the other side of the car, whispering, "I'll call you."

I caught her lips trembling as I stood straight. My dick was hard, mouth dry, and chest pounding. After a few seconds of standing over the limo dazed, my phone rang. I didn't need to check it to know it was my office.

"She's ready, Calvin." I backed up and closed the door shut, hoping like fuck her words weren't literal.

Tori: Hey...

Ashton: *Hey...*

Tori: Took you forever to respond. I was expecting to read 'new phone who dis.'

Ashton: *LMAO. Nah. My phone fell into water last night and I'm just getting back online. Had to get a new one this afternoon. Anyway... Hey to you! What's up?*

Ashton: *Now it's you taking forever to reply. I'm about to doze off. Should I go to bed and wait till tomorrow? LMAO*

Tori: My bad. Just stuck. Don't know what to say. This feels weird.

Ashton: *Weird humans are my specialty. What were you thinking about when you texted me this morning?*

Tori: I'm embarrassed to say.

Ashton: *Just say it. No judgment zone here. Plus, I'm done with the article. I can't publish your weirdness anymore.*

Tori: I'm literally laying here ctfu!

Tori: I guess I was thinking about seeing you again.

Ashton: *Let's make it happen.*

Tori: When?

Ashton: *When are you available? Let's start there.*

Tori: I'm in Chicago now. I'll be back tomorrow. How about tomorrow night?

Ashton: *NIGHT? Is this a booty call, McNabb? Wtf!?*

Tori: I'm laughing so hard I can't hold the phone to type

Tori: Stop. I'm engaged. Why would I be making a booty call?

Ashton: *You're the one who said at night. LMAO I can't do Thursday. Friday or Saturday works for me.*

Ashton: **Evenings…*

Tori: *You sure you're not married?*

Ashton: *Yup!*

Tori: Engaged?

Ashton: *Nope. Not engaged.*

Tori: You gotta girlfriend?

Ashton: *Uh…yeah.*

Tori: Yeah?

Ashton: *Yeah. You.*

Ashton: *Did you fall asleep?*

Tori: Just having a weird moment.

Ashton: *Why? Because you're engaged?*

Tori: I guess. Yeah.

Ashton: *Well, now you're engaged with a boyfriend. A boyfriend you'll see Friday for dinner.*

Ashton: *I'm assuming at your place.*

Tori: Yes

Ashton: *Are you cooking?*

Tori: I can.

Ashton: *Can I make a request?*

Tori: Yeah.

Ashton: *I once knew this sexy ass tomboy who made the best spaghetti I tasted in my life. She made it with fried chicken. Weird shit, I know. You think you can give it a try?*

Tori: I'll see what I can do.

CHAPTER NINE

Tori

The doorbell chime sounded all the way into the kitchen, spiking my body temperature and heart rate as if I wasn't already nervous with each hour progressing to the time he was due to arrive. I tried everything to fight my nerves, including sipping champagne as I finished the salad I planned to serve with dinner tonight.

"I got it." Treesha placed a set of new cloth napkins she'd just finished folding on the counter. "I think Renata's ready to go anyway."

She ambled out of the kitchen and I hoped she was correct. I didn't want my cousins here. Rarely did I ever have the place to myself, and tonight was my night to. But first, I had to get my rampant nerves under control. I gulped down the last of the champagne, swallowing it all in one shot. Then I glanced down my body and realized I hadn't changed. Not that it was a big deal, but I still had on my shorts and tank from cooking all evening. Ready or not, my "company" had arrived.

I ambled down the hall for the front door, anticipation not only turning my belly but twisting in my groin. This was all going too fast with Ashton. Way too fast. I wasn't supposed to keep in touch with him after the article. I wasn't supposed to cross paths with him ever again after *Blakewood*. And here he was in my vestibule, eyeing me as though I'd donned a *MEEHAR* exclusive gown. My cousins surrounded him as I broke through their line and reached up for what seemed like a normal hug of etiquette from two acquainted friends. That was until I inhaled his cologne. The shit was intoxicating, forcing me to pull back before I was ready.

My voice was shaky when I attempted, "You remember my cousins Renata and Treesha, right?"

His beaming eyes never left me. "We've exchanged our greetings," Ashton murmured. "It's time for you to do the same."

At first, I was taken aback. Treesha emitted a sound of scandal into the air. The type people did to get a fight going on the playground. That's when I was reminded of Ashton's wit. He was an asshole, always on his toes with unexpected jokes.

I schooled my expression. "Hi, Ashton. It's good to see you."

"Hello, McNabb. It's great to be seen at your place. I've heard about this property. Endless NYC views. Impressive and fitting for a woman of your accomplishments."

I rolled my eyes, unable to decide if he was sincere or blowing smoke. "Dinner is done. You wanna wash your hands in there?" I pointed to the powder room about a yard off from the entryway.

Both my cousins' suspicious regards were on Ashton as he sauntered off. Then they landed on me. In response, I crossed my arms, begging their pardons. Treesha rolled her eyes and head in a manner of saying she called bullshit. Renata tended to use more tact than her younger sister, so she kept her thoughts to herself.

"We're out," Renata announced, grabbing her set of keys from the bowl near the door.

"Did you pack NeNe enough chicken?" I asked. "You know how she likes to act like if it ain't coming from one of our pots and pans, she's a starving student."

"Yeah. I have it packed right here." She lifted a paper shopping bag. "She gone be happy as hell."

I opened the door for them. "And what time will y'all be back?"

"Why, Tori? Damn!" Treesha nagged.

My head fell to the side and mouth twisted. "So that I know what to do with the leftover food."

"We all adults. If we come in and the kitchen is dirty, we'll clean the shit up and put the food away." She whipped out of the door. "Damn!"

Before I could reply, Renata was in the doorframe. "Ignore her ass. You know she's been in a foul mood."

Yeah. She had been for a few weeks since she resurfaced right after my fight. But there was no time to rehash our reality. Renata knew that as she followed Treesha to the elevator. Even seeing them out was weird. I never did this. But they so happened to be leaving when Ashton had arrived.

Ashton...

My body heated in a flash again as I recalled he was in the bathroom. Then I remembered the load of hand towels Treesha had just washed and skipped down the hall to the laundry room to grab a few. Treesha may have been a pain in my ass, but she kept the place clean and did most of the cooking, and almost around the clock. It was her contribution to the house, but it had also come natural to her since she was a kid. Aunt Sonya would always compliment her on cleaning up after everybody in their trailer.

I made it back to the powder room as quickly as possible, and just as the water faucet was being shut off. I knew I should have knocked. It would have been the natural and polite thing to do, but between the champagne form of a sedative and the delirium I felt from him being here, I didn't use my manners. Pushing the door open, I angled my head to find him. Ashton was looking around for something to dry his hands with. When he sensed me, his eyes went from my face to the hand towels I carried.

He snorted while taking a towel, "I was about to say: in this luxury half a bath of a six million dollar apartment, there's nothing to dry my hands with?"

Ashton looked good and smelled amazing. His presence unnerved and intoxicated me. From the mirror, he caught my appreciative gape. He shifted, first just his head, to face me. I noticed his eyes narrowing before he fully turned to me with his body.

"This is going to be some complicated shit, just like the last time, isn't it?" his voice low and thick as velvet.

"I—I uh..." I swallowed hard, licking my lips against the pulse between my legs. "I don't want to talk about the last time."

He nodded, nostrils wide as his head bounced over his shoulders, expressing his understanding. "For how long?"

That's when my regard fell, vaulting around the walls and floors. I shook my head. "I don't know, but I'm not ready," I whispered.

"Then what do you want from me, KaToria?"

My nipples tingled at the sound of my name. I felt a gush of endorphins dizzying me and shame for my arousal at the same time.

"I—"

He arched over my body and kissed me. It wasn't the normal, introductory kiss that would have been typical for first-timers. No. Ashton's lips brushed over my mouth before his tongue pushed inside to find mine. I didn't dally on why. It was because we were beyond the introductory phase and straight into the fire of forbidden passion. His touch felt new, though, just like the other night: lighting my whole body on fire.

The towels fell from my hands as I grabbed him at the wiry beard on his gorgeous face, the shade of hickory, and kissed him with wild abandon. Suddenly, I needed to be closer to him, feeling his heat against mine. My thighs climbed his tall frame until we were pelvis to pelvis and I could feel his hardness against the pulse of my sex. I couldn't tell which was louder: that or the galloping of our hearts, chest to chest.

He moved so my back was against the wall. Greedily, I reached behind and beneath my trunk for the waist of his pants for his belt. Within seconds, my tank was over my loose breasts and his pants were unfastened. The vibration in my groin and ringing in my chest were louder than the voice of good judgment.

"Please tell me..." I panted between licks. "...you've got a condom."

Ashton dipped and leaned us to the side. When we were upright again, he showed me a condom. Excited to the point of trembling, I threw my arms around his neck and deepened the kiss. When I felt the crown of his head between my slippery lips, my torso collapsed into the wall.

"You sure about this, KaToria?"

Between the coarseness and authority in his cords, gravity was heavy. And so was his dick leaning against me. I reached between us, grabbing his unbelievable girth and pulling it inside of me. Ashton's expression went lax as his heavy eyes stapled into mine. When I could no longer feed myself more from the pulsating pressure, he took over, making small, but impactful thrusts until the root of him met my lips. My body felt so full, my heart could burst.

What the hell was I doing? This was Ashton Spencer. *The* Ashton Spencer I had no business having in my home, much less my body. This wasn't me. I wasn't the type of woman who dated men simultaneously or cheated. But something about being this close to a "familiar soul" felt so natural, it couldn't be wrong.

When Ashton pulled out, I caught the creamy white visual of my excitement from him. Embarrassed, my eyes squeezed closed and I dropped my head against the wall.

"It's okay that you've been craving me." He pulled my head toward his and kissed me slow and sweet after that arrogant, accurate assumption.

Then he was thrusting inside me beautifully, stretching my

pulsing pussy in a way I couldn't remember feeling before. I grabbed the back of his shirt, enduring his impales, and angled my pussy, not to miss a single inch of him. It was happening so fast: his heavy breaths, sharp teeth, and slithery tongue on my hard nipples, his hard body and strong arms—and my orgasm.

"Oh, *shi*—" I cried out, leaning back while throwing my sex into him as I came hard, unpredictably, and dangerously.

His nostrils widened and lips pursed as he drove into me with generous determination. I came so long, I thought I broke midway through my orgasm. When I finally came down, I felt needy...greedy.

Slowly, as he grounded in circular motions into me, I opened my tight eyes and saw him peering deep into me with his head cocked to the side and a satisfied gleam in his eyes.

I licked my lips. "I want another one."

A grin broke on his face as he snorted. I wasn't ashamed, awaiting a response.

Ashton pulled me from the wall, closer to his chest. He dipped to gather the waist of his pants and ambled to the door with me snaked around him.

"Where's your room?'

love ∞ belvin

Ashton

With a full belly and gloriously nestled in her fragranced sheets with Tori as my main view along with the nighttime City as the backdrop, I howled in laughter.

"How much in pay-per-view?" I egged her on.

"You heard me!" Tori's head bounced with full-on arrogance as she sat facing me with her legs crossed and a plate of food on her lap. "One-point-one billion dollars in pay-per-view and almost eighteen million paying customers, my nigga."

I laughed again. A sexually satiated KaToria was a funny Tori. "You know that was one of Thomas' selling points to take over the S.I. piece?"

Her eyes widened in shock just as she fed herself more salad. "Really? I bet it took him weeks to convince you."

I shook my head, recalling that afternoon in his Ojai home in the mountains in Ventura County. "I told him yes in the same conversation."

She blinked a few times before she nodded while chewing her food. My eyes fell to the empty plate, but for bones on my lap. I had so many questions but was too afraid to ask. I even noticed her curious stares at the scars on my shoulders, but she didn't spend much time there when she did. My better judgment implored me to go at Tori's pace.

"I think what you've done in your tenure was sheer genius, and as delayed as I am, I'm happy to have been a part of it, even if it was just to follow you into your final fight."

This time, Tori's regard fell somberly to her plate and immediately, making me regret my praise.

"Well," Her eyes returned to me. "Quiet as it's kept, you were a part of my journey more than you know."

"How?"

She placed her plate on top of mine in my lap, then transferred them onto a nightstand. "A couple of years after leaving school, I stood in front of..." She gestured with her arms. "...this black hole. I'd been walking beside it for a while and then finally, it got so big and... inviting." She took a deep breath, eyes on the comforter below. I tensed, grossly familiar with taking dips into the black hole myself. "I considered jumping into it. To be honest, I was supposed to, considering the resources—or lack thereof—I had before *BSU*. But while deciding, my eyes ran across a book that lit a match in me. It reminded me of...hope." Her eyes were on me again. "It reminded me I had options...choices...a responsibility. Care to take a guess at the title or author?"

I had no clue. "I don't know."

"Tyler Thomas' *Up in Black Arms*." My head jerked in surprise. "The sight of that book reminded me of his words of leaving Cumberland County, and courting the world came to mind. So did seeing the magic of Brielle on stage and in person. That..." She scoffed. "That was a huge part of my awakening. What made me walk away from that inviting black hole and go back into boxing was Thomas' belief of how our people should be up in arms about dying and never having discovered our purpose."

Damn...

"Hit me with some shit, why don't you?" I sat up in bed.

Tori nodded. "When I was told he was interested in interviewing me for the piece, my first inclination was no. But I couldn't not give that man my time. I couldn't pass up an opportunity to be a 'fellow-villager' of his."

"And now you're here." I gestured to her floor-to-ceiling windows, long and spacious closets, and impeccable view.

She shrugged with a smile. "I don't need to be, but I get what you mean."

"So, this property you're looking for: will your cousins be with you?"

Tori took a deep breath. "That's not the plan, no."

"I'm sure that'll be a hard split. How long have they been with you?"

"Since I won my first thousand dollars and could afford an apartment, for the most part. Renata was discharged from the Army and was between my place in North Jersey and Treesha and NeNe in Millville. I was happy to have her back for more reasons than one."

161

"Were you lonely, fighting and making a name for yourself up here?"

"Not really. Raj was around...until he began taking his talent seriously and focused on his music. But keep in mind, I'd already known Cut and the people at the gym. They were like family. The problem was Treesha and NeNe."

"NeNe is?"

"Treesha's daughter."

"Oh..."

"You probably don't remember Treesha had a daughter. But NeNe was the family's baby. After I left school, Treesha and NeNe stayed with us—*me*—for a little while until Treesha met a guy, and called herself falling in love. She and NeNe moved into an apartment with him in Bridgeton. It turned out he was a bad mixing for her."

"Why?"

"He was a pill head; Xanax, Percocet—opioids. And after a while, Treesha joined him. She spiraled out of control; all the while I was up here, trying to make a name for myself. I called and went home when I could, but addiction was a full-time job and so was boxing."

"Where were Treesha's parents?"

"Her father's in prison, and my aunt, Sonya, didn't do the best job with keeping up with her. She had knee-replacement surgery back then and it didn't exactly lend itself to chasing after an addict. She kept NeNe as much as she could. My other cousins, Treesha and Renata's siblings, half looked out, too. So when Renata came home, I could relax a little more."

"Is that why Renata retired from the military?"

"Probably. That and she didn't feel safe in there. Lots of reports of rapes and no justice. One of her closest friends there was raped by a higher ranking officer and no one did anything. The girl committed suicide. Renata didn't come back the same. She didn't leave for the Army with a clear heart either. Her boyfriend...likely the love of her life, was murdered about a year or so before I went away to school. That *shi*—stuff turned my cousin blue before my eyes. Her light dimmed. Then when she came home with even more trauma..." She shook her head. "I was just happy to have her back. I wasn't making money yet then but worked hard so she didn't have to be burdened by bills. Between her going back and forth, taking care of me, Treesha, and NeNe, as my money grew, the need for Renata to find work was less and less. She's like the Mother Hen of the three of us."

"If she's Mother Hen, who are you? The provider?"

Sadness colored Tori's face as she nodded. "Treesha still struggles with addiction. She's been in and out of rehab and she's barely thirty years old. Renata has been my executive personal assistant since more money has been coming in than I could count. My agency helped me select the right attorneys and accountants, but everything else, like recurring bills, traveling, family needs, raising NeNe... Renata naturally picked up those responsibilities."

"Where is NeNe?"

Her sudden smile was contagious. "She's in her first year at *Rowen University*. She's so smart, Ashton. Oh, my god; she's bright. The girl was skipped. I wanted her to go away to school. Even encouraged my baby girl to apply for *BSU*. NeNe is a family baby. She didn't want to be far away from her father's family in Philly or her mom's side. So I didn't push, but I do pay the bills." She giggled.

"Reminds me of my Keyonna," I shared. "She actually got accepted into *Blakewood* and *Yale* offered her an academic scholarship without my influence."

"*Blakewood*. She doesn't have your last name, so they wouldn't know off the bat."

I nodded. "She turned both down. Said she didn't want to be away from me."

"You?" Her head swung back.

"Yeah. I know. Keeping my word to Brick has been a gift in a curse with Keyonna. On the one hand, seeing her excel past where she would have gone without my influence or resources has been the most rewarding deed in my life. That girl has made me the proudest man in the world, watching her grow in spite of all the odds." I couldn't help my fatherly glow.

"And the curse?"

"The fact that the girl thinks she's my caretaker and boss. Right now, her only ambition seems to be *my* personal executive assistant—similar to what Renata has been to you."

"That's sweet!" Tori beamed so un-Tori'ish. "What's so wrong with that?"

"Perhaps the fact that I'm a single man who doesn't need his niece exposed to every detail of his life. And that I need her to fly. Not to stay in the nest. She has to do what Tori McNabb did, which is find her purpose in life. But so far, she's been too damn stubborn."

"What does her mother say?" She rubbed her chin. "I can't remember her name."

"Precious."

"I thought it was more generic."

"Karen?"

"Yeah. That could be it."

"Of course, Precious is her nickname, but I often refer to her as Karen. Karen is Karen. She's still in Newark, on her shit. Heavy drinker, but she's been working at one of the *B-Way Burgers* since before I came aboard. She's a manager there. I just wish she and Keyonna got along better."

"They don't?"

I shook my head. "They're two different women." I pulled in a deep breath. "Gift and curse. Keyonna has been around the world, studied in the best academic program in the state, met famous and wealthy people—gone to school with their children—and has never spent a day in lack, other than having her parents full-time. Karen's story is vastly different and makes her low key resent Keyonna for transforming into the queen she's becoming."

"You blame yourself for that?"

"At first, I blamed myself, then Karen. Now, I simply accept it for what it is. I would do nothing different for that girl. She's one of a

164

kind and prepared me so much for parenting. I just wish she didn't view me as the dependent and enjoy her privilege."

"That reminds me of NeNe. Her respect for her mother has been so compromised over the years and it shows when either Renata or I'm in the room with her and Treesha. It's uncomfortable, but all I can do is take it for what it is. I didn't give up on that girl. She made me want to be a parent, too. I'm sure when you have kids, you'll be a better father for the sacrifices you made for Keyonna."

My stomach turned over and chest heaved as I regarded her with narrowed eyes. I struggled since we stopped fucking after her third orgasm and began to hold each other in her bed as though we'd been friends all this time. There was so much shit we needed to discuss.

"You sure you don't want to talk about *us*, Tori? I have a few more minutes before I have to get out of here."

A wicked gleam sparked in Tori's eyes and a casual smirk lifted on her beautiful face. She reached over and pulled the comforter down my waist. My dick sprang to life in the cool air. Her hand wrapped around me and Tori stroked up and down.

My eyes closed, succumbing to what I knew would be erotic pleasure. She crawled up the bed, settling her knees between my legs. Her ass touted in the air in just a thong.

"Are you married?" She whispered over the head of my dick. Tori's warm tongue circled the opening. I shook my head. "Engaged?" I wanted to remind her she was, but with my cock in her hands, if Tori didn't want to recall that very well documented fact, I sure as hell wasn't going to remind her. She kissed the shaft of me as I shook my head again. "Do you have a girlfriend, Spencer?"

This time, while rubbing my lips together, I nodded. "You," I croaked out. "You're my girlfriend."

Quickly, I reached up to grab her. After a few rough movements, I managed her to straddle my face so I could eat her pussy properly. While Tori began caressing my dick with hugs, kisses, licks, and sucks, I grabbed her ass cheeks as my tongue explored her pussy from another view. The taste of rubber from the condom was present, but nothing could keep me from enjoying her.

I had no idea what was going on between us. This experience this evening had been a hybrid of a first date, creeping, and catching up with an old friend, all of which I had experience in. But never with Tori McNabb. At *BSU*, I didn't feel like we were creeping. Because of where my dorm was, there was very little chance of running into Aivery. The same with hanging with Tori off-campus. We'd go to remote places so I could chill with her, not keep her a secret. Also, that was Tori McNabb, my friend—although she didn't consider me one to herself.

"Mmmm..." Tori moaned sweetly over my cock while cupping my balls, reminding me she was, unfortunately, a savant at giving head.

This was Tori McNabb, the accomplished, world-recognized champion. The woman who was wealthy, cultured, and clearly unafraid to pursue what she wanted. And the fact that it was me made me work harder when fucking her pussy with my tongue as her ass cheeks trembled against my forehead as she bounced. This blissful erotica went on and on for what seemed like an hour, though it wasn't. And just as I was preparing to blow, believing Tori had possibly tapped out earlier, she began moaning hard, humming while strangling the fuck out of the neck of my cock. Her abs tightened over my own, and her tongue swirled and swirled over my head.

As I blew in her hot, talented mouth, Tori's delicious juices exploded in mine.

She had me pinned up against the front door. I was supposed to have left over twenty minutes ago, per my text back home. But having Tori's warm, eager, and open sexy body pressed up against mine had me all fucked up. She kept inviting me to kiss her glossy lips. After our joint explosion, she handed over a washcloth and a toothbrush, and let me shower in her bathroom. I couldn't go home smelling like pussy. I'd always been a better man of the house than that.

"Thanks for having dinner with me," she smiled goofily under my chin.

My face tightened playfully. "Is that all you wanna thank me for?"

Her soft hand cupped my dick through my pants. "This wasn't too bad either."

I chuckled, enjoying Tori's light-heartedness. She was pure. Carefree.

"I want to get to know you."

"I thought you knew me."

"According to you, I don't."

"Well," She reached up and kissed me. "...seems like you got a nice orientation tonight."

"So, does this make me your jumpoff?"

She unlocked the door behind me. "According to you, I'm your girlfriend." Pushing off of me, she whispered sexily, "Good night, jumpoff human."

As I rounded the open door to leave, paying her my final lingering gaze, I thought, *'I'd be that only for you.'*

Only I didn't know how long I'd be able to endure.

Tori's engaged...

Tori

I sat at the island in my kitchen with my laptop and tablet open. Sipping on much-needed java, I viewed properties on my laptop while reading an article on a friend of mine in a boxing magazine from my tablet. Leona Bethune announced her desire to fight my second to last opponent, Tonya Garcia. That didn't sit well with me. As talented a fighter as Bethune was, I didn't think she was ready for Garcia. It was common in women's boxing that when a fellow-boxer saw you win a fight, they felt they too could have the same results. It was foolish on Bethune's part.

But I'm retired. Let them have it...

"Oh, good!" I heard from behind me. Renata's slippers clip-clopped against the floor. "I was coming in here to see if your laptop was fully charged so you can see the houses the real estate agent sent over. And look at you, all up and at 'em early, and shit," she teased in her motherly tone.

"I know how to behave off the leash," I mumbled into my mug.

As she opened the cabinet for a coffee cup, she asked, "Are you excited about any of the properties? I saw she sent you one in Budd Lake. That's up yonder by Raj."

"You hate where Raj lives."

As she poured her coffee, she countered with, "You don't."

"What are you going to do when I move?"

Renata shrugged, leaning against the counter. "I don't know. Something."

"Hey..." I turned my body to face her, guarding my mug to my chest. "I meet with Jerry this week. You should see an increase reflected in your next pay."

Jerry had been my accountant for many years. Now that I'd officially retired, my plan of downsizing in staff had taken effect. I no longer had use for Lidia like I once did. Renata would resume what little of her role I still needed. Even my time with Drea would decrease significantly. I had no desire to do red carpets or formal public appearances like I used to and, therefore, had less of a need for a personal stylist.

Testing the temperature of the coffee, Renata shook her head. "That ain't necessary, and you know it. You've always paid me well. Used to be more than I deserved. My life is simple, and I imagine once you settle into your new life—whatever it'll be now with this Deon bullshit—you won't be so demanding."

I nodded, happy to see her understanding of my transition. But it bothered me that it sounded like we were coming to an end, too. Did I like living with family? Not mostly, but my need of them, even emotionally, superseded my desire to finally be independent of my cousins.

I'd just turned back to my devices when I heard, "Hey, mommy one and mommy two!"

That familiar twang had me swinging my body backward. "What are you doing here?" Her beauty always struck me first. Not only was she a healthy, genetic balance of her mother and father, but NeNe was aware of her strongest feminine features and played them up very well. She wore a wig this morning she managed to pull into a natural—as natural as one can get with a wig—ponytail on the top of her head. Her fake lashes were always a reasonable length and width, and waist and butt proportion was still remarkable, thanks to my pushing of track in high school despite her disinterest.

NeNe floated over to the cabinet to retrieve a mug when I asked again, "What are you doing here on a Saturday morning?"

"Why wouldn't I be, my favorite champ of a human?" She mocked me, laying an affectionate kiss on my cheek.

"Because I just sent food to you last night via your mother and aunt."

NeNe shrugged, pouring coffee. "I ate half of it on the way up, and left the other back in my fridge." She grabbed a leftover biscuit from the cake stand and bit into it. "It was banging, as usual!"

"What about work?"

"I didn't have any."

My chin dropped. "On a Saturday?"

"On a Saturday, gorgeous." She blew me an air kiss on the way to the entryway. "As it appears, someone needed overtime, and we worked it out with my supervisor to get it to him. Apparently, the court is on his *ass*—butt—for child support. I'm glad I was able to meet his need like the Christian gal my dear auntie, T, taught me to be," she singsonged, winked, and then was gone.

"Get your Christian ass—*butt*—on that treadmill this morning, too!" I shouted behind her. "You think those biscuits're gonna melt away like me with your charm?" Renata laughed behind her coffee cup. "Since when does *B-Way Burger* give anyone off on a Saturday? Especially not the one in Bridgeton. They stay packed!"

Renata's only response was a shrug before I turned back to my laptop and began clicking through photos of a property in Wanaque. It was spacious, but too old and disproportioned for me. I hated house shopping. It had been over a year of constant house-hunting and I'd gotten nowhere.

"Did Ashton like the spaghetti?" I registered Treesha's smoker's rasp right away. We didn't call it spaghetti and fried chicken in my family. It was just spaghetti, and you could skip the mention of salad. I added that on over the years as I became health-conscious. "Last night..." She made clear. "Did he enjoy the food?"

"I imagine he did." I acted as though distracted by my screens.

Deep down inside, my pangs of loneliness rang louder. I couldn't believe I slept with him last night. Well, not sleep, and that was my hang up. How could I be so weak that I didn't want him to leave? I was so close to asking him to stay the night, needing to extend that unparalleled intimacy with him just a bit more. Last night, I was brazen...and so unexpectedly. In my wildest thoughts leading up to the night, I anticipated a kiss and simple words expressing I'd be interested in taking it further in the near future. I just didn't know the future had been now—*last night*. I wasn't that type of girl, being so free with sex.

And we talked...

That was unplanned, too. My intention was to feed Ashton and feel him out. I'd only known him to be a complicated guy. I wanted to gauge his current level of complexity, to see if it was worth me risking my dignity, but I ended up falling into a web of lust instead. We talked about NeNe and Keyonna, components in our lives that were similar.

Then we spoke about my next chapter plans regarding my cousins, that contemplation following me into my morning thoughts. This was nuts. Ashton was now in my head beyond what was reasonable because his sex was just as I remembered, if not better. I came four times last night; just as unsuspectedly as our chemistry. I was hoping my morning coffee could help clear my hazy mind so I could gain ahold of myself before speaking to him today.

"*I* imagine he enjoyed more than the food." Treesha wanted to be a pain in my ass this morning, I understood.

Turning toward her, I saw she had on her cleaning gloves, obviously having begun her Saturday chores. "What are you talking about?"

"About what he was doing here in the first place. It was weird."

"I'm sorry. I think I missed the part of two people who just wrapped up a professional endeavor being weird for simply having dinner."

Treesha's head swung. "First of all, it wasn't a simple dinner. It was spaghetti. You—we—made him our spaghetti. Since when do we do that for random people?"

Renata whined in warning, "Treesha—"

"And secondly, what does this type of foil have to do with spaghetti?" She pulled a condom wrapper from her pocket, and my eyes damn near popped out of my head. "Did you *wrap* his leftovers to-go with this?" My eyes were stapled to the opened wrapper held in the air. "Speaking of which, are you sure you're not his leftover, T?"

My eyes shot to her face. "You're skating on thin ice with me right now."

"Yeah, Treesha. That's none of your business," Renata reminded her.

"It ain't? I live here and cook and clean." Treesha faced Renata with those soft facts. "And when I saw one, I thought to let it slide. Tori's allowed to slip. But when I made it to her bedroom, there were two more of these. Now, I can't let her bump her fucking head while down there. What the fuck, Tori!"

I shot to my feet, flying to get into her face. "You're still here in my good graces only on a wing and a prayer, girl. If I were you, I'd practice the same act of grace." Out of breath, I measured my volume, not wanting NeNe to hear this.

"Y'all need to chill." Renata drew nearer to us. "Treesha, you know you still foul for not showing up to the fight—"

"I missed *one* fight! Sue me!"

"My last one. One of the most significant of my career."

"But did you lose?" Treesha challenged.

"That ain't the point. You know I've supported you over the years in more ways than one. When you needed anything, I was there. I gave to you before I served myself. If all I ask in return is to support the one and only thing I love, why can't you not get high *one* day and show up for me?"

"Like I showed up for you with Aunt Dot and baby Bobby?" Her chin pushed into the air. "Wasn't I there for you when she was sick and then passed—*God, bless the dead*. Wasn't I there when you cried at night, thinking nobody heard or when you threw up in the mornings on your way to work, struggling to act normal. No, I didn't always jump in your face to comfort you, but I was there, waiting to catch you. And you know I did a few times!"

Renata's head fell over her shoulders, face to the floor. Treesha had pulled out a big gun this morning.

"Why are you doing this?" I was officially wounded.

"Because since you told us about *BSU*, Ashton Spencer was put on the fuck boy for life, no-fly list. And now that he's back, it was only to do the stupid article. He did it, and look how fast he fuck you. Fucked you, Tori? You don't even fuck with people like that. I know this shit with Deon is fucked up, and as far as I'm concerned, fuck his fuck boy ass, too. That nigga on the no-fly list now. But Ashton? He just flew in here. How? Do we know he ain't manipulate his way into the *Sports Illustrated* shit? And you said he runs *B-Way Burger* now. Do you know that for a fact? Just because his daddy started the business don't mean his son can just slide up in that bitch, owning the shit." She grabbed her cleaning bucket and headed out. "Not even all white people with money can do that."

Treesha left the kitchen with her fumes of self-doubt and insecurity wafting into my psyche. Renata stared at me with both muted apology and possibly concern of Treesha being right.

I turned to close the laptop and grab my coffee and tablet. "For the record." I stepped in front of Renata. "*I* fucked *him*. Each time."

And with that small fight for my integrity, I left the room.

CHAPTER TEN

Ashton

It was still dark out when I made it to my kitchen. I began a pot of coffee, then began plucking ingredients for my buttermilk pancakes, per the text I received yesterday just before leaving the office for Tori's. Pancakes were a staple in my home. Fresh blueberries, strawberries and bananas set the tone, and I couldn't forget the thick-cut bacon. It was a must.

As I went about laying the bacon in the pan, my mother walked in with her kimono flying behind her, and straight to the coffee pot.

"Caffeine for the queen this morning?" Typically, she was a dessert coffee drinker.

"Mmmhmmm," she hummed. "Had a late night last night." I froze. "No big deal there. But once I got done with story time, Aunt Hattie called me."

"About what?"

"Aunt Allegra is sick. Cousin Evelyn just had knee-replacement surgery and can't get Aunt Allegra's business done."

"Business like what?"

"Well," she exhaled. "paying the taxes on three properties—you know she ain't doing no online payments—collecting payments from the farmers, inspecting one of the houses that she's about to renovate."

"What she gonna do?" I asked, tossing my pancake mix into a bowl.

"I'm not sure there's much she can do. She's usually at the mercy of cousin Evelyn. You know she don't trust many to do her business. But cousin Evelyn's gonna be down for a few weeks."

My mother's aunt, Allegra, was an eighty-two-year-old woman with several properties she still tried to keep up with. Her not changing with technological times and going electronic hadn't been working to her benefit. Now, she was at the mercy of her daughter who, too, was aging. My mother was right: her aunt didn't trust but two people with her "business."

"You need to go down to help out? I can move a few things around in my schedule to clear up time with the girls."

Taking her first sip of coffee, she released a contented breath. She shook her head. "No. That won't be necessary. You know they have off from school next week for the Jewish holidays. I'll take them with me."

"Thanks." I smiled. "But you know that isn't necessary."

Swallowing, she lowered the mug from her face while catching the sunrise. "Mmmhmmm. It is."

I paused on my buttermilk pouring and scoffed. "What do you mean, it is?"

"You, my son, need a break."

"A break from what?"

"From the lifestyle of a middle-aged man. You work too much." She rolled her neck, grimacing. "And do you forget you're a single man? Go somewhere. Have a one-night stand—shit, an affair—so long as it's healthy and consensual."

I chuckled, going back to the task at hand. I was on a tight schedule this Saturday morning. "I don't think I need Ms. Wanda's coaching on getting some ass."

"I can't tell. I almost got excited last night when you said you'd be late coming home. Hell, I was happy when you went to that party a few days ago. But you walked in before four in the morning, so I knew it wasn't a good night for you."

Flipping over the bacon, I couldn't help my humor. "Actually, I enjoyed myself last night very much." So much, I refused to think about it.

"Mmmmhmmmm..." She gaped my way with a raised brow line and twisted lips. "Make a couple of calls, Ashton. Go away. You can afford to go anywhere you want, and lord knows, you have an exhaustive list of female volunteers. Go! Have fun!"

The sound of heavy plops in the hallway grew nearer.

"This discussion isn't over." I went back to my batter on the counter.

"Oh, yes, it is, bruh."

She turned away, sipping her coffee.

My legs bounced on the balls of my feet as I waited in a small lounge outside of his office. His actual office at *B-Way Burger* headquarters. My eyes brushed over the lavish place: burgundy carpeted floors, earthly hued panel walls, leather padded bench, and sleek maple wood furniture for his executive secretary, per her nameplate facing me.

Eddie, the security I arranged to travel with me today, stood near the elevator, on his phone to look less...security'ish. I couldn't wait for the day I didn't need a bodyguard. The time when no one cared to take up my time when in passing; they'd just wave and keep it moving. But today wasn't that day. I'd only been weeks out of the final fight of my career and still had press to do.

My head popped up when Ashton's office door opened. Out came an average height Hispanic man wearing a suit without the jacket. So far, I could tell headquarters was formal. Everyone I encountered since being permitted upstairs wore hard bottom shoes. So, I had to surmise this guy's suit jacket was in his office—or in his cubicle.

He sidled up to the receptionist counter, leaning into it way too casually for the way he was dressed—the way this place was outfitted. "Yup. Boss man's in a foul mood. Any idea how he got there?"

The woman whispered and, at first, I thought she was telling him who I was. That was until I heard, "He's been like this for almost a week. Where have you been?"

The guy's head bounced over his slender shoulders. "Well, if you need anything...anything I can circumvent around the big guy, let me know. If you want to hang out after work for some pointers, hit me up for that, too."

When he stepped off dramatically, I quickly diverted my eyes and lowered my face. If I hadn't been recognized by now, I wanted to keep it that way. The elevator opened as soon as he punched the call button. With my head still hung as though I was peering into my phone and legs crossed, I watched him onto the elevator. When the door closed, my eyes wandered lazily back over to the receptionist corner, then to Ashton's door.

He was there in the doorjamb, looking at me. His expression was neither excited, surprised, or disappointed. It was...familiar, as though I'd done this a million times. And damn, did he look good in his cologne-colored brogues, suit pants, dress shirt, and tie. After a short stare down, Ashton pushed from the frame and turned back into his office, pushing his door open wider.

"McNabb," he called out over his shoulder, inviting me in.

My attention went to Eddie. He was already peering my way. I nodded to communicate where I was going. I'd already told him earlier it would be unnecessary to attend this "meeting" with me. He should stay near, but not attend.

I stood and sauntered on wobbly knees inside. Though the office was large, it smelled like him. His essence was here mixed in with the carpet freshener, wood polish cleaner, and *Windex*. Ashton's presence was large and looming, just like the man himself here at the headquarters of *B-Way Burger*.

"Kindly close the door," he ordered while going for his office chair.

Wanting to roll my eyes, I obeyed. Then I stood in front of his desk expectantly with my hands clasped at my pelvis line.

"So, you *are* the CEO." That stupid observation was the way I foolishly decided to open this conversation.

"Did you think I wasn't?"

Treesha's mention of it last week still burned, but I honestly didn't doubt him. Ashton Spencer was born royal. He didn't have to lie to be appealing: he was Mr. Untouchable, and I seriously doubted I was alone in feeling that way.

I plucked my brows. "I don't know much about you, but your dick game is still as stellar as it was twelve years ago."

Ashton pulled at the collar of his shirt and stretched his neck. "I would hope it's improved, but I guess I'll take it. Is that why you're here? To make that assessment?"

"I'm here because I haven't heard from you since last Friday night when you left my place."

"You haven't called to express this."

"I shouldn't have to. *You* should have called!"

His face fell toward the red tie on his chest and Ashton chuckled. "You still don't know shit about punctuation," he murmured.

"I think and finally believe I *do* know what you mean by that!"

"Then why haven't you called and shared this? It would have been less dramatic than you sitting in my office, fuming in heels and lipstick, and risking my staff knowing there may be something between us."

"Because I needed to look you in the face."

His expression tightened as his fingers tented at his chest line. "For what?"

"To check for any signs of the old childish, selfish Ashton who doesn't have the balls to communicate he no longer wants to be..." I shrugged while shaking my head. "...cool anymore."

Ashton leaned in with one ear and squinted eyes as though confused. "You mean friends? You still can't say we were friends back in college, Tori?" He sat back in his seat. "Damn."

I no longer had the patience for the icebreaker. "Why haven't you called?"

Ashton chewed on the inside of his cheek, eyes falling to his desk. "Can I be honest?"

"That's all I came for."

He stood from his desk and ambled over to the large windows of his office. "When I left your place, I asked was I your jumpoff. It was a literal and rhetorical-hybrid. On my way to my car, I decided I'd be that for you. Then on my ride home, last Saturday, and into the week, my thoughts began to change." He poured himself a glass of water using a larger pitcher with fresh citrus fruits and mint leaves. "You drew a clear parameter."

"What's that?"

"That we can't talk about what happened then and who we are now."

"What's wrong with that? I thought we were embarking on something fun."

"Fun is hard for me to have with you. *Fun* is something I can have my pick of the night of as a single man. You and I can't just have fun."

Irritated, I asked, "And why not?"

"Because as much as you want to ignore it and as much as I've tried to downplay it since agreeing to take on the *Sports Illustrated* feature, we have a history, KaToria. It was evident the night of your party."

"I let you go down on me. I think you should consider yourself as lucky. I'm engaged!"

Ashton took a long sip of his water before focusing his regard on me. "And I paid for the alcohol and food at that event while the only thing from the menu I had that night was you. I think you're the lucky one here."

I was gutted.

How?

"Did you work that out with Deon?" I was confused.

"I don't have to run shit by your fiancé, sweetie. As you can see, I am the CEO of one of the fastest-growing fast food chains. I can make shit happen on a mere itch."

"So, you manipulated your way into my life for a final fuck?"

My cousin was right...

"Newsbreak, Tori: I don't need to fuck you. I'd much rather be taken serious by you." His neck twisted, eyes narrow. "Do you know what I went through because of you, and you up and disappeared?"

My heart twisted painfully, lungs seized, and an unexpected tear fell. "I left that school broken!"

"No." He shook his head, eyes pinned to me. "*I* left broken! I still have the bruises to show. I went to my graduation on crutches, high off opioids to combat the pain of being vertical. You talk about the extensive therapy you've received over the years; I can show you endless receipts of the physical *and* mental health therapy I endured!"

And then I broke physically. An unexpected torrent of emotions threatened to shoot from my stomach and exit through my eyes and mouth. I barreled over, covering my face to catch it all. Thankfully, it was a miss. My recovery cost me seconds of weakness, but I rebounded.

I'd, indeed, seen his scars. They were on one of his muscular shoulders and even ugly ones on his beautifully sculpted knees when I was in a six-nine position with him. I sucked him with passion, expressing my sympathy for whatever had happened to cause it. Ashton's body was more slender, exposing his athletic muscular frame. He was more cut and less beefy than he was as a quarterback.

He shifted closer. "You went from cold and disgusted being on the same plane and resort as me, to hardly giving me the time to do my job, to being rather forthcoming, to letting me serve you dinner then asking about who I'm fucking, to letting me flirt with you, to letting me taste your pussy, to fucking me—all the while making it clear all this time you're not available and unopen to discussing our past. But you've damn sure made it clear several times that you're engaged." His head fell to the side. "How am I supposed to know you're not fuckin' with me?"

"*Wha*—what do you mean?"

"How do I know you're not some twisted, crazy ass broad with an unrooted vendetta from *Blakewood*?"

I stepped back, reacting to the blow. "Why would I do that?"

"Why would you not want to talk about real shit? Why would you wait for me to call to not have to 'talk?'" His head cocked to the other side and he blinked. "Just to fuck? Is that all you want from me, KaToria? To be a fuckin' tool? Oh, so you want my johnson *and* Johnson's johns—"

I caught Ashton's eyes growing wide at something behind me. Turning quickly, I noticed Eddie and the Hispanic guy from the reception area earlier looking into his glass wall at us. It dawned on me how loud we must have been. The guy, who had to be a whole foot and a half shorter than Eddie, opened the door and leaned inside.

"Everything okay, big guy?"

My head whipped back over to Ashton, having processed he was being looked after. Realization of our throw-down must have hit him because Ashton closed his eyes, shaking off the anger.

"*Ye*-yeah, Julio."

"You okay, too, Ms. McNabb?" His tone was less cavalier than it was with the receptionist.

Not knowing how to exactly answer that, I nodded, regard going to Eddie. I gave him a more affirmative nod.

"Holy shit," the Julio guy snorted, big smile on his bubblegum-colored lips. "You two know each other?"

Having a new source of irritation, I gaped at him like he was an idiot. Then my face relaxed as I got a good look at him. There was something familiar about him. "You are?"

He chuckled with a mixture of surprise and excitement at my question. "I'm—"

"Julio," Ashton cut him off, his regard sweeping the ceiling. "this is *the* Tori McNabb. McNabb, this Julio Hernandez. He's an executive on our operations team." He visibly struggled to keep his cool.

The fuck—the friggin' nerve...

"So, I don't know you?"

With a bright beam still in his eyes, Julio shrugged.

"Julio is the grandson of Muriel, my former housekeeper." Ashton still refused to look my way.

Once I registered the connection, my eyes ballooned, then my heart leaped. "I'm so sorry about your grandmother. I only met her the one visit, but she treated me well. She was very sweet."

Now, Julio's face tightened. "Wait a minute..." His head pushed over his shoulders as though taking a deeper look at me. "You're not the girl..." He looked to Ashton for help. "You're the girl he brought home the one time? I remember you!"

"How do you know it wasn't someone else?" I asked.

"Because other than Aivery, Ash never brought another girl to the house that I saw." Julio peered over to Ashton again. "*Right*, bro?"

Ashton expelled a deep breath. "Correct, but I don't expect

McNabb to believe that. She's insistent on believing I'm what you call an evil, neglectful, selfish, childish, and apparently heartless human." Finally, his head twisted with hiked brows and he narrowed his eyes to peer at me—daring me to challenge him.

"Wait..." Julio's fingers dug into his forehead as his eyes squeezed closed. "Does that mean you two are—"

"KaToria McNabb is engaged, Julio," Ashton growled. "Let's show her a little respect here."

His tone intimidated even me.

Julio's hands shot into the air. "I forgot. My bad. I'm not that good at following pop culture."

"I'm gonna go. It was nice seeing you, Ashton." Feeling an unexplainable deflation, I turned to leave the office.

Ashton

"A suite at *Vista al Mar Negro* or *Agua que Brilla*." Keyonna asked. My eyes perused the empty landscape as I listened to her. "I know you love the *Vista al Mar Negro* property, but prefer the food at *Aqua que Brilla*."

That made me pause my circular movements. My head fell to the side. "Narvaez left *The Black Ocean View?*"

"First of all, its name is *Vista al Mar Negro*. You hating the term negro won't change that. And yes, Narvaez left for a resort in St. Lucia years ago. You sent him a parting package."

As I eyed my realtor's patient posture, I couldn't recall the gesture. "When was that?"

"About a year after Aivery."

Ahhhh...

That made sense. Not much stuck to memory for me around that period.

I moved the phone away from my mouth and asked Jaquana, "How much?"

She glanced up at me. "Ahhh...one point-three, Mr. Spencer. Well under budget."

"Considering."

"Yes." She smiled. "Considering."

I turned away from her to close my conversation with Keyonna. "Fuck it. Get me a house."

"A house?" She parroted. "In *Saint Justin*?"

"Isn't that the location at hand?" I asked with sarcasm. "Okay then. Something small, but with a competent—"

"I know," she interrupted. "A chef's kitchen, Jacuzzi, bar, and privacy. Yeah, yeah, yeah. I got you. My question is what type of mattress."

I froze. "Are you being nosy?"

"I kinda need to know to book. Are you going alone or no?"

"No."

"Okay. So unless you're taking a guy friend—which you aren't because you didn't request a second bedroom—either you're going alone or with a woman, which means you're sharing a bed. And for the record: the purpose of my question was not to get into your business, it's simply to find you a place to stay this weekend and have you properly accommodated. As you know, a California king will give you the leg room you need and keep you close. A Wyoming king will give you the leg room you need and space you prefer from a woman. And an Alaska king will do if you're feeling...like throwing a party. Again, I'm not asking to get in your business. I just need to know what to arrange."

I could hear the eye-roll in her tone. Already frustrated for more reasons than I could count, the last thing I needed was Keyonna's shit. Teaching her shit over the years had been a pleasure and a goddamn pain. She was an excellent pupil and knew too much at the same damn time. I had no idea if I'd be going alone or not. It was fucked up that I kind of didn't want to go alone.

Fuck it...

"California."

"See. That wasn't hard, was it?" Her tone was patronizing. "You were able to give me information and I still don't know your business. See how that works?"

"Yeah, whatever." I rolled my damn eyes. "I'm keeping Jaquana waiting. I'll hit you with a food list later."

"I got you, dawg!" she gruffed sillily before the call disconnected.

"Now, you," I exhaled. Then I glanced around the empty lot once again. Bold green and dense trees outlined the ready-to-build portion of the property "I get what you mean about the space, endless options for customization, and a cut in overall cost, but..."

"But." She turned to me, humor in her chestnut eyes.

I exhaled, glancing around at the vast and gorgeous empty property. "I'm so damn overwhelmed with work and keeping up with my girls. I don't have the capacity of overseeing having a home built. It's not something I want to delegate either. How many people have you shown this to?"

"No one else." She dangled her keys while giving the property a final gaze, too. "I have another client with a similar dilemma as yours that I'll be showing it to. The seller is an old man who bought up quite a few lots in obscure locations in his ambitious youth. He's nearly eighty-five with no children or close family to bequeath them to."

"Bequeath." That made me laugh some more. "How long do I have to answer?"

Her face tightened. "I think you just did." We both laughed at that. She was right. I wasn't interested in building.

I took off for my car, where Calvin was waiting to zip me to a meeting that was soon to begin in mid-town Manhattan.

"I'll hit you by Monday if I change my mind."

Ashton: *You still don't know shit about pacing.*

Tori: I understand punctuation. OKAY? I also understand when someone doesn't want to be bothered. But you wait two hours after I leave to text me. I came to see you! You could have said whatever it is you need to say then!

Ashton: *You didn't listen to anything I said.*

Tori: Oh I heard everything. You think I'm out to hurt you as though that's possible.

Ashton: *You still don't get it.*

Tori: Oh I do!

Ashton: *You don't. And you don't want to fuckin talk about it either.*

Tori: Talk about what?

Ashton: *About me Tori. About what I've been through. About who I am.*

Tori: You know who I am!

Ashton: *And yet you don't know who I am as a thirty-four year old fucking man!*

Tori: One with a nasty attitude. That's all I see.

Ashton: *One with feelings and a heart you'll never know.*

Ashton: *Oh. Your fingernails wet McNabb? It's been a whole hour since you last responded!*

Tori: I don't have discussions via text. I came to see you for that.

Tori: Now who's not responding?

Ashton: *I'm just leaving out of a meeting and headed into another. Do you want to talk face to face but have a real conversation this time? I can stop by your place around 9:30-10.*

Tori: That late sounds very creep'ish to me.

Ashton: *Seems like that's all you want from me anyway. It's the best I can do. I can explain why if you want.*

Tori: NO! I'm in a photoshoot now. I can be available at that time. We just can't do my place. Why not yours?

Ashton: *Do you really wanna know why? I'm more than willing to share.*

Tori: NO! I can text you the address.

Ashton: *Which dark alley are you having me killed in?*

Ashton: *Tori...*

Tori: No dark alley. Jersey City. I'll send the address in a minute. They're calling me.

Ashton

"Here you are, sir." The concierge motioned for me to enter the apartment directly from the elevator.

I nodded as I stepped off into quite an artistic foyer of black and white, checkerboard marble pattern flooring. The dual colors so stark, the shiny panels were almost reflective. The creative ambiance from the distinct black walls with large, gold-framed artwork and a round table topped with a huge bouquet of an array of fresh silver and black roses. This was different. I hadn't been in an elevator-entry apartment in some time, and certainly never in Jersey City.

"Silver roses," I broke the ice, seeing Tori leaning against the wall opening the foyer.

Stiffly, she nodded. "Raj keeps the place stocked with fresh flowers. I had these arranged."

"Any significant meaning?"

"Silver's supposed to represent sensational."

"And black roses?"

"Sophistication, power, and mystery." She crossed one leg over the other in heeled slide-in sandals and a flowing maxi dress.

My brows hiked. "What inspired the selection? And why do you look like you wanna fuck me?"

Slowly, one arm stretched and lifted in the air, and Tori extended her index finger my way. She was answering my first question. "And it's because I do. As embarrassed as I should be—as shameful—I do."

My dick lurched in my pants and I exhaled, looking away. "You're going to make this painful, aren't you?"

I didn't know what the night would entail, but I could feel a tsunami of unspoken emotions coming our way. The question was only who'd get run over by them.

"Follow me." Tori turned into a corridor.

I followed her into a sitting room. It held the same pattern of black and white flooring and walls. The furniture was douses of bold colors. Candles lit the room, music set a vibe, and the smell of marinara sauce and garlic reminded me I'd missed dinner, trying to make it here at a decent hour.

"Hungry?"

"I can eat," I murmured, looking at the bottle of rum, another of *Coke*, wine, glasses, and a platter with mussels in red sauce and sliced French bread for dipping. I met her gaze. "You really wanna fuck, huhn?"

Uneasy about her truth, Tori rolled her eyes. "The bathroom's just out the room to the left, if you want to freshen up before eating."

Paying her a long regard, I left for the bathroom.

CHAPTER ELEVEN

Ashton

When I returned from the bathroom, Tori was standing, waiting with a large index card and marker in her hands. Her thoughts were visibly heavy under the romantic sounds of eighties and nineties R&B classics.

"Before we eat, I want to address the elephant in the room." Her voice was honeyed, shaky. I had no idea why Tori was so damn nervous. Should *I* have been? "You want to talk about...us, and I need to respect that. I can only stomach so much of revisiting those *BSU* days. So, I figured we both ask *one* question about that time period."

"Just one?"

She nodded. "I'd like to see you again. If this works out, we can ask more—*another*—at some point, but just one for tonight." She handed me the card and a green marker. "I've written down my question. You can write down yours and I'll answer it with full honesty."

I received the card and marker, then sat on the mustard chester-field sofa and began to consider the single question. I'd interviewed Tori and was even given a glimpse into her life, but still felt I was missing significant details about the force behind her career and life-style. I had no idea who this woman was. As I pondered, Tori moved over to the coffee table and poured drinks. She chose two servings of rum and *Coke*. When she turned to give me one of the tumblers, the flicker from a candle exposed the unrest in her eyes. Right away, I took a long sip of the rum, then wrote my one burning question.

"Good?" she asked, sitting down next to me.

"Always," I exhaled, feeling tense myself. "I'm done." I placed the marker on the table.

"Perfect." Tori brought the tray of food closer to us, arranging the empty bowl for the shells. "How was your day, dear?"

I laughed quietly, watching her grab a mussel, beginning to eat.

"Why does this feel like déjà vu?"

"Hmmm..." she hummed before licking her lips in between chewing. "We're missing the pool at *BSU*, maybe?"

That's when the memory returned. When we snuck and used one of the indoor pools at school. Actually, I arranged that with the maintenance staff working that evening. "You remember that?"

She licked her thumb. "I remember everything. It's pathetic how much of the culture and lifestyle I've been able to adapt as a successful boxer derived from the few months I spent at college around a certain snobby human."

I grabbed a piece of bread, then dipped it into the marinara sauce before biting into it. "Do you know how much I paid Garlin, the maintenance guy, for that area on that shift?"

Tori shook her head. "I'm not sure I want to. I thought we were there because you had pull."

"Yeah," I scoffed. "Five hundred dollar-pull."

"We weren't allowed to use it?"

"Not exactly. They needed to be reserved and I wanted to do something creative to impress you, but it was too late to book by the time I came up with the idea of seeing your thick thighs and juicy breasts naked in the water."

Tori snorted. "I guess I was an expensive piece of ass that night."

"The best piece of ass." I went for a mussel. "Had my damn nose wide the fuck open."

"Oh, whatever!" Tori laughed.

"Seriously." I took another pull from my glass. "Did you make this?"

Tori shook her head just before slurping the meat from the shell. "I had it delivered. Told you I had a shoot tonight. *You're* talking about last minute planning in the pool room. That was me tonight."

"Raj gave you his place for the night?" I laughed. "We're *definitely* creeping like broke college students."

Grinning, she licked her fingers again. "That's the way I feel. But no. He gave me the keys the night before my fight with O'Connor. That dude's got a sick way of predicting my need to hide away."

"Why couldn't we do this at your place? We're only going to talk. Is your fiancé there?" I teased.

Tori rolled her eyes at my grin, catching it. "No. I just didn't want the judgment of my cousins. They found the condom wrappers from your first visit."

I wasn't expecting that. "Oh."

"*Oh*, is right. I almost knocked Treesha out over it."

"Well, that's another thing we have in common."

"What?"

"We answer to people living in the homes we pay for."

Tori visibly froze. "Maybe we should get into our question. This is sounding very *BSU*'ish to me."

Chuckling, I reminded her. "I don't have a wife, fiancée, or girlfriend."

"So you say," she exhaled, unconvinced while reaching across the table for her card. "Ready?"

I grabbed my card. "You wanna show them at the same time, like a game?"

Tori rolled her eyes. "Give me your question. I guess I can go first." She gasped after flipping my card over. "Oh, my god..."

I took another drink. "What?"

"Our questions are the same."

"What?" Tori handed me her card. It read *why didn't you call me after the fight with the guy when you left the hospital?* She was right. My question to her was *why did you leave and never reach out?* Sadness weighted my shoulders. "At the risk of sounding like a bitch, I'll ask my true question. Why did you leave me?"

It was fucking sad how hard my heart began to drum in my chest.

At first, Tori struggled to look me in the face. "You want the professional reason after years of therapy?"

"Give me anything that makes sense."

I watched her swallow, eyes dancing below. "Because I was a young, dumb coward who wanted to avoid rejection. I actually thought you were done with what we had. I thought the bubble we'd created since that stupid stunt I pulled on you in the therapy room had finally burst. I always knew it would." Tori was referring to the first day she sucked my dick. That experience was the most bizarre, and unknowingly, my crash course into her enigma. "But when I called that day after hearing about the fight, and you said you didn't want to talk, I took it as the end to what we had."

She shook her head. "I was hurt, angry, embarrassed and..." Her eyes appeared on me again. "...and I ran. It was such a quick decision for me. I just wanted away from the embarrassment. Ashton, I was so young, so naïve. And it happened so fast, my stubbornness. Until one day, I came up for air and wondered why hadn't you reached out. Everyone else did—"

I lost Tori's eyes again; this time, she squeezed them closed as though she'd misspoken. That was odd.

"Who reached out to you?"

Shaking her head, she rubbed her lips together contemplatively. What was going on in that brain of hers? It drove me crazy back in those days when Tori didn't talk to me. I now understood how back then, she was unable to articulate her feelings. But adult Tori did that very well. She ran a formidable empire and was one of the savviest and wealthiest women in sports: lack of articulation was no longer a handicap.

"The school...Trisha." *Oh.* "She tried for a while to get me to come back. I mostly ignored her. My life was too complicated to go back to being a student."

"Even after your mother died?"

Tori nodded. "There was no way I could ever go back after... Aivery found out about us. I'd gone through too much at that school. It was the place where I found my heart and lost it just as fast. I was humiliated, Ashton. And again, I thought you were done with...whatever it was we had."

"Friendship," I murmured, chest twisting. I scoffed, "I would've thought after all these years, it wouldn't bother me as much that you downplay what we had—"

"What did we have, Ashton? *Fun?* Yes. *Sex?* Yeah. *Lies?* Yea—"

"We had something pure!" I hated raising my voice. Hated I had an emotion to. "I can't define it for you. Couldn't then and can't now, but I can tell you the same shit I felt then. You were my friend, Tori! You were something so rare, beautiful, and pure." I laughed, unable to believe I had to explain this to the person who was there with me growing these feelings. "You were like my best friend. I felt like you were the only person penetrating the grief I could have been lost to from Brick's death."

"You didn't seem like that. I didn't think you were grieving."

"That's the thing, Tori: I avoided so much of it because of you. You were my distraction until you left me."

She shook her head, face tightening. "You never called." Her voice cracked.

"Do you not know what I dealt with? I needed surgery for a couple of years. I was chasing a fleeting career in the *League* from hospital beds. I was trying to fight for my sanity while recovering from each procedure. I had the *Kings'* front office and the media calling like every damn day until finally, a specialist—top of his game —gave me the news that shook my entire fucking world. Being told I'd never get my dream career fucked me up so bad, I was numb for years. And don't think for one second the fact that you didn't call or fucking write didn't pick away at my fucking heart for a long while."

I took a moment to breathe through my anger. I knew what to do. I could handle physical and emotional pain if I focused myself. "I called your cell for months." My voice was croaky. "I'd wait late at night when no one was around. I figured if I could just hear your voice, I'd toughen the fuck up. I had no one I could be honest with about how I got in that situation. I never told my mother the fight with Benjamin was over you. I had no one to share that passion with: *of course*, I wanted to talk to you. When I got my hands on your phone record and saw there was no activity for months, I knew you'd tossed the cell. I resented you from that point on."

When I saw the first tear slip from her eye, I couldn't shut the hell up.

"Called myself stupid for not believing the very truths of your heart you shared with me freely. You kept saying we weren't friends. You didn't believe I saw you as a real human being. If I couldn't convince you when we were hanging out, I damn sure couldn't, laying up in hospital beds and therapy offices. I was fucking lost to my circumstances. And worst of all, I was left holding the bag alone." I scoffed. "So, you ask why didn't *I* call. My fuck up was blasted on just about every sports news outlet there was. You knew what *I* was going through. *You* should've called!"

Her lips parted and Tori shook her head steadily. "I didn't know. *I*—"

"How could you not?"

"Ashton!" she cried. "I was in no-man's-land in South Jersey, trying to make ends meet. Cable was a luxury. Sports was a foreign country for me. I worked multiple jobs, made sure my mother saw her doctors, took her meds...had food to eat. I didn't leave *Blakewood* the same girl I was going in. Ashton, I couldn't even stay in that trailer. I worked my ass off to get us out of there, like right away. My world was so disconnected from even my heart because if I wasted a moment to feel it, I'd break even more."

I turned away, unable to stay in that place with her. She didn't deserve my empathy. There was no getting around our abandonment. Even if we could go back to twelve years ago, our circumstances were unimaginable and too difficult to navigate.

"Don't turn away from me, Ashton. I don't know what I'm doing being here with you, but I do know it's where I want to be. Call me foolish for wanting to spend time with you again, but my world has been so crazy to the point of loneliness lately, and being with you distracts me from it. It makes me *feel* something I haven't felt in so long. This may not be like me, this 'creeping,' as you called it. But it's what I'm feeling now."

"What you're feeling? Who are you even? All I've been getting since our first sit down in the summer has been ice queen vibes."

"I'm Tori. Margherita pizza is my favorite food—even more than spaghetti now. I like swimming naked and drinking dry, bitter wines, rum, and am partial to champagne. When I don't want a full meal, I eat mussels and French bread." Her lips trembled. "My favorite places to vacation are cabins in wintery locations. I like tall guys with football builds—preferably quarterbacks, even though my fiancé isn't." Her face folded at that realization. "I like reading books promoting Black consciousness, and love financing movements bene-fitting Black people. I enjoy concerts. Basically, Ashton, I'm who you made me in those short few months." With tears in her eyes, she stretched her arms and shrugged. "The culture shock that was you became my culture."

My lungs seized and forehead stretched. That shit was heady. I hadn't seen this depth of vulnerability from Tori since she was a girl. And then she leaned over and kissed me. Face wet with tears and hands trembling with unspeakable fear. Tori grabbed me by the side of my beard and put her mouth on me. Her lips were timid, and even the slip of her tongue couldn't mask her anxiousness.

And powerlessly, I couldn't leave her hanging. I grabbed her at the waist, gripping her tight muscles. Our breathing was loud and heavy. At first, I couldn't close my eyes, still reeling from her admissions and my rawness from the conversation. What did this mean for me? I had no intention of continuing to see this woman. Tori McNabb was not on my list of complications in life anymore. My world was already filled with consequences I still faced from meeting this woman thirteen years ago. This could be catastrophic.

"You're engaged," I reminded her in between tongue lashings.

"I know."

"Aren't you afraid of ruining that?"

Finally, Tori's eyes opened and her mouth released mine. "My relationship with Deon is not what you think it is."

"You're engaged," I repeated.

Tori shook her head. "I'm not marrying him. It's a lot to explain, but that's the short of it. And I can't think of him right now when I'm feeling so much so strongly. I don't care about anything you and I did or didn't do twelve years ago as kids. It's nasty." Her voice cracked with tears. "...very nasty. But right now, I want you to make me feel like you would if we never made those bad choices back then."

She didn't get it. "Tori, we're making a series of bad decisions eerily similar to what we did back then, and look where they got us? I'm not a very emotional man. I don't have much experience with exclusive emotional relationships with women. I don't do anything resembling passion or commitment outside of fucking, and yet I'm here, feeling the same degree of rawness I felt for years as a result of our recklessness at *Blakewood*. This can't be good for me." I fought for a steely veneer.

There was no fucking way I was going into shit with Tori McNabb without guarding myself.

"I don't want to hurt. I don't want to hurt you." She shook her head when whispering, "I won't. Just tell me what to do to prove it."

The sound of a candle cracking was crisp against the soft music playing. Her hot body was a perfect balance of soft and firm leaning over me. My dick cried out in need, it throbbed so hard. I couldn't say no to her, even if it was the best call to make.

"My reckless hope is this shit won't blow up in our faces and leave us just as broken as we were from our first encounter—"

Tori leaped toward me, capturing my mouth, and gone was my stamina to fight. Annihilated was my will to play it safe. Her hands were at the sides of my shirt, gathering the material to pull it over my head. I pushed beneath her maxi dress, reaching for her ass swallowing a thong as we kissed like rabid fools. When I slipped a finger between her folds, Tori cried out with her lip caught between my teeth, I wouldn't let her pull away. I rubbed her clit until she danced on my fingers, moaning so deliciously.

My other hand traveled up to her back, looking for an opening. Tori helped me by pulling down a zipper under her right arm. Impatiently, she pulled out of the top of her dress. The moment her robust breasts were released, I left her mouth and kissed her chin and neck until I landed on her firm, globular breast. Thrilled by the size, I pulled it into my mouth and nibbled. Tori's body tensed over me as my hand strummed her clit and tongue beat her nipple.

I was growing harder by each thrust she made over me, the need to be inside her a painful one. My free hand reached into my pocket for a condom. I was able to manage my wallet while keeping my face busy on her bouncing breasts. The moment I found the rubber, Tori was flashing one in my face, being a responsible partner. I moved mine close to her face, so she could see it. Then she shifted down my body, my hand slipping from her soaked folds.

"I'm so ready," she breathed, hands to my waist.

I watched her facial expressions while ripping open the foil and removing the lubricated latex. Tori damn near snatched it from my hand. My boxers and pants were pushed down, and I watched her apply the condom over my heaving abs. She bit her lip, using laser focus as her bare tits shifted with each movement she made. When Tori was done, her heavy eyes rolled up to me. Expressionless with her bottom lip hanging on her tear-stained face, she mounted me. I watched as she positioned herself over my stiff cock. She lowered onto me enough just to swallow my tip and bounced. I couldn't see shit of where we met, thanks to the material of her long dress. But those full, swollen breasts that still were so perfect they looked cosmetically enhanced sprang with her movements.

"Ooooh..." She moved, eyes closed and head rolling over her neck from pleasure, the rubber creating a sound and sterile friction. "Mmmm..."

Her volume was of a lover's whisper and arch perfect as she teased both of us with this half-mast act of penetration. The sensation of her tight squeeze made my neck lazy and my eyes close. I took it until I could no longer and flipped her ass until she was gripping the back of the sofa and I entered her from behind.

"Uhmmmm..." She suppressed a guttural cry on my first thrust.

At this point, I'd lost all patience and widened my knees, driving into her. Holding her at the waist, I surged into her for depth, wanting her to feel my impression deep. Tori didn't have to tell me she was lonely for me to know. The most dangerous woman for a man to have is an underwhelmed one. Tori was hungry. As I peered at her through the oval-framed mirror hanging over the sofa, she hid none of her mundanity and even less of her passion.

"Asht*uhn*..." she cried, rolling her head to the side.

Her eyes were closed, features hanging lazily as she reached behind for the back of my head. Tori positioned herself to take everything I gave her. She was coming, and so quickly. The perfect arch and squeeze...tits. This hungry woman had no idea how beautiful she was. How tempting and forbidding.

"*I don't want to hurt. I don't want to hurt you.*" Her words echoed in my psyche as I pounded into her.

Lie to me...

I'd accept anything she promised, even if I didn't believe it.

"Fuck!" I choked out before biting her shoulder.

I came so damn hard and unexpected, my toes curled in my damn shoes.

A ringing phone stirred me in my sleep. Tori's nesty hair lifting from my extended arm fully awakened me.

"Hello?" she slurred.

Hearing masculine wispy sounds from the caller had me wiping my eyes clear.

"Why?" Tori asked unwelcomingly. More wispy sounds. "There's no need." I rolled over to leave the bed. We ended up back in one of the several guest bedrooms here, fucking more some time ago until we both tapped out. She shifted on the bed. "That's not necessary because I'm not home." I searched for my clothes under the glow of a single candle.

When I found my phone, I discovered the hour. I didn't intend to stay so late but wasn't tripping. I could still get home and be ready for my morning ritual.

"No. I'm not home," Tori was clearly informing her "fiancé." "That's no longer your business."

It took no time to locate my things and slip them on. Tori did a good job at gathering my shit after our second round in here.

"No, I don't," she continued to argue, her voice raspier than normal. "Are you drunk? No, I'm not being heartless, Deon," she whined.

"I don't want to hurt. I don't want to hurt you. I won't." is what she said earlier.

I'd slipped up, revisiting my worst pain with Tori. She didn't deserve my painful truth. This was clear from her exchange with him.

Lie to me. I'll take whatever you give.

Even if I don't believe you.

"Ashton, where are you going? It's late!" her tone alarmed.

Just as I made it to the door, I turned back for the bed. "You wanna know? Are we going beyond the one question tonight?"

When I didn't get a response, I understood her answer.

I left.

"You think I'm crazy." I nodded, having come to the conclusion.

"No, Tori, I don't think you're crazy." My therapist's head swung left to right slowly. "I think I would have qualified that diagnosis many moons ago if it were the case."

"Okay." I continued to nod, lips pushed out. "I guess foolish would be less extreme, yet still accurate."

She scoffed, standing from her armchair. I watched her smooth down her cognac, wide-leg slacks. Placing her tablet on the desk, she grabbed a marker and strolled over to a dry erase board. She wrote the words *sex, August, closure, anger, resentment,* and *truth.* I rolled my eyes and folded my arms against my chest at the last two.

"You're here on a last-minute requested visit. Something's wrong. I get it. That's not crazy, and foolish would have been for you to sit in this without making sense of it. I'm familiar with the history between you two. I just need to know everything you're thinking and then we can possibly upend your dilemma. Does that make sense?" I nodded. "Okay. So you were in touch again in August for the interview and by the end of September, you were intimate."

I recoiled in my seat, almost unable to look at her. "Yeah," I murmured.

"Mmmhmmm." She circled the word *August*. "And although the sex is incredible and you two should be in a superficial honeymoon stage with your rekindling, you sense tension from him."

"More than sense," I corrected. "He left me this morning crazy incensed!"

She circled the word *anger*. "And this was after a night of passion."

"Yes."

The word *sex* was circled next. "And he knows you're engaged."

"Who doesn't?" I told her all this already.

"Tell me about Ashton—*what you know*." Her inflection changed when she amended her request.

"He's fine. Like hella fine: walnut skin, full and manicured beard, tall and still built like a warrior. He still has all of his teeth and they're all healthy and a fair shade of white. Oh, my gawd," I cried dramatically. "and he's like the smartest man I know—still. He's a student of life. The guy absorbs so much." I nodded, lost in my thoughts. "I bet he still reads a lot. He has to, he's a writer on the side. Writers have to like reading like fighters enjoy being challenged physically. And the muscles in his pelvis area are so damn fluid. But I feel like he's holding back on me."

"Holding back?"

I nodded. "This is going to sound weird, but he's touched me like a stranger. No matter how much of a kid I was, I knew then and know now Ashton touched me with passion. There was more exploring back then. Now, he touches me to satisfy the moment."

"Have you asked him about that?" I shook my head. "Has he brought up boundaries during sex?"

"No. That's been me. Ashton wants to talk."

"About what?"

I shrugged. "Things that don't matter." I turned away and scratched my nose, murmuring, "Although he swears it does."

"Like what?"

"Our *BSU* days..." My eyes rolled. "What happened after. You know...the things we can't change."

She turned for the board again and circled *resentment.*

"But those things that have shaped you two into the adults you are. When you have the type of complicated history you and Ashton have, there's no healthy restart button without revisiting what previously ended your relationship."

"When you say relationship..." I flapped my hands in the air. "you mean like two kids exploring?"

She shrugged, chuckling dryly. "I can't define what you had without speaking to him for his take. Whatever it was and however you want to classify what you had twelve/thirteen years ago, the way it ended, and what succeeded its demise needs to be fleshed out. Sounds like you want all the glory of an affair you once knew him as capable of without the benefit of knowing who he is. How do you know he's comfortable carrying on an intimate relationship with an engaged woman?"

"We're not engaged."

"Unofficially." She circled the word truth. "Have you told Ashton this in plain terms? Have you asked him if he wants to be a part of your complication?"

That made my stomach flutter.

"So, you're saying I should've ended things?

I didn't want to stop this "thing" with Ashton.

"I've been known to prescribe no sex in the past." She placed the marker on the lip of the board and ambled back over to her chair. "Sex between two people with sensitive, complex factors such as yours and Ashton's is an extra layer of complication."

"If things between us are already complicated, why add more?"

"Why not just talk about what happened?" she pushed.

"Because I'm embarrassed by who I was at nineteen."

"Why?"

"Wait. Don't get me wrong; I'm proud of my humble upbringing.

But who he knew mixed with the decisions I made embarrasses me at thirty-one. I don't want to 'sit in that mess' because it's the opposite of who I am as a woman now."

"It sounds like the woman you are now has no qualms with mess. You're in it with him all over again. Why not make neat of it this time?"

"This is only temporary."

She shrugged. "Doesn't matter. Air out your truths and move on. You did it before, so you can do it again. Right?" There was a trick-component to that one-word question. "What's the worst that can happen to learn about who this man is and what has shaped him into the burger magnate and accomplished journalist he is?"

"Because..." A tendril of jealousy wrapped around my heart like a vine.

"Because what, Tori?"

My head snapped toward her, forcing us both to realize I was irrationally offended by her urging. But she once again had done it. This woman propelled me to the ugly ledge of undeniable truth.

Emotions shot to my eyes, blurring my vision and choking me at the neck, making it a challenge to breathe as I dropped my head.

"Because I don't want to find out my future was stolen from me."

"By who?"

"His girlfriend." My throat burned at her name, "Aivery."

Her forehead stretched. "He had a girlfriend?"

"I told you...years ago when I told you about him."

"I'm sorry for forgetting that detail. But you said he's not married. Why is she still a factor?"

"Because he was with her when I was so young and let him have anything he wanted from me. I never said no. Never said stop. I let him take and take, knowing he had a girlfriend. When she found out about us—from his former porn star lover—they got into it. The guy she was friends with fought Ashton with a bat. It ended his career in the *League*."

"Did they stay together after that?"

"I don't know what happened after that because I left."

She stood and sauntered over to sit next to me. With her hand on my thigh and tone soft, she counseled, "This is why you need to *talk* to Ashton, not just want to take passion from him. You need to close the last chapter, even if you agree to leave your ending there. You have to flesh out whatever it was you once shared."

My lips trembled when I whispered, "I don't want to learn about my first forfeiture of what belonged to me."

Truth hurt like hell...

CHAPTER TWELVE

Tori

While listening to Raj's latest radio hit, I giggled gleefully as the girls sang the last riff of the song.

"*Be my whoooooore!*" They attempted all the notes he hit passionately in just those three words that ended the song.

The riff was long and vehement, compellingly powerful. I was proud of the guy each time I heard the radio smash. Elle twerked against the countertop. Jade did some sexy-thrusting number in the air. And once done, they all began to laugh, too.

"Yooooo," Jenise, a friend of Elle's, shouted dramatically while hopping on one heeled foot. "Raj's catalog is turning nasty as fuck, and I'm loving that shit! Not that I didn't like him before—who in his peer group is as vocally superior as him?—but now? Hit after hit. Sensual innuendo after sensual innuendo—"

"Overt freaky line after overt freaky line like that one!" Elle interjected.

"Have you seen this video? Raj is even more cut up than before," Jade added. "His swag is different in those videos and his shows. Oh, my god, and that album cover. He's posing like he's looking down on a woman giving him a blow job!"

"Right!" Jenise cried. "Like what the hell happened when you got married, bro?"

Jenise's curious gaze found me, and Elle and Jade's followed. That made me laugh even harder. There was no way I'd confirm Wynter's sex game. He would never admit it to me because Raj's pride wouldn't allow him to. But from side conversations I'd had with Wynter when out shopping or just alone chatting, I could tell she liked the type of sex that was pretty bold for Raj. He'd had sex before her, of course, but it was in small doses and crazy irregular. The man trusted no one. But Wynter had him unrested, which was a great place for Ragee to be emotionally and mentally. There was nothing mundane or irregular about his inspiration anymore. That was reflected in his art.

"What do you know?" Jenise demanded. "Everybody knows you two are tight like Black on Black."

The doorbell rang.

My arm shot into the air. "I got it!"

They laughed at my obvious need for an escape.

"That should be Lex!" Elle called behind me over the music.

I jogged down the dark wood flooring of the corridor to the entrance of Elle and Jackson's home. Lex's big hair could be seen from the mostly glass door.

"I know I'm late," was the first thing Lex admitted.

I took the gift bag from her hand and she greeted me with a hug and kiss on the cheek.

"You're fine."

"Girl, that Mia Grace of mine!" she groaned.

"Is she okay?"

"She will be." Lex followed me into the kitchen. "My husband got his daughter his first time out. Our second daughter favors Ms. Remah. This third and last little one thinks I'm her only parent and guardian!"

"Is everything okay?" Elle asked with concern the moment we entered the kitchen.

"Her fever finally broke around noon. So, thank God that's over with," Lex answered, walking the room for hugs, starting with Elle.

"Fever?" Jade cried.

"Yeah." Lex hugged and kissed Jade's cheek. It was like watching a giant smother a midget. "She got an ear infection. I'm so sick of those things!" When she arrived at Jenise, she waved. "Hi. Nice to see you again."

Jenise smiled, bright pink lips over her beautifully brilliant white teeth with a dim smile. "Same here. Same here."

Lex could be so shady when she wanted to be. It was comical. When she liked you, she loved you and if she was unsure, she was a frigid one. It was something we'd talked about a time or two. We'd likely talk about tonight at some time in the future.

"All is well?" Lex asked Jenise while backing up to put her purse in a chair in the corner.

"Yeah," Jenise replied, fighting off Lex's blasé greeting. "Sorry to hear about your little one."

Lex waved off the worry. "Child, they'll be just fine. Mommy's off duty tonight. Where's my *drank*? What are you drinking, Jade?"

"This bangin' ass rum Tori brought," Jade licked her lip expressively. "It's my first night out since forever, and I plan on letting loose!"

I dipped low, keeping my drink in the air. Elle twirled and Jenise did the whop dance. We cheered Jade on. She'd been so strong since losing the baby.

"And what are you sippin' on, Tori?"

"Just wine for me tonight." I lifted my glass of Cabernet Sauvignon.

Rum and *Coke* with Ashton had me coughing up painful truths last night that had me waking up alone this morning.

Truth is overrated...

Lex turned to Elle. "And you, Mrs. Hunter?"

Elle twirled. "A little bit of this and a little bit of that. Jackson's flight has him getting home in approximately four hours. I'll be ready for him." She ground her hips in the air again, having us all laughing.

"I guess it'll be a shot start of the night for me. What ya got?" Lex asked.

"Try the rum," Jade suggested. "It's so good."

"Let's do it."

"You think Jackson's going to be ready to go at two in the morning?" Jenise asked. "He's thirty-one, not nineteen where that jackrabbit was at its prime."

Elle giggled. "Jenise, you're telling me more about your sexual experience than you think you're advising me about my husband."

"No." Jenise shook her head. "I don't mean it that way. I'm just saying don't be disappointed when he comes home tired."

"Please," Jade snorted. "Trent's thirty and with his schedule, I can only sleep with one eye open when he's coming home. Even if I'm up in Connecticut at our apartment for a night, it's understood my time there isn't to rest."

Lex high-five'd her. "I know that's right."

Jenise's face wrinkled. "Aren't you married to a minister?"

"A bishop, actually," Lex corrected just before downing the shot Jade prepared for her.

"There's no way—" Jenise corrected herself. "Let me not speak out of turn. I've only heard about your husband for years."

"Please don't." Lex giggled. "My husband's a beast in every pursuit of his." She dropped her chin. "Each. And. Every. One. Of. Them."

We all fell into laughter—everyone, except for Jenise, who appeared to be confused. It was weird hearing about Pastor Carmichael this way, but Lex made it very clear from the jump: if she was going to hang with us, we'd have to see her as she sees us; regular people. She wanted us to leave her title in the four walls of the church. I had no problem doing that with Lex. Her husband was a different story, though.

"I'm just saying," Jenise waved her hand in the air. "I've been married enough times to know none of us are fucking men with the same stamina as we did when we were nineteen years old."

"I'd agree with you to an extent." Lex motioned for Jade to pour her another shot. I observed her body in navy blue, high waisted culotte pants, a cropped ivory turtleneck sleeveless shirt, and *Asè Garbs* wedge espadrilles. "My one argument is none of the guys I was bangin' at that age and even after, laid it down like my husband. Not even close."

"I've had jackrabbits and they were all anticlimactic for me." Jade rolled her eyes.

"My point is we women need to readjust our expectations of men," Jenise tried to explain.

"I ain't gotta readjust shit." Elle's arms formed X's in the air.

"Whoa!" I yelped. "Language—"

Elle's blonde curls flew in the air as she shook her head. "When my husband gets home, he's laying *big, big* pipe!"

"Okay..." Jenise relented. "You have good sex with your husband—"

"Great fuckin' sex, ma'am!"

"Hey!" Lex clapped her hands. "If I'm committed to working on eliminating my favorite language, you gotta be, too!"

"Right!" Jade agreed.

I did, too. We were all working on our profanity for the betterment of our spiritual walk.

Elle rolled her eyes. "I been drankin'."

"But it's bigger than sexual chemistry," Jenise pushed. "We're all women here, and no longer girls. While our ages go up, our expectations of men—especially husbands—should go down."

"How so?" Lex asked.

My phone vibrated in my hand. When I saw his name on the screen, my pulse raced.

Nasty Human: *Where are you?*

Jenise's regard arrived to me. "Tori, I've heard about your issues with DJ."

Me: At a friend's place.

Suddenly, I wanted to be anywhere but here. I enjoyed hanging with the girls like this, but Jenise was an outlier. She came around once in a awhile and could be a hifalutin know-it-all. That was why Lex didn't greet her as warmly as she had the rest of us. I knew Elle had been on a mission for years to find female friends. It was a part of her treatment plan from her therapist, Pastor Carmichael. That was how she and Lex became friends. When Elle had gotten to know me, and saw we had people we knew in common, she began to soften to me as a friend...against my resistance. Elle was high-maintenance and with a vibe of elitism that had historically made me insecure like in my *BSU* days. No matter how real she was, she was a freaking cover model-looking diva, one who was aggressive and the best in the public relations game.

"How?" Elle demanded.

"Entertainment lawyers talk!" Jenise rolled her eyes. She was right. As an attorney, she likely did rub elbows with her peers. It happened in just about every industry. "And I have no idea why you're upset about him being accused of something that may not be true."

"Because it *may* be true," I countered. "I deserve better than those odds."

Nasty Human: *Send me your location.*

Cute...

But I couldn't focus on texting: I needed to see where Jenise was going with her spin on my life. So, I half-mindedly sent Ashton my location as my attention returned to the know-it-all, marriage-blowing attorney.

"He's an athlete." Jenise's head fell to the side. "My first husband

211

was an athlete. You know they're not with just one woman at a time. They're not built that way!" She shrugged with her chin. "And when they're finally ready to get married, it only means they're ready to love one woman, not just fuck one woman. They need what they need when they need it. These men travel the country for months and relieve themselves when needed. I think it's unfair to balk at this one accusation so soon. You're not even married. What if this happened when you were married? You can't just run every time an issue with a woman arises. Athletes—hell, men of power and wealth —aren't built for monogamy. Expectations need to be adjusted."

The room was silent for a while, and before I could address her diatribe, Lex asked, eyes low from just shooting back another shot, "And how many times you been married?"

Jenise's shoulders wiggled with confidence as she smiled. "Twice and engaged three times. I have experience with high profile men."

"That's not experience," I explained. "They were failures."

"Amen to that!" Jade raised her glass. "I've only been married once, but if I had two behind me before fifty, I'd been looking at me."

"Right," Lex agreed. "And not telling others how to do it."

Elle sputtered a laugh and Jade followed. Lex didn't. She opened a bottle of water with her face screwed. It was one of those 'I said what I said' gestures. She could be cutthroat when she wanted.

"I don't consider them as failures." Jenise shrugged, then swiped her shoulder-length hair behind her shoulder. "Marriages end for a myriad of reasons."

I nodded in agreement. "One could be choosing the wrong man. Ignoring red flags."

"Or assuming they can't fuck after twenty-one years old," Elle added.

Jenise shrugged again. "Okay. So along with presuming all the married women here will stay married to their current husbands forever, I'm to assume you're getting dicked down like you did in your late teens/early twenties, too?" Her eyes rolled as she took a big gulp of her drink.

"I wouldn't say that," Lex explained. "It's my prayer to be married to my husband till death do us part. Hell, I had no expectations of us lasting a year when I said 'I do' a few years ago. But one thing that has never—*ever*—been an issue is my husband's stamina. I would say in the bedroom, but our sex isn't limited to that one place." Slowly, she shook her head with pouted lips. "Now that you've brought it up, I don't think I could've handled that man in his twenties."

That made me laugh, and hard. I bent over toward the floor, cracking up.

"I'm serious, Tori," I could hear Lex's humorous cry. "Y'all don't understand because I don't share, but that man's a beast."

When I was able to straighten, I saw Jenise didn't find Lex as funny as we did.

"Well," I pushed one finger in the air. "I will say, the best sex I've ever had was when I was eighteen/nineteen years old."

"What!" Jade yelped. "Are you serious?"

I nodded.

"With who?" Elle asked, a sly smirk on her face.

"I'm so glad you asked because I didn't want to," Lex breathed out. "And I certainly wanna know."

I dropped a piece of cheese on a cracker, then topped it off with a green olive. "No one you know. A muted reckless mistake." Then I plopped the whole thing in my mouth.

"What made him the best?" Lex asked.

"Did he make you come?" Jade asked. "I don't think any man before Trent made me come on purpose." Jade's face tightened as she processed that information.

I nodded. "My first."

"Damn," Jenise murmured. "And still your best?"

"Yup." I emphasized the P. "Till this day!"

"Okay, Deontay Wilder!" Jade shouted.

"What made him the best was..." I let my thoughts run for a second. Ashton was a different lover than he was back then. He was still skilled, but his lack of trust for me surfaced when we had sex. "...his confidence and...ability to express passion. When we were young and fucked—" I apologized to Lex and Elle as the three of us struggled with profanity. I didn't believe Jade cared. "—he was so bold and expressive. He didn't care about how he looked or sounded. He wanted me to have fun and feel good. He was selfless and generous. And oh, my god, he was patient. That boy could go and go, waiting on me to come. My pleasure was mandatory. You know?" My eyes narrowed as I nodded my head, trying to find the words. The girls swooned. They were with me. Lex hi-fived me. "I ain't never have that before."

"So, Deon's never made you come?" Jenise asked before taking a gulp of her drink, her eyes on me.

"I didn't say that. If it wasn't for my first, I wouldn't know how to make myself come with a man."

"Damn!" Jade choked out.

Elle giggled.

I continued. "All I'm saying is my participation in joint pleasure was a must with me and the kid. And I haven't had a man to match that." I shook off the sentiment. Ashton and I were once again in an awkward place and in reckless waters, so to speak. It was messy and I was too comfortable in it. "Anyway. Let's switch gears here and talk about someone who matters and is dear to our hearts."

Lex and Elle's attention turned to Jade. Her expression fell, holding a shot glass to her face.

Elle trudged back into the kitchen, carrying a huge *Chanel* shopping bag.

"What's that?" Jade asked, alarmed. "It's not my birthday."

"It's not," Elle confirmed. "And neither is it Christmas, but we're playing Santa's helpers tonight."

We followed Elle to the kitchen table, where she placed the seemingly heavy bag.

Lex nudged Jade's arm with her own. "Somebody's missing their Jelly." She winked.

Jade sucked in a heap of air. "What's going on?"

"Open it," Elle demanded.

Elle assisted Jade with unbagging a box. As Jade took over with unwrapping the tissue paper around it, Elle spoke.

"Your sweet husband knows this has been a rough season for you. He hates that he hasn't been home to comfort you the way he wanted to after losing the baby. When I tell you Trent Bailey's every thought is his wife..." Elle rolled her gorgeous eyes dramatically. Jade's beautiful hazels watered while she covered her mouth. "It's all my client talks about. Anyway, he's been working on a gesture to make you smile, and I believe this is it."

Jade finished the last of the black tissue paper and revealed a black, quilted leather box. She managed to open it with a small golden key, finding four *Chanel* mini purses and gasped, "No, he didn't!"

"Yes, he did!" Lex and I shouted at the same time.

Trent was truly a good guy. One of the best husbands I'd ever seen. This act of romance was very touching to bear witness to.

"Four bags!"

"Yup." Elle nodded, smiled brightly. "Aren't they beautiful?"

"That man loves you, Jade," I shared.

As she gazed in awe at the box, she murmured, "Not as much as I love him." Then she turned to Elle. "You picked this out?"

Elle shook her head. "I was only a tour guide. Mr. Bailey did the selecting."

"And that's not it," Lex called out, stepping away from the small crowd we'd formed at the table. She grabbed the bag I took from her at the door on the other side of the kitchen. "He sends this to express his adoration of your body. He says he honors it and can't wait to demonstrate that again." Lex handed her the bag.

Jade covered her mouth in shock again. "He said that?"

"And more." Lex gave a cheap smile. "I can't remember it all, but there's a card from him in there. Open it up."

We watched her unravel more tissue paper from the *Asè Garb* shopping bag. Inside were several pieces of bras, panties, lingerie, and hosiery.

"These are gorg—" She held up the tag on one of them. "Tori McNabb line! Oh, my god! You finally got the line with *Asè Garb*?" she shouted before coming to hug me.

Jade's little frame jumped up and down, jerking my tree-ass while doing it. "I did!" I laughed.

She let me go, then ran back to the table. "These are gorgeous, Tori! Look at the lace on these boyshort panties! What color is this?"

"That's the russet bold hue. I thought you'd like that." I winked.

"Ohh!" Jenise picked up a magenta bra. "I want some."

"Bomb, right?" Lex agreed.

"This is nice." Jenise complimented while observing the table of gifts. "And I thought the rumor was Trent was cheap." My head whipped to her. "Or maybe he is, depending on how you look at it."

"What is that supposed to mean?" I asked.

"Trent is the most fiscally responsible client on our roster," Elle made clear. "In fact, he's one of the most responsible in the *League*. The *Kings* use his budgeting as a model for incoming players."

"I didn't mean it that way," Jenise argued. "I'm just saying, maybe because I don't know him, maybe this is splurging for him."

"And what's topping *Asè Garb* and *Chanel*?" Lex challenged.

Jenise's neck rolled while her lips pouted in the air. "I don't know. Maybe a *Birkin*—"

"I don't need a fucking *Birkin*," Jade enunciated with specification. "I need Trenton Bailey. *Chanel* and *Asè Garb* is all wonderful, but he is better. There's nothing cheap about his love for me."

"Easy!" I jumped in front of Jenise when Jade moved to charge at her.

"No," Jade shouted, attempting to point over my shoulder with a short reach. "I can take a lot of catty shit, but when it comes to my husband, I'll choke a lawyer bitch!"

"Okay. Let's take a break, shall we?" Elle suggested.

"You know what?" Jenise put her glass on the table. "I'm going to leave. My words are being twisted to be derisive, and that's not who I am."

"But what you are is not a good friend or a woman who manifests friendship," Elle qualified.

Jenise's face wrinkled. "What is that supposed to mean?"

Elle put her glass down and hung her head, rubbing her face. "Look. I'm trying here. I'm no therapist, but I know you. Know your type. I used to be you, which is why I've been inviting you over when I hang out with my friends."

"I'm no charity case, Elle."

"No, you're not. You're a good woman with so much to offer other women. I thought I didn't need women before my therapist got his hands on me and tore down the veneers of insecurity I thought were my dopeness or...my wisdom to protect myself. I was wrong. A huge piece of my evolution came when I made myself vulnerable enough to seek out friendships in women." She gestured to the room. "None of us are weak, needy women. Neither are we likely to get along. But thankfully, we understand our insecurities and need to commune with other women to help overcome them. None of us are perfect matches. Hell, the two things we all have in common is our committed Christian walk and calling each other out when we use profanity."

"Not me." Jade's mint green index fingernail shot in the air. "I don't hold myself to that expectation. Trent does and y'all do, but I only cuss when it's needed. I don't have a vulgar personality."

"Sounds like you judging to me." Lex rolled her eyes while

leaned over the island counter. "I am who God made me to be, and that's not to take no bullshi—"

"Hey!" Elle barked at her. She shook her head dramatically as Lex shrugged.

"This is cute, but I don't like being ganged up on," Jenise noted.

"While we're not above that energy," I added. "that's not what we're about to do tonight. You have to accept some responsibility, too, Jenise. Just chill."

"And keep my man's name out ya mouth!" Jade's arms went into the air and she shrugged.

When Jenise's displeased regard went to Elle, Elle's head fell to the side to emphasize Jade's request.

"Let's each have another drink and start all over again." I waved them back over to the drinks on the counter where Lex had been. "If Elle constantly invites you to hang out with her, I'm gonna show grace."

"Okay, but you guys need to know it's hard being the odd one out. You all seem to have a bond I feel I'm impeding on."

"We all have the same pastor. That's it," Jade explained. "And one is married to him."

"Yeah. That part, I get." Jenise tossed her forehead toward Lex. "I don't know how you did it. I can't imagine being married to a minister. You're too young and fly for that, from what I've seen of you. And I'm sure he won't approve of you drinking like—"

"See!" Jade said. "You're fucking up already."

I hung my face.

"You're making unfounded assumptions again, Jenise," Elle informed. "If you would observe and absorb, you'd know Bishop is far more fashionable than Lex."

My legs gave out as I howled in laughter. Jade's little frame fell onto me as she cracked the hell up, too. Carmichael was not only good-looking, but he was fly, too. Those were just features you'd forget about when face-to-face with him, because of his odd nature.

He always seemed to look through your exterior right into your core when interfacing with him. Weird, but necessary.

"Damn you," I managed to hear Lex grumble before throwing a small block of cheese at Elle.

This felt good. Being with these women was good for my heart, especially on a day like this when it was troubled.

"I'm just joking," Elle chortled. "But for real. I remember the first time I saw him. He wore this dope ass, dookie brown suit that was contoured for his body. Not only did he pull off the bland color, he made me go out looking for it. I wore it to StentRo's recognition dinner a couple of months later."

Even Jenise joined us in laughter. I managed to pour each of us a shot of rum.

"Okay!" I tried speaking over them. "Let's take another shot. This one's for Jenise's training wheels in this circle." I raised my glass. "May she not fall off the bike and in the mouths of sharks like Jade Bailey and Alexis Carmichael while riding over the dangerous sea of Elle Hunter and Tori McNabb!"

"Here, here!" Jade cheered.

Jenise rolled her eyes, unable to hide her grin. We all gulped down the spicy liquid, most of us in decent speed.

"Damn, I'm going home drunk," Lex howled as her massive body of kinky hair fell back in a cascade. "and I'm gonna get my ass beat!"

I laughed so hard, I felt a cramp in my side. We were loud and rowdy at this point, many of us barreled over the countertop. My phone chirping interrupted my laughing spree.

Nasty Human: *I'm outside. Let's go.*

I blinked hard, reading the message a few times. When my gaze lifted, Elle's attention was on me. Her smile faded. My pulse began to sprint. I bit my lip as my brain sped faster than I preferred when needing to make a call. Ashton was outside. That wasn't something I expected.

Elle motioned with her head to talk away from the girls. I grabbed my purse and headed out of the kitchen. Elle was on my heels and when we made it into the corridor, I turned to her.

"I gotta go."

"Where?"

My mouth opened to muted words. I didn't know. Rolling my eyes, I came clean. "Ashton just pulled up out of nowhere and wants me to go with him."

"Spencer, the writer?" I didn't answer her. "How does he know you're here?"

"I sent him my location accidentally, but intentionally." I let out a breath, feeling the shot encroach my good senses. "I'm gonna go."

"What about your car?"

"I'll text you about it."

When Elle didn't respond, I took off to the door. After she opened it for me, Ashton stood outside the backseat of the limo he'd sent for me last week. With modest speed, he turned to find me on the porch. His posture with his torso leaning on the open door was casual, yet his energy was impatient.

Half his face lifted at Elle's recognition. "Mrs. Hunter." He nodded. "Good to see you."

"Quite a surprise to see you, Mr. Spencer," Elle kept it pleasant. The adorable chuckle Ashton emitted as he turned away and rubbed his beard had my nipples sting. I started down the stairs. "She's been drinking."

Ashton shook his head softly. "She won't be driving...any vehicles."

That had me stumbling a bit on my way to him. I walked into a cloud of Ashton's compelling scent before being in arm's length distance to him.

"I don't think I realized I was sending my location."

"And yet, I'm here." He moved from the open door to invite me inside. "I have somewhere to be in about"—he checked his wrist for the time—"thirty minutes. Take a ride with me. I can have my driver bring you back here for your car or to your place."

I was confused.

"What is this? A parting...closure ride?"

It couldn't have been about sex because I'd decided after the session with my therapist I would stop with Ashton. Things were getting too dangerous.

With his empty gaze down the street, Ashton stated lowly, yet clearly, "If closure's what you want, don't get inside the car."

My lungs seized as I tried pulling in a breath. Slowly, Ashton's narrowed eyes rolled down to meet mine. There was a torrent of bold emotions in them, vulnerability and anger being the two leading ones. My eyes squeezed close in frustration. I was going with Ashton. No matter how cold he was toward me, I couldn't say no. Instead, I turned back toward the house where Elle stood on the porch. She leaned against a post at the top of the steps, one shoulder exposed in her russet, off the shoulder sweater. Her long nod said it all. Elle knew. She knew I'd crumble to weakness and follow Ashton on a whim.

Rolling my eyes at his unfairly self-possessed posture, I ducked beneath him, climbing inside the limo. Within seconds, Ashton was crawling inside behind me.

I flipped my hair, looking away from him. "I could have been with my fiancé."

Did I really just say that?

"I got out of the car respectfully to greet him."

My head whipped to him. "Did you come get me to give more attitude than you did this morning?"

His eyes were lazy as his head shook softly. "I came to fuck you before my flight. I'm leaving for Tampa for a couple of days." I couldn't speak to check his arrogance. As I sat inhaling his delicious cologne and absorbing his thick vibrations, I was shrinking. The lights in the car began to recess. Soft string notes grew in volume. I recognized the artist. Ameerah's strings could set the mood for any occasion. Already, my senses were manipulated. The wine and shots had caught up with me at a time I needed resistance against the most formidable opponent of my life.

"Come here, KaToria," he commanded throatily, pointing toward the area between his long spread legs.

Without hesitation, I obeyed, taking to my knees. When I made it to him, Ashton released my ponytail, fingering out my hair. The act was relieving and arousing at the same time. His other hand caressed the side of my face, his thumb trailing from my cheek to my lips. Weakened by his touch, I closed my eyes. I felt his hands trail down my neck, brushing against my nipples, then to my waist. He pulled this shirt from my jeans, then slowly over my head. My hands curled, sexual anxiety crippling me.

My belt was next, then jeans. Ashton's warm, soft lips were on me as he pulled my panties and jeans down. Nervous energy had my hands flying to his bearded face. I pulled him into me, tasting his lips and smooth tongue. When he managed my jeans and panties to my knees, Ashton scooted up the seat and grabbed me to him by the cheeks of my ass. His touch was possessive and impatient, taking me over the edge. Greedily, I moaned, clutching the hair on his head. I resented the space between us, needed to melt my skin against his. But I was undressed and Ashton was still fully clothed.

He lifted me from the floor and, instinctively, my thighs opened for him. It was as though I'd done this for him a million times. My naked back hit the cool leather seat, legs pushed over his shoulders. His kiss transported me to deceptive places. It made me feel secure and I was so lost to it that when Ashton pulled back, I tried going with him. When his tongue left my mouth in a long stroke, I exhaled from the bottom of my belly.

Ashton's spine straightened while on his knees and, unexpectedly, his dick thwacked my wet sex, landing perfectly centered against my throbbing clit. My head pushed into the seat and eyes rolled to the back of my head. He wasn't fully erect. I knew this, feeling him thicken against me as he dragged his cock up and down my slit. I moaned, neck going weak. I wanted him. Needed him...in my mouth, inside me—anywhere I could have him.

I watched with lazy eyes as he rolled on a condom. My pussy pulsed and nipples burned in tortured pleasure. He leaned over and sucked my right nipple hard, then ran his tongue around my areola. I squeezed my fists together painfully. The car rocked, going over potholes and bumps in the road, making my breasts bounce in the air. I was doing this. I was letting a man fuck me in a car, against the back of his driver. But this wasn't any man. It was Ashton Spencer, the man I could never tell no. The only man whose lead I followed hopelessly.

Ashton grabbed himself by the thick, hairy root, pushing his crown inside me. I could feel my walls quivering. He was so big, I could feel the ridge of his head just inches inside, stretching me. My body vibrated, breath stolen as I gasped from the broad intrusion. He stopped and pulled it out and back in. Holding my legs over my head, he teased me with just his swollen crown. It was effective, but torturing in more than one way. I hated the rubbery feeling between us. With Deon, I didn't mind, understanding the need for the barrier. With Ashton, barriers felt clinical. It set a parameter in an area of my life I wanted none with him.

In no time, I felt my groin churning. I was senseless, delusional in pleasure.

"Ashton!" I whispered hard.

"It's okay," he advised, voice authoritatively soothing and thick. "Come."

Before he released that one syllable, my hips began bucking, embracing what was coming. Ashton's measured hip rolls came faster, only giving me his head. A violent orgasm rolled over me, causing my shoulders to shift manically against the leather, going nowhere. He had my body curled into a ball as he drove me wild until my body stopped shaking.

He released my weakened legs to dangle over his shoulders and grabbed me at the waist. When he pushed into me, filling me to the hilt, I thought I'd lost my mind. I was still swollen from last night into this morning. Ashton was packing a sizeable tool; a recovery period was needed when having sex with him. Even understanding that, I craved the pain. And the thrusts went on and on until I lost count of how long we'd been at it. I welcomed the broken clock, enduring whatever Ashton gave. He didn't slow when he pulled my breasts together and reached down, licking my hard nipples. With each swipe, I felt wetter and wetter, his dick driving in and out of my swollenness. My second orgasm was unexpected and not as powerful as the first, but appreciated nonetheless.

"Fuck!" Ashton barked. And before I was done, he pulled out of me. "Too soon."

Ashton lugged me from the bench and arranged me with one knee on the floor and the other on the seat. I gasped when he rocked into me, not giving me the benefit of several thrusts to adjust to his size in this position. He didn't gain speed for a while but took his time. His hot palm grasped onto my shoulder, anchoring his pelting, the other hand gripping a fist full of my hair as he rocked into me. I was reminded of his masculine strength when he impaled into me, the fat of my ass smacking into his hairy thighs.

"*Be my whooooore!*" broke through the speakers, bursting a bubble in my ears.

I didn't hear Raj's song come on, which was likely best. I didn't want to have him in mind when having sex.

He chuckled above me. "That's what you want from me, McNabb?" Ashton taunted, voice strained, "You wanna be my whore and nothing more?"

That was cruel and he wanted me to feel it. Ashton was angry, it was clear to me now after my session with the therapist. He wanted to release the barrier of the knowledge of our past, something that could have broken me like the pounding he'd begun with my ass in the air. His impales were strong and rhythmic. My breasts slapped against the leather, stars flashed behind my closed lids. I was thriving on the precipice of pleasure and pain.

Then he pulled out again. My eyes burst open wide, seeing colored shadows in the dim lighting. Ashton tugged me around the middle of the floor. When I faced him, he was shirtless, pants down and sitting on his heels, pulling me toward his dick. In a flash, he rolled off the condom and stuffed the head of his cock in my mouth. I used my hands to break my fall before taking him all the way in. Ashton directed my oral strokes with the lock of hair he still held in his hand. Rubber. I tasted and hated it, but it wasn't enough of a deterrent from me enjoying the feel of each ridge of his pulsing dick against my tongue.

Ashton tried muffling throaty mewls as my head and mouth plunged down on him. I wanted to see him, peer up and witness his torture. Bobbing and bobbing and bobbing, I pulled with my jaws and licked with my tongue, focusing on not gagging. My pores began to sprout sweat, body hot all over for him. I was his whore. Willingly. Shamefully. Blissfully. Time jumped again and I couldn't tell how long I'd been at it. I didn't care. It was Ashton's show. He was giving me a thrill I hadn't had in so long.

After a long, delicious slurping sound from his mouth, Ashton grunted, "Shit!" and lifted me from his throbbing dick.

I sat on my knees in front of him with throbbing lips and wet eyes from straining. He reached into his jean pocket wrapped around his long legs, pulled out another condom, and pulled it on. I watched as his eyes strained while peering out of the dark windows to gauge our location. When he was done, he had me lean over the seat and entered me from that back again. No kissing the rubber-breath mouth, I figured, and it hurt. But when he grabbed my hip and slammed his thickness inside of me, I couldn't feel any pain except the ache from my swollen walls. My face dropped onto the leather seat, spine arched as he held me in place. So quickly, I was lost to him again. My wails fell into the seat beneath the music.

I felt everything, his pulsing inside me, the ends of his wiry thigh hairs poking the back of my legs, and his labored breaths hitting my curled back. His pounding reverberated in my spine and chest, seizing my lungs. His grips on my hips turned more vulnerable than he likely wanted to expose. His grunts turning deeper and deeper, Ashton was losing his composure, and I welcomed it. I pushed back, arching my spine deeper, and lifted my head. My walls tightened as I felt him thicken even more inside me.

As he impaled my misted frame, I yammered, "Don't stop! Don't stop!"

With heavy, lazy swinging lips, Ashton rocked into me with so much commitment, not even sensing how close I was to another orgasm. An unexpected groan shot from my core and I cried out. I felt the car shake as I rocked into his hard thrusts.

"Shit!" he croaked, coming right behind me.

His pelvis jerked and his squeeze on the fat of my hips loosened as he became undone. It happened so fast. As my sex throbbed around his pulsing dick, the car was coming to a slow drive. Lights from outside pierced through the tint of the windows, and I could hear hurried voices and beeping horns. We'd arrived at the airport.

Ashton pulled out of me with one smooth and quick motion, leaving me empty in more ways than one. He grabbed a jacket from the other seat across from us and managed to wrap it around most of my naked, trembling body. I had the shakes, body performing successive shuddering every few seconds. I was chilled all over, and my pussy bruised and unusually satisfied. My heart was wounded and spirit thwarted as I watched Ashton get dressed at casual speed. I could hear the trunk being opened and presumable luggage being pulled.

He was leaving. Leaving me like this. I was Tori McNabb, the undisputed champion of the world. I had millions in the bank and countless more in post-retirement endorsements. I'd met world leaders across the shores, and even had dinner with the first Black president and first lady of the United States. I'd influenced young girls and women by the thousands and even given millions of dollars to countless organizations who serviced them. Yet, I was here, curled in a fetal position in a limousine belonging to the man who acted as my raw weakness, shivering like a lost pet. I felt lost. Was lost. I had no decorum or dignity to even try and set my body to a graceful posture as he scooted toward the door and let himself out. Ashton had taken it all from me in these thirty minutes or so into the ride.

He didn't speak as he rose from the car with athletic grace. Ashton didn't look ruffled or compromised from the orgasm he'd had mere seconds ago. He was calculated and recovered, making it clear I wasn't in control as much as I assumed I was when taking this ride. Agreeing to the *Sports Illustrated* interview with him had its consequences, I was clear of that in this very moment.

A voice no more than a murmur spoke to him. And just like the corporate man he was, Ashton appeared unruffled when replying, "Very well," with a nod. He moved to close the door, ending my potential indecent exposure to the airport passersby but caught it just before the click.

He didn't lean in when he uttered, "I'm going away this weekend. *Saint Justin*. I'll return Monday evening. My accommodations are enough for you." His neck rotated for emphasis. "But *only* you. No assistants, no stylists, no cousins, no work. Only you." He stepped back. "If you're interested and can adhere to that, let me know by Thursday night."

The door slammed.

My eyes closed in shame.

CHAPTER THIRTEEN

Tori

"Where the hell are we?" Treesha inquired throatily as we turned onto a dirt lot.

My finger hovered over the blue *Follow Back* button on Ashton's page. I was ready to do it. I was finally prepared to learn more about his world. I wanted to know more about the man who had my head spinning at eighteen, nineteen, and now, thirty-one years old.

"The fuck! Jaquana's ass tryna set us up to die?" Treesha continued. "Don't pull in there. Stay by the road!"

"Would you stop, Treesha? Damn!" Renata scolded.

That had my head shooting up to see what the commotion was about. Treesha was right. It was an empty lot of dirt. I'd forgotten my real estate agent wanted to show me land. I'd been so preoccupied lately, I'd forgotten all of what I'd agreed to today during our last call.

I pressed the table to blacken my phone. It was time to figure out what was going on here. Besides, I wasn't as ready as I thought I was to learn about how glorious and storybook perfect Ashton's life had been after *BSU*.

As I ambled through uneven orangey dirt to get to her, Jaquana's million-dollar smile and impeccable poise were on display. "Now, I know what you're thinking."

"That you're a crazy human," I posed. "Yeah."

I could hear Treesha mumble something I knew wasn't polite behind me.

"You good, Tori?" Renata asked, out of breath so quickly from hiking through the rolling rocks and soil. "Those your new sneakers, ain't they?"

"Apparently, my real estate agent couldn't care less about my new kicks. Otherwise, she'd be showing me another house and not open air."

Jaquana laughed, ignoring my crankiness. "I may not be, though. We've been at this for so long, and have seen countless places fitting many or most of your criteria, but none satisfying your total desire. So, in the spirit of specification..." She extended her arms in a manner of presentation. "...we have this option. Build your own. We're in one of your desired counties of Northern Jersey. This is several acres of your six bedrooms, four to five bathrooms, family room, library, theater room, four car-garage," she accurately counted on her fingers, "balcony off the master en suite, the classic-English hybrid style chef-capable kitchen, state-of-the-art gym, outdoor pool, and Deon's detached football suite." Her palms smacked her thighs when she dropped her arms, shrugging.

I took a deep breath, caught off guard at the Deon mention. Few knew there would soon be no more of Deon in Tori's life. But as I gazed around the empty tract of land, I couldn't deny her point.

"Building a house?" Renata asked her. "That's a lot. How long will it take? Who's going to build?"

"So glad you asked." Jaquana flipped open a file folder and pulled out a document. "My office keeps a list of reputable builders, many of which we've worked with. I had my assistant update it a few days ago, arranging my preferences at the top of the list. Building is far more economical than buying as-is. It's less costly and customized for your preferences."

"How many acres you say, again?" I asked, knowing I didn't look over the specifications she emailed for today.

"Four acres...possibly a smidge beyond that behind the tree line back there on the south end of the property."

Renata showed me the color-coded list of builders as I asked, "And how much?"

"It was originally listed at one point three, but I just got word the seller's willing to do a price adjustment of two hundred thousand for a quick sell."

"One point one? I'm feeling it. It's enough space for all of us to build something on." Treesha nodded as she inspected the land. "None of us need a big ass house like Tori. We can even build some-thing on here for NeNe!"

"Come on, Treesha. This is Tori's call," Renata interjected. "It ain't about you, me or nobody else—"

I turned to my real estate agent. "I'll take it." Jaquana blinked hard and successively, her head swinging back. "What? You showing it to other clients?"

"*I*—uhhh.." She shook her head, opening her file folder again. "I only had two clients in mind for this property, you being the second I've shown. I don't think he was in the right mind space that day, something I was really hoping was the opposite for you. I see so many opportunities, especially because of your celebrity status. You like privacy, and can have that here."

"Well, too bad for him." I winked playfully, sans the smile. "You think I can have a moment alone to chat with my cousins here? Do you need anything from me right now?"

"No. Not at all." She stopped typing into her phone and reached into the pocket of her blazer for her keys. "Your word is all I need to put in the offer. We'll be in touch." When she took off, Jaquana waved to my cousins. "Bye, ladies. You've made my year with this." She playfully rolled her eyes, and I understood her reference of my indecision during this lengthy period.

I watched my realtor make it to her car before turning to Treesha and Renata. Exhaling, I began, "Look..."

"Tori, if you don't want to buy it, it ain't a big deal," Renata explained. "I'll call her in an hour and tell her there's a change in plans. It happens. This is for you: nobody else."

Shaking my head, I rolled and closed my eyes, suddenly feeling off. "It's not that. I'm going to do it. If the deal goes through, we'll set up a meeting between me and one of those builders—"

"Don't forget about your trip to Tokyo," Treesha oddly brought up."

I was frustrated, needed to get this off my chest. "I haven't. I know that's coming up. We can work around my schedule like we always do. Right now, I don't even know what I want in a house anymore. I just need to stop procrastinating on getting one. But I have to tell y'all something about my schedule, and frankly, I don't want any judgment or questions, second-guessing my decision."

"Oh, shit!" Treesha mumbled, eyes narrowed on me. "You're getting back with Deon."

"No!" I shot back through gritted teeth. "Would you let me talk?"

"Treesha!" Renata warned her.

"Okay! Then spill it!" Treesha groveled. "Damn."

"I'm going to *Saint Justin*." Renata's forehead wrinkled. "I'm leaving tomorrow, and I'm going alone. No security, no assistants, and no you two."

"Hold up!" Renata's head fell to the side, face tight. "Ain't no way in hell you going nowhere that far by yourself. You buggin'!"

I shook my head again. "I'm going with Ashton."

"Ashton—"

"What—" they commented at the same time.

My palm shot in the air. "No judgments. No questions. I'll be back on Monday and can call home at any time. No one's taking me against my will or forcing me. It's something I've gotta do."

Treesha was the first to respond. She walked off, heading toward the truck. "The fuck is going on here!" she shouted into the empty air.

When I peered over to Renata, for once there was no sign of an ally in her expression. I was on my own with this one.

With Ashton.

Ashton

Gazing out of the small window of the plane, I turned over my phone on my lap, pensive. The ground crew worked to anchor in a jet that had just arrived. One scribbled into his clipboard. Two controlled the traffic with colored corn devices. A catering truck just pulled up to a jet across the way to deliver food for the flight.

My phone vibrating broke my nervous browsing.

Maurie: *We're in the air now. I feel better. Thanks for the talk. Love you.*

I snorted before replying, appreciating the break in brooding.

Me: Good. I'm glad you're feeling better. Enjoy your flight. I'll check in later.

"Mr. Spencer," the flight attendant startled me even with her soft tone. "I'd like to get you comfortable for takeoff. Can I prepare *Mauve* for you, and perhaps the rum you ordered for your guest while we wait?"

What the fuck was I doing? This was ridiculous. Tori was engaged. Maybe she came to her senses and had changed her mind. Perhaps she never decided on coming in the first place. She hit me up yesterday as I advised, but she didn't exactly follow my instructions. Her text simply asked what time was takeoff. I told her one-fifteen and it was now almost one-thirty with no signs of Tori.

"We can go with the brandy, Mel. Don't worry about the rum."

"Very well." She took off for the back of the plane just as I heard my name being called from the front.

One of the captains had stepped on. "Mr. Spencer, your guests have arrived."

"Guests?" Anxious, I stood, placing my phone on the table.

Just as I'd made it to the door, Treesha was stomping up the stairs with a duffle bag and what looked to be a makeup case. The other captain on duty, Brown, was at a runway cart receiving what I could only assume was identification and passports for the trip. Tori was on her way up the stairs, wearing high heeled booties, jeans, and a cropped hoodie pulled over her head.

She smiled behind her sunglasses. "Raj's jet picks him up in his back yard."

I scoffed dryly. "Unfortunately, I don't have one of those, so the good ol' airport will have to do. Tell me? Do you make his flights on time, and follow his instructions on your entourage?"

Happy as hell to see her, I was disappointed about having her cousins tag along. There was no way I could get to know her with them flanking on either side of Tori.

I turned toward Treesha inside the jet for emphasis. To my surprise, she placed the luggage down and was heading back to the door. The nasty gaze she served while rounding me could kill a weak man. I had no idea what that was about but was satisfied with her leaving. Renata remained in the cart with the engine still alive.

Just as I was about to ask Tori about this weird ass set-up, she blurted, "I wanted you to break up with her."

My face tightened even more, confused by her timid yet determined energy. "Who?"

"Her." She swallowed deep, then raised her chin. "Aivery. I wanted you to break up with her and to be mine."

"When?"

"Christmas break. I'm sure I had nasty fantasies about it before then, but that night, outside, by the Jacuzzi. I was finally intoxicated enough by the champagne and the...sex to confess it. I wanted to break up Mr. and. Mrs. *BSU* to have him for myself."

My chest tightened, heart thundered. So taken aback by this overwhelming information, my gaze fell from her. Treesha had gotten into the cart, and she and Renata pulled off. "You never said—"

"I was about to, but she called. You'd just made love to me— gentle love. You held this tomboy tight, creating this sweet, innocent and protective place for intimacy, something I'd only had with one person before you: my grandmother—only without the sex part. She wasn't a perverted human." Tori shook her head. "You kissed me, made me feel the pleasure between us was reciprocated. You made me feel real and alive and small enough to be protected, but important enough to be treasured. *You* did that." Her lips trembled. "Even as a kid yourself, you made a girl who didn't think she was beautiful feel seen in a desirable way. You made the tomboy admire her own body...appreciative of her breasts that were always annoying attention-grabbers and a focal point of my training as a boxer. You feminized me, Ashton. You." She swiped an errant tear from one eye.

Stunned, I didn't know what to say. This lengthy, passionate confession was the last thing I thought Tori was capable of. My lips parted to speak, but the damn words wouldn't form.

"I can speak now, Ashton. I found my voice after *BSU*. Maybe if I had it back then, I would've left *with* the guy who helped me discover my heart. I couldn't string together words of love, desire, or vulnerability for myself back then. I'm sorry. I was muted and hopeless. Until you." She closed her eyes tightly, attempting to hide her face to fight the tears. Finally, she returned, taking a fortifying breath. "I can speak now, and I'm still afraid to learn what could have been. Who you taught after me. Who you made love to after me." She scoffed. "God, I didn't even know I'd been made love to by the first guy I gave my body to willingly. Ashton, I've sat with lots of women who were sexually abused as kids. I've heard horror stories of consensual sex for the first, second, third—*fifteenth*—time. Very few were able to enjoy it the way I did with you. And I think it's—" She shook her head, laughing bitterly at herself.

"You think it's what?" She wouldn't allow me her eyes again. "It's what, Tori!"

"I think it's because you may have possibly liked me a little like that, too. What if I was more than a charity case to the coolest guy on campus? More than a tomboy who let him fuck her and ruin her peace of mind?"

I was winded by my own words being thrown back at me. Fucking speechless, standing at the door of the jet.

An exaggerated clearing of the throat stole my attention. Mel was standing in the entryway, holding a glass in each hand. One was with gold liquid and the other, clear. "I think it's time to unwind for the adventure awaiting you two." Her smile was stellar. I moved to invite Tori inside. "It's a pleasure to meet you, Ms. McNabb. I'm a huge fan." Mel's tone was sincere, yet detached, as it should have been.

I'm sure she had been around countless celebrities in her line of work. She had the temperament to fangirl in a way to not alarm clients.

I grabbed my drink then tossed my head toward the other in Mel's hand. "That would be for you."

"Oh." Tori sniffled. She took a deep sip right away. "Girl, I'm gonna need two more of these to take on this man."

Mel laughed as Tori moved past her to take a seat. I tarried behind, still stunned by Tori's confession, a barrage of emotions budding inside in a delayed reaction.

I sat on the edge of the pool overlooking the roiling Caribbean Sea. The sun was attentive and generous, and the wind merciful. The sky had to be the perfect hue of blue with not a cloud in sight. Having just showered from a morning workout, I rolled my head over my shoulders, slipping into relaxation. My hair was a bird's nest of a mess, and I actually enjoyed it. While drying off from the shower, I noticed my shrinkage from going for a swim last night. The moles on my face were visible, making me feel more nude than losing the towel could have ever. I was okay with that. Shedding felt good no matter how painful it was.

"A mimosa, ma'am," was announced from above my head.

With a smile, I received the champagne flute from the butler. "Thanks."

"De nada." He bowed and retreated into the house.

I hummed, feeling a sense of comfort from my vulnerability, something I hadn't experienced in years. I was away, on my own. There was no security, no assistants, no managers guiding my way. It was just me, chasing what felt good.

As I took my first sip of the mimosa, a lengthy, hickory figure wade through the shoreline onto the sand. He palmed the water from his head and beard. Each step he took disturbed the muscular pattern in his abdomen, and every time he swiped water from his face, the globular muscles in his arms and chest would flex. I turned away, too affected by his presence. Ashton was too much temptation and danger for me at the same time.

There was a surface of peace above an active volcano in *Saint Justin*. Our stowed emotions and combustive history were going to explode, and soon. I could feel it and knew he had to as well. It was obvious with how quiet yet present we'd been here to each other in less than twenty-four hours. Ashton read between a book and magazine during our flight in. It was close to five when we landed, and quietly we unpacked, then dressed in swim gear before I went for a dip in the pool.

After a few laps, I found Ashton relaxing in the Jacuzzi, listening to mesmerizing jazz while enjoying a tumbler of *Mauve*. His peaceful muted energy kind of reminded me of the Ashton I discovered on Christmas break in upstate New York, where he read and enjoyed silence. The only difference was the element of resentment brewing between us. Still, Ashton was an intriguing individual to me. Fine as all holy hell, too.

Finding the prospect tempting, I quietly joined him, burrowing into his side under his extended arm. We sat in silence for close to an hour. I kissed him and he returned the passion. But we didn't take it further. There was no need, just muted desire being transferred between wounded people. We were disturbed by the butler calling us for dinner. We had it out on the patio with a moon-side Caribbean Sea view. This morning, Ashton leaving the bed awakened me. I waited for him to leave the bathroom before I washed up for a workout.

And now, watching his thick, rope arms swing with each advancement he made toward the house, I was flustered. I was no longer tender from sex with him, but also okay with just lusting. I didn't want to rush anything. My revelation was still raw and I needed time to recover from it.

Ashton sauntered over to the outdoor shower near the pool,

rinsing off the sand from the beach. I turned my head away at the first sight of the undulating muscles in his back and arms as he hand-washed his head and shoulders. I gulped down the mimosa to distract myself. *God...* I tried to recall the last time I'd been so attracted to a man and wondered if I appreciated Ashton's virility back at *Blake-wood*. The meticulous grooves in his lower back and calves were godly.

A sudden splash of water had me leaping on the ledge. Ashton had jumped in while I was caught up in a lust reverie. He stayed beneath the surface for a while. When he finally came up, he wiped his face and found my admiring gaze.

"How did your cousins react to your decision to come out here with me?"

Conversation. Okay...

I shrugged, peering out into the ocean. "Treesha was negative again. It's not usually her style, but we've been at war lately, so I've come to expect those vibes from her."

"At war?"

"She missed my fight." I shrugged off the memory of her disre-spect. "She does random acts of selfishness from time to time. It's all good." I lied. "Renata's usually supportive, but I don't think I have that here. I told them while at a showing with my realtor and I'm sure they weren't expecting that announcement when talking about prop-erty features." I giggled.

"Yeah," he exhaled, then turned to swim to the other side of the pool, capturing the concrete ledge. "Believe it or not, I'm sick of talking houses, properties, and features with my realtor, too."

"Is yours any good? I feel like I'm exhausting mine."

"Yeah. Mine is the best. It's really me, being aberrantly indeci-sive. This decision seems more...permanent to me."

"Permanent. You're filthy rich!" I laughed. "Nothing's permanent for people like you. How many properties do you own?"

He swiped his nose. "You know I've got my father's spot." I nodded. "I bought a place in Vail."

My eyes bulged. "Colorado?"

Aston nodded. Then he cracked an arrogant smile. "I forget you're new money." I rolled my eyes, taking another sip of my mimosa. I knew *this* Ashton all too well. "Got muscled into that. Haven't been there in a few years now. I had a home built for my mom on her parents' property down in South Carolina." Then he mumbled, "Got a ranch in Texas, too." Then only his eyes roved up to me.

Weird human...

I didn't focus on that. "That's a lot."

"How 'bout you? Please tell me you own properties."

Swallowing down my drink, I nodded. "Yeah. I do." As the butler handed Ashton a remote control, I motioned for another mimosa. "I bought a house for Renata, Treesha, and NeNe down in Millville a few years ago. That was my first purchase. It's small, not attractive for retail, but it's theirs. Most of my properties are investments. Ragee wouldn't have it any other way. I've got apartment buildings and single-family rentals all over the state. Thanks to him, I invested in commercial real estate, too. Bought about three business parks. I may own yours," I teased.

"Never that." Ashton grinned. "I own the land for headquarters."

"I wouldn't expect less from you." I winked.

Ashton tapped the remote and Latin music cranked from hidden speakers. He pressed a few more buttons before a familiar R&B tune flowed.

"So were the showings you did at least successful?"

I thought about that for a minute. "I don't think so." Then I laughed. "I really don't know what I want at this point." I gestured toward him. "Clearly, because I'm here in *Saint Justin* with the guy I think I fell in love with as a kid."

"What's changed in terms of your needs of a house?" It was clear Ashton didn't want to engage in humor. By his stoic expression, I knew he wanted answers.

I shrugged, annoyed by the prospect, and feeling silly for what I was about to share. "I want my own family. I want a baby—something I wanted since high school. I want to be a mommy. I want to grow and nurture my own. So when I thought about what I wanted in a home, so much of it included space for that."

"What's changed?" he asked, accepting a drink from the butler.

I watched distractedly; the butler quickly ambled my way with my mimosa. He took the empty champagne flute in exchange. Right away, I gulped down a bit of it. Ashton was across from me, body submerged in the water, sporting an expectant posture.

"He's changed. My fiancé isn't ready to share a life with just me. He likes to have his cake and to eat it, too."

"And what's the problem with that?"

"The mere fact that I'm the cake and edible at the same time. I deserve monogamy."

"Monogamy comes at a price." He took a casual sip of his drink.

"And what's that?"

"Soul-tying."

"*And,*" I emphasized. "what's that?"

"It's finding that person you can't live without. Connecting with that person who not only shares with you everything about themselves, but helps you learn you, too."

"You ever had that?"

He nodded. "I have."

See!

That hurt. Why did it hurt hearing Ashton had loved a woman like that? I shouldn't have been affected. This trip was proving to be as difficult as I feared.

"Does he know you're here?"

"Deon?" Ashton nodded while swallowing his drink, eyes piercing me against the sun. "I spoke with him earlier while I was working out. He's just happy I'm taking his calls at this point."

"What does he want?"

"In a home? Just his own space off the main house."

"No. How do his personal goals align with yours?"

"It doesn't matter now." I shook my head. "We won't be living together. No home. No wedding. No baby. No family." I couldn't hide my sulking if I tried at this point.

This mimosa is life!

I sipped again, tasting it a bit more this time.

"I'll give you a baby."

My head swung ahead to face him. I blinked hard. "What?" I laughed nervously.

Ashton gave a casual shrug. "Just being the generous giver I am."

Ashton

"Yes. Give her the phone. I'll talk to you later." I smiled. "Okay."

As I waited, my attention went outside the sliding glass door to McNabb. She'd left her seat on the ledge of the pool and toed around to where I'd left to pick up the remote. I watched her try to figure out the buttons with rapt interest and chuckled.

"Okay! Hang on. I'm coming, baby!" my mother shouted to the room on the way to the phone. "Hey, Caribbean mon. You picked up any fun yet?"

I snorted a laugh. "My fun'll always be where you are, Ms. Wanda. Everything good?"

"Yup. We're good," she sighed. "About to go over to Levi's farm. They're roasting a pig over there today."

My face wrinkled. "Sounds like gross fun. Send me pictures."

241

"Will do. Go off and dance in the sun, son," she tried to sing just as I got a glance of Tori doing a two-step with her arms in the air.

Those mimosas definitely had her going.

Or your impulsive proposal...

I snorted soberly. "Will do, baby girl. Have fun."

"You have fun for once!"

I'm having something...

"Hit you later."

The call disconnected and I leaned against the peninsula in the kitchen, watching my fun.

Painful fun...

"Señor." I turned to the sound of the butler's voice. "The fish man should be coming up soon."

I nodded. "Cool. Gracias."

"De nada."

My gaze rolled back to the best show in town, and I found Tori in full-on Brielle performance. That prompted me to join her again. I stepped outside and sidled up behind her.

"This is reminding me of your unexpected twerking skills at the homecoming bonfire," I shared loud enough to get her attention over the volume of her bestie's radio hit.

Tori laughed, still dancing while peering at me standing behind her with my hands in the pockets of my trunks. "Unexpected? You didn't know me."

"I damn sure didn't expect that skill from a tomboy."

Tori began a twerking number, going down on her haunches until her ass damn near met the heels on her raised feet. Then she sashayed up and bent over, giving me a lude view of her ass and pussy in her slim-cut bathing suit. Why my mind was blown again, I didn't know.

Tori caught me dazed by the smooth, rhythmic bouncing of her ass and laughed. She fell out of sequence and turned to face me. My body stiff...hungry.

"Ashton, chill. I'm a tomboy from a trailer park. We couldn't afford concerts and consistent cable, but we could imitate pop culture. I've been twerking since like seven years old. Making babies, working in the casinos, and twerking were goals." Her breathy laughter warmed me as I peered down on her. "And did you not watch this video? Brielle had me in it. It was a blast." Then her face sobered. "I forgot. You blocked me out."

I closed my eyes, not wanting to go there. "I ain't block—"

Tori leaped around, bending over to her knees and giving me another lewd show of her bouncy ass.

Fucking perfection...

I wanted to touch her, but for now preferred the show. Tori's ass could really dance.

As I watched, I heard my name being called behind me. The fisherman was approaching the pool landing. Colorful fish wiggling off his shoulder from a recent catch.

"As much as I could view this show all day, our lunch has arrived."

Slowly, she stood, still twerking that ass directly into my groin. She turned my way then vined up my taut body, still able to twerk. Tori wrapped her arms around my neck and leaned into my face to whisper in my ear, "Take me to the fish man, *The Banger* wanna-be-baby-daddy."

Cheapened by that jab, I reached down and bit her right boob as I turned us to meet the fish man. Her shrieking cry thrilled me. With her arms and legs clenched around me, Tori's head tossed back and she tittered.

"Oh, my god. I love it here!" she trilled into the air while sprinkling breathy giggles. "Let's move to *Saint Justin!*"

She moaned into my mouth, squirming beneath me. The scent of our freshly washed skin, her scorched, blow-dried hair, and crying pussy had my dick aching. The woman obviously enjoyed fucking me, but I needed to get her to appreciate more than this one aspect of my capabilities. There were only two things I could offer her in *Blakewood*: an abundance of luxury gifts and exploratory sex.

As she grabbed the back of my head and hiked up my thigh in an attempt to draw nearer to my cock, I realized those two tricks wouldn't work for a thirty-one-year-old KaToria. Yeah. I could sling a mean dick for her enjoyment, but that was it if she didn't open to me. Tori could buy her own *Loubs* and *Asè Garbs* now. As a millionaire several times over, she had her own. I needed a way to compel her to get to know me as a man.

Her arm shifting across the bed beneath me caught my attention. I opened my eyes in enough time to see it retract with a square, silver foil. I pushed her arm back out, rejecting the notion.

"Ashton," she cried in a whisper, her left hand gripping my ass cheek.

"You still fuckin' Johnson?"

Panting desperately, she shook her head. "Not since the night I left your apartment."

She left my place aroused?

Do tell on yourself, KaToria...

"Do you plan on going raw with him again?"

"*We*—" She licked her lips, puffing with a strained face as she brushed her pussy against my standing cock. "We've... I've never not used a condom."

"Come on, KaToria," I growled deeply, scraping teeth on her chin. "*We* hardly ever used condoms back in the day."

"That's...why I don't..." Her face wrinkled and she cried, "Ashton, please. Come on. That's why I don't go without them anymore. We made lots of sloppy mistakes back then," she whined. "Deon hates that I won't let up since I'm on birth control, but it didn't feel right unless we were married."

I roved my ass back until my dick could gauge her opening. "We don't need them. I haven't fucked without them in years." Then I sank down inside of her, circling my head in her opening.

Tori gasped under me. She squirmed again, trying to take in more of me. "Ashton!" she begged for me.

"I'm your boyfriend." I dipped farther inside her and pulled out until just my head was left inside her soaked, palpitating pussy. "Tell me what you want."

"I'm engaged," she panted, reminding me of our unfavorable reality.

"Yup." I smiled against her open lips, her tongue in search of mine. "And now *you* get to have your cake and eat it, too." I sank into her warm deepness again, filling Tori to the hilt.

A pungent, skunky scent wrestled me out of my sleep. I twisted, then turned over to my left. The coolness of the sheets and thick distinct odor had my tight eyes opening and peering down the bed. It was Ashton, at a small table obstructing the doorway of the balcony. His gaze to the moon illuminating into the suite was terribly lonely. The drift of smoke emitting from his nostrils and rolled cigarette in his hands had me sit up, grabbing the sheets to my bare breasts.

"Ashton?" I called out coarsely.

He didn't answer for a long while, almost as if he didn't hear me. But he had to. We were the only two in the room, how could he not?

"Every time I fall and admit to you I'm willing to change who I am just to be connected to you, you don't catch me. I did it at *Blake-wood* as a kid and here I am, doing it again as a grown ass man."

"*Whe*—What?" Just when I thought he'd explain smoking a blunt, he went left and brought up *BSU*.

He finally turned my way slowly, reminding me of the boiling volcano beneath our surfaced peace. "I told you I lived in Texas."

"I don't know what that means."

"Yeah. And you never asked. You never care to ask. I've dropped a few subtle hints of who I am as a man and what my life has been." He took a deep pull of the blunt, held it in his lungs for seconds long before releasing curly patterns against the moonlight from his nostrils. "I fuck. I have emotionally distant relationships. They have their places behind a barrier, and it works for me because of my life-style. And I'm good with that...I'm good at it. I'm really good at not lending myself to women. I'm good at what I do at my jobs profes-sionally. I've won awards in journalism and I'm not even a journalist. *B-Way Burger* has had more growth since my taking over than it had in all the years my father has been dead. I know I'm good at what I do —was even good at what I did in football. I'm excellent at playing the game of life. What I'm not good at is playing the game of KaToria McNabb."

With a deep, rapid pulse, I asked, "What is that game?"

"Erasing the past twelve years between us. I can't. I was a boy then and I feel like I'm still being taxed *as the boy*—"

"It's not that." I shook my hung head. "I'm just afraid—"

"Afraid of what?" He scoffed. "The reality is here. We have another situation, only it's now reversed. We have this combustive passion, but one of us isn't available. You're engaged; just like back then, I had a girlfriend. While neglecting those passionless relation-ships, we're avoiding what we can be to each other. You're not with Johnson like that—"

"I'm really not!" I rushed to be honest with him. "I've never lied to you about him. I've always been honest with you—mind-bogglingly honest."

"And I do believe that. Just like I never lied to you about Aivery. Not one time. But *still*, I feel like I'm being penalized for my behavior as a twenty-one year old kid."

"I told you, Ashton. It's not that. It's my fear. I'm afraid—"

"Afraid of what?" he spat with disdain.

My lips trembled when I answered, "Afraid of learning what happened. What I possibly fucked up."

"Fucked up," he snorted, paying a cursory glance to the open air before returning. "You wanna know about fucked up?" He chuckled lowly. "I'm sitting here smoking a blunt. You know I can do it legally back home? I do have a prescription. *Although* I don't use it...haven't needed it in a while to mellow me out, I've done other things to help balance myself. You mentioned the black hole when I visited your apartment." He took another drag from the musky blunt and let it out. "I've swam shallow laps in it, drowning...fighting for my damn sanity. So, it appears to me I'm far more versed with it than it seems you are."

"Ashton..." I was cracking inside, heated all over and trembling.

"You know I've not spoken to NormaJean since I cussed her ass out for telling Aivery about you?"

A shower of tears fell from my eyes, forcing them close. Fighting back mewls, I nodded. "I know."

"How do you know?"

This time, I caused the delay, trying to find the courage to be honest with him. "I talked to her a lot after *Blakewood*," I whimpered.

"*What?*" His deep vocals reverberated around the dark room. Big body pushed back from the table, causing a deep screeching sound, too.

I couldn't control my sobs. Didn't even know where they came from.

The volcanic eruption...

I buried my face in my folded knees over the bed. "Ashton, you didn't even come to her funeral."

"No, I didn't! She betrayed me. She's the reason I lost you—"

"Yeah, but I was able to forgive her and move past that."

"How the fuck could you after what she did to you?" he demanded. "To us—"

"She reached out to me!" I seethed, shouting over him. "I was not forgotten to her. She remembered me no matter how much of a mess I was. No matter how insignificant I was. No matter how much of a nobody I was. No matter how much of a tomboy I was. She remembered me! She had someone find and follow me, and she kept reaching out. Even though I was cold to her...mean to her. She kept reaching for me!" I slapped my chest.

His voice was raspy low and body inclined toward the bed when he asked, "What are you saying?"

"NormaJean was the one who helped me start my organization. She gave me the money for *Bobby's Hope*. She funded my life's commitment to change the world."

"Do you not realize what she represents? What she did *to me*? To us?" Ashton's voice warped into one of a petulant child no matter how thick and commanding. It made me think of the guy who resented his deceased father for being gay. His stamina on this wouldn't change, just like it appeared it hadn't on Robert.

"I do—"

"You don't!"

"Ashton, I was there when the shit hit the fan!" He needed to remember. Gritting my teeth, I needed him to know, "I still have wounds from knowing you less than two *semest*—"

"*I FUCKING MARRIED AIVERY!*" he roared, spitting fire across the room. I tried breathing, but my lungs disappeared. This was it. My worst fear materialized. She'd won. She'd gotten her happily ever after with her guy. Aivery proved who I was among their aristocratic unit. My existence in Ashton's life disappeared into an abyss of nothingness once the bubble of the parody of a real relationship with her boyfriend had burst. She showed me I was nothing but a whore. "Did you hear what I said? I married Aivery! She was there —every day."

Ashton leaped from the chair, the blunt being a forgotten ally. "Every day after I had a busted shoulder and banged-up knees. She was there every day and I didn't want her to be. I think I hated her. Fucking hated her every day! But she was there...every day. And you know who wasn't?" he shouted without breaking for air. "You! And you know why? Fuckin' NormaJean! That is *not* a friendship. Was *never* a friendship. Not someone I'll ever speak to and I've got no fuckin' regrets. I did *not* go to her funeral. And she did call after the fight with Pettiford. She kept calling me, too. She even tried to tell me she could help find you, but I didn't give a shit because I hated her fucking guts. Because I lost you!

"I went there to Aivery's dorm to defend *you*, and I ended up losing my career. My life! And then I had to settle. I had to settle, Tori! I had to settle because she was there every day you were *not*! You were *not there*. So you know what ended up happening?" His head angled as he took another step away from the chair. "I had to be a prop in Aivery's ongoing fantasy of being with me. Less than two years after *BSU*, I finally moved down to Texas. We got married. Had a wedding I didn't want to have. Five hundred sixty-two fucking people I was ashamed to be before giving vows. And where were you? You never called! For years, I stayed in Texas, near a damn peanut farm. I just got back from that hellhole three years ago.

"And you know what? All those years...every last one of those eight fucking years and three months, I swam in that damn black hole. I walked around like a zombie inside because I was lost. Lost because the trajectory of my future—career in the *League*—had been derailed. Derailed because I went to defend the one person I actually loved especially—peculiarly. Someone who made me want to be a better human being. She made me feel like I was worth more than being the prince of fuckin' Zamunda. It took me all those years to leave Texas and resume a life that had no traces of Aivery. You never called. You never reached out. *You left me!*"

Trembling and misted all over from the colorful trip through hell he'd just walked me through, I dropped the sheet clutched to my pounding chest, scrambled on my knees to the foot of the bed, and ran to him. I jumped onto Ashton, climbing his tall frame until my arms were wrapped around his shoulders. That's where I held him unbelievably tight, allowing him to cry dry tears into my naked bosom.

CHAPTER FOURTEEN

Ashton

Peering at the ocean view beneath us, I thought of the temperature contrast between the roaring sea and the silky hot water we sat in. *Saint Justin* was a peaceful marvel.

"Tori." I flexed my arm hanging around her neck.

"Hmmmm..." she hummed, either asleep beneath me or super relaxed.

We'd gotten very little sleep last night. She let me make love to her at the crack of dawn, a necessary act to assuage my ego from my bitchy rage last night. While I shot inside of her with a wobbling spine, she showered me with soft words of apology in between kisses. The next thing I remembered was being awakened by the sounds and scent of sizzling bacon. When I ambled out into the kitchen with a sheet wrapped around my waist, Tori was flipping buttermilk pancakes in my wife beater.

We ate in silence, but this morning and at lunch, her small hand pushed across the table to caress mine. She would smile soft and mutedly, even sprinkled warm kisses on my fists. We snorkeled this morning and went for a jog on the beach shortly after lunch. Tori wasn't competitive or pensive. She was present and gentle. Maybe this was Tori, the grown woman.

"It's time to prepare for our flight."

She turned her glorious nude body into me, her globular tits brushing silkily against my chest. "Can we stay another day or five?" she cried with closed eyes.

I kissed the side of her face. "I've got work and you've got Tokyo."

Her arms wrapped around my torso. "And I've got a boyfriend. I need to enjoy him, here on this island."

"So, I'm still your boyfriend?"

"For a long time, I hope." I gasped and her eyes opened, focusing on me. "Can I ask you a question?"

"Sure."

"I guess before I consented to sex with you last week, I didn't ask all the right questions."

"What do you mean?"

"I asked if you had a girlfriend, fiancée, or wife, but never asked were you married. Are you and Aivery still in touch?" My entire body steeled. Tori sat up, sloshing water. "Ashton, what's wrong?" I tried finding the words as though they were bouncing over the rolling billows below. "I hope I proved last night you can talk to me. I'm still here. I still want you."

I finally peered into her eyes, and immediately, I saw it. Tori wasn't ready for all of my truth. She'd run. Yeah, hearing about my depression and failed marriage was one thing. Learning all the working parts of my life was another.

Shaking my head, I admitted, "I don't think I could trust that. I tried sharing what I couldn't keep bottled in. Telling you everything..."

"Ashton, look at me." She placed her hands on my chest. "I know we have mess; I helped create it. I listened last night and heard you. Keep in mind, I never told you about my journey without you—at least not all of it. But as long as it's over between you two, we're good." My gaze dropped to her cranberry-hued nails on my chest. "Ashton!" she cried in a panic. "Your heart is galloping. I swear: you can tell me any—"

"Aivery died." The muscles in her face dropped at the second word. "Five years ago. She passed away."

Her mouth opened, eyes bounced across my chest. "How?"

"Car accident. She was hit by a sixteen-wheeler on the highway."

I could see Tori's eyes roll beneath their lids after she closed them. "*I'm*—I wasn't expecting to hear that."

She couldn't say sorry, because it wasn't a natural emotion when talking about Aivery's misfortune, even in death. It stung a bit, but I understood.

"You're allowed not to express your condolences."

With her eyes still squeezed closed, she whispered, "I *didn't*—I don't mean to be insensitive. She was your wife."

"And your nemesis." I got it. "Your bully." When Tori still didn't speak, I felt the need to comfort her anyway. "ShawnNicole flew into the funeral. She brought Andrea's condolences. Andrea and Aivery never recovered from their little beef on *Macen Beach* during spring break that year. I think you defending her made Andrea realize she needed to drop Aivery. I guess it was easy to, considering that was our last year in college."

Looking away, Tori murmured, "Five years ago." Her mouth balled and twisted. "Drea's my wardrobe stylist now. ShawnNicole's my contracted hair stylist. One of the terms of their contracts was they couldn't discuss *BSU*. Not you or Aivery." *Damn.* Her heavy gaze returned to me. "I guess they've been the consummate professionals."

Silence stretched between us for some time.

"What does that change?" I asked.

Tori met my gaze. "Between us?" She shook her head. "Nothing.

Listen, I'm sorry you're a...widower, and you were one before thirty. I can't imagine what that feels like. You're so young."

"I was young when I married, too." I snorted. "The therapist I was seeing in Texas told me my life was novel-worthy and I should consider getting someone to write it." Tori laughed dryly with hiked brows, nodding her head in agreement. I sighed, stretching my arms out. "Nah. No one would believe it. They'd say it's hyper-dramatized."

"True," she giggled into my shoulder. Then, after a minute or so, Tori shook her head, whispering, "NormaJean and Aivery are gone."

I nodded. "The two women standing between us twelve-thirteen years ago."

"As much as it hurt and I felt like life had turned dark on me, I would have never wished that on either of them. NormaJean's death was hard on me. She had two services: one for her Hollywood people and another for just her family and personal friends. It was set up in her will to be that way. I went to both."

"Damn. How much did you two talk?"

Tori's mouth twisted and she nodded. "A bit. I couldn't get rid of her for years. After a while, I started to see how you made her a friend. She was charismatic and crazy sharp about her brand. She taught me a lot, once I let her." She shrugged. "And I did because it helped me remember the good in you. She was good to me, and I figured that *good* was what you saw in her and why you were able to stay friends with her for so long. It was like she knew the cancer was killing her and she'd die, but while fighting death, she fought my stubbornness and groomed me for wealth. She had me set up relationships with my first lawyer and accountant. She was regretful, and worked to make me forget the pain."

I couldn't believe this was the Tori McNabb I knew talking. No matter how frustratingly incommunicative she was, it was something I expected of her. This woman next to me who strung together words, articulating herself was someone I had to get used to.

"Ashton."

"Yeah?"

"I hate to sound corny, but as we can see, life is short. We have a history, no matter how short-lived it was. Let's embrace what we can of it."

"Okay."

"Great." She perked up. "Now, let's go see Jimmy."

My eyes went wild. "Jimmy? Why? When?"

"Yes, Jimmy. Because he was one of a few in my youth who didn't look past me. He recognized me when you brought me home on Christmas break. Maybe it was because he was trying to reach you, but it doesn't matter. I liked Jimmy, and now that you're my boyfriend, I wanna share the news with him." She stuck out her tongue and gyrated in the water, disarming me.

"Boyfriend," I noted. "You keep using that term." Not that I minded. It made my dick twitch.

Tori winked. "I'm using punctuations you ain't think I could."

I laughed my ass off. "I see!"

"Now, come on. Since we *have* to leave, let's go. I wanna experience the mile high club with my boyfriend." Tori stepped out of the Jacuzzi, her ass jiggling with each step. When I moved to join her, she turned around. "On second thought, maybe I'm too sore for sex right now. We had sex twice yesterday, and you're a big boy, Ashton. You bruise me."

Not you, too. I sulked internally. Then I stepped out of the hot tub. "You're a fighter. Aren't you trained to sustain pain?"

"You two make yourselves comfortable." The woman stood at the door after walking Tori and me to his suite. "I'll go get Mr. Porter."

"Thanks," I expressed before she shut the door.

While I took one of the available seats, Tori paced the foyer of the suite. Oval space and earthy tones with brass rich wood fixtures: It was a showing of elegance and wealth. In the center was a round table with a fresh bouquet of an erotic arrangement. Abstract art filled with robust colors in plush frames lined the walls. I was sure some of them were of Jimmy's work. Art was a feature in the facility's list of activities. Jimmy had been living the life of royalty.

On my dime...

Tori's phone ringing cut her curious stroll and gaping. She pulled it from the pocket of her blazer and rolled her eyes before tapping to answer the call.

"Hey..." Her voice was customer service-effort polite.

"Hi, honey. I was beginning to worry about you." The speaker volume had me lifting my gaze in attention. "I've been calling all weekend."

"I'm sorry. I've been away. I had my calls rerouted. Why didn't you reach out to Renata? She would have told you and taken care of whatever you needed."

"Because," he scoffed, also attempting the façade of warmth. "I want to hear from my daughter when I reach out to her, honey."

Tori's brows shot up at the bite in his tone. I may have been equally shocked. The Tori McNabb I knew didn't have a father. At least, not one to speak of. Not one checking for her. When I began my research of her after *Kamigu*, I noticed her father had been photographed with her after fights and in some *TMZ* shots. I believed his name was Timothy. Sharing Tori with a man would be hard for me. Deon was one thing, her father was a completely different phenomenon.

"I understand that." Tori rolled her neck, her back to me. "But I'm here now. What's going on?"

"I don't like your tone, honey. Is this not a good time?"

Tori turned to me. "Actually, it isn't. I just got back into town and I'm visiting a friend of mine. But I'm waiting, so I have a couple of minutes."

He sighed. "Well, I was hoping to talk to you about Tokyo."

"What about it?"

"Your brother can use some time away. He and Shelly are going through a rough time, and Patty and I thought Tokyo would be a nice distraction for him. Maybe a change of scenery would do them both some good."

Tori scratched the back of her head while pinching her lips together. "The trip for Tokyo has been booked for months now."

"I understand that, sweetheart, but life happens. Your brother can use your help now."

"Yeah, but our tickets were reserved back then."

"Oh," he chirped. "I thought you were flying private."

"No. It's way too costly for my small group. My partners out there are covering the stay, but not the airfare."

"Oh." Again, he paused. "I see."

Tori rolled her eyes. "I can always see if the flight has available seats, but again, this was booked so far in advance, I wouldn't get my hopes up."

"Thanks, honey." I could hear the smile in his voice. "Let your old man be the optimistic one. You'll see when you and Deon have kids, you flip over heaven and earth for your children."

Damn...

I sat up in the chair. He was damn sure right about that, but *this* instance didn't match his claim. Something felt awkward between the two.

"I'll let you know," Tori assured, ending the call.

"Thanks. I look forward to hearing back from you."

Just as the call ended, the door opened. Jimmy was being wheeled into the suite, his face tight, eyes wary. He looked thinner than the last time I'd seen him. It had been a few months but felt longer.

"Well, here you are, Mr. Jimmy." The aide stopped him near me. "Do you need anything else?"

With those beady eyes on me, he answered her. "I'll page you when I'm done."

"Okay." She nodded at me with a smile before leaving us alone.

"Damn. Don't look so happy to see me."

"Sir Ashton," he breathed heavily, the mask of the oxygen tank he had to keep near clutched in his hand. "I'll be whatever mood you want me to be, so long as you're not here to tell me to pack my shit."

My head fell back. "That's why you think I'm here?"

"When do you ever come for a casual visit?"

"I was just here a few months ago."

"Squeezing in time for my birthday party isn't exactly a family visit."

"Then you should've had a family."

"I'm still trying. I send gifts and cards to your home, never forgetting a birthday or Christmas. Except for Wanda. She and I have an understanding. It's the rest of you to whose hearts I'm trying to appeal."

That flared a panic in me and I softly shook my head, signaling him to shut the hell up. Suddenly, Jimmy transformed into the cunning inn-keeper I'd always known him to be and whipped his neck at the sight of my flicking eyes toward Tori.

Oblivious to the near slip, Tori rounded the table in the center of the room, crouching down next to him. I'd die a thousand deaths to have experienced the wonder and welcome in her face when I saw her months ago, for the first time in twelve years. But no. I had to fuck her to be acknowledged as her "boyfriend." Jimmy here did nothing but remained alive after all this time.

"Oh, dear Buddha!" he gasped, face completely filled with shock. "This can't be real."

"I know, Jimmy." Tori accepted his free hand. "I know. I'm so happy to see you."

Jimmy's amazed regard swept back over to me and I shrugged with my brows. "She asked to see you."

"Oh, my! The diamond in a rough." He held her eyes in wonderment. "You made it just as I knew you would. You're a phenomenon...all over the television, news, and radio. I tell the peasants here I knew you, and very few believe me." He clutched his mask to his chest, clearly out of breath from his shock. "I can't believe you're here. And with him" He turned to me. "My days are marked, honey. This queen's at the end of her tunnel." Jimmy cupped the mask to his face, eyes closing dramatically.

"I'm sorry, Jimmy," she murmured. "I'm so sorry."

His grip on her hand flexed as they embraced in silence. That's when it hit me.

"You two been in touch? How could you be so affectionate after meeting each other just for a few days thirteen years ago?"

Jimmy's yellow eyes opened first. They shot to Tori, who couldn't stop smiling.

While peering at him, she explained, "Jimmy found me when I left *Blakewood*, too."

What the fuck...

"Too?" Jimmy asked. "Am I missing something here?"

"NormaJean," was her one-word answer. "She followed me back home, too. I was being stalked by two stubborn humans. I wasn't in my right mind for a while at first. And I was too immature to keep in touch. I'm so sorry, Jimmy," she apologized again, throat thickening.

"I understand, dear heart. I, too, was an immature kid once, believe it or not." He winked with charm.

Fuck that. "You reached out to Tori and didn't tell me?"

"I didn't get the impression you wanted to know. When I heard about your fight up there and was finally able to get you on the phone, you were cold—unusually cold. Also, Aivery was always around. So, I called the school for Tori, and was told she'd left for the semester." He lifted his chin in the air, nonexistent lashes clapping. "It troubled my heart that one: you had those horrible injuries no one could account for. And two: I couldn't find the one person in Sir Ashton's world who could provide answers."

"That doesn't explain why you never mentioned contacting Tori," I argued.

"Oh, but I did, his highness. In my brave, covert attempts, I called your cell close to midnight one night, knowing you were at the hospital recovering from one of your many surgeries. *This was months after you'd graduated and had left Blakewood.* I'd been given updates of your care by, of all people, Queen Rosemary. We still had your estate to guard. She told me she'd just hung up with you this particular night. Said you'd started speaking loosely because your pain meds had begun to kick in, and she ended your call." He shrugged. "That's when I called you. I knew how loose those meds could have someone. To my surprise, you answered, sounding like you had a mouth full of cotton balls. I asked about the beautiful tomboy from Christmas. Your answer was something to the tune of her being the worst human and that she'd left you. Well, I thought it was awful, and confirmed my suspicions about you two."

"Which was?"

"That you were good for each other." He shrugged with wide eyes. "I wouldn't have said soulmates or anything as premature and unpredictable as that. But there was certainly something there. So, on that call, I asked if I could find her, would you be interested in knowing."

"What did he say?" Tori's narrowed gaze was on me.

We were in such a delicate space right now. The last thing I needed was loose-lips Jimmy here to fuck it up, repeating shit that no longer mattered.

"He said you were a fraud..." He counted off on his fingers. "who didn't care for him, and were not a good human." He howled as best his lungs would allow. "I know it sounds ridiculous, and I may not have that 'human' phrase correct, but I doubt I'm far off."

Tori stood from his wheelchair. "I have a feeling you're spot on, Jimmy." Her hard regard pinned me.

Fuck...

Jimmy's amused eyes hit me, sensing I was "in trouble." Then his forehead pinched. "Sooooo, you two are...?"

"He's my boyfriend," Tori shared with less luster than she had this morning in *Saint Justin.*

260

His shoulders reclined in his chair. "But dear heart, are you not engaged to the football stud?"

Tori's eyes rolled. "That announcement is being worked on as we speak. But for all intents and purposes, I have a boyfriend and he's it."

Jimmy's beady eyes roved down my frame, from top to bottom, almost as if he were casting judgment. "Interesting." Then he gasped. "You know... This has turned into the modern day Charles and Camilla love story. I always said, if they just abandoned stiff cultural traditions and let those kids follow their hearts, Diana would still be here today."

Shit. Aivery...

Tori, totally missing the analogy, laughed at that, a girly giggle that teased my groin, relaxing me. She crouched beside him again. "We're probably going fast—or slow." She tossed her chin toward me. "I don't really know, but we're finally going. I was hoping I could have another opportunity at a friendship with you. Like I told Ashton, I'm older now to be trusted with those things."

Jimmy turned to me, eyes beaming. "Oh, dear Sir Ashton, how could you not give a woman like this the world?"

Tori's smile broadened and she broke into an adorable cackle. So damn beautiful.

I shook my head, looking away. "She can give that to herself, in case you've been living underneath a damn rock."

I needed to figure out what I could give Tori that she couldn't get from anyone else.

"Let's go see my quarters, dear. Shall we?" Jimmy placed his mask down to roll his wheelchair to the double doors of his expensive ass suite. "It's divine and designed for a man of my particular taste, you know."

I followed the two, mutedly praying Jimmy wouldn't share with Tori more than his "quarters." As tough as she tried to put on, Tori wasn't ready to learn about all of the components of my life.

Tori

I needed to stretch.

Moaning, I tried switching my weight in the chair. It didn't matter that we had business class seats that could transfer into beds on this flight, I'd much rather had flown private. Commercial flights didn't allow for push-ups, stretching, or simply walking about the cabin freely. And I couldn't get comfortable. I didn't recall being as antsy on the flight to Tokyo, but returning home?

Ugh...

"Can you hand me my laptop?" I asked Renata, across the aisle from me. "How long do we have?"

"Like thirty minutes, T," Renata groaned, probably annoyed by my impatience.

It wasn't my first time asking. I was so ready to blow this joint. There wasn't enough sleeping, playing games on my phone, reading business reports, or watching movies to speed this flight up. Tokyo was always a good time. My partners over there in women's boxing were generous and hospitable when I visited, but I couldn't make this trip often. The commute felt too long this time. I needed to be home, *like days ago.*

"It's fully charged now," Renata informed. "Here." She reached over the aisle and handed me the laptop.

I opened it, going straight to my photo album after signing in. Butterflies took flight in my belly and my chest dropped deeper before my lungs filled again. They were beautiful, and I was the bomb photographer out in *Saint Justin*. The sun gave the best lighting out there, and sky the perfect hue of blue. I blinked slowly, wishing I was back there—we were back there.

"*Mmmhmm*," Treesha hummed. "*That's* why you wanted your laptop, I see."

I glanced over to see her peeping my screen. That irritated me, but not more than the long flight.

I rolled my eyes. "No. It's why I'm ready to be on U.S. soil again, though."

It had been a long six days away from...him. We *FaceTime*'d and texted when we could, but what I craved from Ashton couldn't be provided telephonically. I needed him: his scent, hands, his mouth, taut beating chest when he touched me, and his dick. *And I was ready*. On this flight alone, I was unbelievably horny. I leaked so bad I ran to the bathroom, thinking my period arrived early, only to find a puddle of need. It was insane! I felt like a teenager all over again, except I had no sexual desire as a teen, and thought that meant I wasn't normal and possibly liked girls. That was until Ashton. *And* here again was Ashton, pushing my femininity further than any man or woman.

Treesha sucked her teeth. "Here we go with this nigga again."

My face wrinkled. "What about him?"

"Where did he come from? Like how y'all cool again? He did the interview and now it's over. You damn near didn't want to speak to dude back in *Kamigu*, and now you're fuckin' him like he ain't that same dude who played you back in the day and left you with a bab—"

"That's enough, Treesha!" Renata hissed hard enough to turn a few heads at the late hour. Most were sleeping or watching movies in the dark.

"No. It's okay. Let her speak." I looked Treesha dead in the eyes. "Ain't no way I'mma be judged by somebody like you. You ain't perfect, Treesh."

"Oh, I know." Her head bounced. "But I ain't a fool for no man either. Ain't never been; not even with my baby daddy. And at least if I'mma bump my head and go crazy over one, it's gonna be better than the one you're engaged to. Sounds to me like you're creeping, too."

"I'm not creeping." That was offensive. "How am I creeping, Treesha?"

"He only been to the apartment once," she argued. "How he only been there one time and the first and only time, you give him the cake?"

Taken by her audacity, I jerked my head to Renata on the other side of me. Her expression was apologetic. Again, *and unusually*, she agreed with Treesha.

"First of all, I can't have company the way I want because y'all are always there. Just like you made a big deal about that first time, you're judging me now. I don't have to subject myself to that."

"So, you go to his place to serve him the cake?" She swung her index finger in the air. "Told you, y'all been creeping before *Saint Justin* and when you got back."

I started to speak and defend myself but remembered Ashton and I had been at Raj and Wynter's apartment in Jersey City twice before I left for Tokyo. We'd never had sex at his place. He hadn't said I couldn't come by his place, but I had not since he cooked me dinner last month. I guessed I never asked to and had already provided our "creep" spot.

Treesha's right!

One reason I'd gotten comfortable in Jersey City was because of the privacy Raj had over there. He was a bigger celebrity than me and enjoyed more seclusion. With Ashton, privacy was a must because publicly, I was still engaged to Deon. I didn't think about having privacy at Ashton's because he wasn't a public figure and likely didn't have the measures to accommodate that.

But what if he did and you never thought about it, and *you never asked?*

Sitting back with my legs stretched out, I hissed, "Treesha, shut the hell up. I'm Tori McNabb; what the hell I look like creepin'?"

"The same way you do cursing," Treesha shot back. "We back to that now?"

I shot her the nastiest glare. My cousins and I didn't fight. At the most, Renata yoked Treesha up the first time we found her in a drug house, high off pills and God only knew what else. I definitely didn't fight my cousins because it wouldn't be a fair one. But lately, I hadn't been above slapping her across the face to disable her mouth—Ashton aside.

Turning away from her, I mumbled while clicking through my pictures, "Talking about somebody creeping." Then I swung my head to face her again. "How about no stops on the way home. I'll be packing a bag to stay at Ashton's place tonight."

"Whatever," Treesha mumbled, burying her face in her phone.

"Y'all, stop," Renata intervened. "Tori, I know Treesha can be rude as hell, but you know she only looking out for you."

"Why do I need looking out for?" I wanted to know. "Ashton ain't no stranger I met at a coffee shop and decided to bring home and fall in love with."

"No, but y'all two got crazy history—"

"And?" It was hard to continue the whispering argument, but we understood our fight was within earshot of so many people.

"And we don't want you getting hurt. We know what this Deon shit feel like. Feel like he fucked us all over. We really took him in, T, and you know that. Plus," She kept going. Unbelievable for the one who typically played referee in our trio. "we know you don't be fuckin' around with dudes like this. Yeah, you better than you used to be in middle school and high school with it when you were confused, but you don't wild out like this."

"How am I wilding out? And do we forget the reason I'm better than what I was as a kid with guys is because of this one guy we're talking about?"

Resigning from the fight, Renata reclined in her seat, effectively shutting down. That annoyed my soul.

"Look, y'all. I appreciate the concerns. I'm good, though. At least let me try out something for me. Can I not be so responsible all the damn time? It gets real lonely being that girl all the time. If this works or flunks, at least it's something I want to do." I wouldn't mention Ashton being my boyfriend. "Let me be a careless thirty-one year old for once. Shall we?"

Of course, no one replied. Renata was right: my cousins were my protectors no matter how rude and hypocritical Treesha had been. But for once, I would make a decision with *my* best interest at heart, not the safest one.

love belvin

Ashton

The house phone ringing on my nightstand awakened me from my doze. Opening just one eye, I peered at the clock next to it and saw it was close to two in the morning. I'd been checking the time for a while now. Tori's flight landed last night and she told me she'd call to let me know she'd made it in safely. My plan was to ask if I could come over. But my home line ringing at this hour took precedent over my dick's needs.

I sat up and saw the security icon flashing on the screen of the digital console. That was strange.

"Yeah," I answered after picking up the handset.

"Mr. Spencer, it's Niko from the parking garage. I have Ms. McNabb here, asking for access to your unit."

My eyes bounced around. "Ms. McNabb?"

"Yes, sir." He cleared his throat. "*The* McNabb, sir."

Tori?

Snapping out of my stupor, I rubbed my eyes. "*Yea*—uh. Let her up, please."

"Will do, sir."

I placed the handset down. Now, doubly dazed from being awakened and learning Tori was on her way up, my eyes scanned my bedroom. The television was on low, candles burning in the sitting room, and heavy winds blowing in through the one window I often kept cracked at night.

Dude, wake the fuck up. Tori's here!

Snapping into action, I dragged myself out of bed and rubbed my tired eyes, in search of my slippers. When I made it to the hall, I remembered turning down the place for the night after cleaning the kitchen. I closed all the doors on my way to the foyer, bathrooms included. By the time I made it to the front door and swung it open, Tori was strutting down the hall with her face to the floor in thigh-high heeled boots, tight denim hotpants outlining the curves of her pelvis, a red tank top that displayed her globular, bouncy tits and pebbled nipples, and a swinging trench coat. Trailing behind her was a rolling suitcase. *An overnight bag?* In no time, I knew what it was. Baby girl wanted to fuck.

Shit...

I leaned into the doorjamb, dick twitching while growing. Tori finally peered up and noticed me while strutting my way, and I peeped her eyes grazing my bare chest. Her chin was to the floor as her eyes shrunk and one side of her face rose in a bashful smile.

"Hi, Ashton." Her tone was unsure, yet determined.

I tossed my chin to her as she stopped in front of me. "You bring rubbers?"

Her beam faded and a crease formed between her eyes. "No. Should I have?"

"You still wanna baby?"

Tori snorted nervously. Glancing away, she switched weight on her hips. "*Ye*—yeah. I guess."

My brows raised. "Gotta be. You coming to my crib with those baby bearing thighs out can only mean one thing." I maintained a placid expression, but I was fucking with Tori.

Going half on a baby with any woman was one thing: getting to know Tori as a woman and a trusted lover was a far more challenging and desirable prospect.

Appearing to be suddenly aroused, Tori glanced away again, biting her burgundy bottom lip.

"The hell in here, McNabb," I grated, swinging the door open.

She rolled her luggage in and I shut the door. In the dim vestibule, we stood peering at each other. Lustful electric pulses of erotic energy zapping between the two of us. When she could no longer take it, Tori lunged at me. Leaping up toward my face, she caught my lips like a hungry leopard, her warm tongue caressing my lips and stroking against my tongue. My hands gripped her round ass, molding it to me. She grabbed my beard as I lifted her onto my waist. Tori's pussy grounded onto me, driving me wild.

"I missed you, boyfriend," she joked breathily.

"You ready to show me?"

She nodded with emphatic decisiveness. Dizzy with arousal and another emotion I had no time to decode, I reciprocated again when Tori kissed me. I managed to grab her suitcase and carry it in the air, down the hall to my bedroom. Luckily, I was able to keep up with her mouth all the way to my room and succeeded in closing the door. When Tori finally came up for air, she peered around my faintly lit bedroom. She observed the television running on low volume, the open closet door, the sitting room with candles, the fish tank on the far wall in there, and then finally my mussed bed.

Then Tori stepped back, pulling out of her coat, unzipping and yanking off her tall, leggy boots; shifted down her shorts, sans any panties, then pulled her tank from over her torso and head. As I perceived, she wore no bra and was nude before me. As bold as her action of stripping naked for me was, Tori's eyes still held an insecurity I'd seen many years ago as her first lover. It was a timidity I now reveled in. She may have had lovers since me, but none could blow her mind the way I could; I was sure of it. I had yet to explore her sexual temperament the way I wanted to and had no clue when I'd start. Tonight, I wanted her to lead. I needed for Tori to feel in control and satisfied her way.

Without verbalizing that, she struck first by toeing up to me and pulled the waist-string of my pajama pants, then pushed them down past my ass until they fell down my legs. Tori was right behind them, falling to her knees, then took me into her mouth. My eyes rolled up before closing at the feel of her warm, secreted mouth. Her lips were pliant, tongue so slick. Her hands were unbelievably soft for a tenured boxer cupping my balls.

Tori's head bobbed and the sounds from her mouth were unrepentant, top-grade erotica. She went slow, then fast before slowing again. She moaned longingly, eyes rolling to the back of her head before she bobbed and suctioned hard again. I reached down to the back of her head and squeezed, pulling her back.

"Baby," I breathed when she sucked hard, her mouth pulling from my shaft then swollen head.

From her knees, peering up at me with drunken desire, Tori stood. Planting her hands on my chest, she urged me to the bed. She signaled with her arm, instructing me to move to the center where she straddled me. KaToria rode my cock with earnest need. Her thighs flexed and ass bucked against my balls. Her lewd tits bounced, enticing me into a kiss. I licked and sucked on them as she mewled over my head in pleasure. Her fingertips gripped my head and shoulder as her nails threatened to bite. The scent of her skin, pussy, and hair was an intimate intoxication I wanted to get used to.

"Ashton," she cried. "I'm about to—" Her body wriggled over me, spine flopped as her hair flew into the air.

I reclined and bucked into her wet folds, battering it. Her head tossed back, tits clapped, and her walls pulsated while coming over me. When her soft, guttural moans slowed, I flipped her over onto all fours. Tori managed to quickly recover and comply. I grabbed a pillow, plunging it beneath her pelvis. Then I thrust into her, filling her pussy. With my thighs spread around her hips, I experienced her soft and firm ass. Reaching down, I kissed her back, trailing up to her neck, pounding into her. Her shoulders flexed beneath me, spine curled into my drive. I could do this forever. Mesmerized by her tight warmth, I plunged and plunged and when her thighs began to vibrate, I knew she was close, propelling my own orgasm.

"Kiss me," she demanded breathlessly.

Lowering myself and readjusting my thrust game, I took her mouth. Tori grabbed the back of my head, tonguing me into delirium as she came. Her hips made futile attempts to buck beneath me as she cried into my mouth, clasping my head. With my balls warming and swelling with each slap into her ass cheeks, I followed behind her, rocking to unsteady drives.

"Ashton," she called out to me as my eyes felt crossed and mind gone, coming down from that orgasm.

"Yeah, baby," I heaved, breathlessly suspended over her back in a half-plank position.

"You think we're moving too fast?" she uttered, out of breath, too.

I blinked. "Doubtlessly. Why?"

It was a matter I'd been mulling over in my mind since her absence over the past six days without solution. I didn't even have a desire to change a thing about our pace.

I positioned myself over her to pull the pillow from beneath her pelvis, then invited her to lay on her side next to me. Instead, Tori rested half her body on mine.

"Because I feel the excitement of the rush. All I think about is you: in meetings, at photoshoots, when at events. But it feels too good to stop. Everyone seemed to have that fun period of love when they're young. I feel like it's finally happening to me and..." She shook her head, seemingly lost for words.

"And what?"

"And I don't feel supported." She let go of a long breath. "I snuck in a therapy session before *Saint Justin*, being totally honest about my feelings for you and fears. And you know what I did? I went to *Saint Justin* and enjoyed every moment of sex with you. My cousins think I'm stupid, forgetting about the pain I felt from leaving *BSU*. They think we're creeping. Like I don't really know you."

"Well," I exhaled, stuffing a pillow beneath my head. "you can't exactly be mad at them. They weren't there for our introduction. They know nothing about our raw chemistry as kids. Have no clue about what made us bond in the first place. It's one of those things that if you weren't there for it, you really don't get it. And no one was there for that, but me and you, Nabby-girl." I dabbed the end of her nose with my index finger.

Her brows knitted and she smiled curiously. "First KaToria, now Nabby-girl. I haven't heard that name in so long."

"Who else has called you that?"

"Only you."

"That's what the hell I thought."

She giggled into my neck before kissing me there. "Raj told me it took him less than two months to fall in love with Wynter. I thought that was crazy fast, but look at me forcing my way into your home the minute I get back from work." Her smile was defiant.

My face folded. "Are you saying you're in love with me?"

Tori's eyes held suspended, peering into mine. Her cheeks were spread, but now in muscular form. The smile was absent in her eyes. "I think I should wash up. You're leaking out of me."

Hearing those words turned me the fuck on and had me aroused all over again. I lifted my head and captured her lips. "First I wanna see, then I wanna add some more."

CHAPTER FIFTEEN

Tori

"Going to shower, then cook breakfast." His lips pressed into the side of my head. "Get some rest. I'll wake you with food."

Moaning as I felt the aches from sleeping on his chest to pushing myself up the bed to rest on the pillows against the headboard, I settled on my back, pulling the comforter up my naked body. Being jet-lagged was one thing, but being sore all over from jumping off a fourteen-hour flight and into the bed of Ashton Spencer was my ruin. When we were supposed to wash and play in the shower, we did that and played more, well after five in the morning. My bones ached and my head was fuzzy. I knew there was nothing I could do but sleep it off.

The bed dipped and I went back out.

"Oh, my..." a soft voice bounced around in my psyche, unwelcomed.

I wanted to sleep, not dream. Shifting my body, I turned away from the unnecessary voyage my dream was taking me into.

"Right there!" The kiddie voice was now stronger. "See! Right there, Glammom. I think it's her." *Oh, noooo! No jet-lagged dreams, please...* "I'm going to get *Maggie*—"

"Oh, no you don't, young lady!" That sharper, more authoritative command completely transported me out of the dream.

I struggled to open my heavy eyes, lashes still obstructing my view as I blinked several times to see. Finally, I was able to lift my head and realized I was laid out on my stomach, head toward the middle of the left side of the bed. There was a draft on my back I couldn't muster the energy to address in the moment. I was in a foreign place, hearing voices. That couldn't be good for my psyche or reality. When I turned my neck to look straight ahead, I saw two sets of feet and legs: one shorter than the other.

"See!" I heard an excited cry. "It's her. It's Tori McNobb, Glammom!" she mispronounced my name.

My head propped up even more.

"Maurie, go to your room." The small body was pushed behind the larger one.

Finally, gaining my wits, I leaped up from my belly. "Oh, *shiiii!*" I fumbled the comforter, trying to cover myself.

"*Ooh!*" shot from the little girl's belly as she covered her eyes. "Her privates, Glammom!"

"Maurie!" the woman shouted. "To your room, now!"

Recoiling at the roar in her demand, I recognized the older woman. She hadn't aged much, eyes still as fiery and presence still that of a lioness. This couldn't be happening to me.

The little girl ran as though there was a fire, leaving me with Wanda. "*Daddy! Tori McNobb is in your bed! She has no clothes!*" she shouted down the hallway.

Daddy?

Oh, my God—daddy!

I shivered beneath the thick, white comforter, naked beyond wearing just my skin in her son's bed. I felt indecent. Exposed. This would have been the time to assert myself, to exercise some dignity. Stunned into silence, I didn't know what to say.

With a tight face, Wanda shifted toward the door. "I apologize for that. We're not used to him having company."

"I—I came over..." I stumbled over my words. "It was a last-minute decision. I'm sorry."

Her head shook faintly. "No need to apologize. If he didn't want you here, you wouldn't be."

Wanda left after those soft words, closing the door behind herself. A switch clicked on in my foggy brain, and my weighted body scrambled out of the bed. I needed my clothes and suitcase to go. Phone, too. Texting my car services wouldn't take long at all. My legs couldn't move fast enough to blow this joint. I had no idea what I expected to wake up to this morning in Ashton's bed, but it wasn't this. A kid and his mean, bitchy mother possibly watching me sleep had been something my mind couldn't create as a scenario.

Oh, no...

After the fourth step I made once out of his bed, my bladder thundered. It was the sex. The heavy beating to my uterus last night had an effect on my bladder. Although I spotted my clothes from last night sprawled out over the floor, the distance to the bathroom became more imminent. I took long lunges inside to the toilet. My pee had begun a step away, forcing me to plop down on the toilet.

"*Noooooo!*" screamed in my mind louder than my urine stream did in the toilet.

This can't be real...

Then, in a rush of rewound time, a rasp occurred as faint as a whisper in my ear. "*Events in your life have fashioned you to run in the face of adversity. However, you're a far better fighter than you are a runner. You're a thinking fighter, even in the line of fire. It's your best stance to face obstacles than to turn your back to them. You're more vulnerable that way.*"

My eyes squeezed closed as my stomach turned over. *Pastor Carmichael...*

The door being pushed open had me bouncing on the toilet seat. I clambered to grab tissue from the post. Ashton leaned into the doorway, laying his head on the frame. His chest heaved and eyes were heavy.

"I wasn't thinking, Tori." He swore throatily with his eyes closed. "You pulled up and I saw you, and I couldn't say no. I wasn't thinking."

"You clearly haven't been thinking for weeks...since my party when you knew I wanted you enough to allow you to seduce me. You knew I wanted you. Knew I was attracted to you all over again." I wiped myself and flushed the toilet. "Sorry, but you've had plenty of time to share this important detail of your life since eating my ass that night." I moved over to the sink to wash my hands, hating I was still naked in front of him.

"Baby," he pleaded. "I'm sorry."

"And I'm leaving."

"Leaving?" His body pushed from the doorjamb. "You can't. You can't run, Tori."

"I'm not running," I explained through the mirror. "I'm walking away with a heart that, though is bruised, is still intact this time. I'm never putting myself through a web of complications again."

"I thought you were my girlfriend, Tori."

I shook my head. "No. You were my boyfriend. I don't think you exactly claimed me the way I did you. And now I see why? A child? You're a father, Ashton? When were you going to tell me?"

"Today. I was going to tell you today."

"That's cold and arrogant: the same guy I knew at *Blakewood*. You let me pour my heart out to you last night and your plan was to casually mention you're a father?"

His eyes closed as though Ashton was irritated. "I didn't get that far. I told you I wasn't thinking last night. I missed you and was waiting to hear from you so I could come over to your place. But when you showed unannounced, I went into freestyle mode with decisions. I knew when I woke up this morning, I'd have to tell you about my girls."

"Girls!" I shouted, leaping off my feet.

Truth felt like acid poured onto my skin. It felt betraying. Not just one child, but girls?

His eyes closed again, nostrils widened. "Tori, I have two daughters—twins."

My chest began to heave out of nowhere, lungs on overdrive, but I still couldn't breathe momentarily. Instantly, my body began to tremble, heart galloping, and I felt violent.

"By who?"

Shaking his head while exhaling hard, Ashton's eyes closed painfully again. "My late wife, Tori."

"*Shiiiiiit!*" I whispered hard and forcefully, rage boiling within.

"Tori—" He approached me until I pushed my hand in the air, warning him. "Tori!" His octave changed.

"I need..." I tried breathing. "a...minute." I would be fine. This one wasn't as bad as I'd had in the past. It would take just a few seconds to focus on my breathing.

"We can get through this, baby. Please don't say we can't. We've been through enough, Tori. Now is our time to see if we can have something together."

Feeling my limbs again, I knew I was coming out of it. I managed to shake my head. "Ashton, this is too much. It's not...fair."

"What's not fair? There's equity here. I want this. I want you, Tori!" He tried touching me again. I didn't fight him this time, fearing I'd lose my breathing again. "I swear: I want you so damn bad, Tori. I needed you then and I want you now. Don't let my shit with Aivery win again. There are no obstacles we can't work through. We're adults now with baggage, but we owe it to each other a try."

He made it sound simple, so promising. And we felt so close, almost like the real thing. His arms wrapped around my curled naked body, his hold so tight, I could feel the racing of his heart against my shoulder.

"Don't do this," he whispered—begged. "Don't leave me again, Tori."

Muted energy swelled the room around us for a spell. I couldn't speak. So many thoughts running around in my mind, visions of Aivery in a bridal gown, then of her going into the delivery room with Ashton at her side. *The same way he's at mine now.* Twelve years. I was too late to be his first bride. Too delayed to be the first to give him his first child.

Bobby...

Ashton was right: we'd been through too much. The mere fact that we were here after all these years, after swearing each other off, spoke to that. We crossed paths and found ourselves still wildly drawn to each other.

My eyes closed as I whispered, "Ashton, I need to go. I have to think about this. It's not fair to expect me to fall in line with you and Aivery all over again. I'm not that little girl anymore. I'm a woman who deserves to fully process what you're offering so I can decide if I want to participate."

I meant it. I'd go home and think about what him having children with Aivery meant. I moved past their marriage with instant forgiveness. Her children were another matter.

"You can't leave right now."

"Why?"

"Wanda."

"What about her? I don't owe her anything."

"If we're going to really do this, really be boyfriend and girlfriend, you'd need to earn her respect. She's very much a part of my support system. She helps me out with my babies. If you leave now, her idea of us being back together would resemble what you're dealing with, with Renata and Treesha. We have to earn their respect, too. This is the last piece of my life I've been hesitant to share."

Shit...

I felt my heart relent to this man yet again.

"I don't have any clothes. I need to go."

"You brought a suitcase."

"With nothing appropriate for your mother or children," I hissed, angry all over again.

Gently, Ashton kissed my back. "I'll give you something to wear."

I took a deep breath before rounding the corner for the kitchen. I could hear a television going and utensils banging against pots and/or pans, helping to locate it from Ashton's room. Inside, he was at the stove, a little girl was at the table watching something on her laptop, and another was at the peninsula with Wanda, placing biscuits in a clothed bowl.

"Here she is," Ashton announced, turning to me with the bravest beam. Handing me a cup of coffee, I could tell he was nervous. I was mad as hell. But for him, I'd fake it, too. "Ladies, meet Tori." He placed his arm around my waist, keeping me near him. "Tori, you met Ms. Wanda, though she doesn't remember. But please meet my babies: Maurie and Maggie. Girls, say hello."

"Told you it was her!" the one at the counter with Wanda wore a genuine beam, opposite of her father. I could see him in her cinnamon face. But even more than Ashton's features, I noted her small slit eyes and flat oval face. It was clear to me she had Downs syndrome. It was weird because the girl was...beautiful. She had long braids with only her natural hair and baby curls framing her round face. The barrettes and bows in her hair, and modest size diamond studs in her little ears made it clear she was a well-kept child. "Look, Maggie!" She turned to her sister. "Isn't this cool?"

Maggie was already looking my way with a slant in her eyes. The difference was she appeared as a "normal" child. She too had her natural hair braided into an intricate style, and her earrings were small gold hoops. The shirt of her matching long-johns pajama set read *cheer princess.* There was no warmth or excitement in her expression. In fact, beyond her cold energy that was eerily familiar, Maggie had distinct features of a yesteryear foe. She was lighter than her sister, but not quite as redboned as her mother. Her lips curved into a natural pout beneath her round snout, and dark eyes lit like flames shooting my way. Aivery spit this girl out. She was her twin— and in energy it seemed, too.

"Maggie," Wanda called out. "Aren't you going to greet our guest?"

"Yeah, Maggie!" Her sister swiped her nose while giggling. "She looks the same like all the pictures in our room!"

"Shush up, Maurie!" Maggie hissed before cutting her eyes back to me.

Once again, she gave me the silent treatment.

"Maggie," I almost didn't recognize Ashton's voice. It was his dad tone.

"Hi!" Maggie yanked her little body back toward her laptop.

Wanda's head swung back, reacting to her granddaughter's coldness. I didn't want to focus on that.

"Maurie," I tried for the most unaffected voice I could. "Those biscuits look amazing. Did you help make them?"

With a wide smile, she shook her head, barrettes clacking in the air. "Daddy did them alone today. Sometimes, I'm his little helper. Maggie helps sometimes, too. Not Glammom." She shook her head again. "Glammom says she's too glam to cook. But she does it for us sometimes."

Despite myself, I smiled.

"And sometimes is too much," Wanda hissed in a fussy manner.

Maurie giggled, eyes shrinking while lifting her shoulder to her chin. "She doesn't cook a lot, though."

"Young lady!" Wanda playfully slapped the countertop. "Are you trying to blow up your Glammom's spot?"

That warm act of affection from the woman who intimidated me with one glare had me loosening enough to snicker.

Ashton kissed the side of my face. "Maurie's gonna tell it all in a minute." He went back to the stove.

"What's your favorite thing your Glammom makes?" I asked before finally tasting my coffee; it was the one silver-lining of my crazy morning.

"I like her spaghetti!" Maurie giggled.

Maggie joined them at the counter, pulling out a seat. It was clear from the way she snuck glances at me, she wanted to be felt, but not seen. I was used to awkward moments with people as a fighter and celebrity—something that still felt funny admitting to. Sometimes, people froze in my presence. Other people wanted to glean my energy before interacting with me. Some were intimidated from the jump. Then there were those who'd decided to hate me before ever being in my presence. I was cool with all those degrees of exposure to people. I could take Maggie on if I didn't like her father so. This was going to be hard.

"I like your peach cobbler and oatmeal, Glammom," Maggie mumbled, pushing her head affectionately into her grandmother's arm.

"Speak up, child," Wanda ordered in her no-nonsense tone. "Ms. Tori's speaking to you."

Maggie veered her little neck to peek around her grandmother. I smiled, turning away when my phone vibrated in my pocket.

DeJo: *We need to talk. I'm flying in tonight. Name the time and the place.*

Rolling my eyes, I took another sip of coffee. It reminded me of our social obligation. We had a *Victoria's Secret* Halloween fundraising party to host tomorrow night. My gaze drifted to Ashton's broad back over the stove. Almost as though he sensed me, he turned his head my way and winked. I wanted to roll my eyes again, at him this time, but he turned back toward the stove. He worked between four eyes and had a great excuse to stay out of the line of fire.

"Hey. Is Tori your real name?" I turned to find Maggie giggling. "Sounds kinda funny and boyish to me."

"Maggie!" Wanda reprimanded her with her name alone.

Ashton turned and did it with his eyes. "You've never said that before in all the years you've been a fan."

She was a fan? *Of mine?* Couldn't be. Her DNA wouldn't allow it. Her mother hated me, and her father wanted to forget I ever existed.

Putting on my showman face again, I smiled. "It's actually KaToria. Hardly anyone knows it, so I'm rarely called that."

"That's pretty and girlie!" Maurie's eyes disappeared, she smiled so broadly. "Right, Maggie?"

God, this was not only a beautiful girl but a kind spirit, too. It was so vibrant, I could tell after being in her presence for just minutes.

Maggie rolled her eyes and recoiled in her bar chair next to her grandmother. "I guess."

Another awkward moment...

"So, I hear nicknames for you two, too. Or are Maggie and Maurie your first names?" I took a sip of my coffee as I waited for what would come back from chumming that out there.

"Oh!" Maurie exclaimed. "My name is Maureen Spencer."

Maureen...

"What's your name, little girl?" Wanda prompted Maggie.

"Margaret Aivery Spencer," she mumbled with long eyes. "Maurie, you never said your middle name!" Her tone was more spirited for that as she peered over her grandmother at her sister.

"It's Wanda, like my Glammom," Maurie made it sound so casual.

"Oh." I nodded. "So Maureen Wanda—" Wait a minute. *Margaret and Maureen...* My mug fumbled between my sweaty palms. "Shit!" I whispered.

It was too late. Hot coffee splashed all over my legs and bare feet, and the porcelain mug shattered into pieces. The next thing I knew, Ashton was squatting in front of me, dabbing my legs. When he finally peered up, the embarrassment in his eyes was sad.

"I thought you said you gave up profanity," he mumbled.

"And I thought you said what I woke up to this morning was the last secret you were holding!"

"Daddy..." someone timidly called behind me, crushing me in a different way.

I didn't belong here. This ride didn't come with training wheels.

"Ut! Let's get set up for breakfast in the dining room this morning. You guys go first." Wanda assisted the girls from the high bar chairs.

I'd just finished texting my car service and Ashton was cleaning the last of the broken porcelain from the floor when Wanda waltzed into the kitchen.

"Okay!" she breathed, appearing upbeat. "Now that the girls are finally eating breakfast and distracted with their devices while doing it—something you know disturbs my spirit—why don't we try to figure out what the hell's going on here."

Her eyes bounced between her son and me. Ashton couldn't even look me in the face. Angry all over again, my knees vibrated.

"It's not a big deal. Really," I lied. "I've just been surprised at every turn this morning. I'm tired and will be out of your hair in a few minutes."

"Like hell you are!" Ashton finally turned my way. "Tori..."

"No. I'm tired, embarrassed, and clearly have embarrassed myself here."

"How?" Wanda asked after her head ping-ponged between us. "What is going on? Ashton, did you not tell her about your family?"

"No!" I made clear.

"But you thought she was special enough to bring home. Why would you not do that?" she asked, showing signs of sense. "Is it not a part of the process of getting to know each other? I'm sure she let you get to know her for the article. That's been more than enough time for you to tell her you have a family." Then she visibly cringed. "Please tell me you told her what you do for a living. Like what you really do instead of giving the bullshit evasiveness you usually give women."

"Ma..." Ashton scratched his beard, looking like the kid I met back in *BSU*, only immature. "Tori's not new to me or my world." His hand swung in the air, trying to articulate himself. "I know you said you don't remember her, but Tori and I dated back then."

Her eyes roved over to me. "I don't remember this."

"Because I didn't broadcast it. It was my senior year and I—we—had a lot going on that year."

Her head bounced back and Wanda blinked several times. "Like Aivery?"

I nodded. "Yup. Like Aivery. It wasn't the best decision I ever made, but I somehow did. It was a mess then, and apparently, it's a mess now."

Wanda's regard returned to her son, and thankfully because I would not force myself to stand in judgment. Elder and all, I wouldn't cower to Wanda.

Ashton chuckled dryly. "I believe it was the night before Thanksgiving of the year I'd fallen for a tomboy fighter from a trailer park in South Jersey. I was in your kitchen when you told me cheating is wrong, and will never be right. But the biggest conflict is when you fall in love with someone who isn't yours. You said people fall in and out of love every day, and that most of it is bullshit...being more about passion and temporary emotions. But when the person you're cheating with is worth a commitment and sacrifice, and when you're prepared in your heart and mind to walk through the fire of the mess, it might be something real after all." He gestured to me with his hand. "That was and still is KaToria McNabb."

Tears threatened my throat and eyes. Did he really say that? Did she?

With closed eyes, Wanda shook her head. "Okay. Okay...okay," she whispered. "I can process that later. But what did that have to do with my babies' names? That was the second part of the drama."

"Margaret Maureen McNabb was Tori's late grandmother. Her matriarch." Tears pooled as he spoke of her. "She was the most influential person in Tori's life when I met her, her comfort blanket of a memory, if you will."

"And you named Aivery's daughters after her?" Wanda's face protruded over her shoulders, eyes wild. "A woman you never met?"

Biting his nails with his arms and legs crossed as he rested against the peninsula with his back to me, Ashton gave a faint nod. "I've done some crazy shit since *Blakewood*. Unspeakable shit. But that's something I can't find in my heart to regret. At all." He finally turned to me. "I hated you for leaving me. Absolutely detested your existence. But you made an impression on me like no one else. I was willing to steer clear of your path for the rest of my life—wouldn't even take my daughter to see her favorite athlete—but I'm a grown ass man now. I'm going to get this right this time—*we're* going to see it through, Tori. I'm just that reckless with my hope."

Wiping my soaked face, I left the kitchen.

Ashton

Closing the door from just having seen Tori off to her car down in the garage, I trekked to the back of the apartment until my mother's voice captured my attention.

"What were you thinking?"

She walked from the dining room, where I still heard the girls chattering and their devices going. "I wasn't."

"How long did you think you could go without telling her?" I shook my head, implementing the same answer. She let out a deep breath, then swallowed. "I'm going to cancel my trip to Vegas—"

"No, Ma." I dismissed the thought. "That ain't necessary. Tori and I will figure it out—this time. We've got to." A pang ran through my chest at that.

"Oh, you're going to figure it out on your own, alright. And by that, I mean without my participation. My only role here is to support you with these little girls. As a father, I understand you need time to be a man. That was something I wish I understood as a mother who was single. When you went off with your father, I didn't date. I should have been investing that time without you in *me*, but instead, I worked or studied or got things done for you like checking your homework, fighting with your coaches—hell, even checking your room for drugs and porn."

I kept the porn at my dad's place where I had less supervision because he worked so hard. My workload had been resembling his since I'd been a father myself. Family is truly the mistress for a man with my level of responsibility. My mother here made it so that I didn't fail at it. I didn't know where I'd be without her partnership with the girls.

"Yeah," I chuckled, embarrassed by the reminder of my old porn companion. "which is exactly why I need you to make your girls trip. I'll have to figure this shit out alone. I know I'm a single father. I'll make due."

"You don't have to, is what I'm saying to you." She shifted closer to me once the girls darted out of the dining room for their bedroom to get ready for school. "I may not have been the CEO of a top ten restaurant chain and a practiced journalist, but I was a tenured professor between two universities. Work was demanding and I could have failed if I didn't have what your father could do. *Shit.* Even Rosemary spent time with you regularly...my brother June...Tabitha. It does take a village. I'm gonna be that for you until you get a woman. God, please get a woman! If you do and do it right, I can be a real Glammom and travel the globe, only seeing my grandbabies when I feel like it." She jerked her shoulder, pushing her chin in the air.

I couldn't help but chuckle. "I love you, Ms. Wanda. I really do."

She began to take off to the back of the apartment. "Of course, you do. And you're also in love with that former tomboy of a boxer. Even a blind man can see that."

I closed the door behind me and left my suitcase in the foyer as I winded down the hall to my bedroom.

Renata stepped out of the office, intercepting me. Her eyes roved down my body before she asked, "You okay?"

At the same time, Treesha peered out of the kitchen, eating a pint of ice cream and wearing the same curious glare.

I stopped, knowing I had to provide an answer. Arriving home before eight in the morning after an alleged rendezvous could only mean bad news.

"I'm good. Need my bed to work out this jet-lag ish." I shook my head. "I'm gonna shower and sleep. Don't bother me unless it's an emergency, please. And cancel that call with Elle and the marketing department. Tell her I lost my feet with that long flight." I scratched my head. "And I got your message about the Halloween costume. I still have the cat woman one *MEEHAR* made for me last year. I never wore it. If Deon doesn't have a batman costume, I'm sure we'd still be fine."

"Okay." Renata's face was blank but for her eyes. "You sure you're good?"

I let go of a deep breath, mental exhaustion now rivaling physical. "I just need sleep. I'm going to bed."

And with that, I took off to my room and closed the door. My boots were the first to go. I had no desire to discuss what happened with my cousins just yet. It wasn't because of fear of increasing their doubt in Ashton or sharing it would have been proving them right. Maybe they were right; that didn't matter. But as I toed into the shower when finally naked, I realized issues with Ashton were not matters I wanted to run to anyone with. This was for me to sort first. Problems with Ashton were personal pains I had to process before sharing them. Right now, I would rest.

Ashton and the existence of his family would have to wait until I was ready.

"T..." A knock at my door sounded before it opened. "T, it's late. You ain't eat nothing all day. We can order food."

Lifting my face from the pillow felt like too great of a task for my neck, but I made it. The light Treesha let in from the open door was disrespectful. Not only that, I couldn't process what she said. I heard her but didn't fully understand. She stepped in and sat on the side of my bed. She placed a few menus in my reach. Then she ran her fingers through my hair and down my shoulder.

"Pick one and text me your order. You can't sleep the day away. Okay?"

I nodded. After a squeeze on my bare shoulder, Treesha left out. I turned around for the windows. It was indeed dark out. I didn't feel hungry to say all I put on my stomach today was a few sips of coffee. What I did feel was groggy. Shifting on my stomach, I reached to the opposite side of my bed for my phone on the nightstand. I really needed a new number now that I was retired. Too many people had it. Hardly any of the texts were important—including Deon's—and none were from Ashton. I tossed the phone across the bed, feeling my bladder cry.

After peeing and washing my hands, I dove back into the bed. It was just after nine at night and I had no idea what to do with myself. What should I do? Read? Watch television? I wouldn't know where to begin with that.

Ohhhh...

I still needed to check out Brielle's movie on *Netflix*. It wasn't her movie, per se, but because of her fame, the producers top-billed her. I quickly passed on that. Brielle was one of the most talented people I knew with skills exceeding a microphone and stage, but acting was not her gift. I had no idea how to tell her that. Maybe I never would. She was my best friend and I could never tell her to stop going after these roles that real actors deserved, which was why it'd been out for a month now and I'd yet to see it.

Ugh...

Sleep? I could certainly hit the resume button on that activity. But Treesha was right; I needed nourishment. I picked up the menus. No to Mexican. Blah to soul food. Had loads of Asian foods while in Tokyo, so I put that in the pile of discarded menus. *DiFillippo's.*

Hmmmm...

My door opening startled me.

"Sorry, T." Treesha craned her neck inside. "Ashton's on his way up. You wanna meet him in the living room?"

I sat up, resting my back against the headboard and bringing my blanket up with me. "He can come in here, Treesh."

I went back to the menu, suddenly having a taste for something garlicky. By the time my door opened again, I was lost in the menu. I glanced up to find Ashton coming in with a duffle. He wore half his suit, removing his tie and replacing his suit jacket with a more casual one. Ashton resembled a corporate dad—one that was fine as hell, but a father. It was a side of him I never knew. His chin was to the floor as he looked my way silently.

"Hi..."

"Hi."

"Still mad at me?" I nodded, feeling like a child for my brutal honesty. Then Ashton nodded, too, but in an accepting way. "I'm going to try and fix this. I know I can't 'fix' having my babies, but repair not sharing them with you before this morning."

"How?"

"By not running, and not allowing you to run either." He wiggled out of his jacket, tossing it on the sofa chair. "And beginning dialogue to get you caught up on my family."

He came over and sat on the side of my bed, taking the menu from my hands. My eyes nearly closed at his manly scent. "Food. Great! You didn't eat. I'm starving," he murmured, perusing it. "Lori had just finished up with the girls and their homework when I got in.

I helped with dinner, went over their homework myself, then got them bathed and in the bed." His octave changed every other sentence when he'd focus in on a particular item on the menu, I supposed. "I packed an overnight bag, fixed a plate for Ms. Wanda then put away the food, but forgot to feed myself."

"How?"

He glanced my way, brows meeting in concentration. "I had to prepare for my time with my girlfriend. Food was less attractive."

That warmed me.

I'm still mad as hell at you, though...

"Who said I'm still your girlfriend?"

Ashton took a deep breath. "And that's why I'm here. You can't resist me if I'm here in your face. And you can't break up with me if you can't resist me, Nabby-girl."

Defiantly, I turned my head away from him. This didn't feel right, but still good. He'd lied to me by not being honest. Did Ashton not remember how vulnerable I was when letting my guard down? I was still very much that girl...with him.

There was a knock at the door. I turned that way. "Come in."

Treesha was back. "Have you decided on dinner?"

"I have," Ashton spoke up. "She's going to have the Margherita pizza and I'll have the mussels in red sauce." He stood from the bed to hand Treesha the menu and quickly yanked it back. "You know what?" Treesha froze, face hardening. "I'll have the shrimp scampi, too." He pulled out his wallet and handed her what looked like a business card.

"What's this?" Treesha asked, examining it.

"A membership card," he explained.

"Is it going to give a damn discount?"

As Ashton resumed his seat on the bed, he answered, "No. But it'll pay the full tab, and tip adequately."

CHAPTER SIXTEEN

Tori

"**R**eady?" he asked over my head.

Clutching my mug of hot nighttime tea, I peered up at Ashton confused. "For what?"

"A story of discovery."

I had no clue what he meant by that. Two hours later, we were in my bed with me nestled to his side. Just Ashton's scent alone soothed and aroused me. It was weird. Before the food arrived, Ashton had showered, so his cologne was faint and at this point, his natural oils had lulled me to a relaxed state. He'd worked in bed after we'd eaten in the same spot, and I simply relaxed into the pillows and his taut side, actively ignoring Deon's calls and texts—along with everyone else's. I was still bruised by my "discovery" earlier and plain ol' jet-lagged.

"I guess." As long as he didn't move or decide to leave, he could do whatever he wanted.

"Good!" He brought his tumbler to his lips for a sip. "Sooo... "He took in a deep breath. "we all had plans for after *BSU*, my crew and me. Aivery and I planned ours in our junior year. In particular, I was going to the *League* without a doubt and my pseudo-girlfriend at that time was supposed to follow me and remotely work for her father's peanut farm as soon as she got settled. Of course..." He glanced down at me. "that was until I learned about her losing her virginity to a guy who was an active nemesis to me."

Pettiford...

"And that led us into a series of events, including me falling head over heels for a particular tomboy who hated all humans, but somehow tolerated me enough to get her hooks into me. It was so bad, I invited her to spend the summer with me."

With tensing limbs, I blurted, "Who? Not me!"

Calmly, Ashton nodded. "In *Macen Beach*, on spring break, I asked if you had summer plans. When you said no, I begged you not to make any. I couldn't make any definitive plans at the time because I hadn't been drafted and, therefore, didn't know where I'd land. But I damn sure wasn't ready to let you go, so all the plans I'd made the year before were to be damned."

My heart ripped. I vaguely recalled him asking me that in *Macen Beach*. All I could recall was a sad Ashton. He didn't tell me why and with Aivery and their crew in the house, I didn't have time to pry it out of Ashton. So, his story of discovery, so far, was just that.

"Anyway," he continued. "Let's fast forward to after being told about my shoulder and knees, and being cut from the *Kings* before I even got started. My mother and grandmother sought out the best specialists in the country, and I landed back in Jersey. Healing and repair was a multi-year process with the screws and tearing that had happened. So that meant surviving time in between surgeries and physical therapy. In other words, I was bruised and heartbroken. I thought losing the *League* was the totality of my heartbreak at the time.

"My mother pushed me to talk to someone. Eventually, I did. I was diagnosed with major depression and prescribed medication. So down, I began taking them and saw they made me feel worse. My mother had me stop. In her wisdom, she knew the diagnosis was temporary and not a disorder like some suffer from. And when Ms. Wanda puts her foot down, it's law." He shrugged. "But she kept taking me to a therapist to talk. It was useless, but created a pattern for me and got me out of the house. Uncle June would take me, help me with my crutches and shit. We'd smoke an L right after a session and then go back to my mother's place and eat up a bunch of food. I knew what he was doing. I'd lost a lot of weight and, in his mind, he was fattening me back up."

"How're your uncle and cousin?" I asked. "I can't remember your cousin's name."

"Boobee? They're good. Still around. Happy as hell that I'm back."

"Back from where?"

"I'm getting to that, Nabby-girl," he breathed out as though irritated.

"Okay!" I hissed, nestling deeper into his side. "My bad."

"Okay. So, after I'd reached a particular milestone in healing, which was the end of my surgery cycles, I was no longer tied to the NY tri-state area. That's when Aivery's aggressions kicked in. I guess I didn't mention she'd been staying with me at my mother's place practically full-time. She hated it there—hated it here. My mother's apartment was a culture shock for a southern belle like her, and the metropolitan was too much for her, too. So, after my final check-up with the specialist, she hit me with the news over dinner. She said she was ready to go home and she wanted me to come, too...permanently. You have to remember, I was basically a zombie of myself. I felt nothing but the injuries I was still recovering from and the huge black hole inside my chest.

"My response to her was I'd think about—no. I actually said I'd talk to my mother, which I thought would be an obvious deterrent because everyone knew Ms. Wanda didn't play when it came to me those days, understanding how vulnerable I was. Plus, I was high at the time, thanks to big June. To my surprise, when Aivery brought it to my mom's attention the next day, she agreed. The only caveat was that it should have been viewed as a temporary move. When she put it that way, something inside told me it was the least I could give Aivery. The girl had been there for me day in and day out, while trying to learn her pops' business to one day work alongside him, and eventually take over.

"A few days later, I was in Texas. A few months later, we were engaged. I know this sounds hella weak, but I gave into that, too. Aivery had tried to tread lightly for months about us resuming our plans to get married. So when she cried one night after we'd had dinner with her family and father's associates, about how she felt inadequate for not being married or engaged at twenty-three, I gave in. We were married six months after the engagement."

"That was fast," I noted, lost in this story already: half angry and half sad.

"It was. When you come from Aivery's pedigree, your church and banquet hall has been selected for years. The guestlist takes little time, and money is no object. My grandmother understood that, too. So she practically put in place the list for my side of the family and flew everyone in, but not before Aivery and I flew out to take pictures at a European ice cream parlor named *Pozzetto*."

"*Pozzetto*? I've had their *glace* before. It's pretty good."

"Yeah," he breathed, rubbing the spot between his bottom lip and chin with his finger as he gazed out of the window into the night sky. "Well, I hate that shit. It was flown in for the engagement party—oh, and that was the theme. Everything Aivery wanted, she got. Every damn thing." He shook his head. "The pomp and circumstance were for and all about her. Lucky for me, I was able to afford to fly my family back and forth. If not, I would have likely stood alone. The

Coopers practically paid for the entire million-dollar engagement and wedding ordeal without me, which was fine, because it was planned without me.

"They made it a concentrated mission for months; all the while, I swam in that dark hole. So, before I knew it, I was a married man, and Aivery was an ecstatic woman. That was until a friend of mine arranged for me to visit a hero of mine I'd forgotten all about."

"Who?"

"Who?" He peered down at me.

"Who was your friend? Did you keep in touch with Al and Dre?"

"Sparingly. My friend was an old business associate of my father's. He attended my wedding and noticed something was off, which was weird because I never knew he'd paid me much attention. He was not a relative. And my relatives attributed my moods to my diagnosis and tried to hold on to faith that I'd snap out of it, so when Azmir reached out a few weeks after my wedding, wanting to meet and told me he was bringing a friend, I was shocked as hell."

I only knew one person by that name. "Jacobs?"

"The one and only."

"I didn't know you knew him," I whispered in shock.

"I know. And I didn't have the balls to burst your bubble when we met for the first time about me taking over the S.I. article." Ashton kissed my forehead, expressing pity for me. I refused to let him see how embarrassed I was, thinking I was showing him how "important" I'd become since *Blakewood* that day. "Anyway... We meet, the three of us."

"Who was the third person?"

"Tyler Thomas." *Oh...* "And they began sharing about their journeys into manhood, as it related to their successful careers. I now realize they thought I was stuck in life from being derailed from the *League*. They knew I wasn't an average kid. The men were versed with my heritage of the *B-Way Burger* corporation. It was something, by this time, my grandmother, Jimmy—and even the current co-owner, Lawrence Briggs—had been imploring me to get into, similar to Aivery's obligation to her father's business. The pressure was on, but I was lost in the laps of that black hole. I told them just as I told my grandmother, Jimmy, and Briggs: I wasn't ready.

"In all their wisdom, Jacobs and Tyler went a different route with me. They challenged me to explore who I was now that being an athlete was in my rearview mirror. Thomas recommended I talk to a more engaging therapist than I had back at home. He said I needed help to shape my perception of life so I could begin to experience optimism again. Thomas said without it, I couldn't explore who I was as a man and, therefore, latch onto a meaningful career. He said the professional was expensive and remotely located, but would be a worthwhile investment. So..." He let go of a deep breath. "The zombie in me obeyed, just as I'd obeyed my mother in her lead into my journey of repairing my shoulder and knees. And just as I'd obeyed Aivery's emotional pleas of needing to be married.

"Therapy that time turned out to be impactful. The diagnosis was more specific and the scope more intense. Her focus for me was on hope and inspiration. After a few sessions, we were able to see that obviously the quick and unexpected change of my career choice had set off my depression, but also that I hadn't dealt with the tragic death of my cousin, Brick. When she was able to illuminate that fact, it took just a few weeks to earn my trust. I was eventually able to tell her more. Talking about the manner in which I processed my cousin's death led me to make mention of an energy I'd suppressed for some time at that point."

When his eyes found mine, I asked, "Who?"

"One KaToria McNabb." My eyes went wild. *Me?* "She was then able to explain how you were a part of the trauma of my senior year in college. I'd lost the last thing that had inspired hope. Tori, that shit flipped the light switch on for me. It was when I'd begun climbing out of the hole. Don't get me wrong: it wasn't just you. It wasn't even about you, but it was about learning me. It was about accepting how fragile I was. When you're young, you feel you're impenetrable and even invincible when you have the privilege I was born into. It made me learn how to protect myself, how to honor myself. I was more than a ball player."

Again, he peered my way and I saw the raw emotion in his eyes. I understood what the revelation meant to him, even if I didn't feel it myself.

"I started realizing my other strengths. So, two months after starting this intense therapy journey, I'd begun speaking to and had even traveled with Thomas. I knew almost right away what I wanted to do with myself. I wanted to explore people, regions, cultures, and conflict. I read a lot and wrote plenty. I became a student of the globe. It was a heady milestone I'd reached mentally, spiritually—because my therapist addressed that, too—and emotionally. After two-plus years of being in that black hole, I began to feel close to the guy I used to be."

Ashton took a deep breath, almost in a fortifying manner. "That was until I was reminded of how shrewd Aivery was, how manipulating. She announced to the dinner table consisting of her parents, sister, sister's children, and her sister's new boyfriend that she was pregnant."

With my gaze inside my mug, softly, I nodded.

The twins...

"I'd been traveling with Thomas and conferencing in private with my therapist, totally distracted from her. One thing to be noted about my depression is, it didn't fuck with my libido as much as I'd been told it did others with my level of grief. I still fucked Aivery. It may not have been as often as I once enjoyed fucking, it may not have been my once typical reach of explorative fucking—Aivery preferred the traditional variety. But we'd engage, and I'd even give her the parody of lovemaking when she expressed needing it. However, she'd been on birth control and I'd stopped using condoms after we were engaged."

"Why did it take so long?"

"Because of Pettiford."

"You held onto their relationship?" I never knew if they'd slept together at *BSU*.

"Yes, and no. My mother pressed charges on my behalf for Pettiford using a bat. It was a sucker move, and he was not defending himself when he got it. We're from Newark: we know the rules of war engagement. Not that I needed to, but I agreed with her. I was just too fucked up with my injuries and shit to give the lawyers the energy my mother was able to. But just as I had money, so did the Pettifords. Benjamin's father has been Aivery's father's right hand in business for over twenty years. He had legal guns, too. They tried to negotiate his 'punishment' out of court and we wouldn't have it. His family even sent him away from home—from Aivery—to placate us. We weren't beat for it. It took up until we'd gotten engaged for his sentencing."

Oh my, god...

"What did he get?"

"Punk ass five-year sentence, of which he did about three and a half. It hurt him and his family, though. Pettiford, like me, was born to wealth and influence. He's never paid a consequence in his life and wasn't built for prison. Unlike me, he didn't have family on both sides, with one being able to coach you for prison life. Anyway, he did the time. I found a letter Aivery had written him just before she put it in the envelope. That *bi*—" Ashton caught himself. "She really considered him a friend during that whole debacle. Even apologized for things being as they were. Apologized."

I shook my head, remembering that reckless Aivery.

"And this was before the girls?"

"Yeah. It was right after we'd gotten married. But fast forward mere months later, I'd just come back from a Middle Eastern tour with Thomas for a story he was breaking when she hit me with the news she was pregnant. I asked her how, seeing she'd been on birth control. She told me with a straight face that she stopped just before the wedding day. So all that time, she'd been plotting to get pregnant."

I could feel him tense around me. "Tori, I'm embarrassed by the anger I still feel surrounding my babies' conception. Maybe it was the therapy working and allowing me to feel feelings again, or maybe it was the ability Aivery had to really anger and betray me at the same goddamn time, just as she did when telling me she'd lost her virginity to Pettiford in our junior year at college. I don't know, but I damn near hated her for that."

I tried to understand. "But you stayed married to her."

"As millions do and have done since the practice of marriage. She was pregnant, and I was in the process of an awakening on several levels. Aivery went on with her pregnancy, and I continued with my therapy and progression of learning who I was as a man. I was still distant in many ways in general, but I was improving."

"Were you still sleeping with her?"

"When I needed to." His eyes grew when reading the doubt in mine. "Tori, at that time, the damage was done. She was pregnant. I was still a man, and until you, I never cheated on Aivery. There was nothing romantic about our relationship or marriage, but it was functional."

"You think she was happy?"

His eyes narrowed as they swept against the ceiling. "That's a good question. I don't know."

"She won...in my eyes. She won. She got you. She took you back from the diseased girl on campus and married you...had your babies. That's what my sulking has been about all day. But now that you've explained your time with her, I see why you shouldn't envy people or think they're better off without you. I really thought—the very few times I allowed my mind to venture—that you may have possibly married, which meant she won."

His arm tightened around me. "Maybe she did, maybe she didn't. But I sure as hell did not. The best things coming out of my union with Aivery were my girls. Because of her constant presence during my lowest moment in life, I played along with her every design of her dream world. I didn't get a say in the engagement announcement, the wedding, when we bought a home to live in or the one to vacation to. But when it came to naming my girls, I asserted my voice. Girls are different from boys. They're more likely to be influenced by their mothers. If I could make them namesakes of women who I believed embodied strength, courage, and wisdom, things I wanted them to have, I would. And I did.

"I named my babies, as sick as it was. But I have no remorse. They're my gifts and became my easy inspirations from the first ultrasound I'd seen. We learned in utero one, Maurie, would have Down syndrome. Aivery, predictably, took it hard. My tarrying numbness to life helped shield me from the disappointment in that. I just wanted them alive and healthy. When they were born, my life was irrevocably changed. They were perfect, including Maurie. The week after their births, I agreed to come aboard at *B-Way Burger*. Legacy was happening all around me with the Coopers and their farming business. We lived minutes from them, and Aivery worked for her father. I couldn't waste my legacy away. My girls were a part of another heritage they needed to know. At that time, I'd begun being mentored under Thomas. I took a few online journalism courses, but that wouldn't pay the bills, only feed my soul."

"You finally took over," I noted out loud.

"I came aboard and was groomed for a year or so. Worked hard to really learn the industry, traveling back and forth from Texas. When Aivery died, I stayed in our home for a couple of years, understanding my girls had bonded with the Coopers, but eventually, I recognized the signs of unhappiness. My babies were young and would adapt. I, on the other hand, was a full adult and needed peace of mind *for them*."

"Wow!" I was amazed. "That sounds good. So bold and unapologetic."

Ashton nodded. "Therapy really helped me, I have to say. It brought me back to myself. And I brought my Black ass, along with my babies, back to the East Coast. The Coopers weren't happy, but I couldn't dwell on it. Even let Aivery's sister, her new husband, and children live in the house for pennies. I was done."

"And now you're here. In my bed."

"And now I'm Tori McNabb's boyfriend," he agreed. "And I'm going to be here. I don't know how this will work, but I'm prepared to sacrifice my most valuable asset to see if you and I have that promising thing I should have pursued years ago instead of letting my ego make the call."

His is most valuable asset was his time.

"What about your daughters? I don't think Maggie likes me. And I don't think it's fair to shove me down their throats. I have a history with their mother."

"I understand," he agreed with grave confidence while nodding. "We'll go slow on them both. I honestly don't get Maggie's hang-up. She's a huge fan."

"She's also a spitting image of her mother." My voice was apologetic; haunting, too.

"Some say she is. To me, she's my Margaret, my loving protector. I'll work on her."

"Work on her, work on me, work..."

"Yup. And workout. I have no idea how I'm going to make this shit happen, but I will." He took me at the chin. "I just need you to be here with me. To want it as much as I do. Let's be reckless with our hope. Let's try. If it doesn't work, we could at least say we tried as adults."

Biting my lip, afraid out of my mind, I nodded in agreement. "I want to try, too."

We still weren't in the clear. Ashton and I still had to unravel who we were as adults and if we made sense for each other. I also wasn't ready to tell him about Bobby. Learning Maggie and Maurie existed further complicated my role in his life back then.

"Good." He kissed my lips. "Are you ahead of your calendar yet?"

I shook my head. "Renata still controls it. I do know I have an obligatory event with Deon tomorrow in New York."

"Well, I'll have my assistant contact Renata to try and sync our schedules. I'll try to spend as many nights here as you and I can stand, but I'll be out before sunrise to make it home to see the girls off for school. I have to be there in the evenings for them, too. But I'd like to court you. So even if that means having lunch together or catching a movie or going away on a weekend I can manage a sitter, I'm in."

love belvin

Ashton

"Here she is," Boobee called out teasingly.

Keyonna walked into the bar with the new *Louis Vuitton* bag I bought her around her shoulder and chest as well as the *Asè Garb* sneakers. Rarely did I see her wear the expensive shit she had. Maybe it was a female thing, but the girl had more shit than she wore.

She pouted playfully. "Why don't I get invited for drinks?"

"Because you ain't grown," June adamantly proclaimed.

She rolled her eyes while gathering her arms around him at the bar. "We'll see how grown I am the next time I tell Nish you ain't have a whole damn bag of *Jolly Ranchers* while I'm taking you to the doctor."

He fingered her head affectionately. "Fuckin' lil' snitch."

Keyonna kissed him. "Yup. Play with me." She moved on to hug Boobee, too. "Hey, Santa!"

"Don't play with me, Key," Boobee warned. "You ain't too big to get yo ass whooped, you heard?"

"You'd have to catch me first." She winked, on her way to me over in a booth.

We all clowned Boobee about his gray beard. He went aggressively gray about eight years ago. His face was damn near white at this point. Aging could be unkind.

"Hey." She leaned onto the partition of the booth. "I see you brought your office to the bar."

I snorted, going for my drink. I'd been here at Boobee's bar in Maplewood for a few hours. I'd come here during the weekday when I needed a relaxed office view. I helped him get the place up and started about five years ago. It was a modest size and not much to manage with a reliable staff. June came here often to just chill. It was his way of getting out of the house, claiming Nisha drove him crazy there. They'd sit at the bar, watching the news and their phones, and I'd work in between our chopping it up. A few hours ago, his bartenders helped decorate the place for the Halloween special they had happening tonight. This was mostly how I spent time with my uncle and cousin, due to my impossible schedule.

"I did." I placed the glass down. "I asked you to drop by because I need to kick it with you about something." I gestured to the bench across from me. "Have a seat, princess."

Keyonna eyed me warily, but obeyed, sliding inside of the booth. "Something doesn't feel right."

"There's nothing wrong. I just need to share something with you."

"What?"

"Tori."

"Tori McNabb?"

"That would be the Tori."

"What about her."

"We're sort of dating." I didn't know the lingo kids her age spoke. I also didn't know what in the hell to call what Tori and I had been pursuing.

Keyonna's face tightened. "What you mean 'dating?' You don't

303

date. Do you even know how to take someone out to the movies? Anything other than dinner? And even so, what's the purpose? You don't...'date,' sir."

My head seesawed as I thought of a response. "I guess I kinda do now." I pursed my lips.

This was harder than I thought. Keyonna was protectively attached to me, it was so bad it drove an insecurity.

"You 'bout to have a rich step auntie-mommy!" Boobee teased her, to my dismay.

Keyonna tossed him a glare. This wasn't a joke.

"Hang on!" Keyonna's torso twisted in the booth. "You told them before me?"

"I'd just told them today. I'm telling those closest to me. I wanted you to hear it from me."

"Who the hell else would I have heard it from?"

"Maggie," I answered.

Keyonna sucked in a breath. "She knows before me?"

"It's a long story." I scratched through my beard for my cheek. "The girls found out yesterday, along with my moms. Everyone was surprised, including Tori. Baby girl, I swear, I'm telling you right away. Yesterday was one of putting out fires at work and in my home."

For a spell, she didn't speak. Her eyes bounced all around. "She's engaged. The Deon Johnson guy."

I nodded, taking in a deep breath. "It's complicated, which is why I'm telling only those closest to me."

Her eyes narrowed. "So, the most eligible bachelor I know is a jumpoff? A side nigga?"

"Whoa!" Boobee leaped around in his chair.

"Easy, young lady," June warned. "Fuck Johnson and his pussy ass. If that young lady wanna be with my nephew, she gone be with my neph. Anybody with a problem could come meet the hammer." June lifted his arms to gesture a shotgun, his favorite toy. "You feel me?"

"Peel 'em back." Boobee threw up his set using his fingers.

"Your gangsta family can't fuck with the media, especially bloggers like *Spilling That Hot Tea*. You know that, right?"

I couldn't respond to any gang threats or that of media and blogs. Instead, I reached over my paperwork strewn across the table for her hand. "Which is why discretion is key."

"Tori McNabb, though?" she asked in disbelief. "All because y'all went to school together then bumped into each other for the *S.I.* project?"

"Oh, nah!" Boobee spoke up, unusually chatty. "It goes deeper than that. She came to your pops' funeral."

"Oh, my god," she murmured. "You know, know Tori McNabb."

Hesitantly, I nodded. Of course, I didn't tell Keyonna the real deal about my knowing Tori. I kept it PG by sharing we were fellow-*Panthers* and competitive as hell, although we weren't in the same sport.

"I do, baby girl, and I'd like for you to get to know her, too."

Her eyes widened. "I met her."

I shook my head. "Technically, you haven't. You met a nemesis of your dear old uncle's, who thought you were one of my toys. Tori and I, as you know, weren't in a good place in *Kamigu*. We've talked a lot since then and—"

"Just talked?"

I reclined in my seat. "That's not a line we're going to cross, Keyonna."

Her eyes fell in shame. "I'm sorry, Uncle Ash," she murmured quickly.

I understood the shock of it all. I also understood Keyonna's attachment to me and why it would concern her to see me take on a relationship with a woman in earnest. When I was fucked up in Texas, I still provided monthly for Keyonna to Precious from my trust. It was enough for her expenses and some for her mother, too. But Keyonna needed more than that. Keyonna needed a father. And with me going through my *League* then marriage shit, June in and out

305

of the streets, and Boobee just not being built to take her on the way she needed, Keyonna was neglected.

Beyond that, the girl took a special liking to me since she was small. So when I moved to Texas, she'd want to visit. Of course, I'd let her when she could, but then there was Aivery. Aivery was cold toward Keyonna, similar to how she was with Keyonna's father. Aivery didn't want her around, and although Keyonna was young, she felt it. I'd never left Keyonna on Aivery or alone with her. Precious threatened to whoop Aivery's ass one year, it was so bad. But I did what I could to keep a bridge between the two of us. Things improved once I got my shit together. Unfortunately, it was at the time when I was having children of my own.

Having the girls helped Keyonna a lot. She took to them right away, and Aivery tolerated it, not interfering when Keyonna visited. When Aivery passed away, Keyonna's stays were extended and my babies loved it; I loved it. So, Keyonna's hesitation to the news of Tori and me was peppered by the insecurity of sharing me with a woman who didn't accept her.

I took her at the hand again. "No one will ever come between us. No one ever has. I've explained to you, I wasn't myself with Aivery. My injury and losing the *League*...me having to take on my father's legacy, and some other shit all fucked with my head for years back then." I wouldn't explain Tori's contribution. That was too intimate for Keyonna. Plus, I had no idea if the shit with Tori and me would actually work. "But you, me, Maggie, and Maurie, we're a team that cannot and will never be broken. Right?"

Keyonna's mouth twisted as her eyes fell again.

"Girl, you know your uncle Ashton ain't never leaving your big ass head side!" Boobee interjected. "So knock it the hell off. We a unit up in this bitch. Feel me?"

Keyonna's heavy eyes rolled from him to me. Finally, she nodded. "Okay. I know," she hissed. "But please don't tell me Julio knew before me, too." She pouted. "He thinks he's family, but we're blood!"

Shaking my head, I rolled my eyes toward the ceiling. "I got a project for you."

Her eyes went wild and Keyonna inclined toward the table. "Another one? We're not quite done with Auntie Wanda's birthday party—*wait!* Does it have to do with Tori?"

I chuckled. "Maybe. I want to find a wintery location. Maybe a cabin, but something with snow, village-feels, and isolation."

"Why not your place in Vail?"

I turned up my nose, shaking my head. That was Aivery's place I wasted my money on. "Let's try something without sour memories."

She winked. "I got you."

"Y'all mind giving us a minute?" Deon asked Renata and the hair and makeup artist, Roxy, who ShawnNicole sent with me to the *Victoria's Secret* fundraising event.

We'd just pulled up to my apartment building, done with the evening. Thankfully.

"Sure." Roxy went for the door, scooting across the bench.

Paying me a final gaze, Renata followed suit. They closed the door and hurried inside the lobby. Finally, my eyes returned to Deon. He was truly a handsome guy: warm nutmeg skin, mismatched-sized lips which I found adorable on him, fiery chestnut irises, and dark curly hair. He was tall and thick, huskier than Ashton, but still fit. I guessed I hadn't been the only one finding him attractive. Nothing about him felt exclusive to me now.

"I know I got us into this situation, T, by not cleaning up my shit when I proposed to you," he began, using his hands to communicate. "But you know we happened kind of fast. It was like from the first conversation on a date, I knew you were special and for me. I still do." Still feeling the effects of my Tokyo trip, I had no energy for this dance. So, I waited for him to say whatever it was he had to say. "I just feel like..." He rolodexed his fingers.

"Deon, just say it." The hour wasn't late, but I was ready to go.

"Damn, T!" His eyes rolled to the blackened window. "I just thought that you'd be more understanding. I thought you understood how this celebrity shit worked and were willing to lock it down with me. I just feel like we ain't even say 'I do' and already you letting some nobody come between us. You ain't willing to fight for us." His brown irises landed on me again. "I'm just saying I'm disappointed you're deadin' us before we can get started. Love don't work like that. When you in love with someone, you accept their flaws and weaknesses and help them be better. I thought we had something real. This don't feel like that. This feels superficial."

He took a deep breath before continuing, and all I could think was how happy I was that we'd taken off the makeup from our costumes because I wouldn't be able to sit in dignity and listen to the cries of a fuck boy dressed as Batman.

"I'm just disappointed is all." He shrugged. "This ain't what real commitment is like." He pouted. Actually. Pouted.

I shook my head, unimpressed. "Deon, love and true commitment aren't about excusing someone's betrayal of you. It's not allowing yourself to be put in danger—your health."

"C'mon, T! You know I would never put your health at risk."

"I would prefer your pledge to never cheat."

"Yeah, but we were in love, T," he returned after a beat. "You know it and I know it. Love ain't this."

Cheating is wrong, and will never be right. But the biggest conflict is when you fall in love with someone who isn't yours. You said people fall in and out of love every day, and that most of it is bullshit...being more about passion and temporary emotions. But when the person you're cheating with is worth a commitment and sacrifice, and when you're prepared in your heart and mind to walk through the fire of the mess, it might be something real after all.

Ashton's words from his kitchen yesterday flew to mind. I was that woman for him; the woman Deon was telling me the pregnant girl from California wasn't for him. Then the craziest revelation hit again. Maybe I wasn't just a random "whore" Ashton cheated on Aivery with all those years ago. What if he'd reciprocated the feelings I had for him but was too young and inarticulate to share?

I felt the false lashes I kept on after having my makeup removed slap together. I really needed to go process this repeating theory.

Scooting over toward the door, I shared, "Cheating is wrong, and will never be right. People fall in and out of love every day, and—as you proved to me—most of it is bullshit." Deon looked at me as though I was crazy. I was. Those words were completely stolen, but I'd given him enough of my attention. It was time for me to feel the feels I never allowed myself to. "I'll see you for the next event we have to do as a fake couple."

After closing the door, I skipped inside my building and click-clacked my way to the waiting elevator. The trip up to my apartment seemed to have gone too fast as I checked my phone for a text from Ashton. Denying myself, I decided not to bother him. When I made it to my apartment, I saw Renata left the door unlocked and headed straight for my bedroom, where I stripped, pulled my hair up, and showered. So many thoughts running through my mind: the what ifs and why nots. The thoughts followed me out of the shower and into brushing my teeth.

When I dumped myself naked in bed, I told my mind to shut down with all the noise of yesteryear. Ashton was here now, and so was I. I still felt things for him I never had for any guy in my life. He was right. We could give us a try, finally, and if it didn't work out, it didn't work out.

God, let us work this time...

309

CHAPTER SEVENTEEN

Tori

I sighed, looking away from my phone next to me on the bed as I flipped through channels. It was close to eleven at night and it only vibrated for humans I had no interest in. My chest ached from burning knowledge I wanted to share.

Should I call Raj?

No. He'll say I'm being extra...

Brielle?

Nah. She wouldn't understand. She's on a strike from men...

Elle would pick up.

Then she'll see how weak you are...

I could only call Ashton but was sure he was likely doing something with the girls. *Ashton's a dad.* No matter how unfair a part of that felt, I was happy for him. I wanted that for myself. Only had, had a flash of it, and craved it all over again.

Bobby...

A pang ran through my belly over that. Just when I was feeling optimistic, doubt felt like acid in my stomach.

The sound of the door unlatching had my head swinging to my right. I thought it was Treesha coming in to share her red velvet cake. But he was even sweeter. His tall frame eased inside, closing the door behind himself. His all-black sweat suit with the hoodie covering all but his beard made Ashton look more youthful than he did in his *B-Way Burger* suits. I watched as he pulled his *Asè Garb* man purse from over his shoulders and tossed it onto the sofa. Next, he pulled the hoodie from his torso while kicking off his sneakers. His sweat pants hung low, exposing the band of his boxer briefs, and those revealed the swollenness of his oblique muscles that got me each time.

Then he approached the bed mutedly, his eyes dark and heavy. Ashton climbed the bed, planting his palms on either side of me and reached for my mouth, covering the shadows from the television. His lips were soft and cool, but his tongue warm and hungry as he kissed me. I inclined into his mesmerizing scent, forgetting to cover my naked breasts. I didn't care. I officially wanted nothing between my boyfriend and me. His skin, my skin; his heart against my own.

His mouth released me and slid between my throbbing tits and down my stomach, making me lay back. Ashton peeled the comforter from around my lap and down to my knees until he lifted them in the air. He captured my heel with his teeth, scraping it with soft bites.

"Mmmmm..." I moaned, eyes fluttering closed.

He ran his fingers down the center of my slit, his thumb pressing into my sensitive clit. He used his mouth to nibble from my ankle, down my thigh, creating a trail until his lips met mine between my legs. My back arched, welcoming the pleasure. Deon rarely went down on me. I never pressed him because the few times he did when we began having sex, it wasn't good.

It was never this...

This was...service to my "oasis." It was admiration, reverence,

311

and...dedication with every flick of his tongue. My hands went to his thickly carpeted, wavy hair, feeling like silk on the pads of my fingers. This wasn't just nostalgia. It wasn't a pleasure once known. It was my reality. My favorite lover had returned to me. What had I done for God to grant me this chance again? This time I'd be vocal. No more muteness for me.

Ashton licked against me with swift pressure. My thighs contracted and head rolled side to side. My groin twisted, lifting higher and higher. His big hands rubbed the sensitive area between my belly and thighs soothingly while the cool autumn chill licked my hard nipples.

"Ohhhhh!" I cried. "*Ashton...*"

An orgasm wracked my body. My hips vibrated in the air, over the mattress as Ashton ate me with steadfast dedication. As I came, my mind didn't empty as it typically did, but I was shot into orbit mentally and emotionally. This man made me feel things when he tended to my body that were far more than physical.

When my mewls calmed, Ashton slowed into tender kisses. His beard tickled my inner-thighs and my heart swelled in my chest even more as my fingers dug into his scalp. My spine arched again when his cool breath hit my soaked pussy and wet thighs.

Ashton pushed up from the mattress and sauntered into the bathroom. I heard the water run for some time while I caught my breath. My body still tingled, but my heart throbbed, it was so full and ready to burst. When he came back out into the bedroom, he carried a washcloth and took to cleaning me with care. I was confused, but lay in bed while he went back into the bathroom and returned a second time with a warm cloth to remove the soap. When Ashton came out of the bathroom the next time, he peeled out of his sweats and climbed into bed. He leaned over to kiss my forehead, affording me the scent of his minty breath.

Then he pulled me into his warm body, a swathe of manly fragranced heat around my needy frame.

"Night, Nabby-girl," he murmured throatily.

Night? Night!

"I was in love with you," blurted from the pit of my belly. Ashton's body steeled into a tense rock around me, matching the erection he'd brought into the bed. My throat burned. "At *BSU*. I was in love with you. You were the first person I actually loved since..." I thought of Ragee, but NeNe was born after I'd met him. "Since my cousin, Treesha, had a baby. I loved *and* was in love with you, and didn't know it. I was young and confused about my sexuality because of my childhood assaults. So when I met you and began feeling these things *and* experiencing sex, it was too much for me."

Completely exhausted, I stopped. A burgeoning sense of relief washed over me, and now I wanted to sleep. I turned over in his arm and reached for the remote to power off the television. Within seconds, I was dozing.

November

"Of you, your last defeated opponent said she learned how to box with her heart from watching you in her amateur days. She said, watching *The Banger* on tape while training is less scary than watching her in the ring when trying fruitlessly to beat her." Ebonee put the index card down on her desk and regarded me. "That's a lot coming from someone who's just beat your ass in front of a million people." When the audience fell into laughter, she asked them, "Wouldn't you say? I mean, I was at the fight, three rows back, and practically felt the impact from *The Banger*'s blows!" The audience went up again with cheers and clapping as the host turned back to me. "Tori, Monica *"Four Leaf Clover"* O'Connor is much younger than you, but I knew was shaking in her boots when attempting your title back in September. What do you have to say about that?"

I chuckled, making a silly face at the audience. "Nah. I'm just kidding." They laughed even harder. "What I will say about O'Connor is I did feel her heart in that ring. She emitted an energy of being in the moment and trying to absorb to win. She's a student of the art, and because of that, she'll continue to excel in boxing. And trust me, if she wasn't a formidable opponent, I wouldn't have decided on her to fight."

The responsive audience began a round of applause. Ebonee Williams, a former attorney, was a popular night show host in Canada. As a Black woman, she was a rare force in television, some argued the most popular Black face in nighttime hosting since Arsenio Hall. She was the around-the-way girl who could hold court even with the British monarchy. She'd been at it for about ten years and had continually balanced out her guests and topics with Black culture as much as she did popular culture. It was truly an honor to be a guest here again.

"Well, that's mighty professional of you, and I know you've got to go." Ebonee's eyes narrowed with mischief. She was a beautiful, caramel-skinned woman in her late thirties. The type of features and accomplishments I would despise and automatically reject and judge, feeling inferior to. That was until my days at *Blakewood*. Ashton. *Did I just speak his name mentally without cringing?* Boy, had things changed for me. "But before you do, I have to ask you about your personal life."

Although I didn't find anything funny about the mention of my hella-complicated personal life, I laughed. "Okay."

Ebonee's energy was that contagious, I couldn't help myself.

"We know you're retired and will soon be married to *League* phenom, Deon Johnson—" The audience's applause rained over her voice. "Yup. Yup." Ebonee nodded. "What type of wife do you think you'll be?"

"Hmmmmm..." Good question. "A committed and dedicated one. A supportive one is my goal."

"Interesting," Ebonee noted. "So long as you didn't say a jabbing wife, I think it's safe to say you'll be okay." I laughed with the audience at that, eventually shaking my head when she threw a few air punches. "Last one! Last one. You and Deon don't have a date yet."

I shook my head. "We don't."

"Well, do you, at least, have a vision for what *season* of bride you may want to be, and will Ragee or Brielle sing you down the aisle?"

I laughed along with the audience. "Your last question was three."

"Well, technically two because both Ragee and Brielle are your besties, so they can roll together."

I chuckled more. "Well, I see myself as an outdoor bride." The crowd cheered and I bobbed my head up and down. "Yeah. And as for who will sing, I'm not sure if I have a choice. Dude sings waking up in the morning and falling asleep at night." I threw Ebonee an exasperated expression.

She shook her head. "I know very little about the R&B crooner, but one thing I am very convinced of is him falling into bed and making a noise that may not be quite as melodic as it was before he got married." She turned to the audience, who'd just exploded and laughter. "Have you guys seen his new album cover—have you heard his last two albums? I'm surprised he doesn't have a factory of babies by now!" I found that so funny, I had to cover my face, which egged the crowd on even more. "I think it would be sweet. Like really sweet of him."

"And bossy, yeah."

They laughed.

"But that's best friends, right," she asked. "I mean, weren't you bossy at his wedding, wanting it perfect?"

"Ummmm... No!" Because I wasn't invited to his sham of a wedding.

I cussed him out so bad for that for months. Even once I met and fell in love with Wynter, I didn't let up on Raj. It took some time for me to get over him not cluing me in on Mike Brown's stupid idea. Thank God, it ended up working in Raj and Wynter's favor.

"So, if he comes to yours being bossy, that's when you'll be the jabbing bride." Again, I laughed with the audience as Ebonee turned to the cued camera, fighting for a blank expression as she announced, "Well, folks, that's my time with the undisputed, heavyweight champion of the world, Tori *The Banger* McNabb!" The audience exploded with applause. Ebonee stood, reaching for me, and I offered her my hand. "When we return, I'll announce the winner of last week's bake-off challenge!"

As the band played the outro music, Ebonee pointed to a couple of waiting photographers behind the big video cameras, prompting me to pose. Fluidly, I raised my fists in the air, giving the typical fighter pose as the cameras flashed.

"Thanks, Tori!" Ebonee turned to hug me. "You did amazing, as usual!"

Returning her embrace, I replied, "Thanks for having me again."

When we broke apart, her makeup artist and producers were behind, vying for her attention. There was another producer waiting for me just off the stage.

"We love you, Tori!" a few shouted from the audience as I walked behind the curtain. In motion, I waved and blew kisses.

My feet were on fire, yet I walked so no one knew. Drea wanted me to wear the latest *Bottega Venetta* sandals they sent over for me. The problem was, they accidentally sent the wrong size. When Drea notified the company of the problem, they immediately shipped my correct size, but it was too late for today's appearance. So, here I was, taking obligatory pictures with the producers and staff backstage with burning feet. Nonetheless, I smiled and posed through it all until the last one. Renata was there waiting and guided me back to my dressing room.

Drea and her team were there as well as ShawnNicole and her assistant. When we walked into the room, they were packing up their things.

"You did great, girl!" ShawnNicole praised, doing a celebratory two-step.

"Yes, you did!" Drea agreed. "And I was so happy with the way you maintained your posture, showing off all of your ensemble!"

Brielle had actually taught me that a few years back. No one had poise like that woman. She was a human barbie doll, nimble and proper.

"Yes, girl!" ShawnNicole rasped as she fingered my curls. "Let's go out and celebrate. Montreal has this cute pub with some banging ass fried shrimp. *Oh!* And Lord and his wife are in town."

My eyes grew big and a cheesy smile did, too. "I can't. We have a flight to catch like...soon."

"Sho' do," Renata confirmed, pulling out my clothes I'd wear to the airport.

"What?" Drea's face was screwed.

"Hey," I turned to their crew. "You guys mind giving us a moment in private?"

"Sure."

"You got it."

"I've gotta hit the bathroom anyway."

They cleared the room almost right away as I sat down to take off the sandals. Straining, I began, "Listen, this is not easy to share, but must be done."

"Oh, god!" Drea dropped herself into the director's chair in front of the vanity.

"No." I shook my head, handing Renata the shoes. "It's not bad. At least not for you—for me either, I guess." Frustrated, I shook my head as I started to strip out of the pant suit. "Let me just start. It's something we're keeping under wraps for rather legal reasons, but Deon and I are done."

"Oh, my fawkin' gawd." ShawnNicole held a curling iron to her mouth, eyes wide.

"Long story I don't want to get into, but I have to mention that before sharing this. I've got a boyfriend."

"The hell, Tori!" Drea cried.

I rolled my eyes as I pushed the dress pants down my legs. "Yeah. Messy, but that's our little history, I guess."

"Whose?" ShawnNicole demanded.

"Ashton Spencer," Renata blurted. She was usually a fly on the wall, good at not making herself known in the room. But here she was, snickering at my...mess.

"The fuck!" Drea trilled.

Renata couldn't look my way as she handed me a pair of jeans. Rolling my eyes from her, my attention went back to the girls.

"Yes. Ashton," I confirmed. "We've been spending time together since the *Sports Illustrated* piece, and while it was a slow drip, I'm finally caught up on his life since I left *BSU*."

Drea's eye shot over to ShawnNicole as ShawnNicole's met Drea's.

I shook my head, then rolled on the t-shirt Renata handed me. "As much as I want to say Aivery won—the one fear I had and why I never wanted you two to talk about them—I can see how we've all lost in some way: Ashton, Aivery, and me. And I'm sorry about the loss of your friend." My eyes bounced between both of them. "I swear, I'm truly sorry I imposed my rules, forcing you to follow them while you were grieving her. It was wrong of me...immature."

"Yeah, but you didn't know that, Tori," ShawnNicole tried throwing me a bone.

"I didn't know because I've been manipulating our relationship, threatening to end our professional one if you went against my wishes, and friendships don't work that way," I made clear. "I am wrong."

"You didn't know, Tori," Drea pushed.

"Because I was too selfish to even imagine the possibility. I mean, no one would have been able to guess Aivery would pass away, but my fear was the marriage...the kids—" When I saw ShawnNicole gasp, I nodded. "Yup. I know that, too. I met them a week ago. Maggie doesn't like me."

Drea's face tightened. "That's the one who looks just like Aivery?"

I nodded with my eyes to my toes, heart heavy. "My karma probably, but I deserve it."

"Tori—" ShawnNicole tried.

"He's worth it," I needed her to know. "Ashton is worth me dealing with anything connected to Aivery."

"Yo, do you know how crazy this shit sounds?" ShawnNicole dropped herself on the other side of the couch. "This the shit you see in movies. Un-fuckin-believable!"

"I know." I nodded, feeling crazy insecure, seeing it from their perspective. "I'm crazy, right?"

Renata handed me my phone. Ashton had just texted me seconds ago.

Nasty human: *Great job, Nabby-girl. I enjoyed every-thing except for the Johnson mentions. Hurry your ass home!*

See!

Reading his words zapped me back into what felt good to my heart. I wanted Ashton. He'd been in my bed just about every night since I learned of his twins a week ago. The nights he couldn't because of Maurie's ear infection, he arranged for lunch in his office. Ashton was crazy romantic with flowers filling my foyer and cute little notes he'd leave in the morning while I was still asleep, rating my sexual performance. It was fun and meaningful for a woman like me, who clearly still had issues connecting with humans.

"Girl, I'm thirty-four years old and been married and divorced!" Drea's head swung around her shoulders. "Crazy is in. And you know what? If it doesn't work, then you try again with someone better. You're a goddamn millionaire, you'll eventually get someone who deserves you. Do you know how many goofies I filter each year? I ain't judging!" She stood from the chair. "I'm just glad you know about everything and we can be...normal."

"I heard you didn't go to Aivery's funeral." I cleared my throat; the fact was an uncomfortable topic to mention.

Shaking her head, Drea took a deep breath. "I didn't want to be phony. Aivery reached out to me, inviting me to their wedding. This was about two years after we graduated. She never apologized, never asked to talk about where things went wrong. Even the invitation seemed braggy, if that makes sense. I outgrew Aivery and our friendship. So, when she passed, I sent my condolences."

My attention turned to ShawnNicole. "Through you, I heard."

ShawnNicole nodded. "It was sad. Their girls were so small. Karmen and Al were there and took it hard. Aivery and I kept in touch sparingly, but because that's what happens out of college. She went back to Texas after Ashton was done with his surgeries, and I went to Philly for just a few months, then eventually ended up settling in Jersey. When I did speak to Aivery, she seemed so happy, but I never got the impression she was. Plus, I'd heard Ashton was never the same after the fight with Benjamin." She shook her head. "I don't think she made him happy. Ashton changed. A lot."

"I agree," Drea added. "When I've run into him over the years, he's been cool, but...different."

Ashton explained his laps around the black hole. This seemed to be confirmation of that. It wasn't something I cared to discuss with them. Much of it was personal and Ashton's business.

"Well, I just want to apologize again." Now dressed, I stood to leave. "I'm really sorry."

"Awwwwwww, boopee!" ShawnNicole hugged me. "I hope this works. Putting your trust in a man is crazy nowadays, so if this thing works with y'all, crazy done did good!" She laughed.

I hugged Drea next, feeling even more guilt. ShawnNicole knew more than Drea because I'd always viewed Drea as Aivery's girl. Yeah, I knew they weren't in touch, but that was how I'd met Drea: as Aivery's friend. I held it against her all these years.

"Man, I'm sorry, Drea."

"*Mmmmhmmm*," she hummed playfully. "Now, I can sit at the cool kids' table with you."

"I'm going to do better, Drea." I murmured while holding her. "I swear."

"Tori," Renata warned behind me.

"Okay, guys. I gotta go. Food and drinks on me tonight. Send me the bill." I waved back at them while pulling my crossbody over my head.

Renata led us out to the security we traveled with.

Drea called behind me. When I turned to her, she murmured, "If this works and he gives you your first child, Andrea and Andre are beautiful names."

Then ShawnNicole appeared next to her in the doorframe. "Shawn sounds good for a boy, and Nicole is awesome for a girl." She winked.

My belly fluttered.

Babies with Ashton?

It brought to mind him offering to give me one, and I felt butterflies all over again. I winked and smiled just before being pulled in front of one of my security guards.

Babies...with Ashton.

Ashton

"So," Tori's beam was in her eyes as she engaged the twins. "What were you two for Halloween?"

Maurie's face lit up. "I was Willa Lykensen, the werewolf! Daddy let me get the white extensions and wear the makeup, too!"

"Ah, man! I bet you were beautiful!" Tori looked over at me. "Did you take pictures—I mean, of course, you did. I would love to see."

I nodded before forking chicken from my plate.

"And what about you, Maggie?" Tori's beam didn't wane.

Maggie's little eyes slowly rose from her plate, up to Tori, then to my mother at the head of the dining room table. She mumbled, "A witch."

"Oh!" Tori's brows shot into the air. "That's cool. I was a witch a lot in middle school. You can get creative as you want with that."

"Daddy and Glammom don't get dressed up for Halloween," Maurie shared. "Did you get dressed up?"

Tori's eyes skirted over to me. "I sure did."

"Wow! What did you go out as?"

"I was Catwoman this year."

"Adults don't get dressed up for Halloween," Maggie mumbled. "That's childish."

Here she was again, trying my patience.

Before I could say anything, Tori explained, "I did it for work. I had an event to host. It was a fundraiser for young girls in Harlem, wanting to be models. But I've gotten dressed up before to go to Halloween parties." She shrugged. "It's fun."

"Wow!" Maurie commented again, chewing her food. My baby was so good for the soul. "That sounds fun, Tori. Maggie was supposed to be you again this year, but she changed her mind. She wanted to be a witch. Glammom had some stuff here to help her."

I sighed internally, not wanting Tori to know about that. She was speechless, her regard going between my mother and Maggie. Maggie would glance up from her plate, intermittently gazing at my mom and me, but refused to acknowledge Tori. It bothered me because we all knew how much she admired Tori, but now that she had her in the flesh, Maggie chose to be rude.

Tori cleared her throat. "I'm sorry you changed your mind, Maggie. I would have loved to have seen you. You're a very pretty girl and would have looked great in shorts and boxing sneakers."

"Hers are purple and black, just like yours on TV," Maurie wouldn't stop.

"Maurie!" Maggie hissed. "She doesn't need to know all of that."

"I don't mind!" rushed out of Tori's mouth. "Again, I think you'll rock it."

"She did. Last year!" Maurie explained. "Maggie had the big gloves and shoes—"

"Maurie!" Maggie shouted.

"Now, that's enough, Maggie." My mother finally intervened. "And all there is, is love and respect at this table, young lady."

Maggie's eyes rolled apologetically. "Sorry, Glammom."

This was Tori's first dinner with us. I was proud of her attempt to get Maggie to warm to her.

"Grandma called us, Daddy. She said she miss us," Maurie shared.

"Yeah." Maggie finished the last of her food. "She said we're going to have fun when we come down this year. We get to pick the turkey. Are you coming again, Daddy?"

"Baby, I told you last year would be the last time I'd come. You should celebrate with your grandparents without me always hanging around."

"And what about Mommy's birthday?" Maggie was sure to look at Tori.

This year, Aivery's birthday fell on the Saturday after Thanksgiving. Each year, the Coopers remembered Aivery on her birthday with a small gathering with the girls. They always requested the twins once we moved, and would even work around their school schedule. This year, the girls would spend Aivery's birthday with the Coopers because of when the turkey holiday fell. They'd be in Texas the entire weekend.

"I haven't forgotten." I nodded. "You girls have been to Texas without Daddy."

Maggie pouted. "And what are you going to do?" Again, her glower was focused on Tori.

"You forget I have a birthday, too?"

"You're going to be by yourself?" Maurie's eyes burst wide.

I couldn't help turning my attention to Tori. "I hope not."

"Are you going to marry her?" Maggie asked, yanking my heart from my chest.

Tori quickly grabbed her water.

Before I could answer, my mother spoke up. "Maurie, I see you didn't touch that salad."

Maurie shook her head with pouted lips. "It's too crunchy, Glammom."

"That's alright. I see you tried with the shredded carrots and cheese." My mother gave her an encouraging nod.

Because of her condition, Maurie struggled with food texture issues. She'd been improving on coarse textures, but preferred softer foods for her palate.

"Great job, Maurie," I followed up with. "Daddy's proud of you for trying." I winked. Her spirited smile melted my heart each time. *Damn*... I loved her soul. "Maggie," I called over to my angry daughter. "I see you enjoyed the lasagna tonight."

"Yeah," she sighed. "It was good." Even moping, Margaret was a beauty to behold.

"Oh, yeah? What did you like about it?" Tori asked, neck extended in anticipation.

Maggie shrugged, rubbing her eye, "My dad put less of that ricotta cheese in it—or maybe it was just more cheesy..." She shrugged again, avoiding contact with Tori. "It was just good tonight. He did a good job."

Tori turned to me with a haughty, yet goofy grin. Lasagna wasn't high up on Maggie's favorite food list. She ate it, but never requested it.

"Maggie, baby, Ms. Tori made the lasagna tonight. Your daddy made the salad and bread."

That's when her little eyes rolled up to Tori and narrowed. My baby pretended to gag and rubbed her belly.

She turned to my mother. "Glammom, I don't feel very well. I think I'm going to be sick."

My mother's head popped back and bounced. "Margaret Aivery Spencer!"

Maggie's lashes clapped. "May I be excused?"

"You better!" My mother pointed toward the door. "No dessert for you either."

Maggie drug her little body from the chair and paid me a last dejected gaze. I struggled for a stony veneer. "We'll be having a sour conversation before bed."

Her pout extended as she grabbed her plate, turned, and took off.

"Alright, young lady." My mother huffed before standing. "Let's go check out this tea party you've got set up in your room before Glammom goes. I've gotta stop by Aunt Tabitha's house for some sister time."

Maurie picked up her plate and followed my mother out. Taking in a deep breath, Tori turned to me.

"Has she said why she doesn't like me?" Her expression wasn't much different from Maggie's.

I shook my head. "I don't think I've asked. Maggie's a sweet kid. She's experienced so much change in the past few years. This is one of them."

"My karma."

"What do you mean?"

"Her not liking me. Her looking so much like her mother. She even sounds like Aivery. I feel like I'm back at *BSU* all over again, only this time, I'm pandering. This time, I want to be liked. I want to fit in. But it's my karma. I knew you and Aivery were the real deal and I wanted you anyway. I wanted with you what she had in you. So, now that I have the opportunity, here's yet another obstacle. And guess what?" She reclined in the chair. "It's Aivery's baby girl. Beautiful, clearly smart and articulate...privileged beyond what I could understand at Maggie's age. And she's telling my big, thirty-one-year-old, rich self I don't fit in."

I pulled her chair next to mine, scraping the floor along the way. Her body was limp when I pulled her into me.

"Maggie's never seen me with a woman, much less into one."

Tori peered up at me. "She doesn't know you're into me. She just sees me around."

"Just like at school, you have no idea how crazy I am over you—and so quickly."

"It's kind of hard when your child makes me feel like I'm encroaching."

"I feel that way sometimes, too."

She looked up again with confusion in her eyes. "How?"

"I feel like an interloper around your cousins. I'm not quite sure if I'm ready to meet your friends because to everyone else but me, you belong to him."

"Deon? I don't belong to Deon. My circle knows that."

"Doesn't feel like it when I hear him being asked about in your interviews. When I have to see you out with him for the next few months. That shit's hard for me to look at, no matter how much I know what's between us."

Searching my eyes, she murmured, "Now, you're walking in my *BSU* shoes."

I considered that for a second. "Wow!" I whispered. "Is this what it felt like? Because when I was with you, I was with you whether

Aivery was around or not. I played a role for what I thought was the greater good."

"Touché," she replied so softly. That shit hit like a ton of bricks, making me turn my head away to process it. "I'm not with Deon. My cousins know about my history with you, which is why they're so protective. It's not the same as being bullied."

It was my turn to reply, "Touché." I sat in that for a minute. "Salt and pepper."

"Huhn?" She lifted her gaze to me again.

"It's a saying—more like a decree—Brick and I had. We were blood relatives, but were constantly told we were different. He had one lifestyle and I had another, but together, we viewed our kinship differently. Instead of accepted, he was the black sheep and I was the white angel, hence salt and pepper. We agreed to take what they saw and blend it to a new hue."

"A new color?"

"Gray. When we felt that divide among us, one would say 'salt and pepper.' The other would reply 'gray.'"

"So, who's our divide?"

"Whoever or whatever we feel. Tonight, for you, it's my baby, Maggie. Two nights ago, for me, when you were doing the Ebonee Willilams' show, it was Deon and the general public. But when you flew home and crawled into bed on top of me, all I could think was 'gray, bitch.'"

Her eyes flew open. "Bitch?"

I laughed. "Look. You wanna be down or not? That's how it goes. The world is a cold bitch."

The muscles around her eyes softened and she murmured, "I wanna be down with you."

"Which makes you an exceptionally bright woman." I kissed her.

Tori returned the gesture readily, pushing up to meet my mouth. Her tongue pushed through the seam of my lips with hungry desire. Her hand pushed up into my beard as she changed the angle of her

327

face to deepen the kiss. Her strokes were broad and wildly expressive. My dick swelled immediately.

"You bring your overnight bag?" I tried asking around her seductive mouth. She shook her head, breathing heavily. "Why not?"

She pulled back, lazy gaze on me. "I wasn't invited to."

"You're expected to."

Tori's regard swept the room. "I don't think Maggie would agree."

Shit. "Maggie doesn't pay any bills around here."

"Maurie's already seen me naked. I can't be around here traumatizing your daughters."

"I've already told them about the new knock rule."

Tori rolled her eyes. "That's why Maggie hates me. You've drawn the wedge."

I took her at the chin, bringing her face back to me. "No. I drew a boundary, which is necessary."

Then I kissed her again, my mouth trailing to her neck, just beneath her ear. Tori squirmed in her chair. "Ashton," she cried.

A knock across the room had her leap and freeze in the chair. Slowly, my head ascended.

I smiled. "Lori."

"Hey..." Her cheeks burned. "I'm sorry. Something dawned on me as I was about to sort the girls' schoolwork. Did you ever get my time off dates I left on the calendar in the pantry?"

Inhaling deeply to control my fucking swelling dick, I answered, "I haven't, but will be sure to tonight."

"Okay!" She slipped out of the doorway. And just as my attention was returning to a frazzled Tori, Lori slid right back in. "Hi, Tori McNabb, although you're not really here." She winked, giggled, and left out again.

"She's signed an NDA, I assure you."

Tori laughed, reaching for my face with slanted eyes. "Gray, bitch."

CHAPTER EIGHTEEN

Ashton

"Maggie, where's your brown jacket?" I asked, flipping through the spinning rack in their closet.

The girls were playing in their room, waiting to leave. They were rightfully carefree as children, but frustrating for me.

"Which brown jacket, Daddy?"

Which brown jacket?

"The one you begged me for, for a whole week last month! That brown jacket."

"Oh!" *Oh...* "I left it in Lori's car, remember?"

My head dropped and eyes closed. I had a business dinner in less than two hours, and I needed to get the girls off to the airport before then. Trying to calm myself, I sauntered out of their closet.

"Maggie, what did we talk about just last month about responsibilities?"

She glanced up from her device. "That I'm about to be ten and if I want more, I have to be responsible over the things I have now."

"Exactly. So when you beg me for a jacket and get it, I expect you to be responsible with it, which doesn't include forgetting it in the car."

"I'm sorry, Daddy." She tried assuaging me, because for her, it was easy to do but she didn't mean it. My girls simply hated disappointing me. "I can wear my pink one."

"You're going to have to, even though you said it's too girlie."

"I like my pink jacket," Maurie added with a smile.

"You like everything," Maggie grumbled.

"Not nice, Maggie." Maurie frowned.

"It wasn't." I agreed with Maurie. "C'mon, girls. Time to roll. Glammom and Auntie Tabitha are probably at the airport already." And looking forward to their first cocktails. My mom would be escorting the girls to Texas for the holiday weekend and was taking her sister with her as a companion. "Maurie, do you have your *Beats* and charger?"

She smiled. "All in my book bag!"

"Okay." I turned back for the closet and grabbed Maggie's pink jacket. "Here you are, young lady." I found her book bag near her bed and placed the folded jacket inside. "Remember, it's here in case you get cold on the plane."

"Then we can get warm blankies!" Maurie announced, hugging herself.

"Daddy?" Maggie called out near the door.

"Yes, baby."

"Is Tori McNabb your girlfriend?"

"No, my love." I lied because Tori's ass had better been my girlfriend, although she was now in L.A. taping a morning holiday news segment with her fake ass fiancé.

"Because that's the way it seems, and I don't want you to have a girlfriend." She scratched her nose, expressionless.

I brought Maggie's bag over to her. "Girls, Daddy's thirty-four. Do you realize how old that is?"

Maurie laughed. "Yup. Old."

I tried keeping a sober expression. "It is, and on top of that, I have two princesses. I have companies I run, too. Daddies usually have one job and then a few kids with mommies to help in all that. Your dad has far more than the average. I would like to one day have a wife, but will likely start with a girlfriend."

"Tori McNabb?" Maggie needed clarification, it seemed. "Because *TikTok* says she's engaged to that big football player."

Oh, baby, he ain't big at all...

"Tori and I met a long time ago. We were really good friends back then and somehow lost touch with each other. We saw each other for the first time in so many years just a few months ago and decided to hang out again."

"So, she's not cheating on her football guy?"

Shit...

I sat on Maggie's bed, relenting to my messy reality, as Tori would call it. "Can I tell you two something in secret?"

"Yes, Daddy!" Maurie was quick to agree.

Maggie nodded, eager to understand.

"So, yeah. Tori has a guy she told a while ago they could get married. That was before we ran into each other again after that long time of not seeing each other. Well..." I took a deep breath, knowing I was probably fucking this up, but couldn't be an irresponsible dad and ignore it. "I like her...for myself. I don't want her to marry the football guy. And the good thing about being engaged is you're not married, which means you can still change your mind. So, when I spend time with Tori, I try to be cool with her to see if she wants to change her mind."

Maurie sucked in a breath. "To marry you, Daddy?"

Downs syndrome where?

Maurie could be sharp as a tack. I paid a premium for her therapies and tutoring, but the girl was truly a natural marvel.

"No." *Possibly.* "For right now, I just want to keep getting to know her to see if we could be more than friends."

Maurie's eyes shrunk in a smile. "That's nice, Daddy."

"Yeah, but I would also like you to like her, too. She's really cool." When my eyes traveled over to Maggie at the door, she looked away. "Okay. Enough of Dad telling his secrets." I stood. "This is something I don't want shared with anyone. Tori is a famous person and I don't want to hurt her by letting my secret get out. If there's something you don't like about her, you can talk to me. And if you're not comfortable sharing it with me, you can always talk to Glammom, or even Lori. But that's it. We can't talk about Tori to anyone else."

Yup. I'm fucking this up...

I'd never asked my girls to keep a secret for me. I never believed it was healthy to.

"Okay, Daddy." Maurie hugged my leg.

When my attention went to Maggie, her eyes fell and she ambled out of the room.

"And Lord, we bless you for the gift of gathering. Fellowshipping is truly a privilege enriched by those you've handpicked to be in our lives."

Tori gave my hand a tight squeeze. "Amen," she whispered under Ragee's prayer.

Raj continued, "Let our hearts to each other and conduct on each day serve as worship to you. And God, we give thanks for the food that was prepared. Beyond it being nourishment for our bodies, may it add to the fatness of our grateful souls. Bless the gifted hands who prepared it. And may the joy experienced from it be shared by those less fortunate than us on this day. All these blessings we ask in Jesus' holy name. Amen."

All of us around the table echoed, "Amen."

I was one of the last to sit, taken by the sight of the radiant moonlight glistening against the lake. We were eating in a heated greenhouse of sorts with the best autumn view of water and falling leaves. There were pumpkins and haystacks inside and outside the structure and a bountiful feast at the beautifully decorated table. It reminded me of the festive experiences I was robbing my girls of by having them in a NYC apartment.

Shit, I need to touch bases with Jaquana about my own *property...*

It appeared to be a lowkey event with just Ragee, his wife, Wynter, and their boys, Benji, Mathew, and Devon. And then there was Tori and her crew: Renata, Treesha, and me. We began digging in right away.

"Treesh," Raj called out from the top of the table. "I was looking forward to seeing NeNe. I was planning on giving her that spanking in Dominoes."

"She's still talking about when y'all played on Easter. She was like, 'Uncle Raj was mean to me for the first time over that game!' I cracked up!"

"I had to learn when coming into this family, there are no niceties during board games," Wynter added while laughing.

"Yeah. And I'm the king here." Mathew pretended to flex his muscles.

Tori whispered to me while holding a forkful of food to my mouth, "Try the sweet potato soufflé."

I tossed my chin in agreement before allowing her to feed it to me. It was good, though I would have done the dessert rendition, changing the texture for sweet potato. I gave her a nod of approval.

Raj laughed. "She would've been a good distraction from my disappointment."

"What's wrong?" Tori asked.

"You know the Thanksgiving meal and huge giveaway Trent Bailey does every year with the church? Well, Ezra has been recommending it be expanded for years. Now, StrentRo and I had been contemplating doing something similar: him in Newark and me and New Brunswick, which is why Ezra said expand instead of recreating the wheel. We were good with that...TB was good with that. So, TB sends us the paperwork. You know, the mission, budget, the blueprint. StentRo and I had our lawyers look at it and do the preliminary work.

"We were ready to get aboard this year and when TB finally talked to the planner, a chick he's had on board for mad years—like before he got locked up—she said she wanted more money. No problem. Even though Stenton and I both had our own boards set up to engage our respective cities."

"Why you need your own?" Treesha asked. "Sounds like that's stealing ol' girl's thunder."

"Oh, you have to," Tori correctly explained.

"Yeah," Ragee agreed. "You can't go into a random hood saying, I'm gonna do this, that, and the other. You'd get run out before they find out it's of no cost to the community." Raj laughed. "And we were ready. Our boards consisted mostly of people from our cities. All she had to do was to coordinate with them so we could get it poppin' today. Well, this chic waited until two weeks ago to say she was going to charge us five times what she charges TB to do it."

"Oh, wow..." Tori was taken aback.

"Could you believe that?" Raj asked me directly. "Now, I'm sure *B-Way Burger* does charities because when my people did a scope of search, I saw the company. How do you guys do it?"

"Well, we do it as a subsidiary," I explained. "It's marketed as sponsorship for the public eye. My mother started it when I came aboard. She launched it in her hometown of Newark and a few other large cities across the state. After the first year, she wanted to expand. We had the resources, so I told her to go for it as a fulltime employment gig. The problem we incurred wasn't the cost we couldn't afford: it was the time to identify community stakeholders. My mother already had the blueprint. A year after she started, she recruited help, creating a board." My aunt, Tabitha, was the first she brought on once my mother saw she was serious about her sobriety.

"Well, maybe I can jump on with your organization," Raj proposed. "It's not for recognition for me. It's about getting the work done. If it's all legal, I don't mind silent-partnering."

"Fair warning of my mother's sexual harassment-capabilities." I tossed my hand. "You remember her from fight night."

"Oh, yeah! I do now." Raj's eyes grew large. "Man, I was so tight that night because..." His eyes cut over to Tori. "...of all that was going on."

"He knows about Deon," Tori made clear before feeding herself more food. She turned to me and murmured. "I found out the night before the fight."

Damn...

"Anyway." It was clear Ragee didn't want to dwell on it. "My spirit convicted me the next morning. I humbly apologize if I offended you with that energy. It's just..." He pointed toward Tori, who rolled her eyes playfully in the air.

"Just that it's hard protecting the undefeated heavyweight champion," Wynter dutifully finished for him. "These two have the weirdest chemistry." Renata and Treesha agreed with mumbles while eating. "It's so unique, I misread it when I came into the picture. I so thought my husband was crushing on Tori."

"Gross," Tori quickly retorted, having us all laughing, including the boys.

"And little did she know," Raj shared with a dramatic sigh.

Wynter followed up with, "And little did you tell." She added a head bounce. "But even when I was wrong, I never gave Tori bad energy, and it ain't because she could drag me in the ring either."

"Well, I'm a big brother." Raj shrugged. "It's what I do. Deon still can't look me in the eye—" He shook his head. "Anyway, back to today. Not only were StentRo and I salty, TB and his wife, Jade, were, too. Jade called her up—and I lie to you not—told that woman if she finds out she's trying to rip TB off, she betta have that 'Tori *The Banger*' shoulder roll ready!"

As the table went up in laughter, including the boys, Tori bowed her head while shaking it. "That damn Jade!" Her arms shot into the air as she shouted. "I don't know what I'm going to do with her!"

"Nah." Ragee shook his head. "We need to make sure Trent knows what to do with her."

Tori brought the stogie to my mouth from her seat behind me. Her long legs astride me, one curled the other with her foot planted on the lounge chair. I pulled from the cigar at her silent request. We were on the balcony off of the study in Ragee's home, having a cigar with him and his wife.

Dinner was delicious and a far better vibe than I anticipated when Tori asked me to come today. Admittedly, I was hesitant because of the energy the night of the fight. But from the moment I arrived with Tori and her cousins, Ragee and his wife were down to earth and seemingly anticipating my company. I now wondered what Tori had shared about me. There was no mention of Deon or it being strange she'd been spending the holiday with a man who wasn't her fiancé.

We'd been spending so much time together around our hectic schedules that the month of November had sped by within a blink of an eye. Being Tori's "boyfriend" had been somewhat of a challenge for me. Not only was she a busy woman in her post-retirement life, she was also a woman with very few needs. Beyond that, although Tori was wealthy, likely beyond her dreams, she was still a simple woman. She had a mean bag, shoe, and clothing collection, something that according to her, Tori had learned from me in our *BSU* days as well.

And we enjoyed our private time together, sneaking all the time. Creeping was to different degrees when your "girlfriend" was a celebrity who was engaged to another celebrity. This meant, all the restaurants we patronized had to have private dining rooms and, preferably, entrances, too. I'd even played the background to a few of her business meetings when they were video-conferenced, as she did mine. Tori's business portfolio was diverse and growing. She had the *Asè Garb* lingerie line that had sold out in most of their boutiques within just hours. Her sexy and incredibly fit body was on television in commercials, in magazines, online, and on billboards. Imagine me taking a meeting with a tech company about software for employee wellness and having one of its members comment on my "girl-friend's" tits and ass. No? I couldn't either until it happened to me.

She also was working with a cookware company. They initially only wanted Tori to be the face of the new line of products, but she was determined to have her heart in even the design of them. She'd been working with them on the technology of cookware that would be a part of the McNabb brand. Tori gave lots of time to her charity organization as well. She'd had lots of meetings to prepare for the holiday season. She was determined to not have a detail about their activities not approved by her. The woman was shrewd.

Tori's popularity swelled my chest with pride and concerned me at the same damn time. Her work schedule had caused her to miss my mother's birthday party last Saturday. I wanted her on my arm although it was impossible considering our need to keep a low profile with our relationship. Pathetically, I kept looking at the door for a surprise appearance by my girlfriend that never happened. Tori was at a movie premiere in New York City. My feelings for her had been growing exponentially, and to a terrifying rate with each time we'd talk late at night while snuggled into the pillows or making love in the car, clandestinely in the bathroom or kitchen pantry. As a father, I now mastered quickies at home. But sometimes, sex was about more than a mutually gratifying experience.

At times, sex was more emotional for me, involving my

burgeoning ego. Tori did lots of appearances for Thanksgiving and had begun some for Christmas this month. Some of them included Deon. Those two deserved Oscars for how well they pretended to be "together." Deon's small touches and nicknames for her were convincing and telling of his desire for Tori. Tori, on the other hand, behaved as a woman wanting to get along for the greater good. That was to the eye of those of us who knew the real deal. To an unsuspecting eye, Tori was a passive woman in love with a possessive man. So while the month had been filled with learning more about the champ, it also left me trying to determine where I fit in, in her demanding and somewhat public world.

A soft bite on my earlobe tore me from my reverie. "What're you thinking about, Spence?" Tori whispered in my ear playfully. Then she chirped, "Wait. You missing the girls?"

I did, but my heavier thoughts were not on two nine-year-olds running buck wild on a southern ranch estate. I'd spoken with them twice today. Maggie and Maurie both were having a blast with the Coopers. They always did, even if it was at the expense of my being there bored out of my mind. I'd made a good call sending them down instead of going with them this year.

"It's our first Thanksgiving apart, but I think we're all enjoying it."

Her arm around my waist tightened as I sat between her legs. "I'm going to make sure you have a great weekend or else Maggie will really hate me." She turned my head to land a kiss on the side of my mouth.

"Damn!" Ragee maundered. "Y'all in deep, huhn?"

He, ironically, was standing across from us in Wynter's arm as she sat on the ledge of the balcony, both enjoying their own cigars. Though I understood the politics of engaging in a stogie smoke and had done so several times in my adulthood, cigars weren't something I fancied. Apparently, it was a particular pastime for Ragee, considering his cigar room. Nonetheless, he was a *Mauve* man like myself, which was satisfying alone for me.

"Oh, I'm space cadet'in it," I readily assured.

"Daaaaaaaamn!" Ragee whistled.

"The hell, Tori!" Wynter demanded. "The fuck are you doing over there?"

I could feel Tori's cheek on my back and her body spasmed from laughter. She was being shy. My candid answer had surprised her.

"You know..." Tori tried against her laughter. "It's so easy for married folk to get all up in single people's business. I'm tryna get like y'all. Chill!" She couldn't stop with her nervous sniggering.

Cute...

"Get like us how?" Wynter asked.

"Yeah." Ragee's forehead tightened as he smirked. "Married, Tor? You wanna marry Spencer?"

Tori groaned behind me. "You know I want a family, big head. Why are you trying to embarrass me in front of my boyfriend?"

"Awwww! He's her boyfriend, Blue," Ragee teased. "Ain't that cute? You know they met thirteen years ago at *BSU*?"

"At *Blakewood*, yes," Wynter answered. "But damn. That many years ago? Listen, I'm no relationship expert or nothing, but life's too damn short to fuck around with people's souls. If you want to be good to each other, do it. Plus, I still have this dope ass gown I bought with Tori's wedding in mind I need to get into before I blow the hell up."

Ragee rolled his eyes, though Wynter couldn't see it. "Hey, I think we should talk about collaborating, Spencer. Aside from the charity piece, I think Wynter would be great at writing a jingle for *B-Way Burger*. I think y'all owe her that for all the years she OD'd on your doubles with cheese when I met her."

Wynter slapped him on the shoulder.

Chuckling, I agreed, "I'll have my people set up the meeting."

"Are you serious?" Wynter's eyes were wild and slanted from drinking. "Like, just like that?"

"Of course," Tori assured with confidence.

"It's how deals get made every day, B," Ragee explained. "White people been doing it forever."

"I've got to remember I married into a family of bosses." Wynter winked.

"But..." Ragee began, getting our attention before taking a pull of his stogie and blowing it out, "back to y'all. I just wanna say it seems so fast, but I'm happy for you."

"It has happened fast—is happening fast," Tori corrected herself behind me, "but I deserve the rush. Do you know how much praying I've done over the years?"

"Amen," Ragee murmured, nodding his head.

"This guy had me praying like crazy before I even believed in God!" Tori exclaimed, having Wynter and I busting out laughing. "That's how neurotic church boy has always been."

Ragee repeated, without an ounce of offense, "Amen."

"Nah, but really." Tori slowed her own mirth. "Just before we left for training in *Kamigu*, and definitely when I got back, I started realizing I've been looking out for everybody but me. I'd been on pilot mode, making sure everyone's safe and happy: NeNe, Renata, Treesha—hell, even my partners at *L.I.A.* Yeah, they've made me money over the years, but I'd been an easy partner for them, rarely saying no. I need something for me." She kissed the side of my forehead and whispered to me, "You better not mess this up, Spence."

"Hey, Tori!" Renata appeared at the French doors. "Ashton's plane is in the area."

"Oh," Tori chirped. "Let me pee."

That's when it dawned on me I'd left my phone in my jacket pocket inside the house. I should've received notification, too. I stood to let Tori up.

"Everything's in place?" Ragee asked. "I can have Leech pack your luggage on the cart. Are they by the door?"

"Yes," Wynter answered. "I had Ashton's driver put them there when they arrived."

Tori followed Renata into the house, confirming my driver was taking them home when they were ready. That left me and the McKinnons alone on the balcony. Wynter was now wrapped in

Ragee's arm, head on his chest. I had no idea why that made me think of all the gay rumors of him over the years. Back when I'd met Tori, I'd seen Ragee once in passing, but had never gotten those vibes from him. Even when he began to blow up in his singing career years ago, I never picked up any feminine vibes from him. I did believe he was weird as fuck socially. He gave the world very little off stage. Now, having spent time with him in his home, I got the impression he was solid, just not for public consumption. I felt that, which was why dating his friend had been a challenge for me. I'd given up the prospect of fame when my shoulder and knees blew on me.

"Birthday weekend, huhn?" Ragee tossed his chin my way.

"Birthday weekend."

"I remember what happened that first birthday weekend. How you gone top that?" He squeezed Wynter. "Blue, Tori lost her virginity thirteen years ago this Sunday. Why couldn't you wait for me?"

Virginity... Thirteen years ago... Sunday's my birthday—

I cocked my head to the side. "Is there anything she hasn't told you?"

I remembered that shit. Tori wanted to fuck on her birthday, but selfishly, I wanted it as a gift for mine. Plus, I wanted to do the right thing and at least had been officially broken up with Aivery before going there with Tori. I wasn't a total ass about something as sentimental as a girl's first time, even if it didn't seem as such for Tori.

"Yeah." Ragee nodded his head. "It's something I discern, but will let her tell you first."

Wynter's mesmerized eyes swept slowly from her husband and over to me.

Strange humans much?

Tori

He tapped a panel on the wall and the room illuminated a large gym room. The television powered on as I perused the stations around the place. Elliptical, stationary bike, treadmill, bench station, TRX station, a weight rack...the whole shebang.

I turned to Ashton, unable to hide my amazement. "Wow! This is nice, too."

Not wanting to scratch up the rubber flooring with my heels, I toed further into the room, but didn't go too far. The wall on the far opposite of the entrance was a floor-to-ceiling window with a view of a stone fountain and benches outside now covered by snow.

Ashton was still at the door when I turned back to him. "Is that a juice bar?" I referred to the small station beneath the television. "Nice. Maybe a workout before we checkout?"

He nodded. "We've got another room to see. C'mon."

I quickly obeyed. Maybe because I'd been in the market so long for a house, I found exploring this cottage fun. It was my birthday staycation, and a very thoughtful one of Ashton. I enjoyed a tropical climate, but a woodsy, mountainy, cozy winter wonderland had been my favorite setting since... well, since Ashton brought me up to this region on Christmas night years ago.

"This way," Ashton directed, looking delicious as hell in his charcoal wool slacks and black cashmere sweater. I felt shameful for how attracted to this man I'd been. It was something I never allowed myself to admit to when we'd met.

We flew up here to New York from Ragee's estate. He allowed us to be picked up from his runway. Ashton and I landed at a small airport about twenty miles away. I'd been enjoying all the features: high vaulted ceilings, modest-sized but chef-grade kitchen with an open plan, two floors, two-car garage, gym, four bedrooms, and an outdoor Jacuzzi so far.

There was a second floor, split-level style. A set of French-style sliding barn doors opened to a master suite that was bare, yet making a powerful statement of quiet tranquility. Black walnut wood flooring stretched from wall to wall. A huge ceiling fan centered the room. An oversized bed with white, fluffy quilted bedding similar to Ashton's place lay against a wall with a tall leather headboard. There was a dresser, chest of drawers, and a standing mirror. Ashton turned on the lights to a small walk-in closet. The bathroom was next door to it. I ventured inside and peeped the freestanding, acrylic clawfoot tub, doorless shower, and double vanity. A portion of the wall was floor-to-ceiling with an outdoor view. Hanging on the linen closet door were two chenille robes. One with the words *champion human* embroidered on the back, and the other read *healed human*.

"Nabby-girl!" he shouted from the bedroom just as a chill tickled my spine. I walked back out to find him at the patio doors. "Take a look." I stepped into the frigid temperature to find a small balcony with a table for two to the left and a Jacuzzi to the right. "Look up, Nabby-girl." There was gruff to his tone.

Still, my attention lifted to a bed of white flooring all around. Within seconds I spotted it—them. There were small white lights dispersed beneath me. Stars, white lights, and foggy skies. A village. A wintery village was the view.

Stargazed, I whispered, "This is breathtaking, Ashton." When I didn't hear a response seconds later, I turned to him. Ashton's chin was down, wild eyes high and unsettled. My heart melted and sauntered over to him, pulling his hard frame into mine. "Why are you acting like tonight will be our first time?"

"You like it?"

"I love it."

"You sure?"

I laughed, now snuggling into him for needed warmth. "Why are you so nervous about me liking this house?"

"Because it's your birthday weekend and I want you to be happy."

"It's your birthday weekend, too." My smile broadened. "And I think I'm going to make you happy. Just don't tell Maggie how I did it." Giggling, I reached up and kissed his soft lips.

"Hungry?"

"Not yet."

"Go get undressed and return your gazillion texts and alerts. I'm going to get this baby going, gather some snacks, and pop open a bottle of champagne. There's supposed to be a fireworks show starting soon."

Excitement burst in my belly. "Well hurry up then!"

Warm, velvety strokes against my clit had me stirring from sleep. His big hands spreading my thighs, the cool air replacing heat created beneath the fluffy comforter pebbled my nipples. I let a moan release from my throat, the ends of his coarse beard hairs tickling the bottom of my ass cheeks.

Ashton...

I smelled him, felt his generous touch, was tortured by his talented tongue. Ashton was a big presence, a strong energy even as an adult. A little moody, too. Last night, we had a relaxing time in the Jacuzzi outside, listening to Ameerah while sipping champagne well after the fireworks show down in the village had ended. He wasn't cold, just a little off. In my haze of happiness, I ignored it, just happy to be with him. We showered together and fell out the moment our naked bodies hit the bed at close to three in the morning.

And to now wake up to his mouth on me, slurping. His tongue pushed inside of my oasis, brushing against swollen nerves. My back arched when it butterflied against my throbbing clit, his long thumbs flickering over my nipples. I lifted to meet his lashings, then began to swing into them. What a way to be awakened!

"Ashton," I moaned, unable to see anything.

We'd slept with masks under his advisement. The bedroom had no curtains or shades and the sun, he was told by the rental agency, shone brightly in the mornings, reflecting from the snow. And one wall was a floor-to-ceiling window. It was too late to look down at my moody lover now, my groin imploded, melting into a warm, boneless pleasure fest. As my body fell into a fit of spasms, Ashton's grip on my breasts tightened, intensifying my orgasm. The pleasure roll wouldn't stop. My feet heated, the pads of my fingers tingled, and my heart raced out of my chest.

Ashton...

Then everything stopped and his mouth retreated to my thighs. I needed a moment, just one to catch my breath because I wanted him now. He'd awakened more than my mind with his mouth. I wanted him inside of me.

My hands lifted to my face and I peeled the mask from over my eyes. So many blinding features hit me at once. The sun was bright, illuminating the stark white walls of the room and revealing it's massive size. Also, the wintery outdoors seemed to be in the room, minus the frigid temperatures, with the pine trees dusted in snow. There was snow everywhere, even climbing up the glass wall. But inside were balloons—white and gold ones—spelling out *Happy Birthday Tori* across from the bed, in front of the patio doors. Bouquets of floral arrangements were spread beneath the balloons, all over the floor.

When did this happen?

Then there was the hickory-hued god with a bubbled, tatted chest and rolling abs, standing to his knees. His dick springing in the air, thick, throbbing, and with a drop of precum at the swollen head.

"Happy birthday, Nabby-girl," his voice husky and guttural while appraising my open, naked body from top to bottom.

My body was humming from an orgasm mixed with a hungry

need. I bit my lip and tried to hide my face under my up-stretched arms. "Thank you, boyfriend..." I hesitated, then pointed towards his dripping cock hanging in the air. "You gonna make me wait two days for it this year, too?"

Expressionless, Ashton shook his head. "Nah, baby. I'm ready for you now."

Ashton descended upon me, covering my antsy body with his own like a shield. My mouth opened to him the moment his lips neared me and I tasted myself on him. He reached between us to guide himself into me. I gasped in his mouth at the breach. Ashton was thick, filling me each time. I met him mid-thrust, wanting him so bad. It didn't take long for that ache deep within to ignite. With each of his kisses and thrusts, I felt my sex getting wetter and wetter. Arching my back, my tits pushed to his muscular chest, my nipples stimulated by his movements.

And Ashton stroked and stroked as I kept him clamped to my body. His beating heart over mine and his strong arms encapsulating me protectively. It was easy to get lost in time with Ashton inside of me. I was entranced by his slow, long stroke filling me to the hilt then pulling back, dragging against my swollenness, milking me. This was it to me. It was close, personal, unavoidable, scary, and intimate.

I looked into his heavy eyes. "I'm gonna cum."

"Come for me, KaToria," he groaned, eyes closing.

That was my undoing. I planted my feet on the mattress and pelted upward. My stomach muscles tightened as I lifted, meeting his every plunge. His cock thickening inside me, our grunts together turned into helpless moans as I clawed his broad winged-back. Ashton steeled over me, pulsating deep inside my walls. Out of breath, I was spent, desperately wanting to be one with him. I loved when we came together, it made me pretend we were.

Panting over me, Ashton pulled my arm from his back and placed it on the mattress. He then pushed it up under his pillow to the left of me, until the tips of my fingers hit paper. My face tightened and I reached for it. Ashton, exhausted, buried his face in my neck and shoulders. Over his head, I unraveled the tri-folded papers, my eyes quickly scanning the first paragraph.

"Wait," I croaked, slightly confused. "Is this mine?"

"Happy birthday, KaToria," he muttered into my skin. "If you don't like it," he panted. "you can always sell it."

And that's when I figured out why my boyfriend had been so moody since leaving the McKinnons last night.

"Haaappeeeeeee buuurthdaaaay! Happy birthdaaaaay!" Nene twerked as they all sang. "Happy birthday to ya! Happy buurth-daaaaaaaay!" Treesha ended her note with a pose and Renata smiled sweetly.

"Thank y'all for that good ol' Millville rendition!" I placed my palms together in gratitude.

They laughed. My attention went above my screen to Ashton over the stove shirtless, the muscles in his back swollen as his arms flexed at minuscule tasks.

"Are you having a good time?" NeNe asked. "I miss you. I thought we'd be together today, shopping?"

"For me or for you, Ne?" I asked.

"Sharing is caring!" She performed an air hug.

Rolling my eyes playfully, I hummed, "*Mmmmhmmm...*"

"*Are* you having a good time?" Treesha asked. "What y'all doing in upstate?"

"It," I quickly offered, grabbing my latte for a quick sip.

"Ilk!" NeNe cried.

She was at her place and Renata and Treesha were at mine. NeNe was right: this was different for us. We typically spent our birthdays together. I felt bad for my lack of guilt. I was where I belonged.

"Incoming," Ashton announced from behind me as his *iPad* chirped.

"Okay, guys." I pouted to the ladies. "I gotta go. I'm starving."

"Wait!" Renata called out. "What should I do with these flowers Deon sent?"

"Take out any notes and have the concierge pick them up. They can decorate the lobby with them."

"Have you spoken to him today?" NeNe asked.

My eyes trailed up to Ashton, who was talking with someone on his device. "Not yet. Maybe later."

"Okay! Bye, Mr. Good-looking Ashton!" NeNe shouted. That got his attention. "Can't wait to see you again."

"Same here, sweetheart," Ashton replied. "Take care 'till then."

"Don't be flirting with my boyfriend, Ne!"

"Bye!" she returned.

Laughing, my cousins waved. "Have fun. Bye."

The three-way *FaceTime* was over and Ashton was replacing my laptop with his tablet.

My eyes went wild at the face on the other side. "Jimmy!"

"Madame Tori!" he sang, sitting in front of a beautiful painting. "Why, aren't you glowing on this special day!"

"Yeah. It's because I'm speaking to you. You look great, Jimmy."

"Thank you, dear heart, but I doubt that glow has anything to do with me. This old queen can't give you what that shirtless stud has. Even in my youth, I'd be of no use to you." He winked.

And that's how my thirty-second birthday began.

CHAPTER NINETEEN

Tori

"Alright, guys! Hit us if you need anything." Eddie tapped the outside of the car as he laughed. "We'll come do a wellness check in a few hours. I'll call first."

"Sounds good!" Ashton, still laughing himself at the skiing jokes, waved off the security we'd brought up here. The two of them stayed at a rented cottage a quarter of a mile down the mountain. This house —*my* home—was the last one on the road, so presumably, any vehicle traveling up this way had to pass the house they'd been staying at first. Ashton helped me through the heaps of snow to the walkway of the house. My snow boots were cute but not practical for the occasion. "Nabby-girl got on the slopes today!" he praised while holding me at the side and arm. "Who finally got your ass to ski?"

"You mean to try and ski," I corrected. "As you can see, I'm no skier."

"You're right about that!" He laughed.

"I've gone out twice with Elle and Jackson. They own in the Catskills and throw parties there." I left it at that because admitting to him the reason I finally tried was because I regretted not doing it with him my first semester at *BSU* would have been too much. I'd already told him he'd basically given me my whole culture in just a few months of knowing him. I didn't want him to know just how much of a weird human I was. "I have no desire to be as good as her or Jackson, but I'll go out for fun...or to entertain the folks around with my clumsiness."

"You did good, McNabb. At least you tried...even if Eddie almost had a heart attack keeping you upright."

I tried hitting him. "Shut up!"

"C'mon. Let's get you inside. I'll draw a bath and open that *Taylor Fladgate Tawny* port. That'll warm you up."

"Oooh, yeah!" That sounded perfect.

Ashton let us in and I inhaled the woodsy scented heat from the fireplace mixed with the floral aroma from the flowers he'd gotten for my birthday. He was definitely a flower man. They were beautiful, too. As we peeled out of our heavy coats, the unmelodic sounds of alerts and notification of devices grew overwhelming.

"That must be the birthday girl's." Ashton's brows hiked teasingly.

As a parent, he took his phone everywhere. Ashton explained there was rarely an "off the grid" occasion for him. He'd even had pictures taken of himself on the slopes and sent them to the girls while we were out there. He was right: it had to be me. I unplugged from the world, without a second thought, once we left out for the slopes.

After Ashton helped me out of my boots and pants, I toed into the kitchen, loving the heated flooring feature. The amount of notifications was mind-blowing. I could immediately sense something was wrong by seeing Renata, Treesha, NeNe, Elle, Jade, Brielle, and Raj's names in the mix. I'd spoken to them all, with the exception of Elle, before leaving out.

"Everything alright?" Ashton asked from the living room.

"I hope." I chuckled. "Lemme call my 'boss' to confirm."

I decided to *FaceTime* Elle since she'd done the same several times earlier.

"What's going on?" she answered alarmed.

"I could ask you the same. Why are you laying down? You sick?" Her nose was red.

"I'm at the doctor's." Her eyes squinted and lips pursed together. "I'm waiting on the nurse to come back in the room now."

"What's wrong?"

"Been sick for over a week, and I'm sick of it." She shifted, turning over to her side. "Enough about me. Have you heard? Where the hell have you been?"

"It's my birthda—"

"Shit!" she swore, eyes closing to a squeeze. "I forgot, Tori. I'm so sorry! You're out of town," she recalled out loud.

I kept swiping away new calls and alerts as they came through.

"Yes." I smiled proudly. "With my boyfriend. But I saw the *Chanel* you sent over. Guess what I got for my birthday?" Before she could answer, I blurted, "A cottage on an upstate New York mountain! Ha!" I extended my tongue and twerked, though she couldn't see me. "And I got a *Birkiiiiiin*! Oh, and I got—well—I got a lot of stuff. I just thought you'd appreciate those two."

"Dag. He totally outshined the *19* and boots I got you."

"Ohhh! A *Chanel 19*! I hope it's like yours!"

"Tori!" she grunted.

"Yeah?"

"The girl saying she's pregnant by Deon went to the media. *Spilling That Hot Tea* broke the story late this morning. They posted pictures of Deon with her back in March. She came with receipts and says she has a video."

"A video?" *Wow...*

"And according to her, it's damning."

My head snapped back. "Damning how?"

"It's supposed to be of them naked, or almost. Or in bed or something like that—it doesn't matter. Deon and Dawn have paid her the demand to not release it."

"Until she wants more money. This is getting so ghetto to me."

She shook her head, making the simple act appear painful. Elle was really sick. "No. Tomorrow's December, which means you have two and a half months of contractual obligations to get through until we can be done with Deon. He's needed you for this exposure he's been getting, not the other way around. You can announce your breakup a week or two after the Valentine's Day appearances you have booked with him and your name is in the clear. He's the one who will have a baby at the same time, which will explain why you two are no longer together. Yes, tongues will wag at the drama of it all, but you'll be the woman women all around the world can relate to. Deon'll have to figure out his next move to remain relevant. Honestly, from what I hear, by that time, he may not have a job in Connecticut."

I nodded. "Okay."

"Are you sure?"

"I am."

"I'm sorry."

"I am, too. I'm sorry you're working on this while in an exam room, on the table. Feel better. Drinks next week?"

"For sure. I owe you for this birthday mishap." She pouted.

"Technically, you didn't forget. Your gift is at my place."

"Chileee, what's at your place is the impeccable work of a competent assistant. I, on the other hand, have been close-to-death type of sick. Drinks on me next week."

"Ciao, baby!" I smiled before hanging up.

I put the phone down and grabbed my head, listening to its vibrations and chirps. Frustrated, I powered the stupid thing off. Taking a deep breath, I closed my eyes.

"McNabb." His concern wasn't lost in the thickness of his voice.

I turned to him, still crouched over the counter. "Hey."

Ashton walked over to me, his big hand on the small of my back warmed me immediately. "I heard. Keyonna sent me links. I'm sorry."

I cringed, eyes closing and all. *His family knows!*

It was bad enough I missed his mother's birthday party last Saturday. They'd spent months planning the formal event. I would have loved to have been there, but thought it was best not to bail out of my commitment to attend a movie screening for a friend of mine. I didn't feel welcomed by anyone but Ashton. Wanda had been...cool, but I'd been waiting for the shoe to drop with her once she realized her granddaughter would likely hate me for life because her father cheated on her mother with me. Now, they knew I was a fool for being engaged to a man who cheated on me.

"I am, too." I obeyed when he pulled me into his chest. "I can understand if this is messy for you."

"I'm not worried about me. I just wanna make sure you're good."

"This is all messy." I wanted to be with Ashton. All the time. Every day. "If you and I are found out, it can be even messier. You don't deserve that." I couldn't properly articulate my feelings, but they were so strong. I wanted us to work.

"Similar to how I wished back then I could have met you without the expectation of being responsible to my relationship with Aivery. It's hard loving someone in secret."

My head shot up. "*You* loved *me* at *Blakewood?*"

Ashton kissed my head. "How do you think I was able to identify *your* handicap of not using punctuations other than periods? Fast and hard."

My head spun as he walked away.

Taking a sip of champagne while lost in the flames of the fire-place, I hummed. Tomorrow would be our last day here, and I wasn't ready to leave. I had plans for Ashton's birthday I wish I could do here at the cottage. I'd definitely be returning soon. Two days had gone by way too fast.

Last night, after hearing about Deon's drama, Ashton cooked me a delicious birthday dinner with dessert. Then we went back out, touring the area including the village. I loved the shops and the people. Most thought Ashton was my bodyguard along with Eddie and Ralph, Ashton's security. It was hilarious and painfully neces-sary. Earlier today, we went out to a few of the distilleries we visited years ago. This time, I didn't fear being carded. The people were nice and welcoming. I took pictures and requested they not be posted or shared this weekend, until I got out of town tomorrow, something I'd been dreading.

I could spend the rest of the fall and into the winter here...with only Ashton if I could. This was a glimpse of the retirement life I looked forward to when I made the call. Only my plan included a husband and a gut full of a human baking. But leave it to Ashton to distract me with something new.

The chirping of his phone on the coffee table startled me.

"Answer that," he ordered. "It's Keyonna and I don't want to miss her before we go."

He sauntered from the kitchen to the stairway and up to the master suite, adjusting his belt. I could stare at his tall, muscular frame all day. He wore dark dress pants, a simple eggplant collared shirt, and shoes. I wanted to jump him, rip his clothes off, and sit on his face and dick over and over and over until I came over and over and over again, something I did a couple of weeks ago. But I used restraint and answered his phone.

My nerves flared after I tapped to take the call.

"Hey, Keyonna," I greeted when her image appeared.

"Oh! Hi…" Her eyes enlarged. "Oh, my god, Tori…"

"He asked me to answer. He'll be right on. But I'm glad he did because I need to apologize for *Kamigu*."

"It's totally fine." Keyonna was beautiful. I didn't recall much of her features when I met her as a child, but as an adult, she was gorgeous: brown skin, shoulder-length hair, thick eyebrows beautifully arched, cute gap between her two front teeth giving her features added personality.

"It's not. All of that negative energy you got was directed at your uncle. We were immature for that display, and I'm sorry."

"Really." She couldn't stop smiling. "Uncle Ashton told me everything."

Everything?

Everything wasn't what I wanted people to know about me. Ashton knew the old, undeveloped me.

"Okay. Well, I'm looking forward to the opportunity to re-introduce myself to you."

"Tori's ass is just looking for an ally to help win Maggie over." I didn't sense Ashton having come back into the living room.

Keyonna laughed. "I actually spoke to her earlier. I called down there to check in. She whispered into the phone she had to talk to me about something once she got home, and that she couldn't do it while down there." Ashton and Keyonna laughed, Ashton's being more exasperated. "Is she really struggling with dad having a girlfriend?"

"I don't get it," Ashton grumbled from behind me on the couch. I was curled up in a nutmeg, cowl neck sweater dress and tights, waiting to leave for dinner. Ashton suggested we try one of the local restaurants, and I was down. "I truly don't understand what my baby's hang-up is."

"It could be that I'm new. You said you've never introduced them to anyone before me," I added.

Keyonna nodded. "That's true. You know how protective we all are. Aunt Wanda's been lowkey warning us about this for forever now."

I twisted my lips, expressing helplessness as I looked at Ashton over my shoulders. "Well, I'll leave you to him. I'm looking forward to spending time with you. I know you've been busy with school."

"I know. It's been killing me. Can't wait until winter break. *Oooh!*" Her eyes blossomed wide. "Maybe Christmas since you like that winter feel?"

"I don't know," I glanced up to Ashton again. "I got Thanksgiving. We'll see if I'm lucky enough to get Christmas, too."

She laughed as I handed the phone to Ashton.

I glided in the air.

Nestled into his chest, feeling his spiky beard hairs on my forehead as we danced on an old wooden floor in the dining room of a restaurant, I glided in the air. Dinner was delicious, a small Italian menu that was satisfying. We shared our dishes and peeled off nearly two bottles of red wine as the small band of three played in a tight corner. Out of the nine available tables, only four were occupied while we ate. Now, only three remained, including us. Our security ate at the bar, watching whatever sport was on.

After polishing off dessert, Ashton asked for a dance and I couldn't deny him anything. The band mixed Christmas numbers in their act, now playing Vince Guaraldi Trio's *Christmas Time Is Here*. It was magical: the ambiance with candles and white lights; his heat, heartbeat, and scent; and the music. This felt good. So good.

"What are you thinking about?"

"About how life can be so simple if we chose simple." I kept my eyes closed, enjoying letting go.

"How so?"

"I know we were young, but we could have done this so many times over if we'd chosen to be honest with our feelings instead of hurting or neglecting others."

His voice dropped an octave. "You're not about to out us in spite of your public relations team's plan, are you?"

I didn't answer right away. "I'm tempted to."

We swayed, creaking the wood beneath us. It was perfect. Peaceful. The music flowed around us for a while.

"Who did we hurt...neglect?"

"Huhn?"

"You said we could have done this so many times over if we'd chosen to be honest with our feelings instead of hurting or neglecting others."

Oh... "Aivery. We hurt Aivery, and NormaJean felt neglected by you. Also, D.J. Paulie." My eyes blinked open to the cheesy Christmas décor I found adorable. "I saw him the day I left campus. He admitted to really liking me. He'd heard about us like everyone else had. The worst part about seeing him was facing the truth. I kept going out with him, knowing I was in love with you, even if I couldn't articulate it at the time. I hurt that guy."

"I'm sure he got over it. Paulie got gigs as Fergie's deejay then went on to invest in music technology and did well. He's been married three times and now resides in the Virgin Islands, where he owns a shit load of properties. He produces music for a lot of reggae artists." *Oh, wow...* "Enough about Paul's corny ass. Aivery nor NormaJean were victims of our unsuspecting attraction and chemistry. Aivery was going through her growing pains just as much as I was. The difference was she wanted to hold on to me while she explored the possibility of more with Pettiford. And NormaJean was manipulative. We'd been too close for too many years for her not to tell me she still held romantic hopes and feelings for me. Again, no damsels in distress there."

357

I swallowed hard, eyes dilating. "Yeah, but they're both dead now."

"Regretfully, but that mere fact is symbolic for never letting anyone or anything come between us again if this is going to work."

But there was something between us. As we swayed conjoined and effortlessly in the air, in my alcohol-induced state of mind, I knew there was a stone unturned in our proverbial graveyard.

My Bobby...

December

"Holy fuckin' nuts, yo!" Rut screamed loudly, reclining on a stool. "Tori fuckin' McNabb is a *Banger*, for sure! Yoooooo! My sis is the illest bitch around, for real!"

I laughed, flexing my deltoids in the air, even air-kissed them. Leaning against the bar, Ashton laughed, too.

"I'm taking notes, sis!" Parker hi-fived me.

"Yoooooo!" Rut glanced around the suite at *Hotep Black Financial Bank Arena.* "I can't believe this! Who else know this shit? TB know?" He couldn't hide his astonishment.

I nodded. "He was here earlier. Jade was with him."

"Yo, is it even legal for us to be here?" Rut asked. "Now, don't get me wrong, I ain't never fuck with his goofy ass—nobody do, really. But this is some gangsta shit, sis!"

"It's what a champ does for her boo." I shimmied in my seat.

"Her what?" Rut looked at Ashton pointedly. Then he stood and walked over to Ashton, giving him dap, holding him in a hug for an exaggerated period of time. When he released Ashton, he came back and pointed to his wife, Parker. "As much as I love me some Tori, I 'on't think I want you chillin' with her no more." He turned to me. "This is the gulliest shit I ever seen, yo!" His arms lashed in the air. "I'm surprised Eli let you do this?"

My head shot back as my eyes narrowed. "Why wouldn't he? This is business. Eli knows business if he don't know nothing else."

"But daaaaaamn, T!" Rut howled. "He let you buy a suite for a whole ass season for your boyfriend when your fiancé plays for his team? *Daaamn*, T! That's how we stunt on niggas who do us dirty?"

I shrugged. "Hey, it's my boyfriend's birthday. I want it, I got it, I get it."

"That's right!" Parker hi-fived me. I saw Ashton take a call, giving his back to us while walking farther into the suite. "And the most amazing thing about this is her boyfriend can buy this suite for himself. He ain't broke, trying to blackmail nobody over here. He owns *B-Way Burger*, Rutledge. *B-Way Burger!* Bosses only parlay with bosses."

She was referring to Deon's alleged baby's mother who had been extorting him for money. No. Ashton was not a man for the come up. There was no clout chasing here. My money may have been long, but Ashton's was old, and that was a different type of wealth class.

"Yeah." I nodded. "My boyfriend's already paid," I stated cockily, the way Rut and I typically got down.

He was from Trenton, NJ and I'd always felt a kinship to his raw energy. Rut was funny, fun, and extremely smart. He'd come into the *League* already a baby millionaire with a low-ball salary from the *Kings*, but played exceptionally to earn his increase and respect from the organization. His wife, Parker, and I clicked from seeing each at various events for endorsement partners Rut and I shared. She was what his wild boy persona needed. Parker could check Rut and get him in line like no one else. And he needed it.

"Yo," Rut approached me with his hand in the air to dap goodbye. "I gotta go. Gotta get my baby to this OB visit."

I watched Parker rub her expectant belly, pouting playfully. Then my eyes rolled up to Rut. "You really think I'm your nigga, tryna dap me up like I'm a dude!"

"Oh, shit," he snorted. "My bad. You just pulled a real nigga move, my G. I can't help the gangsta vibrations you giving off, making this money move right here."

I shook my head and stood to give him a hug. "Thanks for coming by, Amare."

We'd been here in Connecticut for a few hours. As season suite holders, you were given a festive red carpet welcome ceremony. It was hard trying to figure out what to get Ashton for his birthday today, but I managed. When he woke up this morning, I served him breakfast in bed. I gave him his first gift, which was a *Hublot Classic Fusion* watch. He loved it, as I knew he would. Ashton had a mean car fetish, owning eight luxury vehicles. The only thing second to that was his crazy watch collection.

We talked in bed for a few hours around the birthday calls he received. My heart stumbled a little with jealously when he took the *FaceTime* call with the girls. It was hard spending day and night with him for a few days and then being as quiet as I could to stay out of sight to them. Aivery's girls. It hurt, though I never mentioned it. It was my karma I accepted it, almost right away when I learned about Maggie and Maurie.

After his calls, we lazily showered together. I could tell he wanted me, but couldn't beg him to wait. I didn't want to blow the tricks I had up my sleeves. Kissing and touching all over his body tortured me, but I made it through. We packed up *my* house and left for the airport just after twelve noon to fly here to Connecticut. We had lunch in his new suite where Ashton met the owner, Eli, and his executive staff. Throughout the afternoon, players hand-picked by me visited and welcomed Ashton to the franchise for next season, when the suite would officially be his.

Yeah. Maybe it was cold of me to gift him extravagantly and something so close to my ex, but I didn't care. This was for me. Pleasing Ashton was a personal mission, and I knew the sentimental value the *Connecticut Kings* held to him. He'd lost not only his career, but his passion and genuine love when defending me against his girlfriend at the time. It was the least I could do to bring this love affair full circle.

"Here you go." I felt Rut's hand in the pocket of my blazer. "Yo, you want me to fuck him up?" He whispered to me before I released him. "Just say the word and I got his ass."

"Love you, guy," I murmured back, releasing him. Ashton was back, placing his phone on the bar. "How about you come back next season with your A-game and make this purchase worth it to my man." I lifted a brow in the air, challenging him.

Rut went over and dapped up with Ashton again. "Man, you ain't gotta worry about that. We gone bring the heat, now. Please believe!"

We laughed, expressing our goodbyes. I gave Parker another hug, too, before they left us alone in the suite. I turned to Ashton, who gazed at me with heavy lids and blazing eyes. I returned the sentiment, but I couldn't unleash my sexual desire for him now. I knew what he wanted and needed at this point, and we were on the same page.

He jerked his head, summonsing me. I began my way there and once I was within arm's reach, he yanked me to his tall frame. "You're something fucking else, you know that?" he murmured inches away from my lips.

Ashton may have looked angry, but I could tell from the pace of his heart beating against my upper chest he was happy. "A president's club suite for my favorite CEO."

"You're still learning punctuations, I see. Your boy Johnson ain't gone like this. Bold ass human."

"I don't want any more punctuations with you," I muttered breathlessly.

Ashton's eyes closed. "McNabb," he whined.

"I don't. You may think I had no commas with Deon, and that could be true, but I never felt this before. I told myself I'd grow into it with him. With you, I never had to. I never learned punctuations because I didn't learn them when I learned I had a heart." When he still seemed uneasy about my confession, I reminded him. "You said you don't use punctuations well either."

"I don't. If you'd asked me what I wanted for my birthday, you know what I would have said?"

"Well, it's still your birthday," I reminded him, arched backward in his possessive hold.

"You off birth control."

This time, my eyes closed in frustration. He had a daughter who hated me. How could we have a baby together?

"Let's go, Spence," I murmured. "We have dinner reservations, then we have to get to the hotel suite to wash up then hit the town tonight. I've gotta have you home in the morning for the girls."

"Partying in Connecticut." His face tightened. "You tryna get your fiancé fucked up in his own town? It's bad enough you had his teammates come greet and thank me for investing in their organization." My eyes circled to the birthday balloons all around. We'd celebrated a portion of his birthday at Deon's job. "All these years and I'm still fighting behind you?"

Biting my lip, I nodded. I felt as bad ass as Trent Bailey told me I was earlier this afternoon.

We entered the club from a private, side entrance. Funneling in quickly, I was surrounded by Eddie in front of me, Ralph ahead, and another female security guard we'd picked up for the night with Ashton. We'd finally arrived at the infamous *Arch&Point*, home of the classiest, most skilled female dancers in the North Eastern region of the country and to many of the *Connecticut Kings'* roster. I'd been here a handful of times in the past to celebrate a couple of my athletic peers. Even Brielle had a private birthday party here years ago. Pixie shot a video here months before and invited me on as a cameo.

I'd enjoyed myself at this fine establishment each time. It was clean, professional, yet had an unapologetically lewd culture being played in between the lines of grace and class. It wasn't until my flight home from Canada last month that I considered celebrating a portion of Ashton's birthday here and made a few discreet, investigative calls of inquiry to make it happen. Then came my clever attire. I needed something seductive, appropriate for the establishment, and yet stealthy. I chose a black lace bodysuit, black leather flounce mini skirt with black thigh-high hosiery, and black leather over-the-knee *Saint Laurent* boots. My hair was pushed back into a sleek ponytail, and I wore *Asè Garb* sunglasses with metal tassels hanging from the bottom of the frames, down past my chin, basically masking my face. I didn't know the dancers here and didn't want my identity clear to anyone not in my party.

We were escorted to a private room where the words *exclusively reserved* were on either doors. One was opened for us where Eddie and Ralph stopped just inside and began inspecting the room. I whisked inside, loving when Ashton dramatically brushed against my backside. It was his muted approval. We'd not had sex since the night of my birthday. It was purposeful, and neither of us liked it. But Ashton didn't complain...until we pulled up to the side, curtained off entrance of *Arch&Point*.

When the truck stopped, he growled, "I've been patient, and courteous. When we leave here, those graces will have expired."

A shiver coursed my spine, but I didn't respond. And now we were here, ending his thirty-fifth birthday. I quietly waited until security scanned the room for any electronic devices. I didn't even want the club's normal security's surveillance going. I'd had an agreement of protection for the staff with the club, approved by the staff themselves. I waited with jittery nerves.

"All clear," Ralph announced.

Eddie followed up with, "Clear."

The woman, Nancy, confirmed with a firm nod, then they left the room. Ashton turned to me, flashing his palms to ask *what's next*. I glanced around the room: purple-hued lighting, two poles, two chairs on either side, a small coffee table for drinks, and magically, the music sounded. I moved into his chest so he could hear me.

"I believe your seat is here." I backed him to a specially designed stool with back support.

Ashton sat under a motif of strobe lights highlighting his handsome features. I took a seat across the room, crossing one leg over the other, observing *my work*. I'd bagged a handsome CEO. It was an accomplishment for me. I'd chosen wrong with Deon and before him, I had no interest in men. I used them as public relations pieces while gaining my career. They were faceless men promising me things that didn't matter. Some viewed me as a prize they couldn't match and were good with it. I played the game until I grew into my own needs, which led me to Deon, who wasn't worth my time.

But this...

A waitress in a red satin thong teddy brought in a drink for me. Without giving her too much of my attention, I accepted it, continuing to drink in all of this six-foot, four inches, and two-hundred thirty plus pounds of my work. Ashton regarded me as well, attentive to each sip I took, each leg swing I performed, switching the weight on my hips just to give him an illicit view of my crotch. He was ready. After we left the restaurant for dinner, we returned to the hotel to change and have a few drinks as he made business calls. On the way here, he wasn't expecting the blunt I lit in the back of the truck. But guaranteed the strain of weed would provide the level of uninhibited behavior I wanted for my boyfriend's birthday. We smoked, riding through the city at night with the windows cracked.

Yup. We're ready...

The music changed as the side doors opened, and two women sashayed inside. One tumbled to the floor rhythmically and rolled into a split. The other performed an effortless somersault until she landed directly in front of Ashton. I watched as she restrained his arms at his sides on the chair. His low eyes rolled up to her nude breasts, then back across the room to me as I watched with rapt attention.

The second dancer leaped on the pole, performing a quick spin before flipping directly in front of him. It took seconds for his eyes to grow wild, seconds more, his cheeks lifted in a smile. He recognized her. As the first dancer performed behind Ashton, he caught up with an old associate. After a beat, his slanted eyes raked up to me. Ashton licked his lips, reclining his head back, prepared to enjoy the show.

I drank my cocktail, watching the women with my boyfriend. They wiggled their ass and tits for him and each other. They worked well together, each taking turns creating an illusion of perverse intimacy for just the three of them. And Ashton seemed to be all in, his face turning as they moved, head rolling up when impressed at their skilled sensual acts. But he never forgot about me. Intermittently, those smoldering, low lid eyes would reach me across the room. When they did, I'd swell even more between my legs.

As I watched the trio entertain themselves, I could see Ashton grow in his jeans. It was his cry for me. They may have groped, exposed themselves, and even talked nasty shit to him, but kissing or touching his dick were not permitted. Those acts were reserved for me. My nipples ached, pressing into the lace material of my bodysuit. The strap between my legs grew unbearable against my swelling clit and wet folds. I waited for Ashton's attention and opened my legs to show him the unsnapping of it. When his lips parted and head rolled to the side, the timer was set for their part of the show to end.

It was a fair thirty minutes or so of gymnastic showing of lascivious performances by the ladies I patiently waited through. My drink was long over, glass empty, and sex pulsating. I stood, eyes locked with my boyfriend's. He anticipated me with each step I made to him. Once the dancers were alerted to my presence, they seamlessly parted, giving me room between his wide-spread thighs.

I lifted one cheek. "Say thanks and goodbye."

Ashton's attention dragged down my body and over to the first dancer and gave a nod of appreciation. Then he smiled at the second, "Bye, WetWet. I'm proud of you, girl."

"Love you, Ash!" she returned. "Thanks for always keeping it a buck with me, baby. Happy birthday, sugar!" She stood and kissed the side of his face. Then she slapped my ass before taking off to the two poles in the center of the room. "Get his ass, *Banger!*"

The women began their number there as I squatted between Ashton's long legs and kissed him with a lazy tongue. His felt like smooth velvet against mine. My hands brushed over his rock hard erection as I did. Hungrily, Ashton inclined, reaching down to me. I felt when he tried to engage his hands, but his arms were stuck in the restraints.

I pulled away. "*Shhhhhh...*"

Standing to my feet, I slowly and seductively strutted behind him.

Ashton

As I watched her thick thighs slowly prance behind me, coming into view were WetWet and her dancing companion. They were swinging on the pole, one with her legs and the other her arms. Tori's arms descended from my shoulders to my chest. I was so fucking hard, my dick ached. She reached down while pulling my chin up to meet her mouth. Her first kiss was deliciously slow and sloppy, turning me the fuck on in the worst way. But this time, I was more aggressive, pushing my tongue in her mouth, swiping wildly against hers. I tasted the traces of her citrusy cocktail. Beyond aroused, I growled when she withdrew from me again.

Tori pulled a mask over my eyes, unexpectedly for me. The last thing I saw was the girls coming down from the poles. I felt a small hand on my knee, then another. Long nails trailed up my thighs, nearing my cock. *Shit.* Were we doing this in front of them? Confusion descended upon me. Lips were on my mouth. Her tongue, I recognized. Then hands were at my belt, unfastening the buckle. The button to my jeans was next, then the zipper. Desperate for her touch, I lifted for my jeans and boxers to be pulled down just enough for my dick to spring out of the awful restraints. Soft hands were fisting me, massaging my scrotum. My back jerked at the meticulous touch, tongue lashed faster against hers.

Fuck!

I needed my damn hands to fuck her properly. When she pulled her mouth away, I sighed in frustration. Then when I felt the hot wetness on my dick, I dropped my back against the chair, biting my lips. Whether we had guests or not, I couldn't contain myself. Two days. It had been two long fucking days of not having her. Two days was too long when we spent every waking hour together. The pain of smelling her pussy and not being able to taste it took patience I wasn't sure I was capable of. But finally, I felt her mouth on me tonight. I'd take her any way I could.

Even publicly...

I'd regret it in the morning, but right now, the perfect pressure combo she applied to my shaft and balls stole my dignity. One thing I'd observed since being with Tori again as a full adult was that I didn't feel the remorse I used to when she gave me head. Back then with her, enjoying this act was met with guilt of how she honed her skills. That emotion was faint because it was now hard to see Tori as a victim. She was now a victor; a skilled, consenting aggressor. So using my hips to meet the cadence of her head was not an awful desire, but a frustrating one, considering I couldn't use my hands. Just when I decided to let it go and blow, she withdrew.

A condom was being rolled down my dick. *The fuck...* Then I quickly decided I didn't care. I didn't give a shit if she wanted to go back to them tonight: I just needed her. Fuck condoms, fuck voyeurs, give me KaToria McNabb!

Then she squatted over me. The heat of her body, scent of her sweet breath, and flowery perfume calmed the inner rage just a bit.

"It's eleven fifty-two," Tori whispered into my mouth. "We've got to make this quick if it's your birthday sex." She kissed me, then smoothly withdrew. "Okay, Spence?"

"Can I use my hands for round two?"

She nodded against my head. Then I felt her hand at the base of me, guiding. She lowered herself to take in my head. I sighed of pleasure at her straining. "Round two, three, and four." Her forehead rolled against mine. "I just need to get in round one on your birthday, baby."

Tori flexed her thighs around me, making small thrusts down my cock. My head rolled back at the feel of her throbbing pussy. Tori was so wet, incredibly snug. I leaned away from her, stroking up to meet her plunges. The fucking condom annoyed the shit out of me. I wanted to feel all of her. But I was so damn aroused and Tori's hips were strong, driving my dick to the perfect stroke. Her soft moans and squeezing of my shoulders had me going.

She leaned over and put her mouth against mine. "Eleven fifty-eight." Then she kissed me, her ass moving in fluid motion. It didn't take long before a sheet of heat blanketed my body and goosebumps lifted all over as I let go and let Tori pull my soul from my fucking frame. For seconds long, the music went silent. All I felt were the shakes of her body and flutters from her pulsating walls over me as I shot into her.

The mask was pulled from my eyes. Out of breath, she greeted, "Happy birthday, boyfriend." Her body vibrated over my chest as her legs dangled from the chair.

My attention moved to the back of the room, where it was empty. There wasn't a body in sight.

"Was this a private party?"

Tori giggled, "Sweetie, we will always be a party of just two, like this. Let me get this condom off. I hated having to use it," she panted. "But I didn't want to be messy in here. I'll get your hands out, too. I don't wanna delay round two back at the hotel."

That's when I knew for sure.

I love you...

CHAPTER TWENTY

Ashton

"Done, Nenny!" Maurie announced at my grandmother's table.

"Me, too." Maggie dropped her fork, hopped down from the high wingback chair, and shuffled over to my grandmother at the head of the table for a kiss.

With her shaky arm, Grandmother enclosed Maggie's tiny frame, pulling her into a hug and gentle kiss. "Okay, baby. Go into the court-yard. Take a walk to burn off this hearty meal and maybe Mildred will have home-baked cookies for you before your daddy's ready to leave."

"Okay, Nenny." Maggie swiped an errant curl from her face.

"Okay, Nenny." Maurie hopped down from her chair. "Maggie, let's go get our coats!"

The girls skipped out of the dining room, leaving me alone with my grandmother. She watched after them until they turned the corner.

"Maurie's a dear. So loving," Grandmother complimented. "She's special, that Maggie. Terribly."

"Yeah." I sighed, flapping my tie over my chest and abs. "Special is right. Lately, she's been a special pain in my rear."

"How so, darling."

"She's not been very welcoming of my girlfriend."

"Girlfriend? Ashton Spencer, what's this craziness you speak of?"

I shrugged with my lips lazily. I'd just filled my belly with my grandmother's housekeeper, Mildred's, superb home cooking. The girls and I attended church with my grandmother this morning, something I tried to do at least every other month, sometimes more. All day, I counted down the time when Tori's flight would get in from Atlanta. She'd participated in a weekend retreat with a group of young girls her organization sponsored in that area. I, myself, had just returned from a four-day tour of *B-Way Burger* restaurants in the Midwest to promote our employee support initiative. "I'm in love."

"What?" Her belly bounced at that one syllable. "Ashton Spencer, I've known you for over thirty-five years and have never heard you say you were in love. Not even when you were married— God, rest her soul." She placed her shaky, wrinkled hand to her chest. "Are you joshing me, young man?"

I scratched my chin through my beard. "I am not, grandmother. I've no reason to."

"Then who is she? Am I that out of the loop? I was just with you at Wanda's birthday party. Why did I not meet her that night?"

"Because she was working."

Her chin tucked with disdain. "What type of work does she do?"

"She's actually retired."

Her eyes closed and head swung a little too hard. "Pardon me, Ashton Spencer? How old is she?"

"Thirty-two."

"So how is she retired, sir?"

"She's a boxer, Grandmother. I'm sure you've heard of Tori McNabb?"

"The boxing girl? The one the mens in the church gathered to watch a couple of months ago?"

I half shrugged and nodded. "That would likely be my girlfriend."

"Ashton Spencer!" she warned. "I'm no child. Do not play games with me."

I scoffed. "I'm not, Grandmother. You've actually met Tori before. Almost thirteen years ago, to be exact."

"I've done no such thing!"

Nodding, I chuckled. "You have. She was the young lady you were rude to at my father's place. The Christmas you walked out on me."

She gasped. "The one I caught you with?"

"That would be my girlfriend."

"You said she was a schoolmate. A fellow athlete."

"She was." I opened my palms over the table to express the obvious. "A boxer at *Blakewood*."

"Pardon my language, but that means she was the young girl you were skipping around with when you had a girlfriend, Ashton Spencer."

"Skipping?" I chuckled again. "I guess she would be the one." *Though we did more than skip and were about to do even more had you not walked in on us that evening...*

"Then it stands to reason why my Margaret doesn't take too well to her. She's her mother's child...has her fiery spirit."

My head bobbed, giving her that point. "Possibly, but I'm confident she'll come around. Tori is an amazing woman and a renowned leader and mentor."

"Tuh!" Grandmother spat. "I hope you're not over-exaggerating her reputation. That was not the impression I got from her when I met her."

"She was a kid back then, as was I. What I want to know is if I'll have your blessing when I marry her."

"I think you'd best place your efforts with having your daughter accept who this Tori was to her mother," she chirped.

With purse lips, I nodded. "Duly noted."

I stood and left the room.

Soft knocks at the door roused me from my sleep. With heavy eyes, I glanced around the dark room. The sun wasn't yet up.

"Yeah?" I barked unintentionally, causing Tori to stir above me.

Her breasts shifted on my chest and my side. The doorknob clicked, and my mother peered through.

"It's me, Ashton," she whispered too meekly.

Panic ran through me. "Everything okay?"

"Yes. Come meet me in the kitchen, please." Then she closed the door.

Dazed, my blurred gaze swept the dark room again. I rubbed my tight eyes before snapping into action. Slowly, I pulled myself from underneath Tori's warm cushioned body and shifted out of bed. I grabbed a pair of pajama pants from my drawer, then pushed into my slippers. Before leaving my bedroom, I was sure to close the door tightly. Never did I think I'd be so torn between my fear of my girls finding a naked woman in my bed and having to tell my naked woman she had to wear pajamas in my bed. It was yet another factor I had not worked out.

"What's going on?" I asked as soon as I found my mother preparing a pot of coffee.

My eyes went for the clock on the fridge. It was hardly five in the morning.

"Cousin Evelyn just called. Aunt Allegra passed away."

My eyes bulged. "*How*—what happened? When?"

"Late last night or early this morning, depending on how you look at it. Evelyn called the ambulance last night and they took her to the hospital after reviving her for a short while." My mother kept her hands busy, unable to look at me while telling the story. "Heart attack, they say."

"Damn." I rubbed my face, shocked by this news. My great aunt was an old woman, but that still didn't prepare me for the news of her passing. *Shit...* Mom. I stalked up to her and wrapped my arms around her. "I'm so sorry about this."

She let me hug her. I was somewhat surprised when she grabbed my arm, returning the embrace. I felt when her body spasmed from a silent cry. Mom had always held a softness for her mother's oldest sister. They'd been close since I could remember.

"You know that damn old woman done arranged her funeral already." She sniffled in my arms with her back to me. "Evelyn said the funeral home's coming for her body right now. That lady is—was —so damn persnickety!"

"When do you think her funeral will be?"

"In, at least, two days. She paid for it years ago."

My eyes bulged. "Damn. I've gotta clear my calendar."

When she tapped my arm, mutedly telling me her moment of weakness had passed, I released her.

"You mind if I fly out today?"

"Sure. You know how to charter a flight. Do what you need."

"What about the girls?" She shook her head. "They've got school, but beyond that, I don't think it's good for them to go."

"Yeah," I sighed. "Neither do I." Since Aivery passed, I'd never allowed the girls to go to another funeral. Maggie didn't do well with seeing her mother in a casket, and Maurie, the empath she had always been, became very emotional by her sister's breakdown. The guilt experienced from the day had always stuck with me. I had no idea what to do. It was their mother's funeral, an event that would never reoccur. I couldn't have her children sit that one out. So, since then, and given the fact that my girls had expressed fears of funerals over the years, I didn't want to subject them to any at this time. "But the girls knew Aunt Allegra so well, they have to be told."

"I agree. I can do that," my mother offered.

"We can do it together."

"Hey. Everything okay?" Tori had toed into the kitchen wearing my robe clutched to her chest and mussed hair.

Why must she look fuckable even at this hour?

"Oh," my mother chirped. "Morning, Tori."

I walked up to Tori and pulled her to my chest out of habit. "What's going on?" she inquired softly in my arms.

"My mother's aunt in South Carolina passed away," I murmured over her head. "They were very close."

"I'm so sorry to hear that, Wanda. I really am," Tori expressed, turning toward my mother. "Is there anything I can do?"

"No." My mother exhaled. "I'm gonna arrange to get down there as soon as possible to help however I can. The funeral should be in a day or two."

"Oh, wow." Tori turned to me. "I'm sorry."

I shrugged with my eyebrows. "I'm going to hit up my assistant and clear my schedule for the funeral. I guess I need to find out which day exactly."

"Yeah. I should know the specifics by this afternoon. But what are we going to do with the girls?"

As I inhaled, not exactly having an answer, Tori asked, "They can't get the time off from school?"

"I don't think it's necessary to pull them from school." I scratched my head. "In fact, I think it's best they skip the funeral. They don't do well with them." Then my mind began to go. "I could send them to Texas with the Coopers, but again, I don't want to pull them out of school." Plus, their grandparents would want them for longer than a day or two, and I wasn't having that.

"You could ask them or Sherell?" my mother suggested.

I shook my head. "I don't want to be bothered with her, even if for a few days."

"And Keyonna's—" my mother thought out loud.

"Away with her crew," I answered for her. "And Lori's off this week for finals."

Shit...

"I can watch them." I turned to Tori, finding her arms outstretched, expressing a viable solution.

"Sweetheart, that's unnecessary," I attempted sweetly. "I don't want to impose on you."

"Impose? How?" Her face folded. "I'm your girlfriend who's been 'imposing' on your family from the jump."

"Tori..." I tried.

"Ashton, how long are you going to be away? A week?" she snorted sardonically.

"Less than forty-eight hours, if I can help it."

"I can keep two nine-year-olds for a day and a half, now. Let's not insult me."

"But I know... Maggie..." I lifted my hands, trying to explain.

Closing her eyes, Tori shook her head. "Doesn't like me. Trust me, I know. My karma. But that doesn't mean I can't keep her safe. I've got lots of experience at laying low around people who don't like me. I also have my fair share of experience with NeNe. Maggie'll be with her sister and we'll both be fine. I can keep them at my place, here, or a hotel if that'll make you feel more comfortable."

"They have school," I tried.

"Ashton." Tori dropped her face. "I'm retired with time on my hands: I can get them to school and wherever else they need to be." Her neck twisted. "I'm getting the impression you don't trust me with your girls."

My eyes bulged. "Don't be ridiculous, Tori! Why wouldn't I trust you with my babies?"

She rolled her eyes. "Good, because that wouldn't make much

sense to me considering your wild offer to me in *Saint Justin* and on your birthday last week!"

Offer? What offer—

My tensed shoulders dropped at the memory of proposing to give her a baby, something I was still down for. If I wasn't so stuck on the care of my girls, my dick would be hard at just the thought of spilling my seed inside of Tori. She wanted a family, and I wanted to be the one to give it to her. Me only, and only her.

"Tori," I approached her, but she backed up. "I don't mean to make you feel I don't trust you. Of course, I do. It's just I'm still working on Maggie's attitude around you."

"We'll be fine, Ashton." Tori rolled her eyes while giving me the hand, not wanting to look at me.

Was I being unreasonable here or was she making a big deal out of nothing? I didn't want her upset over something so ridiculous.

Taking a deep breath, I found myself turning to my mother. For what? I had no idea. It was a subconscious act. I didn't expect anything from her. *Or did I?* I didn't know. But when I did, she'd just finished pouring her coffee and lifted the mug from the counter to go.

"Boy, let her keep the girls! She needs to earn Maggie's respect." And she left the kitchen.

Pinching the bridge of my nose, I looked over to Tori, whose head was shaking.

"You want to give me a baby, but don't trust me with the ones you already have? Shame on you, Ashton." Tori was the next woman in my life to leave the room irritated.

Tori

"Goodnight," I whispered at their door.

"Night, Tori," Maurie yawned, turning over in her bed.

I waited a few seconds before prompting, "Goodnight, Maggie."

I'd be damned if she didn't wait until seconds later to grumble, "Good night, Ms. Tori."

Taking a deep breath, I caught my eye roll midair and turned to close the door, leaving just a crack of space. Maggie's rudeness was in her icy veneer. She didn't get fresh with her words, per se. It was her cold regard for me that I refused to let get under my skin. I tried shaking it off as I took off down the hall for Ashton's office.

I picked them up from school today using Ashton's driver, their normal transportation. Instead of taking them straight home, I arranged for a reservation here in the City at the *Melanated Girl Doll House*, a store housing Black dolls of all melanin hues. There, girls could custom make their dolls by choosing their complexion, lip and eye colors, texture of hair, and clothes. The store had a coffee shop and general restaurant to eat with the dolls or while waiting on them to be made. There was also a clothing boutique to purchase outfits and accessories for them, too. It was a Black-owned company I wanted to support and couldn't think of a better way to do it than with Ashton's girls in an attempt to get to know them better, and have them warm up to me as well.

While there earlier, Maurie marveled at the whole experience. She oooh'ed and ahhhh'ed at every turn of the venture, and even opted for two dolls and several outfits and accessories for them. Her features of them were adorable, and I was all in with her creativity. Maggie, on the other hand, had to be pushed by her dad over the phone to loosen up. She ended up with just one doll and no clothing other than the outfit it came with. At close to onehundred-fifty dollars per doll, I didn't complain about saving a few dollars, but it wasn't about the money for Maggie. It was about the control of the vibe. She knew she could kill my joy by simply not giving in to the moment I tried to create. Even without being able to articulate that Maggie knew.

What was most torturous was how adorable she was. The girl was a beauty—inarguably. Truly the spitting image of her mother, I'd get goosebumps seeing her snarl. It was the same expression Aivery gave me when calling me diseased. This was hard. Damn hard. But I was determined to make it work. I was committed to Ashton—addicted to the man, at this point. And his children were a hill I would have to get around.

Lightning caught my attention just as I sat down in his thick leather chair, reclining immediately. The storm outside hadn't let up in hours. Harsh winds, rain, sleet, and even lightning that had just begun less than twenty minutes ago had been what caused Ashton to move his flight plan up earlier. He wanted to beat the storm or else he may not have made it to his great-aunt's wake being held tonight. It was ugly out and weather inconducive to my next task of the night.

My phone rang.

"Yeah."

"She's ready," Renata informed.

"Thanks." I disconnected the call and tapped into my text app for the number Renata had sent earlier.

The line rang and on the third, a soft voice answered, "Hello?"

"Samantha?"

"Tori?"

"Yes. Hi!" I smiled, butterflies erupting in my belly. "It's me."

"Hey! How are you?"

"I'm..." I had no idea why I had to consider that answer, but it was truly an instinctive reflection. My eyes circled his office, images of his journalistic travel spread all over as well as awards and proclamations. Ashton was consistently handsome in all the pictures with nameless faces of significant people in his line of work. This space was Ashton, the journalist's. His scent and spirit were here, too. "... blessed. I'm blessed and grateful."

"I'm glad to hear that. I heard you whooped that Irish girl's ass back in September."

I laughed. "Well, it's the one thing I'm actually good at."

Samantha snickered, too. "I find that hard to believe. I've seen some of your interviews. I know you like to cook, too."

"I do. Thanks for caring enough to watch me."

"Why wouldn't I? I get cool points from my soon to be teen. I even have her telling her friends, 'Hey. My mom used to be room-mates with her in college!' Do you know how hard it is to impress your own twelve-year-old?"

Thanks to Maggie, I have an idea...

"Girl, I can only imagine!" We laughed until that awkward span of silence was realized. "Listen, Samantha..." I took a deep breath. "Thanks for talking with me tonight. The reason for this call feels so selfish, but I'll be honest: my therapist recommended it."

She sighed dramatically, "You have one of those, too? A colleague of mine swears it's been the best thing she's ever done for herself. And my aunt recommended I invest in one, too, but... You know."

"I get it. It could feel like admitting to weakness or inadequacies you don't want to cop to. The secret is, we all have them. I just needed help sorting mine when my career took off. Well, I should have actually done it long before then, but didn't have the resources. It's paid off, that and spiritual mentoring for me."

"Is this KaToria McNabb? The same Tori that struggled stringing two words together to my science crew friends because she hated humans?"

Giggling, I admitted, "That would be the Tori. God!" I shook my head. "That leads me to the purpose of this call. I've been in touch with a few people from *BSU*, and it's forced me to realize how signifi-cantly impactful those few short months had been on my life."

"Really?"

"Really, girl. And when realizing that, I couldn't ignore the one friend I made on that campus so effortlessly. Samantha, I'm sorry for how things ended. I was a dumb kid, trying to survive life and not always figure it out. I didn't know who I was, neither did I know how to value others. I'm sorry if you felt you extended yourself to me in a way I should have reciprocated—"

"Tori, stop. Just stop right there. You forget I was a kid, too. I totally threw a hissy fit instead of being a friend to you. I left you to deal with the wolves alone. Instead of me hearing your side of it and not judging, I let my immature brain tell me you betrayed me. It was wrong, and something I regretted after leaving school. It was me. I was the drama queen. You know I went back, right?"

"You did?"

"Yeah. My mother told me I couldn't quit at the end of the semester. So, she called to arrange for me to finish my last assignments and finals remotely for the professors who were lenient. The ones who weren't made me show up to class. The last week of school, I finally got the nerve to come and apologize. That's when I heard you'd left."

Twisting my mouth, my gaze fell and I nodded mutedly. The pain of twelve years ago felt so damn visceral right now. "I did." A sudden thunder cracked the sky. Involuntarily, I swallowed nervously, recoiling not at the disturbing sound, but the memory of young, muted, and hopeless Tori. "I was in a lot of pain and didn't see a better solution."

"Same. Girl, I was pregnant with no support from the father."

"Dre. How is he? Did he come around?"

"I guess, but only in an obligatory way. My mother called his parents. And being the steadfast Christians they are, they stepped up right away by sending money for my prenatal care. They didn't come to the shower, but coordinated with my mother and practically paid for her whole nursery. They flew in to see her a week after she was born. Dre didn't come for another month. The next time he saw her after that was Easter, then Christmas, then Easter, Christmas and—you get the pattern." She chuckled.

"Has he gotten better?"

"Not really. He's married with other kids and sends for her a couple of times a year. Sometimes, she's invited on their family vacations, sometimes she's not. On paper, Dre's her father; in action, not so much. But we're adjusted. His checks are regular. So..." Her humor was bitter.

It made me wonder about Bobby and how different my experience would have been. If I'd told Ashton, giving his resentment for me at the time, would Rosemary and/or Wanda have been sending checks? Would Bobby have been brought up with Maggie and Maurie, or would he have been an occasional invitation? Aivery would not have accepted my child, and she had the power. Aivery had won. She married and had a family with the only guy I loved.

Another clap of thunder rented the sky and I cleared my throat. "I'm sorry you have to go through that. What's your daughter's name?"

"Emily. She's amazing."

A soft smile cracked on one side of my face. "If she's anything like her mother, I have no doubt she is."

"She's better than me. Smarter, Tori. She's my teacher of life."

"I wish her grandparents and father could experience that."

"She's a tomboy. Like more than you were. I think they believe she may be gay and for that reason alone, they don't take after her much."

"That's *fuc*—messed up."

"It is. And maybe she is, or maybe she isn't. It doesn't matter. She's a beautiful soul, and a gift to me. Do you have any children?"

I nodded slowly, my eyes closing. "I don't." Unfortunately. "As it appears, I can't snag a man to make them with."

"They're not all some say they're cracked up to be." I laughed. Hard. "No. Seriously. I'm a hardworking, single mom. I have a Master's in chemical engineering and own my own home. I even own two timeshares. Did all that on my own, and I'm not overweight. Girl, I attract the biggest fuck boys known to man!"

"Tell me about it." I rolled my eyes. "But I'm glad you have Emily." Like how I wished I still had Bobby. I'd trade the belts, titles, money, fame, and career to struggle to make ends meet for that boy. My joy. My hope.

"And what about you? You seem happy with Deon."

"Deon and I broke up months ago."

She sputtered a breath. "Are you serious? But I just saw you two on that awards show last week..."

I rolled my eyes. "PR. I think the world knows he's a dog. I've been okay with them thinking I don't agree. I've been playing the stupid human. It's the Hollywood way, chile."

Samantha burst into laughter. "Tori!"

"Seriously. I'm good, though. I really am."

"Wait!" she trilled. "Why do I believe you?"

The picture of Ashton and me in *Saint Justin* on the corner of his desk caught my eye. We were on the beach and drunk, taking usies that actually came out cute. I sent him a few pictures I'd taken of us out there once we returned. This was obviously the one he liked enough to get printed and put into a frame.

Shaking my head, I closed my eyes, trying to snap out of it. I had no plans on sharing my world with Samantha, but suddenly, I felt compelled to. "This is going to be wild, but can I tell you something?"

"Sure! I just spilled my guts to you beyond what you've asked," she joked.

"I'm actually seeing someone else. It's been...recent, but real." I bit my tongue.

"Another celebrity?"

"No." I couldn't fight the grin trying to break on my face. Thank god I was alone. My eyes brushed against a few of the many candles he had around the office. It was him, subtle signs of who Ashton still was. Even back to the first night I spent over here. The morning I met the girls, I saw the massive wall fish tank in the living room. It was a feature of his apartment I missed the first night I'd come over for dinner because Ashton didn't show me around. He didn't show me around because I'd have seen evidence of his family, like pictures of girls on the walls, and their paintings from the refrigerator he'd managed to stow before I'd arrived. This had been an unbelievable ride. *So* unbelievable.

"Okay. Now, I'm lost. Who?"

I closed my eyes. "Ashton." They opened again as I braved myself to face my truth. If I was in love with the boy, I was now obsessed with the man. I had to own it. "Ashton Spencer."

"No fucking way, Tori!"

I nodded, "Yup," eyes sweeping his smart and hella cultured office.

"Didn't he marry—"

I squeezed my eyes closed again. "Yup! And had two beautiful girls with her."

"Yeah. Dre mentioned that when Emily's visit came up. He asked to push it back a week because he was going to their wedding. Oh, wait! Didn't Aivery..."

"She passed away." My head kept bobbing at the reality of my love story.

"Holy smokes, Tori! Are you shitting me right now? Are you really with Ashton Spencer, the *B-Way Burger* tycoon?" She gasped loudly into the phone. "Oh, my god, Tori! I'm about to gossip!"

"Please do."

"Doesn't he write deep thinking articles or something like that? Because Lyricah told me she finally had her chance at him a year ago at a brandy distillery conference. He was there researching the company she works for and she had a table at the exhibit. The way she described Ashton was a fine mutherfucker! Even better looking than at *Blakewood*! Lyricah talked about his beard and how he seems more chiseled now than he did as a quarterback. The girl raved about his thick waves and white teeth. Girl, she was beside herself. She said she shot her shot, or however the kids are saying it. But she definitely said she finally had her go at Ashton Spencer."

I sat up in my chair. "Did she now?"

"Yeah, but that doesn't mean anything. Lyricah is a known over-exaggerator. Plus, you said you two started up again a few months ago. Even if it's true, it has no bearing on what you have. The biggest shocker to the campus, learning that you two were creeping back then was that Ashton wasn't the cheating type. No one had ever heard of him cheating on Aivery. I even heard he was faithful to her when they married. Maybe I should have kept it to myself. I just got caught up in my old college life. I hope I didn't upset you." She sounded so apologetic.

"No." I stated simply. "But I'm going to beat his ass when he gets home tomorrow."

"Tori!" Samantha begged. "You better not. Shit! He's going to hate me. That's what I get for having this drink to calm my nerves before your call."

"A drink? For me?"

"Yeah, girl. You *are* Tori McNabb now!" she giggled.

"Samantha, I was Tori McNabb back then."

"And weird, too. I had to prepare for it."

I hung my head, silently laughing. A small knock at the door had my head swinging up.

"I'm scared." Maggie stood, looking smaller than I'd ever seen her. Her shoulders were practically to her ears and she was shivering.

"Samantha, I've got a visitor. I have to go. Thanks so much for taking my call. Now that you have my number, feel free to call again soon."

"So this isn't your burner phone?"

I snorted, waving Maggie over to me. "No. I need one, but wouldn't give you that number if I did."

"Okay. Yes, let's talk more. I don't want to leave on that cheap, gossipy note."

"I'd like that."

"Good. Bye, Tori."

"Bye." I put the phone down, giving Maggie my full attention. "What's wrong?"

Her face was wet, curls fanning her little face. "I keep having bad dreams."

"Bad dreams about what?"

"Nightmares." Her teeth chattered.

"Yes, but about what, sweetie?" She was visibly shaking and I wanted nothing more than to hug her, but I didn't think she'd like that. So I tried to get her to explain her fears instead.

"About everything."

"Like what, though? Maggie, you're shivering. What's going on? What's everything?"

"Chainsaws. I keep seeing them every time I close my eyes."

That's when it dawned on me. "Did you watch that horror movie after your dad said no, Maggie? Your father specifically said no scary movies, and no to that one in particular."

With the saddest eyes, she nodded, admitting her guilt. I had a feeling she did it to spite him and me. I decided to cook when I saw the weather wasn't letting up. My plan was to end our girls' day with dinner at *DiFillippo's*, but I decided to get them home safely instead. I made spaghetti, which included chicken. Maggie picked with her plate while Maurie and I cleaned ours.

Ashton *FaceTime*'d and when he asked her why she wasn't eating, Maggie said the food wasn't good. He didn't fight her, but when she asked to watch a horror flick, he said no, it would give her nightmares. Eventually, we left her alone in the kitchen for me to go over Maurie's homework before shower time. When I returned to check on her, Maggie's plate was cleaned and the last piece of extra chicken was gone. The bones were on her plate. The poor girl was stubbornly starving. She must have watched the movie while her sister was in the shower and I was cleaning the kitchen.

"And then this clown. I think he's hiding under Maurie's bed!" she cried.

My neck snapped back. "Under *my* Maurie's bed? Oh, no! Let's go right now!"

I took her by her little willing hand, grabbed my phone, and headed out. Making sure to feed her confidence in my presence, I walked hard and tough. Her little hand squeezed mine tighter the closer we made it to her room.

I turned on the light and glanced around boldly, making a show of it. Maurie was fast asleep, snoring lowly. Then I turned on the flashlight of my phone, dropped to my knees dramatically, and searched under the bed.

"Nope. No clown. Just shoes." I glanced back at her. "Wanna see?"

Maggie didn't answer. She cowered close to me and took to her knees. Pressed to my side, she looked, head swinging left and right as I moved the light.

"I don't see him," she whispered.

"Good." I stood. "Because if I had, *The Banger* would have to come out and demolish him!"

Maggie's eyes flitted away, blinking successively. She then nodded, agreeing. "My daddy, too," her voice was small.

"Of course, but as you can see, he's not even in the house. You can now fall asleep in peace." I walked her over to her bed. She crawled in, eyes still expressing she was unsettled. "You'll be okay. I'll be right in the next room."

"Could I sleep in my daddy's room, too?"

I thought on that. Ashton had been working on making his room less inviting to the girls. They still didn't know how often I stayed over because I wouldn't come out until they'd left for school on the weekdays, and on the weekends, he stayed at my place.

"What if I lay here with you until you fall asleep?"

Before I could finish, Maggie flipped her comforter open, inviting me in. Relenting, I exhaled and climbed into bed. I figured I'd wait till she fell out, then creep into Ashton's room for his gargantuan bed.

Maybe it was her whispery voice that awakened me. Or perhaps it was the thick bass I loved hearing in the morning, but I was rushed to consciousness at the sound of voices. The light of the morning sun shone through my lids. My body was curled into a fetal position with my knees off the mattress. *Oh, noooo...* I didn't mean to fall asleep in here.

"She's sleep, Daddy."

"Sleep? Where, if you have her phone?"

"I let her sleep in my bed last night. It was stormy and we should be together to be safe."

"Oh!" he whispered back. "Okay. Can I see her?"

There was shifting in the bed, then a little body lay over mine, likely the sweetest gesture she'd given me to date.

"My daddy wants to see you." Maggie's tone was even gentler to me than I'd ever heard it.

"Hey, girlfriend." I hated how my body responded to his morning coarseness while I was in his child's bed.

Forcing my tight eyes open and seeing him shirtless and still in bed, too, I smiled pathetically and cooed, "Hey, baby..."

CHAPTER TWENTY-ONE

Ashton

"So, it's Vail?" I asked, leaning over with my elbows on the countertop. "Are you sure we can't do it here at the apartment? Or!" My voice hiked when struck with a thought. "We can get a hotel suite here in New York City, like we did before and do a Christmas in the City theme with ballgowns, and I'll pull out my tux!"

"No!" Maggie's head swung adamantly.

"There's no snow here in New York for Christmas, Daddy," Maurie argued.

"Good point." I scrubbed my face with my hands.

"Remember you said we compromise, Daddy." Maggie's little hands flipped in the air as she shrugged.

"Yeah!" Maurie agreed. "You don't want to go to Texas. We don't want to stay here."

Lori, at the table collecting their book bags, snickered.

They were right. This morning, as they were leaving out for school, I'd finally broached the subject of Christmas. I'd been stalling the conversation because this year, I had another factor to consider. Tori. I wanted to be with her for Christmas like I had been for Thanksgiving. Thanksgiving was easy because of Aivery's birthday falling near it and the girls needing to be at their mother's memorial. I'd left them hanging with that as I knew I would last year when I made the call to stop going with the girls each Thanksgiving they visited the Coopers. Maurie and Maggie were old enough to maintain that relationship without me now. But I didn't want to miss Christmas with my girls, and I damn sure wouldn't spend it in Texas. So the conversation needed to be had; Christmas was less than two weeks away. Plans needed to be solidified.

Letting go of a long breath, I relented. "Okay. I'll let Glammom and Keyonna know, and start working on the arrangements right away." My tone was spiritless because I was being a fucking pussy.

"Okay, Daddy!" Maggie jumped off the barstool and sauntered over to me for a kiss.

Maurie followed her sister's actions, standing on her toes for a kiss. "Have a good day, Daddy. Don't worry; we're going to have fun." Her tight smile loosened some of the tension in my chest.

"Alright, girls," Lori called out, bringing them their book bags. "We need to head out or we'll get behind schedule."

"Bye!" Maurie waved again.

Defeated, I blew my baby a kiss and waved back at her as she followed Lori out.

I was just about to turn back toward the counter when I heard my favorite name to date. "Dad..."

"Yeah, baby?" I beat the pen still in my hand from signing permission slips earlier against the counter.

"Ms. Tori can come, too."

My spine straightened, having me stand on my feet. "That's very nice of you, baby. Are you sure?"

Why did I ask that?

She nodded her little head. "I know you like her."

"I do." A lot.

"And she was cool the other day when I had a bad dream."

No, baby. You had a nightmare because you disobeyed daddy's decision on the scary movie.

I nodded slowly myself. "She really is a wonderful woman, and she makes me happy." Why the fuck did I feel so much relief from a decision this little girl made?

"I know. That's why I said you should invite her."

When she headed for the door, a thought hit me. "You know Tori has a family of her own, don't you? Inviting her to Colorado would be inviting those she wants to spend the holiday with, too."

Her face fell into a glower. "Like how many?"

"I don't know. Maybe five?"

"Any kids?"

I hadn't considered that. "I doubt it."

"Well, as long as there are no kids, it's okay. I'm not sharing my Christmas toys." Her brows shot into the air.

I couldn't help the grin splitting my face. "I got you, baby."

Maggie took off down the hall to catch up with Lori and Maurie. I jumped in the air and performed a fist pump before going in the opposite direction to my bedroom. When I opened the door, I saw Tori sitting up with her legs crossed, holding the comforter to her bare chest while talking into her phone.

"Christmas is the week after next, honey. And you mean to tell me you don't know if you're working or not?" A male voice mildly argued. "This is odd."

"I know." Tori dropped her head into her palm. "Things have been crazy on this end, but like I said, I should know something by tonight—" She turned to me, questioning. "—or tomorrow, the latest." Again, Tori was questioning me with her eyes.

Initially, I thought it was Deon on the line, but I'd heard his voice before, and I knew Tori's tone with him wouldn't be so compromising. It had to be her father, someone I'd heard very little of in the past few months since Tori and I had reconnected, neither had I'd seen him.

"Okay, but we really need to revisit the conversation about a joint account or account access with Patty as the matriarch of the family. That would have allowed us to move forward with our plans in case you can't be with us."

The fuck?

Tori shook her head, eyes rolling with pouted lips. "I'll call you tomorrow with my plans."

He created a spell of a pause before relenting. "Okay, honey. I look forward to hearing back from you."

"You will," she assured. "I promise."

"Okay, sweetheart. Talk to you later."

"Bye." Tori tapped the phone, then tossed it across the disheveled bed, rolling her eyes. She tried perking up when asking, "The girls are gone?"

I nodded, then ambled to the bed and sat on the edge. "What was that about?"

"My father, tripping about Christmas."

"What did you tell him?"

"Well, they want to do something, of course, but can't plan anything because I said I may be working. And, of course, that makes me the hold up because I'm the sponsor."

"You pay for their holidays?"

"And vacations," she mumbled, shaking her head. "I didn't have the heart to tell them to just plan something without me."

"Why? What did they do before you reconnected with your father?"

She shrugged. "I'm sure something all together. They're a close-knit family. And that's the problem. I don't feel we've *reconnected*. To me, it feels like my father connected with me and forced me into his family. Me and my money. I hate to sound like that, but I don't feel like I fit in. His kids are cool, his wife is sweet, but I'm not one of them. No matter how much my father tries to make me a part of his family, the fact that I benefit nothing from it bothers me."

"You're saying it feels one-sided?" She nodded. "Well, now that you're off birth control, you're officially working on your own family."

Tori grabbed a pillow and hit me with it. I fell backward on the mattress, laughing my ass off. She was so incredibly shy about the topic. It was cute, and also fun as hell to tease her.

"You're gonna always be an asshole?"

"I don't know, but my child support payments will never bounce —" I tried dodging the next pillow throw unsuccessfully.

As I laughed, Tori playfully pouted. "Why do I feel like a charity case with this pregnancy thing? Now, I feel like *I'm* using you."

I sobered, now stretched out over the bed, and shrugged. "I don't mind."

Tori's smile was sad when she muttered, "You're sweet, Spence. Thanks for this lack of punctuation act."

I gave an affirmative nod. "My pleasure." It damn sure was a rash, reckless hope, but I was down. "I've got good news."

She perked up, eyes lit. "What?"

"I'll be spending Christmas with my girlfriend."

Tori's forehead wrinkled. "Really? You talked to them?"

I nodded. "This morning."

She gasped, leaning over her crossed legs. "What did they say?"

"Well, they're hell-bent on Colorado. That shit's grating my balls." I sighed. "But they're good with leaving the Coopers out this year. I guess that was our compromise."

"And where do I fit in, in these plans? Because I know Maggie—"

"Invited you." She blinked and I confirmed, "She invited you."

I hated this rift Maggie created with Tori. It was so damn challenging. And I could understand it from both their perspectives—I thought. Maggie had never seen me with a woman, and I could imagine her seeing me just as affectionate with a woman as I am with her and her sister was hard on her. And then with Tori—and possibly why I'd been so aggressive with carrying out her desire to be a mother

—I was sure she struggled once again with fitting into my life. I didn't want that for her ever again. Tori was more than good enough to be in my world. Her own successful life was evidence of it.

"Maggie invited me..." she whispered to herself, looking shell-shocked.

"Yup. And my pussy ass didn't even have to ask. She brought it up."

"Wow!" She nodded, trying the thought out for size.

"But I did warn her that you wouldn't come alone. I told her you have a family who wants to spend Christmas with you, too."

The beam on her face fucking thrilled me. "Thanks, boyfriend. I'll keep the number low, but I do have a special invitation request."

"Anything."

I'd give her anything she wanted.

"Good evening, Mr. Spencer," the pilot greeted as I stepped onto the plane with Keyonna on my heels.

"Captain Marks, good to see you." I shook his hands. "Merry Christmas."

"Merry Christmas indeed, sir. Enjoy your flight."

The flight attendant had just made it to the top of the cabin. "I can take those for you, Mr. Spencer. Hi, Keyonna."

"Hi, Lina. Merry Christmas," she greeted.

The first passenger I encountered was the one I didn't invite. "Sir, Ashton." His beam couldn't be measured. He raised a cocktail glass. "It pays when you let Camilla be the misses, you see." He winked.

Sitting next to him was a woman I was sure was his aide this week while traveling with us to Colorado.

"Try not to have too many of those, little Jimmy."

Being the melodramatic gloat he was, Jimmy took a sip and raised his glass again. "'Tis the season!"

Having enough of him so soon, I kept my stride farther inside the plane. I'd sent my mother, aunt, the girls, and their nanny to Colorado earlier. I couldn't make the flight because of a meeting I took a couple of hours ago about a potential story I was considering taking on at the top of the year. Tori couldn't make the flight until this evening also. She'd just flown in from Miami, fulfilling another contractual holiday appearance with Deon, and she had a meeting with real estate contractors right after landing back home. It still blew my mind how we'd been using the same real estate agent all these years and never knew until her birthday weekend when I told Tori how when Keyonna was searching for a rental, she lucked up on one for sale. With the help of Jaquana, I was able to close on it expeditiously.

Tori's cousins, who were joining us for Christmas, were able to fly out earlier today with my family, taking Tori's luggage. So, I arranged for another flight this evening, excited about spending time with her before the rush of the Christmas week with all of our family. I missed her over the weekend, which was nothing new. My punk ass always missed Nabby-girl.

"Hey, NeNe!" I greeted Treesha's daughter.

She pulled an *AirPod* from her ear and smiled with big eyes. "Hi!" she sang shyly.

I turned to give view of my niece. "Keyonna, this is Tori's cousin, NeNe. You two have yet to meet."

NeNe stood respectfully to greet her. "I prefer niece, although she's my mom for sure. God fell asleep at that small detail." She giggled, reaching to hug Keyonna.

It made me laugh. I could appreciate her claims to Tori. I'd been trying to make my own.

"Hey!" Keyonna laughed, then met her embrace. "Girl, I feel you." She whispered when she pulled back, "I lowkey/highkey hate when people call me his niece. And I be ready to fight when they say cousin. I be checking asses all day like, 'Nah, I'm his daughter, son!' You feel me!"

I shook my head as they tittered, immediately finding a common ground to connect on.

"Yup. My momma gets mad, but she know what it is." NeNe rolled her eyes jokingly.

"Damn," Keyonna breathed. "I can't believe my uncle's dating Tori McNabb!"

My attention followed hers to the seat next to NeNe, where it was apparent Tori had dumped her things: her *Fendi* coat, *Louboutin* high-heeled booties, *Chanel* bag, and *Asè Garb* tote with her laptop and other devices stuffed into it. Seeing evidence of her so close pathetically roused me.

NeNe laughed. "Yup, my auntie is a label whore. She told me the other day she got it from you. I couldn't believe it until she told me how when y'all met, you tricked her out with mad designer stuff."

Keyonna turned to me, hand on her forehead exasperatingly. "Sounds about Spence, huhn?"

Shaking my head, I ignored her and asked NeNe, "Is she in the bathroom?"

"No. She's in the bedroom back there, coming down from her Miami trip." She rolled her eyes again with a smile.

"Is everything okay?" She hadn't mentioned anything to me. I'd fuck Deon's clown ass up.

"Yeah. She said she wanted to decompress." *Oh...* NeNe's regard went Keyonna. "I heard you go to *Princeton*."

"I do. It's been busting my ass this semester, but yeah." Keyonna dropped her bag and began kicking off her shoes.

NeNe took back to her seat, then almost remembering I was standing in the middle of the aisle, offered, "You should go back there and check on her. Decompressing can get lonely."

Thank you...

I was going anyway. Nothing would keep me away from Nabby-girl. Or anyone.

While ambling to the rear of the plane, Keyonna asked NeNe, "Where are you, again?"

"I think I know an easier way." Ashton stepped away from the counter, rounding the countless bodies in the kitchen for the pantry. Being the tallest person in the room and with a thin cotton tee on displaying the grooves in his arms and back was crazy distracting for me. He returned with a large *Ziploc* bag. "This'll expedite the process."

I snatched the plastic bag from him and tossed it aside. "This, sir, isn't a fast food restaurant. We ain't at *B-Way Burger*. Snowball pecan cookies are to be made with love. Love takes time—"

"It didn't take you much time," he quipped, fighting a smirk.

My eyes swung around to see who caught that. "Ashton, we're talking about cookies."

"You mentioned love."

I tried controlling my voice. "And if I'm not mistaken, you haven't. Now, back to the cookies. We'll powder them with the tea strainer. Yes, it takes time, but the love is in the time." I moved to begin powdering.

NeNe and Keyonna, who were oddly the only two who'd clicked instantly, were over on the bench of the bay window, snickering at us.

"I couldn't disagree with you more. People think love is a lengthy process is all I'm saying."

"I told you I needed to use the mixer next!" Wanda snapped.

I didn't want to turn around, would have much rather disappeared.

"And I heard you, Ms. Wanda!" Treesha returned. "I also said I'd clean and pass it off when *I am* done with it."

"There's a handheld one in the cabinet I can grab for you," Renata intervened with a humbled tone.

"No. I don't want that one. I want the standing one!" Wanda made clear.

"Yeah. She's the mother; she should get first priority," Ashton's aunt, Tabitha, argued on behalf of her sister.

NeNe and Keyonna crept out of the kitchen: Keyonna shaking her head and NeNe covering her mouth, trying not to laugh. This was getting ugly. All of these people, including Ashton and me in the kitchen, wasn't healthy. Apparently, on their flight in yesterday, the women divided up the Christmas meal. I heard it was a festive conversation filled with snaps and eye rolls, but they worked it out. Then Ashton and I had a few items we wanted to contribute. The problem was, I'd hired two chefs to come out this week to help with food and serving, paying a premium holiday price for it, too. Bad idea.

The kitchen, though massive and beautifully laid out, would have normally been too much space for the family of four it was intended for. But with all of these alpha personalities, it was too small to handle this Christmas gathering. The tension in the kitchen had been brewing since we all piled up in here. Treesha wasn't one to bite her tongue, and Ms. Wanda spit fire like the seasoned vet she was.

"Mother, cousin, dog in the shed," Treesha grated. "we all family this week. Ms. Wanda ain't the only woman cooking for tonight or tomorrow. Unlike you, Auntie Tab, we don't sit around and watch women cook; we work, too."

"First of all, chile. I ain't ya auntie and you don't call me Tab—"

"Daddy! Glammom!" The girls ran into the doorway shouting. "It's time!"

Maggie's eyes were lit like one of the four Christmas trees in the house. "Pierre called up and said the ice rink is clearing up. It's time for us to go now!"

"Child, Glammom is in here *tryna* cook!" Wanda fussed.

"It's Mommy's tradition, Glammom!" Maggie cried.

"Yeah. We gotta go and then we watch the movie!" Maurie mimicked her sister's whiny cry.

My head swung over to Ashton for answers.

"When we bought the place, we acquired all the land attached to it...eight acres. Remember that ice skating rink a couple of miles before the road to the house?" Ashton asked. "That's ours. We're not here every year, so the agreement Aivery made with the township is that the residents can use it at their own risk year round, except for Christmas Eves when we're in town. At that time, everyone has to leave so our family can skate alone and the girls can play whatever music on the sound system they want to hear."

Oh...

I nodded.

"And the movie, too, Daddy," Maurie added.

"Oh." Ashton shook his head. "Aivery created another tradition of watching the video of our first Christmas here when the girls were babies. They like seeing her talk about how we'd use this house." His eyes fell, possibly annoyed or perhaps regretful.

Blinking hard, trying to shake off my feelings, I perked up when offering, "How about you guys go. My cousins and I will finish up a few things while you're ice-skating. When you're done, Ms. Wanda can come back and have the kitchen to herself, and when she's done, we can finish up in here."

The kitchen grew quiet for seconds long.

"Come on, son." Wanda sighed. "They're right; it's tradition."

"But you're coming, too, right?" Ashton asked. "I got you ice skates for this very reason."

I nodded. "I'll be out as soon as I finish with the cookies and helping Treesha with the turkey marinade."

I didn't feel good about this, and I hated it. Vail seemed so

Aivery'ish from the moment we pulled onto the property. This house was magical, traditional wealth on display with eight bedrooms, three floors, and a finished basement. When Ashton had the house prepared for our trip, the property maintenance company used most of the décor Aivery had handpicked years ago as it was still like new. The Spencers didn't visit this property annually, but Aivery had the place tricked out in beautiful furniture and accessories. I was so grateful when Ashton gave the master bedroom to his mother and opted for us to stay in a remote guest room. It wasn't as large, but I didn't need space with him. I just didn't want to experience the ghost of Aivery, which had been hard to do these past two days.

Ashton kissed me on the forehead then whispered, "Hurry up."

When the girls saw he acquiesced, they cheered so sweetly, crushing my heart.

Selfish human.

Me.

I pulled the bottle to my mouth again, filling it with rum that no longer burned. It had done its job. I was finally numb, but I still remembered. Still felt the burn of my emotions. Motionlessly, I sat on top of the large island marble countertop with folded legs, gazing at the snowfall in the moonlight. It was beautiful, mesmerizing in the wee hours of the morning. I could even see the snowman Lori, NeNe, Keyonna, and the twins put together earlier from here. I watched Ashton sneak a few pictures of them out there, lost in the fun of nature...creating memories.

Or maybe traditions.

No. That's reserved for their mother...

Traditions. I was sick of them. Mutedly, I watched them out on the ice rink. Ashton glided across the ice, performing figure eights

400

around his girls. *Damn*, he was sexy. Tall, limber, and with a spell-binding smile...beautiful teeth. How had the man stayed single this long? Pierre, the groundskeeper, covertly snapped pictures of the three of them having what looked like the time of their lives. It seemed inappropriate for me to join them after Ashton demanded I come out with him. To humor him, I skated a few rounds, then claimed I had to pee, leaving them and the rest of the family to their tradition.

Then, later on in the evening, the next tradition happened. The girls, Ashton, and their family were in the family room watching a video. I crept out of the kitchen from working with my cousins just to see what it was all about. Aivery. She was narrating the whole record-ing, and it sounded like Pierre doing the recording. It was their fami-ly's first Christmas here. Aivery documented the property and talked to the girls being held by her and Ashton as they went into the different rooms. Maggie and Maurie couldn't have been older than two years old, almost clueless to their mother's words.

She laughed into the camera. I noted how she continually kissed Maurie, who was in her arms, and she'd often walk up to Ashton to kiss baby Maggie. It appeared Aivery loved her family. Ashton didn't over-exaggerate his state when with Aivery. Other than the occa-sional smiles when she referred to him, Ashton's eyes were blank; internally, he was on another planet. But he was gorgeous as ever, tall, bearded, and manly. An empty human, though. It was exactly how I felt now. I walked away as quietly as I'd come, allowing the Spencers their tradition in peace—

"You okay?" My eyes dropped at his deep timbre behind me. Ashton padded deeper into the kitchen. I took another pull of the rum. "Tori..." When he landed in front of me, I dropped my head to the side and narrowed my eyes, acting like the asshole I'd always known *him* to be. "Oh, so you're going to ignore me? It's almost three in the morning. You must be cold down here in just a damn tank and shorts."

Fine ass, asshole human...

I was fine, nice and toasty. The rum made sure of it.

Admiring his physique in pajama pants and a plain t-shirt, I asked, "You know how I got here? What made me drop all of my guards and text you after the fight? What made it easy to let you bend me over a table at a party my fiancé threw in my honor and let you taste my pussy? It was because I was tired of being responsible and looking out for everybody. I decided to be selfish for once. I pursued you—dropped enough crumbs for you to trail—to do something for me for once. I performed this reckless act of letting Ashton Spencer have access to me to finally have a thrill of my own." I giggled, covering my mouth. "It was supposed to be my self-care."

Ashton didn't find it funny, big body stock-still.

"Then guess what? I peeled back the layer of your onion and found some foul shit. Discovered exactly what I'd been fearing since leaving *Blakewood* had actually happened. My nemesis for life— bigger than Tangi and Raquel—had won the one and only guy I loved. She won. She supported you when you got injured and lost your career, got you to marry her, gave you babies—" My hand shot into the air. "—got you to buy her this dream holiday home. And what did I get? I got death and loneliness. Yeah, I got money and fame in the end. But Aivery got tradition." I squeezed my eyes closed when I felt them tearing.

This wasn't supposed to be that.

But I broke, croaking out, "I'm jealous, Spence."

"Tori—"

Quickly swiping away the flash flood of tears, I told him, "I should have given you your first child. I'm partial to boys. He would have been a nutmeg, hairy boy...like you. I should have made you buy this house in a snowy alpine village of Colorado. I would've included a gym. That bitch didn't even consider your athletic needs." That made me laugh as I hopped off the counter and edged up to him until we were chest to chest. I smiled at his glower; his galloping heart empowered me and I pecked his lips.

"I can climb Mt. Everest to the top up above..." I sang out of nowhere, groping his dick, awakening it from resting.

"Swim the Atlantic from 'Old World' to 'New'.

But tell me, baby, how do I survive my muted love?"

Don't make me invisible...

Don't mute our love,

Don't you forget you're the one I dream of..."

I stroked and stroked him, feeling him grow in my hand.

"You were my muted love, Ashton," I spoke into his lips. "It still feels muted. I hate muted."

I paused the stroke to fall to my knees. Lowering the band of his pajamas, I pulled his stony dick out, taking it into my mouth. Ashton lost his balance for a second before regaining himself.

"You're...drunk...McNabb..." he slushed the words out.

And I slurped him, applied immediately the pressure I'd typically ease us into. Fuck seduction; I was desperate to hold on this time. I'd fight through traditions and the memories of his late-wife to have my destiny with him. Fisting his hard, ridged cock with both hands, my mind, body, and soul wanted Ashton, finally and completely.

"Stop!" he growled, lifting me from my crouched position beneath him.

Ashton pulled me into the air and I landed on the countertop again. With impatient fury, he pushed my shorts to the side and plunged into me.

"Ahh!" a guttural cry shot from my belly.

And he pounded away, right away. Like me earlier, Ashton bypassed the preamble of seduction and went full-on with long strokes. With my spine curled over the marble, I felt my orgasm cresting in no time. He grabbed my chin and positioned my head to kiss me. His tongue was wild, matching my mood. Ashton caught and swallowed my orgasmic cries as I melted onto him, throbbing and swelling. He followed soon after, suspending over me while his seeds shot into my core.

Panting, he turned his face into my neck. "I'll put the house on the market tomorrow."

Problem solved.

No!

Swallowing while out of breath, I sputtered, "*Nu—*No!" I shook my head. "The girls. This is their home, too. Their tradition." Heaving, I reminded him. "My karma."

Ashton steeled over me wordlessly. I'd run out of my own, too.

Then he lifted me from the island and carried me to our assigned room in Aivery's castle.

love
belvin

Ashton

When I knew I'd awakened for good, my first thought was her. With closed eyes, I reached for her, not feeling her in her usual position on top or underneath me in the mornings. Tori wasn't there. That's when I lifted my head. The sun was up, music playing, and food wafting beneath the bedroom door. But there was no Tori in sight. Realizing it was Christmas morning and I'd likely overslept on my babies' second biggest day of the year, I hopped out of bed and made my way into the bathroom for a leak and to shower.

I weaved the halls of the house, noting all the holiday décor and even open doors to empty bedrooms. Yup. I'd overslept, but reasonably. My girlfriend was in a drunken fit last night. When I'd finally gotten her to bed, I rubbed her back as Tori's body convulsed quietly. I didn't know if she was crying and thought better than to disturb her.

So long as she was alive and breathing, I decided to just comfort her. I can't lie: the shit scared me. Would this be our undoing? Tori, jealous of my girls. Was that normal? Or was the pathetic side of me that was always weakened by this girl understanding of her pain of betrayal?

What would I have done if Tori had given another man her hand in marriage or worse, a child? How would I feel if it were someone I was sworn enemies with? Would I be able to commit to that child in the same manner I'd be willing to Tori? This was some tricky shit.

Conversely, when I toured the front of the house, there was an air of peace in the place. Music flowed, pans sizzled, and laughter floated in the air. I noticed my mother and Renata in the kitchen working together without drama alongside one of the chefs Tori contracted. Treesha and Aunt Tab were in the dining room, setting the table. In the living room, NeNe and Keyonna took pictures by the tree with Maggie going in between their selfies. Lori, in the armchair, on her laptop found it funny, too.

"Merry Christmas, Daddy!" Maggie yelped, but not slowing on her picture hop.

I stopped thrilled at the sight, but curious about my other girls and guest.

That's when I spotted them. At the door of the veranda, Jimmy's wheelchair was parked in front of a poster-sized framed picture of him with my father on a dance floor. As he gazed longingly at it, Tori was crouched down beside him, her arm circling his small back, head on his narrow shoulder. And next to her was my baby, Maurie, providing the same comfort to Tori that Tori was giving Jimmy. With their backs to me, my chest tightened. Luther Vandross' *"Every Year, Every Christmas"* pushing from the speakers, a song I'd once loathed, gave the experience a heartfelt vibration. Life could be so damn cruel and, on some occasions, complicated. This view was demonstration of that. My emotions were taken over the top when Tori pulled Maurie onto her knee and rested her head on top of my baby's.

Complicated.

But it made me hopeful.

The holiday season typically sped up the end of the year, into the next. And as much as things were the same in terms of our schedule, there were a few faint, yet present changes as well. We didn't spend the remainder of the holiday week in Vail.

Tori had to work a day before New Year's Eve and I'd decided to call the trip shorter than planned, so we flew home that weekend. Tori, along with her fake fiancé, did a pre-recorded NYE event in L.A. She flew home the morning of New Year's Eve. As planned, the girls and I visited with my grandmother for brunch. Then that evening, I attended *Redeeming Souls for Abundant Living in Christ* in Harlem with Tori. The church held two services for the event. We attended the earlier one, where I got to meet the pastor and mentor of Tori and his family.

Bishop Ezra Carmichael was an eccentric, yet with a radiant mind. He was well-read from what I could pick up in a twenty-minute conversation. My favorite feature of his was his breadth of travel. It was great to name lesser-known countries and villages a local pastor not only recognized, but had his own experience to contribute to the conversation. I was impressed and didn't understand why Tori found him to be intimidating.

That night, we rang in the New Year with the girls at my place, snuggled beneath warm comforters in the living room. The problem was the girls fell out by ten on the couch, leaving a tipsy Tori and me to our devises. Yup. You guessed it. I fucked my lady in the same room as my daughters. Did I feel guilty? *Hell, yeah.* But not past my building orgasm. The girls had already fallen asleep with Tori and I hugged up on the floor. We'd all worn matching pajamas—Maurie's awful idea. Surprisingly, Maggie didn't veto it.

But somewhere between the third glass of champagne and kissing under the harsh snores of my girls, Tori slipped out of her pants and rolled on top of me. Her movements so faint and snug, her upper body appeared stationed under the blanket, Tori lay chest to chest over me with her head on my shoulder. But underneath, her pussy stroked my cock enough for the both of us to shiver and explode in tortured silence.

Terrifying and fucking trifling, but I enjoyed all four minutes of it.

CHAPTER TWENTY-TWO

February

Ashton

A few days into the new year, Treesha disappeared. It was the strangest shit to me, but Tori, Renata, and NeNe seemed annoyed by it. Tori and I had just flown back to town from a weekend getaway at the house in upstate New York when Renata hit her with the news. NeNe had been there with her aunt, making calls to people down in the Millville area on and off. Tori's reaction was... distant of worry. She simply ran off a few names, asking if they'd been contacted. When the women answered yes, Tori headed straight to her room without another word. Meanwhile, I was

408

alarmed, asking if I could employ any assistance, to which Renata declined.

Apparently, this was typical of Treesha as she was an addict. Renata told me that Treesha's last run was the week of Tori's fight. It blew my mind, forcing me to recall when Tori shared that with me months earlier. Treesha was a strange character, but the last thing I labeled her in all the months since rekindling with Tori was an addict. My aunt, Tabitha, ran hard in the streets with her addiction, every day for decades. It was clearly another demonstration of how money shapes experiences. My aunt didn't have the resources Tori was able to afford Treesha. My mother had never given up on her sister, but she didn't have the means to minimize the effects of her illness with lavish trips and overstated roles in her demanding world like Tori.

Again, strange.

Then there was Valentine's Day. I had to be specific in planning it as it was a turning of a corner for Tori's and my relationship. So, one morning when I woke up to get my girls' breakfast started before school, I was relieved my mother stayed over. I found her in the kitchen, putting on a pot of coffee.

"Morning," I greeted before going into the fridge to pull out what I needed. "Glad you're here. We need to chat."

"I'm not," she grumbled. "I was supposed to sleep in my new bed last night, but the shipment got delayed."

My mother stayed at my place most nights, even had a bedroom here stocked with clothes and toiletries. She still had her place in Newark, but when the girls and I moved back East, she wanted to bond with them—and I was sure me, too—and basically moved in. It thrilled and relieved me. But once in a while, she'd stay at her own place, and I understood that, too.

"Sorry about that."

"You don't sound like it. What do you need, son?"

"You this weekend."

She propped her fist on a hiked hip. "What's this weekend?"

409

"Valentine's Day, Ms. Wanda."

"Since when do you need me on that holiday?"

I lifted the left side of my top lip as if to say *duh.* "Since I got a girlfriend."

"And you can't spend it with all of them?"

"That was the original plan until I realized the holiday falls on a Friday, which means the girls have school." My first idea was to spend the earlier part of the day with the girls and possibly invite Tori—with their permission. Then I would parlay into the evening with Tori, having finished my day with my princesses. I always celebrated Valentine's Day with my girls, gifting them with cards, balloons, and sometimes dinner at a formal restaurant. "I'm having Keyonna make arrangements for Tori and me in New Orleans."

By the way my mother shook her head with closed eyes, I knew a tongue thrashing was imminent.

"What?"

"You and Tori."

"What about us?"

"I know y'all are still new, but you have to work to bring her into your relationship with the girls, not work harder at separating them."

"That's not what I'm doing at all. Tori spends time with the girls, Ma. You know that." Last week, when I had to fly out for investigative work on a piece I was working on about grocers mislabeling farm-raised seafood for wild-caught, the girls had a few days off of school. Tori took them to *SeaWorld*. She made arrangements with the park so they could enjoy their time there without waiting in lines. Tori also took the girls to get their hair and nails done at ShawnNicole's salon several times. Maggie hadn't exactly embraced Tori, but she'd warmed to her considerably since the first time Tori watched them for my aunt, Allegra's, funeral. "We have dinner together several times a week."

"Yeah, but beyond that," she argued. "missing Valentine's Day with them to spend it with your girlfriend could send the wrong message."

"I'm not missing it with them, I just won't be able to spend it with the three of them together. Tori won't be available until that night. My plan is to have flowers and candy delivered to the girls in school and pick them up myself. I'll have gifts here for them before my flight leaves for New Orleans."

"And you don't want to take them with you?" Her brows furrowed.

I took a deep breath. "I'd rather not have my babies with me on Valentine's Day while I'm with Tori. Not until I get better with having—managing my..." I tried to think of the right words. "I just don't have behaving myself with her down pat when they know she's sleeping over yet...I learned recently."

"I've never seen you grope her inappropriately. And what do you mean when she's sleeping over? The girls haven't figured out that she sleeps over most weeknights. They only know you spend weekends at her place." Then she returned the coffee pot to its base right after picking it up. "Unless..." My eyes fell to the eggs on the counter beneath me. That New Year's shit still fucked with me. It made me realize I was a novice to this dating as a father game. "You and Tori ain't been around here..." Her eyes skirted around. "Have you?"

"I need a sitter for the weekend, Ms. Wanda. That's what I'm asking here."

Her head swung back. "You're nasty! Who raised you?"

"A single parent who didn't explain this part of the game, and I'm trying to do the responsible thing."

"The responsible thing is to marry her. Again, I know it's only been a few months, but at your age and with your baggage, you don't have the luxury of a long dating period. You're at an age where you should know what you want in a partner. That's what you need; you're a father raising young and impressionable kids in this small ass New York City apartment. It's been four years and you haven't settled on a proper home for them, Ashton. You've been married before and should know what worked and what didn't."

"That one didn't count." I shook my head. "I married the wrong woman."

"Then don't do it again. Hell, at least with Tori, you don't have to worry about her being more into your money than you, like you would with the vast majority of women you've encountered. That girl has her own. Shit. Get prenups, make 'em tight if you have to. But figure it out and make it work for your family. You've got more at stake than needing a babysitter for Valentine's Day. You're raising little people who will soon make big decisions based on what they've seen in your house *and* what they didn't see."

My head bobbed. She was right, but what she didn't know were the intricate complications that made up Tori McNabb. Tori and Deon had one last appearance to do together this week as a couple, and it was for Valentine's Day. After which, both parties could announce their breakup within a reasonable time.

Whatever the fuck that means...

Was Tori ready for marriage? I didn't know. Was I ready was another valid question. But what was of no doubt was I wanted her. *Hell.* I'd been fucking her raw in hopes of getting her pregnant. That was some shit I'd never imagined doing in all my years of fucking. I just wanted her, and I believed she wanted me, too. She'd been working on her "jealousy" of my fatherhood, not showing an ounce of it to the girls—because I'd been watching.

Tori also made sure her feet were planted in my world by spending time with my family outside of the girls and my moms. She'd been to the bar a few times with Boobee and Junie. For Keyonna's birthday last month, Tori took her to see Brielle at the *Garden*. Keyonna had seen her in concert several times before, but when she was escorted by Brielle's bestie, the experience hit different. She was able to go backstage to meet her and even hung out with Brielle after the show. My baby girl was over the moon at the experience. It wasn't just about the popstar either. Keyonna was taken with the experience of having Tori to herself. It was just the two of them...with security, of course.

Tori was in my life...officially. The faint, yet present change I'd noticed since Christmas was Tori's behavior. On the surface, she was the same woman, tender and attentive, but beneath her lovingness was an unsettled spirit. I hadn't been able to articulate the emotional orgasms moving her to tears or the questions about my experiences with the girls as infants. It was strange how she'd be on another planet icing, heating, or applying the *TENS* machine to my shoulders and/or leg when they flared up. Tori would be gentle, yet with empty eyes. It was strange. I hated thinking of it because it made me feel weird about making a big deal of something so subtle.

"Let me go wake them up." My mother collected her coffee and headed for the door. "And don't let my babies tell me they done seen some nasty shit between you and Tori either." Her last words before turning the corner were, "I'll keep 'em this weekend."

Her arm shot from the water. "There's another Moorish idol! Right?"

I nodded. "Yup."

"Man!" she breathed.

"The African Moors believed they're the giver of happiness."

She turned to me. "Is that why you had them?"

"I had lots of fish. Still do."

"I know." Her chin dropped and eyes narrowed on me. "I'm still kicking myself about missing that big behind tank my first visit, and how you introduced Lori to me as 'one of my assistants around here' instead of the nanny to your girls."

"*Shiiiiiiit,*" I muttered. "You would've run like hell out of my apartment."

Tori rolled her eyes, attention going back to the gigantic floor-to-ceiling aquarium tank in the suite I'd reserved at a new hotel in The

Big Easy for Valentine's Day. The three million gallon tank with a little more than twenty-five thousand exotic sea creatures had been the ideal experience for me. We had aquarium views in the bedroom, bathroom, dining room, and living room. The hotel had only been open for two months and booked into next year, but I had Keyonna call a few people I knew, and we were booked in a day or so. After a hectic day of travel for the both of us, Tori and I had a delicious dinner, then retreated in here to soak and relax...and experience a portion of the exhibit surrounded by tealight candles and rose petals.

"They're so beautiful. I never forgot them from your dorm in *BSU*." My head bobbed again. "That's when you were the prince of Zamunda." She giggled, bringing her chin to her shoulder.

"What am I now?" I took a sip of my brandy.

Tori waded through the scented bubbles and warm, silky water of the hot tub for me. She wrapped her arms around my neck and kissed me. "The man I can't stop thinking about."

"Oh, yeah?"

Her head bounced slowly. "Yeah." Then Tori kissed me again. When she pulled back, she smiled. "I was thinking. The girls have off a couple of days next week. Right?" I nodded. "Then why don't we take them up to the house in New York and go sleighing? I know they'll love it. They're snow angels like me."

I tilted my head back to scratch my nose. "They wanna go to The Bahamas next week."

Her shoulders deflated visibly. "Am I invited?"

Instead of answering, I asked, "How are you?"

Tori's face fell. "How am I? What do you mean? I'm with my man. There's no place I'd wanna be right now than with you."

I shook my head softly, admiring the curve of her breasts before the bubbles covered her nipples. Her hair was up in a ponytail on top of her head, and Tori wore red lips and diamond studs in her ears.

Simplistic beauty...

"How are you mentally, emotionally, spiritually?" I asked. "And not just in the moment. Look at where we are. How could you not be calm here? We're surrounded by nature. I want to know how you are on the inside."

"I guess I'm fine. This thing with Treesha is annoying, but what else is new?" She rolled her eyes. "But I've been praying." Then her regard rolled up to me. "And I'm thankful. I've been meditating on that a lot when talking to God. I'm really thankful for you, Maggie, Maurie, Keyonna, Wanda...and Jimmy. I'm..." She used her hands to think of the word. "...inspired. Thankful. I feel...empowered. Bold and fearless." Her eyes rolled toward the ceiling as she considered her feelings. "I feel like I can do anything. Like... Actually convince Maggie to love me. Or...maybe get pregnant?"

I reached behind me and felt my way underneath a towel. When I returned to her with a small velvet box, Tori's smile disappeared and her chest began to heave. I opened the box to reveal the nine-carat, Asscher-cut diamond ring.

Her expressive eyes swept the room. "Are you asking me to marry you?"

Slowly, I answered, "Not yet, but this will be my assistant."

"What are you waiting for?"

"For you to tell me you're ready."

Her face contorted. "Ready for what? To waste another twelve years of not being honest?"

"To finish up your business with Johnson. I've been patient." *Too fucking patient.*

Tori's eyes closed as her head shook. "Our last gig was yesterday. You know that."

"But the world doesn't. I don't want to bring drama to your life. I understand your world is a little different from mine, and I have another ounce or so of patience in me, but I have to be sure you're ready."

"I am."

"For what?"

She scoffed. "What the hell are we talking about here, Ashton?"

"I need a wife, Tori, not just a passionate fling. I have kids—one with Trisomy Twenty-one, a condition that will never go away. She has constant medical needs. Maurie will never be independent, unlike her sister. She will always remain in my care. I have Keyonna, who has terrible insecurities about her position in my life. She considers me a dad, full stop."

"I have NeNe. I get it—"

I shook my head. "The difference between Keyonna and NeNe is that, no matter how many issues Treesha has, she's still alive and well, and will always be NeNe's mother. Keyonna will never have Brick back. Not only have I picked it up, but she's placed the burden of patriarchal needs on my shoulders, something my late-wife detested and made known. Keyonna is a part of my package. Our relationship has been unregulated since I've been a widower. I need to stop using my niece as my personal assistant, giving her tasks that my wife should handle—or an assistant to my wife and me who isn't a young relative. I've got to stop living like a bachelor for her, too."

"Are you doubting I can do this? Be in their lives?"

"I'm still living in my insecurities created by a nineteen year old tomboy who single-handedly made me feel the most abandoned in life." I scoffed. "I thought I had daddy issues because of his neglect. At least he showed up, even if it was with his doting boyfriend."

"Ashton..." She blinked, shaking her head.

"You used to be so intimidated by my mother. She's the least of them. *My* Margaret may never fully accept you. It may take Keyonna a long ass time not to feel insecure about me loving you more than her —or whatever crazy thing a twenty year-old's mind can conjure. *My* Maureen will always be a shadow in our union. And in spite of all of those competing detractors, I'll still be here with my own shit, needing you solid beside me."

With a trembling lip, Tori softly swung her head side to side. "I'm never losing you again. I can be anything *you* need me to be to your girls. And I can't wait for the day to be what they need me to be, too." I watched her throat bob as she swallowed. "I'll call Elle first thing in the morning about our plan to announce the break up with Deon. I don't care if we're photographed together the very next day. I can't wait for my belly, full of your baby to be posted on every news media site. I'll walk through the fire for you, Ashton. I'm not nineteen year old Tori. I'm your girlfriend, and if you want, I'll be more."

When she said shit like if I want or walking through fires for me, a tremor of hope ran through me, tingling my balls. It aroused me, making my body burn for her, my heart yearn to blend with hers. I pulled the ring from its holding and tossed the box behind me. When I placed it on her finger, Tori exhaled hard, eyes closed, and tears slipped from them. She wasn't the only one emotional. My tears may not have fallen down my face, but internally, I was so raw; it made me vulnerable.

She opened her eyes again, finding me, then leaped my way, latching onto my shoulders. My swelling dick brushed near her lips as she wrapped her arms and legs around me. Tori kissed me wild and hungrily, her tears soaking into my beard. Backing up to the stairs, I tried to crawl backward out of the tub but Tori reached between us, grabbing my dick. I tripped, catching the ledge as she guided me to her opening.

"I love you, Ashton." Using her core, she plunged down onto me. Her pussy was so fucking wet, bold and rapid movements so needy. It concerned and thrilled me at the same fucking time. My head tossed back and my eyes squeezed closed as she began to ride me on the ledge of the tub. "I did then, and I hopelessly do now."

Then Tori pulled my head toward hers and kissed me feverishly as she rolled her hips, stroking me into oblivion.

Tori

It was just about ten o'clock at night when Ashton and I made it back to my apartment from New Orleans. He'd stopped by to pick up a pair of shoes he wanted to wear tomorrow. And of course, I didn't want him to go. Since we left Teterboro airport, I'd been trying to figure out ways to get him to stay. Just when I was about to simply ask him, I was taken aback from seeing Treesha saunter across the hall from the kitchen with what looked to be a bowl of cereal to her room.

I stopped in the foyer, swinging my head to the side, begging her pardon.

She rolled her eyes. "I'm tired as hell. Don't start your shit, Tor."

My head jerked back. "Start my shit? Are you fucking kidding me? You go ghost for a fucking month and a half and you expect to pop up to my place and tell me not to start my shit? You've got me fucked up, Treesha!"

"Baby..." Ashton tried calming me from behind.

By this time, it was too late. My blood was boiling, head spinning at her fucking nerve!

"Don't try me, Tori!" Treesha warned as Renata shot into the hall. "I ain't in the mood for it!"

What?!

"No more!" I moved down the hall toward her. "Put that bowl down and get the fuck out! I'm done!"

"Tori!" Renata called.

Ashton pulled me by the waist, killing my advancement to her. That shit made me go into a rage. "Get the hell off me! Treesha, get your shit and go now!"

"Who the fuck you think you talking to?" she demanded. Renata yanked the bowl from Treesha and tried grabbing her into the kitchen. Treesha's shouts could still be heard. "I ain't fuckin' NeNe! I'm a grown ass woman. I 'on't ask you for shit!"

"You don't ask me for shit? Really! Okay." I tried wrestling out of Ashton's impossible grip. "When I throw your tired ass out with all ya shit, we'll see how long it takes to ask me for shit. And that's all you'll get: the shit from my ass."

Treesha struggled in the hall as though she wanted to throw hands. I'd beat her fucking ass like I should have years ago.

"Bitch, you ain't God! You can't judge me!" Treesha shouted. "Yeah, I got my shit with me, but so do all y'all muthafuckers. Renata ain't been right since she was in the Army, but you don't judge her! When this muthafucker came back in your life after all that shit he put you through, did I judge you?"

Air hoping in Ashton's arm, I yelled, "You actually did! And you talking about judging. Keep my fuckin' relationship out ya pill-poppin' ass mouth! You don't know shit about me or mine!"

Treesha brows shot up, but she remained wisely stationary. "Oh, I don't know shit about you and Ashton? Or do you mean Ashton don't know shit about how your ass almost went crazy when my nephew died? Ashton, was you there when I helped take care of my aunt, Dot, when she was sick and Tori couldn't work and keep a eye on her? Tori was a fucking lunatic, working two and three jobs while pregnant. She left that uppity school without her mind!"

"Fuck you!" I tried jumping from his arms.

I was going to mop the floor with her dumb ass.

"That's what Ashton did to you, bitch! Sent your ass home with a baby he ain't even help you with. Ashton, am I judging you because you snatched my cousin's soul on that campus? She could have fucking lost her mind burying your son a month after burying her mother!"

My body failed me, limbs went weak, and I crumbled to my knees. Ashton, somehow, let me. His arms released me as I sobbed tearlessly.

"Get your dumb ass in the room!" Renata yelled at the top of her lungs. I could hear a body being slammed into a wall, but couldn't look up to see. "I should beat your ass then let her have what's left of it—" A door slammed.

My body curled and convulsed in acute memory of a trauma I thought I'd worked through.

"If you don't fuckin' talk right now, I'm leaving out that door," that North Jersey twang was not only distinctive, but frightening.

Shaking all over, I couldn't speak. I struggled to my feet and swayed into my bedroom. Seconds later, I felt Ashton looming. I went into my closet, crawling to the shoeboxes on the floor. To the far corner, buried beneath them was a wooden box. It took a minute with quivering hands, but I managed it out. Ashton was waiting near the door, the atmosphere tense with electric anticipation. He received the box of my last and possibly biggest trauma when I handed it to him.

"Asht—*un...*" I could hardly speak his name. "this is my *Blake-wood* memorabilia box." It contained the ticket stub to Brielle's concert, the program from the art show he'd sent me on a "date" to, the *Blackberry* I fished out of the trash the morning after I tossed it in there, the half of heart necklace he gave me, and more. "It includes my son."

Ashton's eyes ballooned.

My stomach toiled and knees bounced nervously as I sat on the opposite side of the bed as Ashton, our backs to each other. The entire rear side of my body burned from the inferno I knew had just been ignited. I fought the urge to curl in the corner, tried to force my mind to go far away from here until Ashton spoke. Chewing on the inside of my lip, I waited, eyes occasionally skimming the clock on my nightstand.

Ten thirty-two...

"Why isn't Renata in any of the pictures?" His throaty tenor was sensitive.

My body stopped rocking as my fingers pressed into my elbows from my arms being crossed. The seam of my lips broke and my eyes danced back and forth over the wall ahead.

I cleared my throat. "Because she was still in the service. She was allowed to come home Fourth of July of that year, but didn't come back for over a year after."

I remembered because it was a time in my life I knew she'd been there for me from top to bottom. When she came to my apartment for the barbeque, Renata admitted to being jealous. I understood it because, foolishly, we wanted to be mothers before we were taught to be women. I knew if Renata had it her way, Cleveland would have still been alive and the father of her children. She would have been pregnant long before I met Ashton Spencer.

"Your mother isn't in any pictures at the hospital," his voice tender to the bone. "...when you delivered."

My eyes closed at the dark memory. "My ummmm..." I took a shallow breath. "She had a stroke a couple of weeks before and was still getting her strength back. I told her...we'd be home in a couple of days and to sit tight."

Then nothing. For so long after my last word, Ashton said nothing.

Eleven fourteen...

In the corner of my bedroom, I sat with my knees to my chest, twirling my hair around my fingers. It was either that or shadow boxing. I didn't want to make noise doing that. It would have disrupted Ashton's time to understand my dark truth.

"How did you deliver?" I leaped a little at the sound of his deep cords.

"Huhn?" My heart roared in my chest.

With his broad back still to me, Ashton elaborated. "How did you deliver him? Caesarean —"

"Naturally," I answered eagerly. "Took twelve and half hours, but *ve*—vaginally."

"And NormaJean knew him." It was a statement and not a question.

My eyes closed, feeling the pain of her memory, too. "Yes," I breathed.

"Did you tell her not to tell me?"

I nodded behind his back. "Yes."

Ashton scoffed, "And she listened."

"*I*—I think it was easy to. You shut her out after..." I hesitated bringing up another bad memory. They were collecting fast at this point. "...*Blakewood*. She said you wouldn't return her calls or emails. After she kept coming around...popping up on me, and I saw she wouldn't stop. I told her not to mention you to me again. I didn't care if you became friends with her or not. I couldn't take it, Ashton," I cried, trying to explain.

Then he said nothing.

Twelve thirty-two...

The tears had returned. At this point, I was using my shirt to dry my face as I curled in the corner, afraid. Hurt. I hated having my sniffles heard, but I couldn't help them. It was hard having someone rummage through the box of my pain. This was Ashton. Ashton Spencer who had never judged me. Ashton Spencer who had a hand in this dark piece of me. He was allowed this time.

The door creaked, startling me. It was Renata. Her eyes wildly searched the room. Ashton's head lifted, his regard on her. I could see her shoulders shrink as she realized the energy of the room. My wet face alone could have given it away, but Ashton's intense mood filled the place, stifling me.

"Y'all good?" she whispered, less protective now, and more sensitive to palpable pain cresting in the moment.

Ashton didn't respond. Licking my dry lips, I nodded my stiff neck. After a lingering stare, Renata backed out and closed the door.

And I waited some more.

One-twenty...

I'd been in this place all these years and never had this room professionally cleaned. The white baseboards were dusty. I wondered if they were in the rest of the apartment. I doubted it. My cleaning service was pretty thorough. I would have asked Ashton who he used, but...he was still sitting on the same place on the bed, ruminating.

This was painful. Was I wrong? Should I have done something differently? The tears began and my heart pounded again. Sorrow swept over me. What more could I have done? He wouldn't have wanted that detour in his career, and I didn't know his injuries had already derailed him. All I did know was that he didn't call. He never sought after me.

"Why did you give him your last name?" he graveled.

I sniffled. "Because he was mine. My last name is McNabb. My mother's last name was McNabb, and my *Ma*—Margaret's last name was McNabb."

It was simple. Bobby was mine. My gift. My love.

After a couple of minutes, he asked, "Then what made you name him after my father?"

A fresh trail of hot tears fell from my eyes. "Because he was yours, too." I could only whisper the last word.

Ashton's face lifted toward the ceiling as he held the birth certificate in one hand and other hospital paperwork in the other. "But my name isn't Robert."

I shrugged, although he couldn't see me. "Your father deserved a legacy, too. You and Jimmy made him sound like a lost, broken, hopeless soul, and I wanted to give him something. Bobby was my hope." I sobbed. "I wanted him to be Robert's hope, too."

Ashton finally turned to me. "Where is he?"

"Who?"

His tight eyes blinked as though he was stuck. "The... My son." He seemed to have regained his confidence. "Where is he buried?"

My throbbing head rocked right to left. "He's *nuh*—not." I could hardly breathe.

"Is your mother buried where Margaret is?" I nodded. "Then why not have him with them?"

"It didn't feel right. Bobby hadn't really lived yet. He didn't plant his feet. Didn't make it to an age where he got to decide where he wanted to live and hang his hat." More hot tears ran down my swollen face. "My Margaret and mother never wanted to leave Millville. It was a decision they made. Bobby wasn't given that opportunity, so it didn't feel right burying him." I managed one shoulder to shrug. "Raj said I should cremate him."

Anger flashed in his face. "Ragee—" Ashton's eyes closed to rein in his temper. I believed it was the Ragee mention. It had to be. So many people were photographed with Bobby in those few short months of his life. That had to have made Ashton feel left out. "Where are his remains?"

My mind moved faster than my body when I tried to jump to my feet. I stumbled from being cramped in one position for so long. Then I whisked out of the room and into the hall for the sitting room. There, over the mantle, was an urn cabinet in the form of a powder blue vase. I unlatched and opened it. My body trembled on the way back to the room. Ashton hadn't moved from the foot of the bed. His heavy, red eyes raked up to me the moment I whisked through the door.

I showed him the urn. "He's here—his remains are here."

Not in a million years did I think he'd be interested in holding it. I could understand if he thought it was weird that I'd kept it here. I could have had it stored at a secure facility, but it never sat well with me. We all knew what the vase was for and what it held. Everyone respected my wishes in having it out. I didn't want Bobby's remains hidden. He was a real, living, breathing human. I'd never forget him.

I was shocked when Ashton took the brass urn Ragee had paid for from my trembling hands. He held it in his big palms, his eyes closed, and I could see them roll beneath his lids. I stood over him for what felt like an eternity. When it finally occurred to me Ashton wasn't ready to part with it, I went back to my corner and waited.

Four eleven...

"I need to go." His thick tenor startled me.

I struggled to my feet, blurred eyes roved over to the clock. It was just after five in the morning. Ashton turned to face me. He looked like hell. That made me feel like shit.

"You mentioned years of therapy," he croaked. "I thought it was for your sexual trauma, the sudden death of your mother, and possibly the abandonment then inclusion of your father into your lofty world. But is it safe to say this had a lot to do with it?"

The innocence in his question gutted me.

I nodded. "Bobby? Yeah. And a little bit of you. The therapist was able to pull out the abandonment I'd interpreted your leaving my life to mean, too."

Did I just admit that?

Either way, it didn't seem as though Ashton cared. He cleared his throat. "I need to go. I ummm..." He hesitated, then shook his head in defeat. "I can't be here right now. I need to process all of this. It's feeling like the old haunting energy of Tori McNabb from *BSU*. The one who never accepted me. The one who kept me at arm's length emotionally and self-protectively. The one who couldn't view me as a decent human being. This shit hurts—"

"It hurts me, too, Ash—"

"*MY FUCKIN' SON! MY FIRST CHILD, FIRST BORN! MY ONLY SON EXISTED AND NO ONE TOLD ME!*" he roared in my face. "Everyone important in your life has met my son, but me." The door opened and, this time, Treesha and Renata were there. Ashton turned to me, hoarse. "I need time to think about this."

He turned to leave. But Ashton grabbed the urn before bypassing my protective cousins, who didn't seem to have rested much last night themselves.

"Ashton, wait," I cried. "Please don't—" I remembered I didn't know how to beg someone to stay with me. Not leave me.

I knew how to blow a man's dick, but not his emotions.

And he was gone. Within a minute, the front door slammed.

"You good, Tori?" Treesha asked.

I moved to my bedroom door and closed it. Then I fell face first on my bed.

Ashton

As I passed through the front door, my mother was the first person I saw. She stopped in her tracks, carrying a cup of tea. After slamming the door closed behind me, I stood frozen. My eyes blinked successively, and suddenly, I was reduced to an elementary school child. Out of nowhere, my face felt wet, beard soaked.

"Ashton," she called out alarmed from about four yards away. "What's going on? What's that vase? Is that a..." She squinted. "...urn?"

I lay across her bed with a cool, wet towel on my eyes. It helped with the throb in the front of my head, but hadn't done shit for the ache in my chest or the damn nausea in my belly.

"This is a lot to chew on, Ashton," she remarked. "It was one thing to learn recently how you carried on a physical and emotional affair with this young lady while you and Aivery were supposed to be living the last year of your most carefree lives together. But to know that affair produced a baby?" her voice hiked.

I'd just told my mother everything. *Every. Thing.* All the shit that happened all those years ago under her nose. Even the details Aivery and I had agreed to keep between us, like the real reason I was at her suite in *Winnie* confronting her. For years, we'd told everyone it was because of her relationship with Benjamin. Very few knew the true reason. Karmen never said, and neither had Pettiford.

I lifted the wet cloth from my eyes and chanced a glance at her.

She held her tea in one hand and cupped the urn inside her other arm as she rested against the headboard. Ms. Wanda was mad. Good. I was hurting.

"This is some *Dynasty* shit if I've ever seen some."

"What's *Dynasty?*"

"A soap opera show that used to come on back in the day. But that shit was entertaining: this is tragic. I was a grandmother long before Maurie and Maggie and had no damn clue. That means while you were undergoing all those surgeries, your son was growing in utero and had been born."

"And died."

"And died," she echoed, haunted by the facts. "So what happens now?"

"Possibly the worst."

"What's that?"

I raised my head from the mattress to peer at her once again. "I still want her. I can't let her go again."

"Well, shit. That sounds like reckless hope."

My head hit the mattress. "That's all we know."

"What's that?"

"Recklessness, muted love, and hope." I recalled Tori's description Christmas Eve and added my own adjectives.

"Are you going to articulate this to her?"

I shook my head. "I can't see her right now. I'd really be reckless if I did and lose her possibly forever. I can't do forever without her this time."

"He looked like Robert," she noted.

"Who?"

"My grandson," her voice cracked. "He looked like that son-of-a-bitch."

Pain dispersed in my chest all over again, and for a while, I couldn't speak. I'd taken a few pictures of the baby from Tori's place. How could I not? I'd missed his whole life.

"I thought he looked like you," I murmured. "Especially in that pic with him in the blue onesie. That scowl is you all day."

"Yeah. Hmmmm..."

I lifted my head and the cloth again. "What does that mean?"

"No. I'm just thinking, she may be dishonest, but she's not a liar. This here is my grandbaby. I don't need a DNA test to confirm it."

"Then how is she dishonest?"

"She doesn't share her truth with anyone—or just a select few. And sharing it with a select few doesn't allow her to live with her truth. That young lady has been carrying a lot of bones with her."

More than you know...

I didn't share about Tori's sexual abuse. That wasn't my business to tell, no matter how bruised I was right now.

"Let me get ready for the girls. They'll be at my door before you know it since you didn't put them down last night. Maybe you should lay low until I get them out for school. Then you can finally rest."

"I've got a conference call in a few." I tried sitting up.

"Have it canceled," she ordered on her way to the door. "That Tori child may have had to walk through life with grief on her shoulders, but not my son. I'm telling you, you need to process this and not go about life carrying it. Ignoring pain doesn't make you a survivor of the trauma. Working through it does. And that begins with not ignoring the fact that you've been up all night wrestling with this pain."

The door closed and, from my vantage point, I could see my innocent son's urn on her nightstand. I guessed this was where I'd start processing his short life and long death. With the two of us alone.

Finally...

CHAPTER TWENTY-THREE

Tori

The second time Renata called me, it was alarming. On my way to the door from the kitchen, I licked the tomato sauce from my thumb then wiped it on my apron.

"Y'all little girls don't scare me." I recognized the abrasive cry. "Y'all may be from the trailer park, but I'm from Stella Wright Projects. Newark, baby." Her chin was in the air, daring my cousins to try her.

I rolled my eyes, though my pulse kicked to high levels. Ms. Wanda had come to fight for her son.

"Lady, I don't give a damn where you're from," Renata made clear. "My cousin don't need no drama right now."

"Then you two need to move aside unless you're taking my coat and purse. Do you live here anyway—"

"Unless you're bringing my son's remains back, I don't under-

430

stand why you're here." I interrupted Wanda's hail of verbal bullets. "Is that why you're here?" I pushed my fists into my waist to put on a brave front.

She looked me up and down, eyes heavy with disdain, it seemed. "No. My grandson is tending to my child's broken heart. And I think you'd agree it's been overdue."

My eyes closed to a squeeze. She referred to Bobby as her grandson. That twisted and tickled *my* broken heart at the same time.

"Treesh, Renata, can you give us a minute?"

"And take my shit while you're at it." She peeled off her coat. "Make yourselves useful!"

"Tori, you better get your lil' mother-in-law before I lose my cool," Treesha threatened.

"Nah, baby. I ain't her mother-in-law." Wanda shook her head with pouted lips. "She blew that two days ago."

I placed an empty plate in front of Wanda at the table. Treesha and Renata were fixing their plates at the stove from the pots.

"I can serve you or you can do it yourself," I offered her.

I put the food in serving platters at the table for the two of us— more for her: I could have fixed my plate from the stove, like my cousins.

With her elbows on the table and fingers tented beneath her chin, she hummed. "I'll do the honors. I don't want too much on my plate. I ain't never had no spaghetti with fried chicken before. What culture is that even from?"

"Margaret McNabb's," Treesha hissed.

Wanda's mouth fell open and I could tell she was about to clapback, but she hesitated. Her eyes shot down to the wine glass in front of her as she pushed the stem through her fingers absentmindedly.

"You know, every time I hear that name, I think of my baby girl," she murmured, less fire in her attitude than she'd had since arriving thirty minutes ago.

That struck me emotionally, too. I was still not used to the idea of Ashton naming his children after my grandmother.

"Tori, we'll be in the dining room if you need us," Renata shared as they stood near the door, holding their plates.

Wanda's head whipped around to face them. "And just what would she need you for? What does an undisputed, heavy-weight champ need your help to do?"

Treesha shook her head, mumbling something under her breath. Renata nudged her, gesturing to drop it and leave. Without another word, thankfully, they did.

"You know I taught them how to fight long ago," I politely warned Wanda as I began plating pasta.

"Yeah, well, that was long ago," she exhaled. "I got nieces still in the streets. One call and this whole luxury apartment building'll be sprayed up."

I dropped the spoon on the sauce bowl, making a clash of it. "Are you here to be trouble or what? Friend or foe, Wanda?"

Ignoring me, she used the tongs to grab a chicken leg. "I ain't neither, but I'm definitely not the enemy here."

"You know..." My brows pinched and I nodded, revelation hitting me. "I've finally figured out you're ratchet and educated."

"What took you so long. That's the best way to go, young lady. I can school you or beat your ass."

Rolling my eyes and exhaling, I went back to fixing my plate. I didn't have much of an appetite, but having Ashton's mother here made me antsy enough to busy myself with eating.

"Are you coming to go off on me about...my son?"

"No, Tori. I came to see if you've healed from my grandson's death," her tone was its usual snippiness, but so affectionate at the same time.

A tear escaped. Quickly, I tried to swipe it away and finish fixing my plate.

"I am."

"You are what, young lady?"

"Healing."

"How?"

I put my plate down and covered my face with my palms. "I'm only a mess because Ashton found out—and the way he did. Otherwise, I'm strong."

"Then what happened? By the way, I noticed his birthday is two days before mine."

I knew that. Realized it when I was away, working with Deon, and Ashton was throwing her a fancy party.

"Ashton." I swallowed hard, fighting more tears. "We've been spending crazy time together, and it's happening again."

"What, young lady? What's happening again?"

My face came up from my hands, and I tried wiping the tears away again. It took a while for me to explain, but I did. "These feelings. It's just like all those years ago, but now I can articulate them better. They're so strong and all-consuming. They're warm and promising—deceitful and...addictive. I've never felt this way about another human. He just makes me so..." My lips tightened and I grounded out. "...weak." *...and fall in love with him like it's second nature to me.*

"Hmmmm..." She bit into her chicken, giving me the side eye.

That was enough to snap me out of my sharing mood. I continued with my plate, done with the topic. Being in love could be so damn painful for me.

"Do you know what my line of work is?" I shook my head. "I'm a professor of women's health and studies. I've taught all over, between New Jersey and New York City, and have done it for many moons. One of my passions is bringing attention to young Black girls from low-income homes, lacking resources. I've encountered so many bright stars dimmed by circumstances. And the one thing I've noticed amongst most is their lack of emotional and mental support." She shrugged, and I realized that was the very work of my organization. "No one ever taught us how to heal, myself included."

"What do you mean?"

"I was born to a poor, uneducated mother and a drunk of a father. He was passive and ever-distant and she was hard-working, yet directionless. They raised us in the projects, which meant we were reared by our impoverished circumstances. I had a brother—the oldest child —who struggled with crack addiction and died by the age of twenty-one. He was found behind my building, in the middle of February, with his pants below his knees and a needle sticking out of his groin.

"The brother just beneath him is a lifer in federal prison. He used to run with the biggest drug gang in Newark, back in the eighties and earlier nineties. RICO got his ass." She shrugged with her head and mouth. "Then there was me, then my sister, Tabitha. She's been through many men and a couple of rehabilitation facilities. By fourteen, she was raped by the janitor twice before anyone found out. Then there's my little brother, June, aka Junior. He and our baby brother, Ross, are high-ranking members of an active, dangerous gang right now. Well, Ross had been until he died. Shot in a turf war about twenty years ago."

"Dang." My head bounced back. That rundown exhausted me. "So, out of six kids, only you avoided the pitfall of the streets?"

She shook her head and took another bite of the chicken. Then Wanda began fixing spaghetti as she shared, "I didn't say that. By fourteen, I had a job running drugs to crackheads. They'd pay the dealer, and I'd drop off the vials to the customer in another area to deter the police."

"You needed the money?"

"Not as much as I crushed on one of the dope boys. He was fine in his leather pants and matching jacket and beanie. Chileeeee, that ass!" Wanda's eyes rolled to the back of her head. "He was my first crush and I'd do anything for his attention. So..." She paused to sample the food. "I knew nothing about sex or appreciating the male anatomy, but that Quaneef...! He just did it for me. And he knew it. So eventually, he made his move and I was game. Now, the problem with my lil' first love was that he had a temper. He watched his daddy beat on him and his momma and took out that frustration on me. It started with pushing, then graduated to open-hand smacks in almost no time."

"What did your father do?"

"Huh!" she shrieked with sarcasm. "He caught my little black eyes and asked if I beat the girl's ass. The man took a sip of beer, then walked off without waiting for the answer."

"All those brothers you had, and no one stepped up?"

"I hid it from them for two years and three STDs I could thankfully get rid of after a prescription. June and Ross got word from one of Quaneef's friends joking about what they'd seen. I was out shopping with Tab and by the time we made it back to Prince Street, the ambulance had just pulled off with Quaneef and his broken skull."

I sucked in a breath, spine straightening. "Did they kill him?"

She shook her head, chewing her food. "They tried. Took a four-by-four to his ass. The last time I saw Quaneef was when Ashton was two. We were leaving my sister's place and he was crossing the street, still with the big gash from his crown, running down his face. He died a year later from a stroke."

I blinked hard. "What a story."

"One that isn't done. After that shit with Quaneef, I was broken —had actually been breaking those two years while enduring it. I had no idea where to pick up the pieces. Guys tried to date me, but everybody was too damn soft for my liking. Many of them knew June and Ross, and were too afraid to smile my way, much less ask me out. I didn't hang out much. Didn't go straight to college either. Shit, I got a job at the damn library!" She laughed. "Who was gonna find me there?"

Wanda shrugged. "But I didn't want anybody. That was until a few months after working at the library, this tall bearded man would come in on Sunday nights and Monday mornings, pulling out books and writing shit down. He would request business and marketing books and draw graphs and other shit while working in a private corner on the second floor. I didn't think much of him physically at first. But the more I interacted with him professionally, I noticed how kind and gentle he was; stylish, too. That man could dress his ass off, wearing designer garb without the garish logos and patterns.

"I'd walk past his trench coat tossed on a nearby table and peep the *Burberry* print on the inside. He had a quiet sophistication to him. Within a few months, I learned he was a businessman. One of the ones who owned the fast-growing *B-Way Burger*. I'd been eating it for many moons and had no idea it was Black-owned. The man, Robert, was researching how to take it nationwide. He didn't want to sell it to the bigger chains. He wanted wealth for himself, a legacy."

"He told you that?" Her words reminded me of what Jimmy had told me about Rosemary Spencer wanting a legacy for Ashton's father when we'd first met. "Did Robert say that?"

Wanda nodded, taking another bite of the chicken. "That man said that and more. We made friends within the first six months. He was so easy to talk to, so simple to trust my all to. He encouraged me every day to demand more out of life. Told me I was special until I was sick of hearing it. Robert was gold. The guy was consistent and dedicated, coming in on his days off. He was creating business models and deciding which was the best fit for his team. He was brilliant and, eventually, talkative. When the place was empty, and especially when it was raining out, he'd sneak food in for me and we'd talk for hours. I actually told him about Quaneef, and instead of judging or showing me pity, he listened. And chileeeee, the man prayed for me." She dramatically twisted her neck.

"I ain't never had that before. But turned out, he was deeply religious, that Robert," she hummed reflectively. "He was a lot of things, and many of those things I didn't know. Robert got to know me well: taking me on dates, introducing me to his controlling ass mother and even encouraged me to go to college."

I gasped. "Really?"

She nodded, twirling spaghetti over a spoon like her son. "He was right there my whole undergraduate experience. Robert was the first to take me out of the country. We visited Brazil, Paris, Croatia...lots of places. He showered me with extravagant gifts, even moved me out of my parents' apartment in Stella Wright."

Wanda slowed on eating and eventually met my fixed gaze. "I fell in love with the wrong man again...the second time in a row. This one wasn't abusive, though. He was more deceptive because he was a liar. From the first time we had sex on Valentine's Day, he lied, and I was too young to know. Then I started getting gut feelings about who he was...like..." Her eyes danced unfocused on the table. "As fine and rich as that man was, why didn't he have a flank of women competing with me? Even the ones who found him attractive when we were out together, he seemed to look right past them. But Robert kept a gang of friends around."

She shook her head. "It was weird. My brothers and sister thought he was gay. So one day, I asked him. Robert, of course, denied it. But that didn't change the spoil in the water, you know? Then, out of nowhere, he wanted a baby. The fool coerced me by giving me a ring—and no proposal." She shrugged. "A young, broken Black girl from Prince Street didn't know the game. I only knew what I felt, and that was my love for him. So, we didn't live together and we weren't engaged, but I believed in him enough to let him impregnate me. His mother was beyond herself with joy. Robert was not. I didn't get it."

I pulled a glass of wine to my mouth for a sip while vaguely recalling Jimmy's version of this story. Less details, but parallel.

"He became withdrawn. Less of a friend, more of a caring relative as I carried Ashton. He threw himself into work like never before. He turned mean and cold after Ashton was born, but not to me and the baby. It was to everyone, like his partners and subordinates. Something had seriously been stressing this man at a time of his life he once claimed he wanted. When Ashton was about a year or so, I couldn't take it anymore. Once again, I found myself being bruised in a relationship; this time, exclusively emotionally and mentally. I had no materialistic need in the world, thanks to Robert; neither did my child. But I'd lost my friend.

"Then I got a call from a frantic ice queen, Rosemary Spencer. She was screaming in my ear, telling me I'd cursed her child. She said Robert told her he was homosexual and would not hide it. Later, I learned he told her he would *no longer* hide it, but of course, Rosemary skewed the truth to make me the blame. I was devastated. Utterly destroyed. I trusted that man more than I had my own father and brothers. He'd lied to me. I saw red, which was a dangerous state for a broken girl like me."

Wanda went back to her food, leaving me thirsty for more details about the drama that was Ashton Spencer's parents. It rang familiar in so many ways.

I dropped my face, annoyed by her elongated break. "Then what?"

She chewed her food while gaping at me, directly in the face. "Start eating your food." She gestured to my plate. "It's getting cold." Grudgingly, I obeyed, mixing my pasta and sauce. I couldn't manage chicken right now. When the first forkful hit my mouth, Wanda continued. "It was ugly. The first thing I did was call up my sister to devise a plan. When that was done, we implemented it—"

"How?" I was too quick to ask.

"Tab and I drenched his home office and bedroom closet with gasoline and lit that bitch on fire."

I gasped, hand slapping to my spaghetti-filled mouth. "You torched his home."

Jimmy's words from almost exactly thirteen years ago were crisp in my memory. *"Child, Wanda Lee is a goddamn spitfire. She set his condo on fire."*

Watching her eat so calmly forced me to believe him. But no matter how unbothered Wanda appeared in the moment, it was clear to me dark emotions still ran hot in her blood behind her painful history with her son's father.

"Well, of course. And then on the way home, I called Rosemary and told her if her ass ever spoke ill against me again, she wouldn't see her only grandchild until he was an adult."

"What did she say?" My eyes were wide.

"I've not had a problem from that woman since. She may have fucked with my baby about his inheritance, but never me. When Robert died, being the generous soul he was, he left me a bundle of cash. He also listed me as a guardian over Ashton's estate, along with Rosemary."

"So, you two would have had to agree for Ashton not to get his inheritance for it to work?"

She winked. "You see why I never got involved with her futile threats against him?" She plopped the fork of spaghetti in her mouth. "Robert knew how controlling his mother was, and while he could trust her with his money, he couldn't with his son. Maybe he knew he could trust me with Ashton and there was a healthy balance between the two of us."

The next few moments were filled with silence. Wanda was clearing her plate while I couldn't taste my food; my head was over-populated with all matters of Ashton Spencer. What was he doing now? Did he think of me half as much as I'd been obsessing over him? Did we have a future together now? God, I hoped so. Having him around lately breathed new air into my world. He'd been a different type of inspiration for my future. Not to mention, we'd been privately working on a baby. The man wanted to propose to me. My destiny. I wanted him to be in my life permanently, finally.

"So, the point of me revisiting my pain was not to entertain you," Wanda's sharp tone woke me from my thoughts. "Let me bring this full circle. For years, I beat myself up for giving my heart to a kid who liked to hit me, then falling for a guy who used me to make his mother happy. I could never see past my disappointment— still can't on many days. I'm still working through my past. Cognitively, I understand it was my humble circumstances and lack of support that allowed me to fall in love with two people I had no business being with. Still, the consequences of those relationships haunt me."

"How?"

"I've had zero interest in relationships since Robert. None." When my head bounced backward, she nodded. "Not an ounce. Now, I've dated a couple here and there, but never with my heart or the intent to use it. I don't want the hassle of one."

"I get that part. Humans are complicated. But do you ever get lonely?"

"How? Since I had my child, my life has been full of adventure. Between raising a Black man in and around the city of Newark, going back to school for my advanced degrees, working in academia, staying on top of Ashton's football career up until *BSU*, supporting him through rehabilitation and mental health therapy after the *Kings* dropped him, and finally with seeing him off to start his own family, honey, I've been busy."

"But you were there with him in Texas."

"Part-time, and that's because I didn't believe he was strong there. Ashton has been living as a shell of himself since his injuries. All this time, I thought it was because of losing his dream career. And now, I'm pretty confident it was because *along* with losing his career, he lost his first love. His heart was broken."

My face tightened. "But—"

"Now, I'm no romantic—*period*. In these past two days since we learned about my grandson, I've come to believe if he'd gotten his chance in the *League*, he could have been distracted from the pain of losing you. Possibly the opposite, too; if he'd gotten you and Bobby instead of his career. Though I'm not sure because I don't see how much you could have given him being a child yourself at the time. But I *am* convinced there's some unrequited shit between you two. I hate that he's hurt all over again."

"I swear, I am, too—"

"But Ashton has to work through that. I'll be in his corner, as always, to make sure he does." Her hand covered mine over the table.

"Young lady, it's your heart I'm more concerned about. Who's nurturing you? You lost your mother just before losing your first and only child. That's traumatizing." Wanda's head shook. "My son is committed to you. He will likely come around eventually. But when he does, and you two decide on marriage and adding you to his family with his daughters, I want to be sure *you're* healthy."

"Why? Why do you care about my mental health?" She sounded like Ashton in New Orleans last weekend.

"Because you're going to be co-parenting my grandchildren. While it's never been my style to involve myself in Ashton's marriage or parenting—ever, I'm still a momma bear. I protect mine. Those girls had a great mother in Aivery, no matter how I felt about her personally. She was good to them and for them. You're not their biological mother, and while you can love them just as good, if you're not right within yourself, especially given the history you have with their mother, it can be dangerous for Ashton's family." Her eyes squinted. Wanda didn't take a breath. "Do you understand where I'm coming from?"

"I think I do. You don't want me to bring toxicity into his world."

"Right. But even more, I'm hoping to encourage and support you in any way I can toward wholeness yourself. *You* deserve that, Tori, and not for Ashton, Maurie, or Maggie. You deserve it for yourself. You would deserve it even if you decided on another man and had children of your own. I want you to be healthy, because whatever broke your spirit as a child doesn't deserve a lifetime victory over you. You deserve wholeness, baby girl."

Unable to look into the beam of light Wanda had just become, I turned my head and allowed unbidden tears to flow.

Ashton

When I walked in, he was at the table near the door of the balcony, drinking tea and eating cookies.

Jimmy turned to me, eyes sparkling with joy until he got a full look at me. Then he tried searching behind me. "Normally, I'd think I'm in trouble, but now that the rightful queen has returned to collect her crown, I'm safe."

Scratching deep inside my beard, I returned, "I don't think so, lil' Jimmy. In fact, I'm two seconds from going down to the admin office to discontinue payments for your luxurious stay here."

"Why ever would you do that, sir Ashton?"

"Because you're the exact conniving, selfish ass weasel I always knew you to be."

He gasped, stunned. "When have I been those things?"

"You knew Tori was pregnant. You knew she had a baby, and never said a fuckin' word!"

He shook his head breathlessly while smoothing down the lapels of his robe. "This isn't completely true!"

"Don't fuckin' lie to me, little man! You both told me you hired someone to find her. I do investigative work, innkeeper! I work with them all the time. You were told about OB visits, pregnancy physique, the hospital stay, and even a baby fuckin' being born." My body flashed hot as I leaned over the table toward him. "Tell me another goddamn lie and today will be the last time you see me and my money!" I stabbed my finger into the table, causing its contents to rattle.

I was ready, on the precipice of flipping my fucking wig.

And this motherfucker didn't appear ruffled enough for me. Did Jimmy think I was shooting empty threats?

"As I said: that is not the complete truth."

"You muthafuc—"

"The day you two left here back in October, I had the staff bring that box up from my storage unit." He pointed across the room, then Jimmy adjusted his wheelchair before motoring it off to a box on a small table. He reached inside, pulling out an overpacked file folder. "I did know Madame Tori was expecting," he finally confessed, causing a pain to lance across my damn stomach. It was the same pain I felt at the mention or thought of him for the past three days since I learned I had a son. Jimmy brought the folder back to the table where I stood. "I admit, I was curious about the paternity of the baby because, even in my not so positive expectations of you, I never thought you'd be irresponsible in that regard. You were always a generous kid, particularly after Robert's death. So while I waited to see if I should even communicate with the eccentric girl, I waited and watched to learn of the father."

His dark beetle eyes rolled up to me. "There was no father in the picture, and my gut told me the paternity was yours. So, I decided to reach out to her. I sent her money to help with the bills. The poor young girl worked hard. Far too hard for her to be carrying a Spencer progeny. Then I waited for her to respond. It took a while. In the meantime, I reached out to you." He dropped his head to the side. "Do you recall that fact, too, sir Ashton? I did reach out to you, and your response wasn't in favor of Madame Tori. Keep in mind, I still couldn't confirm the paternity of this baby."

"You should have told me!" I gritted, violence fighting for supremacy in my raging core.

And NormaJean...

I could have spit on her grave if I knew where she was buried.

"It was not my place, sir Ashton." He pushed the envelope toward me on the table. "I didn't know the baby was yours for sure until now. In all of my correspondences with her after the baby had passed, Ms. Tori never shared his existence with me. How was I to know unequivocally? Now that I do, I believe this belongs to you."

443

He was giving me the reports from his P.I. What good would this do me now? My son was dead. He'd never felt me, heard my voice, or experienced my love.

"I swear, I should abandon your ass right here, right now."

Jimmy's head shook. "You could, but you won't. It wouldn't be right."

I scoffed. "The hell it won't!"

"I reached out to you!" Jimmy shouted at me for the first time in my life. My neck snapped back. I didn't think his fucked up lungs could pull that deep tenor off. Trying to compose himself, he turned away. "I reached out to give you the opportunity to gain this information. I'm not like Rosemary." He smacked the table. "I don't involve myself in the matters of kids' hearts. It's what she did to your father and me. She should have never interjected her religious edicts into our affairs. Whether we went to heaven or hell was our decision, and she should not have had anything to do with our transportation there. I would have never manipulated you into a relationship with a young woman it was evident you loved over the woman you felt obligated to because of your family."

I backed away from the table, feeling even more wounded by the spirit of my son being real. "She named him Robert—" I cleared my throat, feeling the pulsing of my abraded heart. "Bobby."

Jimmy didn't look my way. "Because she's a woman of substance. An unpolished diamond in the rough who honestly just needed repackaging, but her heart was pure gold."

My eyes closed and jaw clenched. I turned to leave.

On my way out, I passed by the administrative offices.

We sauntered up to the front door of the building, the mountains behind felt close enough to touch. NeNe crowded at my side mutedly. Treesha turned toward us sporting a long expression.

"Alright, Treesh," Renata began. "You go in there and get honest so this can be your last time."

Treesha nodded, looking orphaned, carrying nothing more than a book bag with minimum belongings. We'd been down this road before. She'd get none of her comfort possessions until she completed her detox program. Same rules, same addiction, different treatment facility.

"C'mere, baby," Treesha called to her daughter. When NeNe peeled away from me and took her mother's side, Treesha broke down. "I'm sorry to have to do this shit again, baby. I swear, mommy's gonna get better. I'm gonna be stronger!"

I transferred my regard, skimming the gorgeous outdoors of the western portion of New Jersey. This place was supposed to be competent, armed with top-notch medical, mental health, and nutritional staff. I just hoped it worked. I hated dropping off my cousin at these places. She was always so emotionally vulnerable, which is never a safe space to be in around impressionable people.

When I returned my attention to my family, Renata was hugging Treesh. "You gone be good. You gone get through this."

NeNe ambled back around me, her head into my shoulders. My phone vibrated in my hands, hiking my heart rate as it had been doing since Ashton left my apartment with Bobby's remains.

Maggie: *Did you call yet?*

I promised the twins a party at *The Melanated Girl Doll House.* They'd be celebrating their tenth birthday and wanted to do it there with friends. I was thrilled when finding out they actually liked something I exposed them to. It also confirmed Maggie really enjoyed herself and wasn't as underwhelmed as she pretended to be back in December.

Me: Yes. I'm waiting to hear back from their events department.

Renata was still holding onto her sister when Maggie texted back.

Maggie: *Okay. Maurie says hurry! We're so geeked!*

Her emojis were iconic. It made the muscles in my face relax.

"Tori!" Treesha leaped onto me. "I'm so sorry for what I did!"

I hugged her back. "It's all good, Treesh." We talked and she'd already apologized profusely the day Ashton left my place. We were both out of character, and I believed her when she said she didn't know Ashton still had no knowledge of Bobby. I could understand why. It was something I should have told him before we kissed again, though that would have been hard considering *where* he'd kissed before my face.

"I swear, I'mma do better for you." She sobbed into my neck. "I gots to!"

"You need to do this for you, Treesha."

"This for you!" Renata made clear as I said almost the same thing.

Treesha knew this just as we did. Because of her years of addiction, our family knew the lingo well.

She pulled away, face stained with tears and, I was sure, a heart full of regrets. We watched her saunter into intake wounded. Waiting for her to check in then disappear from our lives for a couple of weeks, none of us spoke until Treesha was gone.

"Come on, y'all," Renata commanded, voice deep.

Treesha was on a wild spree. From the first weekend in January until last weekend, no one could find her. That was six weeks on the run, the longest for her. Treesha would text and called Renata and NeNe a few times, but would never say where she was or how long she'd be out there. We only knew she was getting high, based on her sightings and the company she was in. The first few times she did that, it was terrifying, then it got irritating. This time, I didn't realize how scared I was until I laid eyes on her in my apartment. As grateful as I was for the appearance of normality, it infuriated me to see her unperturbed and without consequences. My rage last Sunday when Ashton and I had returned from New Orleans was my fear surfacing.

When we were nearing the parking lot, my car was still running, my security behind the wheel.

"Alright, Tori. We're gonna see you." Renata lifted her arms for a hug.

When we were done, NeNe was next. "Bye, auntie. I'mma call you."

"You gonna be okay with the house?" I asked Renata when she reached the door of her car.

We drove separately because Renata and NeNe were headed back to South Jersey. My aunt, Sonya, wasn't feeling well, and was admitted to the hospital with severely high blood pressure. After checking in on her, Renata would go to the house they technically lived in to do some upkeep around there. The place had basically been abandoned since NeNe got her own apartment. Renata and Treesha were with me most of the time.

"I'll be good," Renata answered. "Plus, I told NeNe to stop by tomorrow in between class and work. Her ass gone help."

Inside the car, NeNe rolled her eyes, already on her phone. Mine vibrated with a call. Again, butterflies filled my belly.

But it was Elle.

I waved them off while answering the call. "Hey..."

"Hey," was her reply as I made my way to the waiting car. "That bug I had?"

"Yeah."

"A bun in my oven."

My feet stopped moving, forehead stretched, and mouth swung open. I was momentarily jarred. "As in baby? You?" I trilled in the mostly empty parking lot. "Pregnant, Elle?"

"Yup. My old, forty-one-year-old ass is going to be a mommy."

She didn't sound particularly thrilled, but I knew she was. She'd mentioned wanting to give Jackson a child a time or two.

"I'm so happy for you!" I opened the door to my car. "You're going to be an awesome, bad ass mom!"

CHAPTER TWENTY-FOUR

Ashton

"So, then he tells the dude from Herefords he'll look into it and get back to him," Julio shared, eyes blossoming. He sat at the edge of my desk bitching. "Get back to him? Muthafucka, what are you looking into for operations when an exec of operations is at the fuckin' table?" he trilled.

I raised my brows, exhaling.

"You see what I mean? Tucker be on some bullshit! He's mad that you put Tim as the head of tech over his dickhead friend, and you're grooming me for a promotion. Does he not know this company is owned and run by Black men?"

I nodded then my attention went to my chirping phone from a text.

Champ: *I need to drop off nail kits to the girls. You mind if I stay for dinner?*

For a moment, I thought to change her profile name in my contacts to something more appropriate like *liar human.*

"How' are the engagement party plans coming along?" I asked Julio while typing back to Tori.

Me: Totally fine. I won't be home for dinner.

"It's all good. Maria wants a damn photobooth and a live salsa band there...running my damn pockets! If there's one thing she's good at—other than cooking—it's spending my cash, bro." He wound his head over his shoulders. "Oh! And head!" His hands flew into the air. "My lady's jaw is priceless." His head bobbed.

Champ: *Okay*

My eyes scrolled up to look at him. "Julio."

"Hmmm?" His chin flipped my way.

"You don't think I'm going to think about that poor girl slaving over your lap, trying to capture your lil' pecker the next time I see her?"

Julio's head tossed back and he howled in laughter. "Fuck you, man!"

"Ms. Muriel would turn over in her precious grave if she heard you speak about your fiancée like that." Chuckling, my eyes dropped to my chirping phone again on my desk.

"You think we can get a surprise popup from *The Banger?*"

Champ: *I miss you...*

My eyes rolled up. Julio was rubbing his hands together. "She ain't available."

"Ah, man! I told Maria it was in the bag for that, bro!"

My brows pinched and lips pushed into the air, expressing my confusion. "Are you serious?"

My father shot to his feet and took long lunges to shut the door, which concerned me. Only my brother, Tim Jr., and his children were in the house with us. My father returned and sat behind his home office desk and took a deep breath.

His eyes closed dramatically before he scrubbed his face with his palms. "Tori, sweetheart, I know this is shocking to hear from your father. It's not how you want to view me, but I'm a flawed man."

"Look..." I pushed my head back over my shoulders. "Far be it for me to judge what goes on in your marriage with Patty, but I'm just taken aback by the request."

His brows narrowed when he demanded, "Why?"

My eyes ballooned. "Why?"

Is he fucking kidding me?

I'd stopped by my father's place this afternoon at his request made last night via a frantic call. It was timely. I had a meeting with the cookware company in Philly first thing this morning, then I crossed the bridge into New Jersey to go check on my Aunt Sonya, who had been admitted to a hospital in Somers Point. It made sense for me to stop by after since my father lived about ten minutes away. But when I got here, I had no idea *this* was what had him almost whispering into the phone, saying he needed to talk.

"Because you're telling me you've been sleeping with this Rebecca woman on and off for four years and now she's had a whole baby, and you need help paying for it."

"It's not like that, sweetheart." His open hands pumped in the air. "That's not what I'm saying exactly."

"If you're asking me to pay the child support for you, it is."

"I'm just asking for *help*—time—until I can sort this out on my own."

"Me, paying for your secret child isn't help to you? It certainly ain't you figuring it out on your own."

"Don't speak to me that way, KaToria." His spine straightened. "I'm your father."

I blinked hard and successively as I sat up in my chair, too. Anger swelled in my belly, and I felt lightheaded all of a sudden. No one called me that name but Ashton. Ever. And now, I couldn't stomach anyone trying to. "Do you have any idea the stress I have on my plate that I have to find solutions to deal with?"

His mouth opened, then he hesitated. "Does this have to do with the rumors your sisters have been whispering about Deon? Honey, the two of you can get through anything. Patty and I are willing to mentor you. I can understand the stress from being celebrities. We can help level that."

I stood, disgusted. "If life were that simple, and if you had offered that when you heard those 'whispers', it would have gone a long way to help me understand you."

"What do you mean understand me? Tori, I'm your father; you can always come to me with any problems you have. It's you who makes me feel otherwise. You can be so standoffish."

"Maybe it's because I don't understand your role in my life or mine in yours. Do you even know me? Like, know me?"

"What are you talking about?"

"I'm talking about how I'm in the middle of a heartbreak right now. Everyone in my inner-circle knows Deon couldn't hurt my heart if he had access to it in the first place—"

"Tori, what are you saying?"

"I'm not with Deon...haven't been since September."

He stood behind his desk, demanding, "Then why did you blow us off for the holidays? You didn't spend Thanksgiving, Christmas, or New Year with us."

"Because I've been with my boyfriend, the love of my life." God, I sounded corny and the worst part of it all was I didn't care.

It was my truth.

"The one your heart is breaking for?" He was being sarcastic.

"Yeah. Him?" I issued a blank face.

My father broke our eye-war first. "Okay." He rolled his eyes closed and took a deep breath. "I don't know what's going on or how we got here. I just asked for a short term favor, and now you're telling me you ditched your family for a guy you cheated on Deon with."

I shook my head. "Let's make something clear: the cheating is what you did. I never cheated on Deon." I somewhat lied. It certainly never felt like cheating with Ashton. "All I'm saying to you is I can't help you with this. I have my own issues and, quite frankly, I find it inappropriate that you've asked me to help."

"How?" he gritted out. For the first time, I saw my father angry, and with me.

I saw it in his furrowed eyes and tight mouth. My typically cool and laid back father now seemed desperate, almost enraged. The aggressive energy emanating from him right now made me quickly decide it was time to go.

My head fell to the side. "Since you've been in my life, you've treated me like I'm your big sister. You engage me to pay for things and make me feel like I'm only included in your tight-knit family because of what I can do for you and them. I'm not even your little sister, Timothy: I'm your daughter. The one you decided all of her childhood to not have a relationship with, then when you finally do, you ask and take. Then you wonder why I'm standoffish?"

I turned toward the door to leave, then something dawned on me. "You know why I was able to get engaged to Deon, a man I didn't love?" When he didn't reply, I still answered, "It's because I've been so desperate for exactly what you have in Patty, Julia, Tim Jr., Vanessa, and your grandkids. I want a family. I want identity. I want to belong. I want to nurture. And I want to give what little good and wholeness I have in me to people who are my own. So I'm sorry if I can't help you clean up the mess you've made in your marriage. I'm trying to get through my mess so I can have what you do."

Then, I left. I had a better place to be, like at Ashton's in time for the girls to get home from school.

My knees trembled as I waited inside the lobby of my building's garage, nerves frayed. When the limo pulled to a stop in front of the entrance, the back door opened. I sprinted out into the cold, clutching my robe. My heart was racing and pussy throbbing. Ducking inside, I sat on the bench opposite of Ashton. It was magically toasty inside. The interior smelled like new leather and him.

Ashton closed the door and the limo pulled off. His eyes hit me longer than they had since we returned from New Orleans last week. Twelve whole days of not touching him...being touched by him had been killing me. I missed his voice. When he got in last night and found me at his place with the girls, Ashton was the master at hiding his animosity and not looking at me at the same time. It hurt like hell. I was in pain; regret was a torturous place. This morning, I twisted and turned in my bed until I got the heart to text him.

Me: I need to talk to you. Drive into Jersey with the limo.

I didn't think Ashton was driven to work much. He drove himself unless he needed to deviate from his normal commute. And he looked good. His overcoat and suit jacket were hanging in from the hook over the window on the opposite side of the car, tie draped over the shoulder of the suit jacket. The few buttons of his white dress shirt were undone, and his blue suit pants exposed the muscular structure of his thighs, belt showed his tailored waist. Suddenly, I was hot.

With trembling fingers, I unraveled the belt of my robe. A cool rush of scented air hit my naked skin and I spread my thighs apart. My heart thundered in my chest. Refusal had become an acquaintance when dealing with Ashton lately. He refused my warmth and regrets at every turn, it seemed. When Ashton didn't move, I almost felt that crushing sense of disappointment I'd had for nearly two weeks.

Ignoring it, I crossed the car for him. Ashton didn't stir. When I kissed him, he let me. I pulled at his beard with my teeth then licked his neck, down to his exposed upper chest. My jittery hands moved to the buckle of his pants and he didn't move when I opened it, then went for his waist. I trembled silently when I pulled at his pants and boxers to lower them. Ashton's point blank gaze burned me. It was daring and indifferent at the same time. I was desperate, similar to my father yesterday. The thought of him kept me focused. Like I said, I was hurting. I was lonely and missed Ashton.

When his thick cock sprang out, I gulped in air, shamefully happy to see it again. *My best companion.* He was half-mast, but growing against the breaths from my nostrils. It shifted in the air each time I exhaled. With a hanging mouth, my eyes roved up to his. Still, Ashton's face only expressed arrogant observation and invitation. Ignoring it, I kissed him. The softness of his thin skin over hard metal soothed me.

Kisses turned into licks and my satisfied humming of appreciation for this part of his anatomy. My breasts rubbed against the hairs of his hard thighs, tickling my core. Fisting him, my hands were soaked with saliva. I built up a good cadence and could typically expect him to cum in any moment. Whether he would or wouldn't was up to him.

When I couldn't take the throb in my oasis any longer, I pulled back from him. My heavy eyes peered up and found his smokey gaze. Impatient about what it meant, I quickly rubbed my hands dry on my robe before mounting him on the bench. Ashton reclined, giving more room and inches of him once saddled. Slowly, I sat on him, enduring his fullness. The hairs of his thighs prickling my butt cheeks was a welcome sensation.

I kissed Ashton again, with my tongue this time. He met my strokes, yet less aggressively than normal. I didn't care; was grateful for whatever he gave. He was hurting, too. His pain was respected by me. I was different from my father; my love wasn't one-sided.

His thickness bruised and aroused me. My swelling left no room between us, something I desperately needed. I got into a rhythm in no time on top of him, adjusting to his size. He felt so good, my feet curled and my palms against the back of the leather bench misted. I squeezed my hips and the walls of my sex clasped and stroked him deeply.

When my back arched in tortured pleasure, I pushed my breasts to his face. Usually, when I did that, Ashton would greedily nibble on them. This time, he only nestled, breathing them in. That mild reaction still provided a sensation as I rolled over him until I felt my orgasm nearing. The car slowed and I knew my time was coming to an end. Ashton had to get to work. We were likely back at my place.

Ashton's big hot hands clutching my ass cheeks was the last push I needed to explode. I was cumming, and hard and fast. I bucked over him, squeezing his thickness to the point of momentary delirium. I stroked him until I could see straight and in full color again, only stopping when I caught his eyes on me.

Slowing down, I asked, "Did you cum?"

He couldn't have. Ashton wasn't shrinking inside me. Plus, I didn't feel his usual reactions when having an orgasm.

"Times up," his tone soft.

I glanced around the tinted windows and could see we'd stopped, even if I couldn't recognize where we were. Not thinking beyond not wanting to impose, I lifted off of him. Ashton tried pulling his clothes together, but couldn't get around his engorged cock.

"Ashton, I can handle that for you." My tone was desperate.

"You've done enough," he grated. "And you've proven to be reckless with my seeds in the past."

My face and heart collapsed at the same damn time. Ashton closed his eyes, leaned back, and took several deep breaths. I sat tense, naked, and trembling from swallowing back a burgeoning cry. It seemed like forever when his erection shrunk and he was able to slip himself into his boxers and pants. He zipped them up and buckled his belt.

"I'm about to open the door. You should close up," he advised without looking at me.

I glanced down at my open legs and immediately felt exposed... dirty. Fumbling with the lapels, I closed my robe, prepared to slip back into the lobby of my garage. When he opened the door, I immediately realized we weren't at my place.

Ashton slipped out, slamming the door behind him. Seconds later, the limo pulled off, and I was finally able to stop fighting the tears.

Ashton

"Damn..." I breathed out, eyes wide in my disbelief. "Daaaaaaamn!" I croaked that time.

A few minutes ago, Keyonna texted me a link imploring me to watch. The last thing I thought it would lead to was a *Spilling That Hot Tea* post with the big homie's wife doing some type of sexy number to Ragee's latest single, "*Come, Handle Me.*" Rayna was killing the choreography game in a black sheer leotard, tights, high heels, and a baby bump. She flipped with speed, landed with grace, twerked rhythmically, and glided over a wooden dance studio floor with effortless agility.

But she's fucking pregnant!

Big sis looked good, though. Rayna had been fit since the day I met her years ago. I knew she danced as a hobby, but with a set of twins running around, I could understand how quickly hobbies dwindled priority-wise. But she was good. Really good.

And seductive as fuck...

A hearty boff shot up from my belly and I laughed my ass off in the hotel bed. Loved Rayna Jacobs with all my heart; she was the light of my big homie's world. I held no attraction to her at all. She was goals for me and nothing more. But I knew that was not the case for ninety-nine point eight percent of niggas watching the same video. Rayna didn't come to play, and it made me wonder how this video had leaked. Azmir wasn't a public figure. Dude was a hidden Black gem, the modern-day version of Clarence Avant. He *made* celebrities, had his invisible hand in sports, Hollywood, and politics. The man was the master puppeteer no one could see. So how did a video of his hella talented wife hit the Internet? There were just over a million views on it.

Oh, shit..

I laughed out loud. Heads were about to roll. And to stir the pot of explosives, I sent a text to the talented and very powerful culture manipulator.

Me: Damn, homie! If I were Rayna, I woulda gone for the Bianca *Louboutin* instead of Fox *Asè Garb* if she was going with those fishnet stockings.

Almost as soon as I hit *send*, my mother's name populated on the face of my phone and it rang.

"Hey, Ms. Wanda."

"How you making out there in D.C.?"

I glanced around the empty hotel suite and remembered my

somber thoughts before Keyonna's text. I'd been traveling alone for years, exploring and researching as a journalist, and never had I felt lonely. For the first time, I wasn't satisfied. It wasn't the story I'd taken on about identity theft in the U.S. It was that I'd had a taste of a new, far more captivating passion recently.

"Good. Met with a few heads at the Federal Trade Commission today." I yawned. "Got another one tomorrow."

"Okay. I just wanted to ask if you knew where Maurie's Powder Girl nail polish is. They're going on Friday, after school to get dolled up for the party on Saturday, and she wanted that specific color." I could hear the rolling of her eyes.

"It should be in her bathroom." My mind raced with where she usually kept her things. "I think it's under the sink from when she—"

"I found it! It was under her sink!" a voice shouted in the background.

"Oh, never mind. We got it," my mother assured.

"Who was that?"

"Who else? Tori," my mother grounded out sarcastically. I closed my eyes, remembering. She was right: who else would it be? *Maybe my aunt, Tabitha, was over tonight with them?* "We finished up dinner. Lori just left, and I'm about to, too."

"Then who's watching the girls?"

"Tori, boy! You sure you okay?"

"I am. I'm just not used to you leaving them when I'm away."

"June done got admitted into the hospital this morning. His sugar shot up to the roof. That man forgets he's diabetic sometimes. I told him, he'll remember when they amputate that leg. You know his doctors have been warning him. Right?"

I shook my head to myself. Uncle June's body had been breaking down for almost seven years now. He was a big man, and with all the risks that came with his robust size. Diabetes, heart disease, and a bad hip and knee from simple obesity. It had been hard watching him decline over the years.

"Yeah. I know."

"Yup. And I don't know what to do. Nisha has been on his ass and so have I. I'm just going to run over there before visiting hours are over and check on him. I told Tori I'll be right back, but likely after they're knocked out. She's okay with it. She knows what to do."

Although foreign, the idea of Tori knowing the girl's nighttime routine was plausible. She'd been coming over for dinners most nights during the week, even when I wasn't there. She had also been basically spearheading the girl's tenth birthday party happening this Saturday for weeks now. The girls mentioned having it at the place Tori took them when my mother and I flew down to South Carolina to lay her aunt to rest. Tori said she'd make a few calls. Then that turned into the girls hounding her about details and making more requests for the party.

One night, at dinner, I told Tori I'd take over. I didn't want her overwhelmed by their demands. Plus, Maggie had not yet fully accepted Tori. She'd been improving, but hadn't been as acclimated to having Tori around as Maurie. I wouldn't allow her to be used. But Tori insisted that she'd take it on, so I backed off.

"Gotcha," was my one-word reply.

"You know she's tough, don't you?"

"Who?"

"Tori. Who else?" She trilled, "Keep up, son! She's been here...in the trenches. That's all I'll say. I'm staying out of grown folks' business—except for June. I'mma cuss his ass out."

Tori had been more than around my place. She'd been around, being seen with the engagement ring I'd given her, sans proposing. That was the link Keyonna sent me over a week ago, the day after I'd left Tori's ass naked in my limo while I went into work with painful groin aches. She had been wearing it loudly and proud, per the blogs. Of course, they speculated if Deon had gotten her a new ring with a bigger diamond. That's when Tori's P.R. team released a statement announcing Tori and Deon's amicable split. That somewhat quelled the bigger rock talk.

And me? I was in pain beyond repair some days. It was a devastating period, but one owed to my son. And I found comfort there; edging that black hole. The longer I stayed in my anger—embraced it —the closer I could feel to Bobby, or feel I was honoring him. For me, there was peace in that. I didn't know if that was healthy—no. I did know it wasn't. But I also felt Bobby had no choice in the matter of knowing me. My son had no choice in the matter of his life at all. He didn't ask to be here as the result of two reckless parents. Nor did he ask to die. The kid had no control of his demise at all. And that shit fucked with me so bad.

When Maurie was born, Aivery rejected her...slightly. She'd take more pictures of Maggie and have longer adoring gazes at her, too. She didn't mistreat Maureen; Aivery just couldn't hide her disappointment in her daughter's condition. Accepting Maurie as God gave her had never been an issue for me. She was perfect in so many ways. The manner in which Maurie showed love and support as she grew were unparallel. So, if I accepted a child of mine with special needs, I could only imagine how I could have loved and adored my first son, who was, for all intents and purposes "regular."

"Alright, Ms. Wanda." My cords were swelling from emotional thoughts of him. "Just hit me up when you get back in so I can have a pulse on what's going on over there. I'll call the girls at their bedtime."

"Aye-aye, captain."

Scoffing, I ended the call with, "Bye, Ma."

Sitting up in the bed, I took a deep breath and contemplated hitting the gym. I focused less on his memory when working out, I noticed. I was sure it would help me sleep through the night tonight. My phone chirping distracted me from making the decision.

A.D.J.: *Fuck you.*

I snorted, reclining against the headboard.

I was late.

Thanks to flying commercially to Milwaukee to interview two couples who were victims of identity fraud, my flight was delayed twice. That made me late for my babies' tenth birthday party. Not to mention, traffic in New York City around the *Rockefeller Center* was unimaginable this afternoon.

But the sight of my girls looking mature and happy abated all of my frustrations. Maurie and Maggie wore pretty dresses and had their hair pressed out into long curls. Their fingernails were painted and lips glossed with a faint pinkish color as they ran to me.

"Daddy, you're here!" Maggie cried, hugging my leg.

"Of course, I am!" I heaved Maurie into my chest. "Didn't Glammom tell you about my flight delays?"

"She said it was two." Maurie held two beautifully designed fingers in the air.

"Yes, baby. Two stupid flights had me miss helping you guys get ready and walking you in to your big extravaganza."

"And look, Daddy!" Maggie pointed to a moving projection of pictures against the tall walls of the warehouse. They were old pictures of the girls as babies and growing into their school-aged years. The pictures were through a projector rotating the room, showing different pictures for seconds at a time.

"Wow!" I was truly amazed. "This place is dope. So this is where you make the dolls?"

"Uhn, huhn," Maurie confirmed.

"Yeah, Daddy. There are different stations for you to decide how you want your doll to look. Isn't that cool?"

"It is." My eyes gazed around the warehouse-looking facility where there were machines literally building certain features for dolls. I'd read about it when the girls decided on the place. They could choose skin tones, hair texture and color, and the same with eyes. Their little friends, some of whom looked familiar, were all throughout the room, cheerily deciding on features and outfits. That's when I thought about the cost. This shit had to be expensive. "Where's Glammom?"

"She went to the bathroom."

"No, she didn't, Maggie," Maurie argued. "She went to the restaurant with Tori about the food."

Because of Maurie's shortness with her sister, I had to ask. "Maggie, is everything alright? Have you been polite to Tori?"

"Oh, yeah, Daddy! I told her thank you a million times today. Isn't this awesome?" Maggie's tone was convincing enough, so I dropped it.

I let Maurie down and the girls ran off to resume hosting their friends.

"Ashton," Lucy Cooper called over.

She and her husband, Dan, sauntered over to me.

"Hey," I greeted. "I'm glad you made it in." I hugged and kissed her on the cheek and shook his hand.

"Yes. This is amazing!" Mrs. Cooper marveled at the warehouse.

Pulling in a deep breath, I caught a picture of me feeding the girls in their high chairs. "It is," I agreed.

"Oh!" Mr. Cooper chirped. "That's you all's place down at home!" He pointed to the picture before it advanced to the next.

"That it is. Did you two come alone?"

"No. Sherell and the kids are up, too."

"Oh, cool—"

"You're here!" I turned to find my mother approaching. Tori was behind her, tapping into her phone. My heart fluttered and twisted at the sight of her. "I bet you won't be flying commercial no time soon, huhn?"

My mother hugged me.

"Wanda, it's cute that this place has these pictures floating around the room," Mrs. Cooper noted. "I've never seen this before."

"Neither have I," Mr. Copper agreed as Tori joined us. "I've been loving seeing my precious princesses' and family faces all over. This place had to set you back, huhn?"

"Well, that picture feature is new to the company, too," my mother shared. "Tori added that special, sentimental touch."

That's when our eyes met. Tori was deceptively beautiful because while she was a stunning woman, I knew when she wore sadness in her eyes.

"I'm sorry." Mrs. Cooper took a step closer to us. "I don't believe we met."

"Mrs. Cooper, this is KaToria, my girlfriend." I did the honors so effortlessly, it shocked the shit out of me. "Tori, these are Margaret and Maureen's grandparents, Dan and Lucy."

"It's a pleasure to meet you." Tori shook Lucy's hand.

"Holy shit!" Dan Cooper swore. "You're the heavy weight champion of the world! I was at your 2017 fight in Vegas against Barnes!"

Tightly and shyly, Tori smiled and bowed with her neck as she extended her hand to Dan. "Thanks for supporting. But for today, I'm just a guest for the best twins on the planet."

"That, they are," Lucy made clear, then looked away with flared nostrils.

My mother's face tightened and I blinked. Dan's face folded, too.

Lucy knew the connection between Tori, Aivery, and me. It was clear in that moment.

"Tori!" Keyonna shouted over. "Come look at NeNe's doll!"

The interruption was timely. Tori turned back to us. "Again, it was nice meeting you two."

As she turned on her heel, Lucy took Dan by the arm and whisked him away, too, visibly angry.

"I swear to god," my mother pledged beneath her breath. "if Lucy thinks she's gonna come up in here and make Tori feel like the interloper, she got another goddamn thing coming. She better leave that aristocratic shit in Texas!"

"She knows," I explained, looking ahead at Tori with the big girls.

Her body language was so tense. As much as I was angry with her, I couldn't hurt or leave her hanging publicly. She still felt like mine—even if I hadn't been behaving as hers lately.

Realization washed over her face. "You think?"

"Aivery and her mother were close. You remember that."

"You're right. I do, but you guys were kids back then. *Shit.* Babies!" My mother peered in a different direction; the one the Coopers left in. "If I ain't holding no grudges for that Pettiford fight being because of Aivery's immaturity, Lucy had better shake off the fact that you're now with Tori. It's called love."

I looked at her through narrowed eyes. Then, behind her, a picture of Aivery laughing with the girls in a pool floated on the wall. It was followed by one with Aivery pregnant, showing off her belly. The next was her alone. I don't know why I was taken by her images being included here, but I was. It seemed weird, yet appropriate.

My mother turned to see what had captured my attention.

"You said this was Tori's idea?"

"It's been a month." My head whipped down to my mother at her words. I knew right away she was referring to me learning about Bobby. She shook her head and began to walk off. "That's all I'm going to say, Ashton."

Tori

As the girls delivered cake to their guests in the restaurant portion of the store, my eyes locked at the carousel of pictures I'd had set up in here, too. I'd tried all day not to focus on them. I asked Keyonna and Wanda to gather them last month when I got serious about planning the party. They were able to come up with over fifty, which I thought was cool, knowing the pictures would populate throughout the entire party.

But the ones, like this, of Ashton, Aivery, and the girls together as a family were one of many I wish didn't grab my attention. Yes. I was an adult and understood they had an established history. But it didn't help to have reminders. The tricky thing about maturity and healing for me was it could have me bipolar. Today, I wanted the girls' mother's presence with them when celebrating turning double digits. They deserved it and so did she. The painful part of it was their mother was none other than Aivery Cooper.

Taking a deep breath, I turned to leave. I had some place to be.

But what I didn't expect was to run into Aivery's sister.

She sidled up beside me, preventing me from moving. Her eyes were on the girls when she murmured, "I know exactly who you are. And you're not as cute as you think."

There was a heavy dose of shade in those words. "Oh, cool. You want an autograph?" I managed a smile.

"I would never. My sister said you were gross. I can't believe Ashton fell for you then or now. Too bad she can't see what a few dollars and a talented plastic surgeon can do."

I scoffed, shaking my head. "Nah, but I can show *you* what these hands can do." When Sherell gasped and pulled her head back, anger spiked in my belly. I hated women who were about that oral toughness, but played victim when about to get swung on. Like, who's going to keep listening to your nasty words? "And I believe the word she used to describe me was *diseased*."

"That's right!" The woman laughed, eyes piercing into me. She seriously found humor in that shit.

I rounded her to leave. "And I'm also that diseased, ugly woman who just dropped twenty Gs on her daughters' party. I should've donated it to your Troll Doll-looking ass for a talented plastic surgeon. It's clear to me Aivery got all the looks."

With that, I left knowing I had lots of repenting to do in the car.

Maybe coming today wasn't the best idea...

Ashton

"Where's Tori?" I asked as the girls were finishing up eating and about to go pick out their doll's clothes in the store's boutique.

"She's gone," my mother answered, passing off goodie bags to the twins to give to their guests.

"Why?" *Did she feel uncomfortable?*

Resentment swelled in my chest. Could she not control her feelings of having the Coopers around for just a few hours? It brought back residual pain from when she left me broken and laid up in the hospital alone.

"She had a doctor's appointment," NeNe supplied as she helped us at the table. "She woke up with a fever this morning, but didn't want to miss the party. She's been off for a few days now. She does this every year around this time. My great aunt, Dot's, death date was last week. She's usually off for most of the month of March, to be honest."

My mother's admonishing eyes hit me.

Suddenly, I felt like shit.

CHAPTER TWENTY-FIVE

Ashton

"Damn," I murmured to myself. "This *is* the place." My eyes scanned the construction site.

There were utility trucks all over, drilling, pouring, and digging. The place was littered with men and women in construction hats. All this activity almost made me question again if this was the property Jaquana showed me five months ago.

I parked the car behind the last truck in the roadway. When I stepped out, I saw Tori waiting in a tan trench coat and rain boots. She waved me her way.

"This is for you." She handed me rolled up stationery. "Hop in," she instructed as she stepped up and into the back seat of a utility truck. With a second of hesitation, I obeyed. "We're ready, Johnnie." She tapped the back of the driver's chair, prompting him to action.

We drove around the countless cars and trucks of apparent workers.

"When did Jaquana show you this property?"

"Back in October, the day before we left for *Saint Justin*." I snorted. "What? Why? She showed it to you, too?"

"Apparently, days before you," I muttered. "She mentioned not having shown it to anyone."

"Did you like it?"

I shook my head, gazing around. "The prospect of building was too overwhelming for me at the time."

"And what about now? It made sense for me. I was honest with you when I said I needed to do something selfish for me. I was a little heady about reconnecting with you. And call me crazy, but I got a visual when she showed me this property. It was the endless possibility of creating something new with you. Obviously, I didn't know about the girls then, but this now makes even more sense with them in mind." The truck stopped. "This is the main house. I approved eight thousand, seven hundred, fifty-two square feet, but it may go a little bigger depending on the attachments."

She pointed ahead to the foundation of a soon-to-be palatial structure. Wood paneling was being installed as we watched. "Eight bedrooms and ten baths, with all the trimmings of a traditional home: formal dining room, living room, family room, den, laundry room— the whole gamut." She tapped the back of the driver's seat again and we moved around the house.

"Here will be a two-story garage for your toys in the form of vehicles. It'll be about twenty yards from the main house, and with a covering. Think the parking garage at the mall. I selected an insulated walkway from the main house to it. Keep in mind, there will be a four-car garage attached to the house for the vehicles used regularly." She tapped the back of the driver's seat.

"And over here will be the family room." She pointed to where the panels were going up. "One side of it will open up to a playroom.

I figured the girls would outfit it according to their preferences, but seven hundred square feet should be enough for them. Then, of course, as they get older, the design and purpose of the room would change." She tapped again and we pulled off to the other side of the outlined structure.

I opened the rolled up paper and saw it was the blueprint of the property. It was larger than Jaquana described, extending *well* beyond the forest outline.

"Here," Tori continued. "would be another insulated walk through—or it can be detached—to the gym. It will be two levels. Over here will be an office for you. We can give it all the features that will inspire your journalistic pursuits. I'm actually meeting with a developer for an electronic map to add, so you can see regions and locales to determine your research. I think one level should suffice, but we can discuss that later." Tori tapped the back of the seat again. "Let's go back to the house."

When we stopped, having returned to the main structure, she shared, "The pool. I want to do something kid-friendly and have almost ten designs to pick from. But it would be here, and I'd like to have a waterfall and slide." The shy smile on her face made me want to comfort her. She tapped again. "That's it for now. I just wanted you to see what I've been working on since the fall. I didn't know when I'd share it or that I would, but I've been hoping to," she explained. "It was my plan to do it when we got back from New Orleans, but..."

Tori was being vulnerable here. It took balls to basically tell me she'd been building a home with my girls and me in mind after the explosive bomb she dropped last month about my son. I'd been coming to a better place emotionally. My anger had been diminishing. Some days, I could think of Tori in a hopeful manner. Then there were days my emotions flared over what could have been if I'd known Bobby, and I couldn't stand the sight of her at my dinner table at night. I'd never been so inconsistent emotionally.

We stopped back at my car and hopped off the truck. I turned to her, taking a deep breath. I was speechless.

"Ashton, I'm sorry."

"You've said that."

"And I can't say it enough."

"No, what you can't do is give me time with my son. That's some shit I'll have to live with for the rest of my life. I've been thinking. This wouldn't be painful if you'd have aborted him or if he was still-born. But no: my child was issued a birth certificate and a damn social security card. He was a living, breathing, eating, shitting, and feeling being!" I growled out, lips pressed into my teeth. Just seconds into the topic and I was angry all over again. I couldn't do this shit first thing in the morning. It was easier facing Tori with others in the room, forcing me to play nice. My hands swung toward the construction. "Look... I don't wanna hurt you—"

"And I don't want to live without you. You wanted me here and not running at the first sign of conflict. Well, damn it, Ashton, I've been here. I've been at your side, in your home, with the women you love the most. Even with this black mark over my head they can see, I didn't run, Ashton! I'm here." She pointed toward the property. "I want you here, too—with Margaret and Maureen. But I need you healed from my mistake."

I scoffed. "Then you're gonna have to give me more time."

"It's been six weeks."

"My son's life extended six weeks." And there was the benediction. Tori's body snatched away from me. I hoped she was processing how real this shit was. A part of me wanted to hold and comfort her. But I couldn't get past the betrayal. "If I'd known you were pregnant, I would have never married Aivery. Did you hear me?" She turned to face me again. "I—" my voice cracked. "would have never felt oblig-ated to her. Yeah, I would have lost the *League*, but I would have had a different future: with you and Bobby. And if we would have lost him, it would have been together. I would have never spent those years taking laps in that dark hole. I would have been Mr. Tori *"The Banger,"* proudly on your journey to being the undisputed champion of the world. I would have found my way...with you by my side."

Seeing the tears fall down her face was too painful to bear. I didn't want to hurt Tori, nor did I want to comfort her. So I took off to my car. By the time I got inside, I saw she'd walked away, her hands at her face with her back to me.

I took a deep breath, eyes closing as I waited for the dull ache in my chest to abate. Then I caught the sight of the blueprint in my lap. I opened it and followed the forest line. There was definitely more open property back there. Giving the construction a final look-over, I cranked the ignition, holding the paper in the air.

"This is the best birthday ever!" Maggie screamed in the kitchen just before taking off for her room.

"Hey!" I barked over the sink, washing dishes. "Don't let that sugar high get you in trouble, Margaret!"

"Sorry, Daddy!" she shouted back, now out of my sight. "I'm just so happy!"

My mother snickered over at the table with Keyonna, having her night coffee with birthday cake. The girls had dinner and birthday cake for dessert on their actual birthday. We even sang happy birthday to them as though we hadn't last Saturday, at their over-the-top birthday party. Maggie and Maurie had just finished their bath time and were headed to bed. I was tired, per usual, but happy they were satiated this birthday season.

"Damn," Keyonna chirped, peering into her phone. "Young Lord may be buying his wife an *Audemars Piguet Royal Oak Perpetual Calendar* as a gift."

"Mouth, young lady!" my mother warned because Maurie was still in the kitchen with us.

"What's the occasion?"

"She's graduating law school this semester," Keyonna answered. "That's so dope! You gonna buy me a *Audemars Piguet* when I graduate?"

"Not a chance."

"But you have one?"

"I'm also wealthy."

"Didn't you get a *Hublot Classic Fusion* for your birthday?" she challenged.

"From a wealthy woman." I winked.

"What's a *Hublot Fusion*?" My mother's face was tight with confusion.

Keyonna laughed. "A watch, Aunt Wanda. You know. A luxury timepiece?"

"Daddy." Maurie was at my leg. Her head was bent and she was pulling at her hair. The nail polish on her cute little fingers had faded since the party. "Can you help me? It's stuck in my hair."

"Sure, baby." I turned off the water and dried my hands on a nearby towel. Then I squatted down near her to see what was causing her irritation. It was a necklace I'd never seen before. A lock of her hair got twisted around the hook. It took a few seconds, but I managed to detangle it. I straightened it over her neck, then inspected the jewelry. It was a simple rose gold chain with a half-heart pendant. Engraved on one side of it was *Maureen* and on the other was *Mommy*. The sentiment was eerily familiar. "Where did you get this from?"

"Tori," she answered, wiping her nose as she sniffled.

"When?"

"She was over here when they got home," my mother noted. "She dropped a few things off."

"Ain't that cake bomb?" Keyonna asked my mother.

"Mmmmhmmmm," my mother hummed, scooping up her last piece of the birthday cake.

"Tori brought the cake?" I asked.

Keyonna nodded.

She made it...

I knew she did. For the first time, I was confident in knowing the adult Tori she swore to me last summer I didn't. Tori would never buy a cake. Not for my babies' birthday. The Coopers contributed the cake for the party last Saturday. It was tall and festive from a baker in the City. I asked because when I saw the cake and all its details, I would have been blown away if Tori had made it. A part of me felt her crazy ass would have tried.

"Does your sister have one of these, too?" Maurie nodded, her eyes heavy. I grabbed her little head and kissed her. "Goodnight, my love."

"Night, Daddy." She took off for the door yawning. "Night, Glammom. Night KeyKey!"

"Night, baby!" my mother called after her.

"Goodnight, Maurie-sprinkles!" Keyonna shouted.

Winded by the countless thoughts and questions shooting off in my head, I stood. "Tori didn't want to stay for dinner?"

"She didn't look herself," my mother noted.

"Maybe she's tired. NeNe said she's been super busy."

Yeah. Having a whole ass estate built...

"Alright." I walked over to kiss them both. "I've got a shit load of reading waiting for me. Good night."

"Night."

"Night, son."

En route to my room, something was nipping at me. I had no clue what it could be. Between work, research, and this bullshit with Tori, I hadn't had the vigor to think through shit like I normally would. Why the hell she didn't stay for dinner on my babies' birthday was hella confounding. I sat on the side of my bed and thought. Was it hard to spend today with them for her? Did it make her think about Bobby?

Then my attention went to my nightstand. Bobby's remains weren't there. I shot to my feet alarmed. That nipping feeling wouldn't slow. But now I had to think about this urn. If my girls played with it or had broken it, I hoped they would have told someone. That couldn't be it. Maggie and Maurie were no longer allowed in my room without permission. They'd even been good at knocking before coming in.

The fuck!

I dropped my face into my palms, trying to figure out what was nagging me. Tori was here, but didn't stay.

Mommy...on the other side of the pendant.

Urn...gone.

March 25th, 2008—

No. It's twenty-twenty...

My head flew up, eyes bulging.

"Fuck!"

I'd never moved so fast, time swallowing me with each wasted second. I may have run a light or two heading out of the City to Jersey. I damn sure cut off a few vehicles in my determined gust. Managing the front door of her apartment open, I trekked to the back with urgent speed. When I made it to her bedroom, I burst through the door.

And there she was, exactly how I feared I'd find her. Tori's eyes were fire red, face swollen and drenched with tears in most places, dried tracks of them in others. Her body spasmed hard as she sat up in her bed, sobbing in evidentiary pain. Bobby's urn was at her side, just as I had suspected.

Regret crashed down over me, and the shit felt debilitating for seconds long. I felt sick, wanting to vomit at the possible sight of a KaToria who'd just learned she lost her son. Broken. My girl was devastatingly broken, and I fought like hell to keep my shit together. But I needed to hold her.

Rounding her bed to get to her, I didn't hesitate to pull Tori into my cold chest and hold her there. Her hands drew up my back and she clutched me with desperation. Damn, I was grateful. I needed her heat in far more than the physical sense. I needed to share in this moment of grief with the mother of my child.

"I'm so sorry, baby." I whimpered over her head. "I'm so sorry I wasn't there for you...with you."

It had finally hit me: I'd never seen Tori as a victim in this. In my selfishness, never had I considered her loss for a child she carried alone, delivered alone, and parented alone. Even on today, the day I celebrated the life of my girls, she thought to do so in her own way, then carve out time to grieve her child. The day Aivery became a mother for the first time, Tori lost her first child. My son. That was some shit I could never get over. And in that very moment, I dropped my resentment. This shit between us was so fucking jaded. So many fears and wasted years.

That ended tonight.

I lifted her head to meet her swollen red eyes. "No more haunting secrets of our past. No more fears. From now on, it's you and me, creating together." It was the term she used when showing me the property two days ago. "And, baby, let's be reckless with this shit."

Readily, Tori nodded. A fresh round of tears sprung from her eyes

Tori

I had no appetite, still emotionally and physically exhausted. Turning over the eggs in my plate, I questioned why love had to be so painful. Almost everyone closest to my heart died or disappointed me. As I peered across the kitchen, eyes inching up his taut back, I knew I'd manage the hurt just to be with him. Love was a sacrifice. Only Ashton made me feel alive, inspired, and hopeful. I'd walk through the fire with him.

"Yeah, Lori. Yup," he spoke into the phone. "And please tell my mom thanks for this. Uhn-huhn. Tell her Daddy loves her, too, and to have the best day ever." There was a heaviness in his voice aside from his usual coarse morning tenor. Ashton was putting on a brave face for home. "Yup. Okay. Later."

He stirred his latte and when Ashton turned my way, my heart galloped and body trembled. To attempt killing the nervous tension, I stood for the pantry. I needed honey and when I brought the bottle back to the table, Ashton was buttering his toast.

He smiled politely, almost formally with his side to me as he worked over the counter. "My eggs aren't doing it for you this morning?"

I couldn't stop shaking as my loose gaze trailed up his body. "I'm pregnant." Involuntarily, I pulled in a quiet breath through my nose, blood rushing loudly in my head.

He turned to me abruptly, looking from my mouth down to my flat belly. Then his chin dipped and a smile opened on his face as he pulled in the same breath through his open mouth, the muscles around his eyes relaxing. "Congratulations. I'm proud of you."

I tried closing my eyes to adjust to the relief he'd just thrown me. "Thank you," only came out as a whisper.

"Was that hard to share?"

My eyes opened. "I thought the timing would be too much for you."

He shrugged with his brows. "We'd been trying."

"Before the storm," I amended.

Ashton nodded in agreement of our grim period I silently prayed was behind us now.

"When did you find out?"

"Sunday."

"Is that why you showed me the property on Monday."

I nodded. "A little. It pushed me to." Taking a deep breath, I pinched the bridge of my nose. "Look, Ashton, I want this baby. I hope you haven't changed your mind."

He dropped the toast and took casual steps toward me. "You want my baby? Why?"

Then he was on me, his bulging erection making itself known. I was embarrassed by how hot my body flashed for him. That instantly, I was turned on. "Because you said you'd give me one."

"I also said I'd do the *S.I.* interview and be done with your complicated ass." The thickness in his voice turned me on, just as much as his honesty.

"I—I," I stuttered. "I don't mean to be, but I really want this."

Ashton backed me into the table until my legs lifted in the air and I saw the ceiling. He pulled up and off my pajama shorts and spread my thighs wide. I was trembling before his mouth met my oasis. Horny human. I'd never craved a man sexually the way I did Ashton. As his lips brushed up my thigh, followed by course trails of his unkempt beard, my back arched. My nipples pushed against the thin cotton fabric of my shirt and my head swirled, blood rushing to one place. When Ashton's wide and thick tongue brushed up my slit, I slushed back the extra saliva my mouth suddenly produced. I may not have had an appetite for food but would always have one for this arrogant, asshole human.

Ashton made love to my pussy with his mouth. He expressed his adoration of it, longing for it, and his happy state having learned he was going to be a father again. At least that's what I hoped it was. I wanted him to be happy, finally. We both deserved it. My hands found his carpet-thick scalp and dug into it as my body heated. My toes curled and back arched deeper, then I exploded.

"Ashton..." I cried, body convulsing over the hard, unforgiving surface.

He sucked and sucked and my titties bounced, slapping against my torso. It went on and on until my cries turned into helpless whimpers. Ashton stood to his feet, eyes low and filled with dark lust.

He righted himself and pulled his t-shirt over his head while peering down on me. "You want a baby, and I want a wife." He lowered his boxers and sweats, then grabbed the thick root of himself without an ounce of self-consciousness. I swallowed as he stroked himself, eyes half-mast. "What another crossroad we meet at again."

When he fed his steeliness to me, his head pushing into my swollen oasis, I didn't have an answer for him. I couldn't think or speak. I could only feel what had gotten me in this latest predicament in the first place.

"And I'm in here most of the time," Treesha shared. We turned the corner, returning to the lounge. She directed us to a round table where she sat, placing her astrology book on the table. "I just be in here reading and learning about myself."

"And eating!" NeNe blurted out.

Renata and I busted out laughing.

Treesha rolled her eyes. "The cooks in here are dope. There's even a baker."

"It costs enough," Renata scoffed. "Something better be good, especially the therapists."

"Anyway," Treesha sighed. "I'm just trying to make the best of the things I can control and letting those things I can't fall into place in the universe."

My head bobbed. "Your room here is nicer than the last two places."

"Yup." Treesha stretched her arms in the air. The mattress, too, 'cause babee!"

NeNe went back into her phone and Renata began playing with her cuticles, killing the conversation. We still had some time left on Treesha's visit in rehab, so I decided to go for it.

"Guess who's pregnant?" I singsonged to dull the announcement.

"Who?" Renata asked.

I pointed to my belly.

"Oh, my god!" NeNe trilled. "Why am I just finding out about this? Does Keyonna know, because if she knew before me, I'mma—"

"Knock it off, little girl." I rolled my eyes. "I'm telling *my* family, those closest to me."

"But that don't mean Keyonna don't know already."

I shook my head. "If she does, he told her today." Ashton and I had basically been stuck at the hip since Wednesday night. He'd taken off the whole week from work and was at my place every day, all day. Just like before Valentine's Day, I'd been staying the night at his place and staying in his room until the girls left for school. Last night, we were at my place and today, we separated for his weekend duties and so that I could come see Treesha. It was the first visit of her stay. "We agreed to keep the pregnancy under wraps until today, so I could tell you guys together."

"How do you know?" Renata asked.

"My period didn't come last month. I didn't think much of it because of my cycle change and the traveling."

Treesha's head swung to the side, brows knitted tight. "Why did your cycle change?"

Dropping my head to the side, I mocked her. "It happens when you stop birth control."

"Ewwwwww!" NeNe cried, eyes wide as saucers as she leaned away from me. "You and Mr. Ashton *been* doing nasty stuff?"

Scoffing at her innocence, I rolled my eyes.

"When you due?" Renata's forehead had been stretched since I broke the news.

"November seventh." My face tightened. "We went to my GYN yesterday. She said we possibly conceived on Valentine's Day."

"Ut-oh!" Treesha chirped.

"What?"

"First, this is another November baby like Bobby. And it's gonna be a Scorpio." She shook her head, turning up her lips. "Them damn Scorpios."

"Anyway!" NeNe dismissed her mother's astrology claims. "You happy? I hope so if you getting off birth control. Let me get off. All hell'll break loose, and I ain't even having sex yet!"

I swung my head. "Let's keep it that way." My death stare game from the ring came in handy when threatening NeNe. She still fell for it. "And yes, I'm very happy." I took a deep breath, unable to believe what I was going to share next. "I'll be even happier when we're married."

"When y'all gone do that?" Treesha demanded.

Renata followed up with, "Do Elle know this shit?"

I shook my head and shrugged. "My life's my own. It's time for me to do me. I'm a private person and will take the licks the media's gonna give. I'm tough and I hope he's tough, too. I don't wanna do nothing on the low. As matter of fact, I want to be an expectant bride."

The whole table gasped.

"Are you fucking kidding me, Tor?" Treesha asked.

"I'm not." I shook my head, unbothered. "I'm so ready for that man."

"What he say about getting married so soon?" Renata wanted to know.

"He's the one pushing for the marriage." I shrugged again,

extending my arm across the table. "He gave me the ring on Valentine's Day. But he told me to wait for the proposal, so…"

"Oh, shit!" Treesha swore, examining the glistening diamond. "Tori, what the hell kind of snatch you be putting on that millionaire?"

NeNe giggled, covering her mouth. "I heard he *been* about 'chu, girl!"

That silliness made me smile with pride. "Yup. You right."

"Damn." Renata huffed. "I know how damn picky you are. I guess I need to start looking for designers for your wedding gown ASAP since you want a bump in it."

"No. *MEEHAR*'ll make that shit for free," Treesha added. "Vera Wang, too. She wanted to do it for the wedding with Deon, 'member?"

"Oh, yeah!" Renata breathed.

I shook my head. "Nah. I want something simple. No heavy beaded ball gown. Something simple and sexy, showing off me and my bump. I wanna see if the Shenedrea woman will do it."

"When you say simple," Renata inquired. "How many people?"

"I'd have to talk to Ashton about that, but on my end, it won't be a Hollywood affair. The day would belong to Ashton and me, and all of our old bones."

"Well, he's gotta propose first," NeNe made clear.

Treesha's index finger swung over to her daughter. "That part!"

Ashton

"What?" Keyonna dropped her phone to her lap.

Maurie smiled widely, liking having no appreciation of my words yet.

My mother straightened her spine, sitting on the sofa.

"A baby?" Maggie yelped, eyes wide, arms stretched in the air.

Tori tensed beside me.

"We say congratulations in this house when people share good news, little lady!" My mother chastised her.

"Congratulations, Tori!" Maurie continued to smile.

Tori's shoulders lifted under me as she gushed. "Thanks, cutie."

I swear that Maurie was my sunshine on a stormy day.

"Congratulations for a baby? Isn't that for her family to do?" Maggie argued.

"Maggie-Patty!" Keyonna intervened. "Let's be nice."

Maggie sat back, huffing. "It was just a question! It's not like Tori having a baby's our business anyway. It's between her and her boyfriend."

I squinted, confused by her assessment. "I am her boyfriend, Maggie."

"Instead of asking that question, why don't you congratulate your father," my mother urged again.

"Congratulations, Daddy!" Maurie issued again.

"Thank you, princess. I really appreciate that!"

"Why?" Maggie demanded. "It's Tori's baby!"

"It's my baby, too," I made clear.

That's when my daughter's face went lax. Keyonna left from her sofa in my living room and came over to kiss Tori.

"I'm so happy for you!" she squealed. "I can't wait! Do we know when?"

While I followed my daughter's expressive confusion, I answered, "November seventh."

My mother was the next to come over for a hug. This time, Tori stood to meet her. It was Sunday night and we'd all had dinner. Afterward, I asked them to gather in the living room so I could break the news. I didn't expect Maggie to perform flips in her excitement, but I also didn't expect her anger.

"Sunshine," I called over to Maggie. "Do you understand what this means? You're going to be a big sister."

"Me, too!" Maurie interjected, shooting her hand into the air.

"That's right, munchkin. You, too." I nodded with a smile. "I think you'd both be great."

"But you're not married," Maggie argued. "Shouldn't people be married before having a baby?"

"I think most people do," Tori spoke up. "It would have been cool if your Dad and I waited, but we...I guess, wanted to be different. I don't think that'll change how great a big sister you'll be."

"And I plan on marrying Tori...soon," I added. "So, we'll be right on track eventually."

"Does NeNe know?" Keyonna's eyes rolled over to Tori. "Like...before me?"

Tori covered her face with her hands. "Lord!"

"I'm just saying! I'm older!"

My eyes stayed glued to Maggie and when she finally looked my way again, I motioned with my head to meet out in the hall. Her little legs pushed off the couch and she left quietly, showing obedience.

When we met in the hallway, I crouched down in front of her, pulling her into my chest. My baby was so small and fragile, I couldn't hug her too hard or I'd crush her.

"What are you feeling?" She shrugged silently. "Are you angry?" Maggie shook her head. "Are you sad?"

"It's just... like... It's happening too fast," she finally shared.

Truly understanding, I nodded. "I get what you mean. I even agree with you. Because you're so young I can't explain yet how this happened so fast. But what I can promise you is that none of this—the baby or Tori—will change the love and bond I have with you and your sister."

"KeyKey, too?"

"Keyonna, too. And Glammom." My attention went to the necklace and pendant on her little chest. I lifted it, observing their names, *Margaret* and *Mommy*, engraved on either side. "We've been such a strong unit for so long. Now, we're adding to it. We're not switching people out. We're gaining a partner for Daddy. And when Daddy got this partner..." I rolled my eyes, bouncing on the balls of my feet at the literal visual. "...he added to the family with her. Nothing changes. Nothing. I still love you and Maurie like steak and potatoes."

"KeyKey, too?" she asked again.

"Always. KeyKey, too."

Maggie leaped onto me, wrapping me in a big girl hug. "Thank you, Daddy."

"Thank you, baby, for understanding Daddy."

"Always."

I blinked back tears. This had been one fucking emotional month for me. I'd held strong for the most part and would continue to.

When I stood to rejoin the room, I saw Tori and Maurie were dancing and Keyonna took pictures of them from her phone. My mother smiled on.

"Alright, girls!" Lori called from the doorway. "Time for your showers."

Maurie charged over to Lori, taking her by the legs. Then I looked over to Tori. She fought through a smile, though I knew she was concerned about Maggie. I took her at the hand, raising it to my mouth for a kiss. We'd have to give her time. No matter how expressive my daughter was, she'd been through a lot and was only ten. We'd have to wait for her to adjust. Tori pulled her arms around me and, standing on her toes, reached up for a kiss.

"Hey, Tori!" a little voice cried out.

Tori's head veered around me. I turned my head in the other direction and found Maggie leaning in the doorway. "My friend, Shelly, got a baby sister last month. She said all the baby does is cry and eat. It doesn't sleep, but congratulations!" She sprinted off.

"Awwww! My sweet Maggie," my mother cooed, standing from

her seat. "But we need to discuss another important matter. I've been to your apartment, Tori, and it ain't much difference in size than this. Where y'all plan to live with three kids—"

"Four!" Keyonna corrected.

"Well, yeah." My mother agreed. "Four kids."

My attention went to my babies' mother. I swiped back her hair that was brushed into a ponytail, reminding me of our *BSU* days.

My tomboy...

"Tori's already got that part covered, Ms. Wanda."

CHAPTER TWENTY-SIX

April

Tori

"Are you looking?"

As my body bounced over the seat from the bumpy, unpaved road, I laughed. "No! I can't see shit and don't understand why. I know we're at the house, Ashton!"

He stopped the car once we turned on to the road leading to the house that was still under construction to place a bandana over my eyes.

"Damn," he muttered. "You're irritated."

I laughed. "I am not! What makes you say that?"

"Because you cursed. You only curse when upset."

That gave me pause. I'd been so much better at my foul language until he returned to my world—that and when hanging out with Brielle. That woman stressed me like none other at times.

"Maybe I'm just anxious to learn why my boyfriend puts a mask over my eyes when we've arrived at a destination I'm familiar with."

"You're going to see in about forty-five seconds."

I felt the sports car shift again. His *Porsche 911* made statements on the dirt road. When I felt us come to a slow, then stop, I let out a dramatic sigh of relief. I listened as his door opened then closed, and a few seconds later, the trunk was opened. After I heard it close, Ashton was at my door.

"Kick your feet out, McNabb. Just turn your body this way." I obeyed, shifting until my feet were dangling in the air, out of the car. Ashton removed my heels and pulled boots on my feet. Then he helped me out of the car, closing the door behind me. I felt leaves being crushed beneath my feet. "Take your time; we're not going very far."

"Then why did I have to take off my heels?"

"Because you can't see and I can't afford you hurting yourself."

"Hurting myself or the baby?" I balled my mouth.

"Either, Nabby-girl."

"But you'll be alright as long as you *let me be your whooooo—*"

His hand was over my mouth, cutting my freestyle bar off. "McNabb!" he growled.

I waited until he removed his hand and we finally stopped walking. "Okay, Ashton. This is getting weird. I'm getting strange human vibes from you."

I felt his hands at the back of my head. "That's because of this."

The bandana was removed and after a few blinks, I saw white curtain string lights hanging from trees, familiar faces, and white rose petals all over the ground. Wanda, Tabitha, Renata, Maurie, Maggie, Keyonna, NeNe, a very pregnant Elle *with her heels still on*, Raj,

Wynter, June, Boobee, Johnnie, the construction project manager, and—

"Oh, my God," I breathed when my eyes caught him smiling, holding his oxygen mask to the side of his face. "Jimmy!" I turned to Ashton. "Are we doing a tour of the property?" Then I spun around, attention fixed on the tall trees and dirt. "Wait. Where are we exactly?" I felt silly, not knowing my own property, considering how many times Ashton and I had been up here in the last month or so.

"Apparently, on *your* property; something you're still learning, I see," Raj quipped.

A few people laughed.

Confused, I turned to Ashton. "Where are we?"

"When Jaquana showed me the property back in October, she said it only extended to the forest." He pointed toward the right. "When you gave me the blueprint last month, I found an odd outland behind that forest line. I drove back here to check it out. As you can see, it's undeveloped, but quite sizable." He dropped his head to the side and I lost his eyes. "Then a few weeks ago, when we talked about weddings, you mentioned wanting something intimate and outdoors. So..." He shrugged. "I wanted to try it out for size. Johnnie got some festive lights, and I gathered family and friends to get a feel. We can fit about a hundred and fifty people back here. What do you say?"

My eyes perused the area again. It was hard to gauge because of the trees. But bigger than that, something dawned on me. At the same time, I heard squeals from the girls. When I turned back to ask him about proposing, Ashton was down on one knee, holding my ring in the original box he gave it to me in on Valentine's Day. I'd wondered why I couldn't find it when getting dressed this morning. I wore it every day now.

"KaToria Linnaye McNabb, I don't know exactly when I fell in love with you, but I do know I've loved you since the fall of two thousand-six when you finally stopped wearing a busted weave and holes in your sneakers." Laughter rang out around us. I was too caught up in the strong memory of it, once again teleported to my freshman year at the school I hated while peering down on the most arrogant, smartest, sexiest human I'd ever met.

"But you were irresistible in a sports bra—my god, did the sight of you in one change my world forever." His face tightened, eyes squeezed closed as though tortured. "But I do know I wasn't always responsible with you. Damn, baby. We were so young and made mistakes that would cost us years of pain. But fate—or Tyler Thomas —brought us back together and"—He gestured my belly—"we've damn sure been making up in no time at all." That made me laugh. "But you owe me. You owe me a lifetime of waking up to you. You owe me arguments over the phone about stupid shit. You owe me dates on random weeknights. You owe me days and nights in the wintery mountains, sipping on rum and soaking in Jacuzzis. You owe me with help raising my girls into the leaders they're destined to be. You owe me more babies. You owe me peace of mind. You owe me partnership. You owe me forever. You owe me...you. Please tell me you're ready to kick off payment by being my wife."

My face was soaked by then, heart ringing in my chest.

"Yes, Ashton." I nodded. "God, yes!"

A heavy applause rang out around us by the small group. He pushed the ring onto my finger and, within seconds, we were crushed by two miniature people.

"Congratulations, Tori!" Maggie shouted with convincing excitement as she hugged her father.

August

Ashton

"A nigga engaged now and can't come out to play?" Launz teased.

"The baby's due in November. No way I'm flying out to Paris for no wedding when my baby's that small, man." I scratched the back of my head with one hand, held the phone to my ear with the other while deciding between two fixtures for the kitchen at the new house.

It had been a hell of a time these past five months since I stepped aboard with getting the house built. I was right: the process was overwhelming! There was always a decision to be made, materials to be picked out, or a process that got delayed. Tori had been a lot more gracious about the process than me. We were three months out from the baby being born, and damn, was the pressure on me.

In so many ways, this pregnancy felt like the first time. Tori had symptoms and changes to her body I didn't recall with Aivery. Yes. I understood why, but when I considered my girls, guilt stirred silently in my belly. Often. Tori had been my obsession lately. Not just because of the blissful period we were in, finally getting together, but because we found out the sex of the baby back in May. Another boy. *Another boy.* What were the odds? It could have gone either way for me because I'd had a boy and then two girls, but Tori had only had a boy. Bobby. We'd been in counseling—premarital and general.

This baby struck an emotional cord for us. I was pensive up until we had the Chorionic Villus Sampling screening back in April. I didn't care if I had another baby with Down's syndrome, but I truly didn't want it for Tori. Then Tori had been voicing fears of SIDS. I took her concerns seriously. My only problem was I couldn't control the occurrence of the SIDS: no one could. That's when I knew we needed help sorting shit. So we began getting help.

So between the girls, the pregnancy, the new house, trying to fit a temporary nursery in my bedroom, and work, it had been a time for me. It seemed to have been a better time for Tori, though. She seemed...peaceful. There had been rumors of her pregnancy, but we'd been local, and even when we did travel, it wasn't to high profile places. We wouldn't be able to keep the pregnancy on the low for long because she had public appearances to make soon.

"Whatever, man," Launz grunted. "I guess I'll be going alone."

"Your introverted, reclusive ass can do it. Take your sister." Like me, my friend kept it in the family, employing and investing in his circle. He was also a quieted, soulful thinker, not with the rah-rah shit.

He chuckled. "And won't she love that."

"*Ashton!*" Tori called me from the living room.

"Launz, I gotta go. Make sure your ass shows up next month. I feel like it's been forever since we hung out."

"It has been, hence me wanting you to hit this wedding with me! The fuck, man!"

I laughed. "We'll see, but my official answer is nah."

Chuckling, he replied, "A'ight, man. Be good to yourself."

"Later." I disconnected the call and went back to the fixtures. "Champagne bronze," I murmured to myself. "Yeah."

Then I made my way out into the living room of Tori's apartment. Most of her things were still here because there was no room for anything but some of her clothes at my place. Renata still stayed here sometimes, but had been spending more time at her house in Millville. She moved her mother in there a couple of months ago after she was finally released from the hospital. Sonya couldn't live on her own anymore, and the family thought it was best that she lived in the house Tori bought her cousins.

Today, we were here meeting up with Tori's friend. It had been long and overdue. The place was now littered with strangers, busying about on their phones. I knew they were handlers and immediately thought how grateful I was to have missed that phase of Tori's celebrity—although I would have endured anything to get back the years we gave away in the fits of our painful stubbornness.

"Baby," Tori beamed beautifully, extending her arm to me when I entered the living room. "Come meet the incomparable queen of pop." Brielle, a starkly beautiful woman without much makeup, remained seated behind a keyboard when I approached them. I'd heard her and her team come in and set up the equipment. Tori welcomed me by her side, immediately nestling into my arm. "BB, meet my boyfriend, babies' daddy, and fiancé, Ashton."

"I'm happy to finally make your acquaintance, Brielle." I proffered my hand to her.

When I thought she'd snap into the moment at any second, Brielle's empty expression tarried. Her mouth went lax and brows slowly hiked in the air. My forehead squeezed and I angled my head.

What the fuck's her problem...

Brielle's disdainful regard dropped to my hand. "You've been in my best friend's life for a year now. I've never met you, only heard about how you've robbed her of her heart again. Clearly, she reserved that honor for another one of her little friends who shall remain nameless—" When her honey irises with specks of evergreen rolled over to Tori, I peered over to my fiancée as well. Tori rolled her eyes, then gazed my way and winked sweetly. Brielle's regard rolled back over to me. "—you greet me with that hand?"

My face tightened even more, forcing me to pay an inspection to my hand. Again, I gazed over to Tori for answers. I'd met countless celebrities in my life—granted none of which, inarguably, were Brielle, who truly was a phenomenon like no other—and none came with the level of dramatics this one had. Immediately, I'd hope she wasn't cold like this to Keyonna. I doubted it or else my baby girl would have told me.

Finally, an unfettered flurry of giggles burst through Tori's lips. "Brielle!" she yelped, head falling back as she clutched my arm for balance. "Would you stop!" Tori couldn't stop laughing and Brielle rolled her eyes stubbornly, turning away.

I dropped my hand at this point.

"I'm so damn lost right now," I had to admit.

"Babe," Tori tried to calm down. "Back in the day when I met this *bitch*, and we got to know each other—"

"Fell in love!" Brielle's body twisted back to face us. "Get the story right, bitch!"

"Yes, girl," Tori agreed. "We did fall in love. But when we first met, I told her about the first time I saw her in concert."

"Okay?" I was still lost.

"Then when we 'fell in love,' I got more comfortable with her and told her about my first orgasm." Tori's face was lit in shameful humor at this time.

I blinked. "Okay?" I didn't get it.

"Ashton!" she screamed.

My brows narrowed. And then Brielle started playing notes on the keyboard. Tori brought my attention to her. Confused as fuck at this point, I returned my attention to her weird human of a friend. Within seconds, the chords came together in a familiar melody. That melody turned into a tune when Brielle began to riff.

"Don't make me invisible...
Don't mute our love,
Don't you forget you're the one I dream of."

My chin was to the damn floor at how effortlessly she played and sang that piece. Her eyes were closed and face taut with passion.

"Don't ask for my heart then demand even more.
Don't ignore my all...
Don't deny you're the sun my earth aches fooooor!"

Blinking hard, I looked over at Tori. There were tears in her eyes as she giggled.

Brielle rolled her eyes. "So you want something with that melody for the wedding?"

Tori nodded, then peered up to me again. "I know. It's the pregnancy."

"Yeah." Brielle exhaled hard through her upturned lips. "We're gonna have to write this one together because I've been left out of this love affair, and apparently, can't write for it alone. Glad I got the time today."

The song apparently touched her emotionally. "I didn't know it held that much significance to you."

"I told you, going to that concert changed my life. One of the first things that made me want to pursue excellence." Tori wiped her wet eyes.

"And it was, apparently, the song you got her off to," Brielle interjected.

My head swung down to Tori.

She cried, stomping her foot. "You don't remember?"

Fuck...

I did then.

September

I watched her across the open tent structured by twinkle fairy lights under the night sky. They were all over the room, along with floating candles in tall vases and cascading white and green floral arrangements. It was magical. With the help of Johnnie and his construction staff cutting down trees and leveling the ground while working on the main property, and wedding coordinator extraordinaire, Pam Hewl, this piece of land was transformed into a fairy tale.

The entire day was magical with just one hundred-thirty of our closest friends and family. Even my grandmother attended. She was even polite to Tori. Samantha White from *Blakewood* flew in with her daughter for the day, too. My wife was pleased to see them.

My wife...

Damn. The thought was natural as fuck.

"Hello, son!" my mother shouted out, twirling past me with Trent Bailey following her in a dance.

My attention flew to Jade. She was at the table chatting with Lex, the wife of Tori's pastor. Then my thoughts went to Brielle. Those two had to be seated strategically. She was on the opposite side of the room, chatting with Jackson Hunter. So long as she was occupied, Tori would be fine. Turned out, Brielle was cool—dramatic—but a sweet girl.

Then my hungry regard returned to my bride. From behind, as she leaned into a pillar in her white dress, she didn't appear pregnant at all. At thirty-four weeks, Tori's arms, ass, and legs were still defined, and she was truly all belly and nothing else—except her boobs. *Goddamn...* Those were unimaginably larger. Before meeting Tori at *BSU*, I wasn't particularly a breast-man. But since graduating, I bookmarked tits in my porn preferences in my online account. She employed a Black, small business seamstress and kept her dress simple: silk tube top, sheath-cut with a hypnotizing display of her protruded belly.

Jimmy had just wheeled up to her. His beetle eyes twinkled at her all evening, and for once, I agreed with the man. KaToria was a stunning bride. I made sure not to leave him out of this momentous chapter in our lives, not that Tori would allow me. We'd forever have significant deaths between us, staining our love story. But I wanted to believe Jimmy represented unity, if anything, in our journey.

"You can whisk her off to have what your priapic eyes are

expressing from across the room." Tyler Thomas took to my side at the bar. "Or we can go back to the eighteenth century and be like Louis XVI and Marie Antoinette, only don't do it if you can't prove your virility to perform."

I snorted, gaining the visual of Louis-Auguste not being able to get it up in front of a group of guests. "That would be some shit, huhn?"

He laughed, slapping my back. "That, it would, son. That, it would."

"Come with me. Tori and I have a question for you."

"Okay."

We made our way through elaborately decorated tables and joyous guests. My Maurie didn't even notice me as she danced with Boobee's daughter. When I made it to my bride and the innkeeper, I took her at the waist as she tittered away at something he said.

Not even startled, she reached up and behind, palming my beard. Then she met me for a kiss. "Hey, Spence." She turned in my arms.

"I told Thomas, here, we have a question for him."

Her eyes lit wildly. "Did you ask him?"

"No. That's why I brought him over."

"Oh." She turned to Tyler, who served as our officiant today. "I asked Ashton did you purposely give him the *Sports Illustrated* assignment to hook us up again or if he thought it was pure coincidence."

Tyler's head tossed back and he laughed hard as hell. "Did you hear that, Jimmy?"

Jimmy's eyes widened as he smiled. "Do tell. I'd owe you a debt of gratitude for securing the correct empress for the job."

"Well, let's put it this way," Tyler proclaimed. "It was a forgone conclusion only after he acquiesced without me having to get on my knees and beg. I was honored to preside over the nuptials of the couple who helped me keep my own marriage."

"Awwwwww! Mr. Thomas!" Tori cried before hugging him.

October

"One. Two. Three. Say cheese, ladies!" Eddie shouted to the pair, showing off their bellies for the picture.

"One more!" Young Lord's wife, Kennedi, requested, falling back into her sexy pose with Tori.

The energy blasting from the crowd out front was palpable. Brielle had the place on fire out there, ending a ballad that had been a radio hit for weeks now. The L.A. night air was special and the atmosphere magical.

"You have about forty seconds, Tori!" a tiny dude with *Coke* bottle glasses, wearing headphones with a mic attached, shouted while clutching a clipboard to his chest.

"I'm so happy to see you again!" Kennedi squeaked with pure excitement. "We tried coming to see you when you did the Ebonee Williams show in Montreal last year, but when I called, ShawnNicole said you were on the plane, heading back to your boo!" She made a silly face with crossing her eyes and flashing her tongue.

"Yeah!" Tori agreed. "Doing this!" She cupped her belly.

Tori looked gorgeous in her black leotard, tights, and thigh-high boots. Dressed in all-black, she still couldn't hide that belly. Her makeup was on thick, yet tastefully done. I almost couldn't detect her swollen nose, a symptom of pregnancy.

"That's what I was tryna do back then, but Isaak was like 'nah, son'!" She laughed along with Tori. "All he was worried about was me finishing school."

"That's sweet!" Tori gushed. "He wanted to make sure you finished before having to change diapers and be up all night with feedings."

She spoke like an experienced mother, reminding me Tori was. She'd been there with Bobby.

"Yup. But as soon as January hit, I got off that birth control. I ain't care!" Kennedi cheered. "And when it finally happened in April, I was like, 'Tada!' Yeah, buddy! The kids are so excited."

"Good for you guys! I'm happy for you, too."

"Kenny!" Young barked behind us. "She gotta go on!" Holding a red cup, he waved his wife to him.

Kennedi giggled and pulled Tori into a tight hug. "Call me, Champ!"

Brielle began her next set; the intro to her classic up-tempo dance anthem had cued.

"I will. My house will be done by Christmas. I want you guys over. Bring the kids, too!"

"Okay!" Kennedi turned to me. "Bye, Ashton. It was so nice to meet you."

"Same here." I waved my goodbye.

Then I caught eyes with Young. "A'ight, man. Stay solid!"

I issued him a salute as Tori was being called on stage. She reached over to kiss me before taking long lunges from the wing onto the stage. The crowd went wild when they recognized her. She hugged Brielle immediately, then waved to the audience of nearly twenty thousand screaming fans. Brielle dropped to her knees, kissing Tori's belly, and the crowd ate that up, too. I watched my wife do an extended dance sequence for the next fifteen minutes or so with my body tensed as a motherfucker. What was I thinking, not saying no to this shit? Yes, Tori was hella athletic. The woman was strong, even giving me a little work with arm-wrestling when I'd had five too many—though her ass never won. But Tori was still a woman in a fragile state at thirty-seven weeks pregnant.

By the time, she sashayed off stage, sweat dripping, chest heaving, yet with an accomplished beam, I was fucking fuming.

When she made it to me, her face dropped. "What's wrong?"

"What the fuck was that, McNabb?"

On the ride back to the house we rented, the energy was vastly different from the *Staples Center*. No deafening shouts from fans begging for autographs, flashing cameras...

No dancing in high heels...

It was only soft music and nighttime lights attempting to pierce through the tinted windows of the limo truck as we rode in silence on the 110, en route to Ranchos Palos Verdes. She was on her phone, scrolling as I did the same. I'd missed the last text Maurie sent, asking to get a picture with Brielle. I'd have to ask Tori for one or find one online; they took a million of them. Right now, I just wanted to get my wife to bed and off her damn feet she admitted were swollen after her little dance number on stage.

Next to me, Tori snickered.

"What's so damn funny?"

"Deon. The baby's his."

"Word?"

"He had that Miranda chick jump through hoops for a paternity test until the judge made him." Tori laughed.

A few months ago, Deon filed charges for extortion, having all the evidence he believed he needed when she requested money for a fourth time. Apparently, he didn't have it, leaving him no choice but to let her go public. They were still tied up in court, but as Tori and I had been getting the house built, planning a quick wedding, and taking on other professional pursuits, her name was all up in the media thanks to Deon's infidelity. Through it all, Tori kept her head up, growing belly out, and engagement ring that was soon joined by a wedding band glistening. She was right. Tori flaunted her new life in her own way. And of course, my identity was revealed last week once wedding pictures were leaked. I had a sneaking suspicion it was done by Tori via Elle, but didn't ask.

"Did you leak those pictures?" I guess I had to know.

Now showered, changed and without makeup, Tori peered up at me. The truth was in her wild eyes as she sat up.

Then a Cheshire cat smile slowly stretched her face. Tori tossed her phone farther down on the bench. She crawled on her knees and walked between my wide-stretched legs.

"If I lie, will you get as mad at me as you did earlier when you cussed me out? Or this time, will you spank me?"

"I don't spank the twins, but I'll beat your ass, Nabby-girl." I used her common threat to me back in school.

"I'd like to see that," her voice low, femininely husky.

"Tori, don't play with me."

Her hands moved to the buckle of my belt, releasing it. Next was the unbuttoning of my jeans.

"I'm a thirty-two-year-old bad bitch, Spence. Playing is for kids."

Her hands worked my growing cock out of the opening of my pants. Tori reached up and kissed me. As her tongue moved in my mouth, her hands fisted my cock, thickening me. Her full, glossed lips moved silkily against me, tongue caressing mine with growing hunger. When she left my mouth, I felt torn between having her pleasure in my mouth or on my dick. My dick won out. Tori kissed my shaft while ringing me just beneath the ridge. She took her time tonguing my head. The visual of her making love to my cock was a turn-on alone, then add her bountiful cleavage in view and I was taken.

Faith Evans' *"Kissing You"* played in the background, its crescendo speaking to my life. As my head rolled to the side, eyes pinched closed, I couldn't believe I was in the back of a truck getting head by a pregnant Tori McNabb. She was a tomboy from *Blakewood*, a trailer park chick I enjoyed making happy and manipulating when she rejected my friendship. She was my crush and the world's champ. And she was kissing me.

What made our love special wasn't *BSU*. Fuck NormaJean and, respectfully, fuck Aivery, too. While I wished they both were still alive and healthy, they were not what made us special either. It was the muted love we shared for each other unexpectedly. The love so powerful, we made a son. Tori and I created together and hurt one another. Now, we had the rest of our lives to live out our reckless hope.

Her mewls drove me wild and slurps had my balls tingling. I grabbed her at the back of her head, guiding her drives. Tori fisted and pumped into her mouth until I felt the back of her throat. My head flew back, damn hips suspended over the leather seat, and I exploded in her mouth. The rolling of my abs was uncontrolled, not dissimilar to my love for this girl.

Tori wiped her mouth with the side of her hand. "Who's playing with who now?"

Still half-delirious and panting, I fell into laughter with her. She was so damn cute.

She returned to her seat beside me and when I could move, I put myself back together. Tori went back to her phone and I was ready to doze the hell off, having been administered my sedative. Maybe I was a bit harsh backstage. Just when I closed my eyes, being lulled by the engine and smooth ride, my phone vibrated. Azmir Jacobs had texted me.

It was a picture of Tori on stage next to Brielle, swinging her crotch in the air, wearing a seductive expression. Tori's eyes were slanted and her index finger was on her protracted tongue lewdly. Funny what a picture could capture. It was what Tori looked like when giving me head. The way she just had. Beneath the picture was a message.

A.D.J.: *Those Asè Garb MeMe's gotta be about 5.5. Checkmate, bitch.*

Fuck...

December

Tori

"Yeah, Treesh. Thanks."

"Alright. Don't forget to call me when y'all decide about Christmas. I miss y'all."

I nod. "Uhn-huhn."

I hang up the phone and a pending heavy breath leaves my lungs as I stare at the wall of my bedroom.

"Hey," he drones behind me, big hands on my naked back. His sound and touch soothes and tempts. "You good."

I turn to him lying beside me in bed, naked, too. My shaken

heart's warring with the peace he brings. Then the sight of a new errant gray hair makes me spurt out a giggle. Ashton's too concerned to join me in my sudden mood change. It could be because I'm fighting tears with all my might.

"You have another wisdom hair." I smile, amazed at his beauty.

Ashton is still the most handsome man I've ever known. It isn't just his looks; it's his style, the swag of his arrogance, and his brilliant mind. I've learned so much in business from him in the fifteen months I've been his wife. This man has expanded me financially, physically, and emotionally.

"McNabb," he demands. "What is it? What did Treesha say?"

My hand sweeps down his hairy chest as my eyes fall. "Paul died of a stroke yesterday."

"Paul?"

I blink, the incoming words feel foreign. "My mother's ex..." My regard rolls back up to his face.

Ashton's eyes bounce until realization washes over him. "*Shit*," he breathes. Then he looks at me. "Does that make you sad?"

I take a moment to think about Tangi and Raquel and what they must be feeling losing a parent. My father and I have been a little distant since I confronted him last year about financing his outside child, but I'd be sad if he were to die. When my mother passed away, it was a loss for me. So, I can't imagine them being immune to his loss.

Then I'm reminded of his touch, scent, taste, and sounds. They haunted me well into my adult years. I can still hear his voice when I allow my mind to go there. Those painful memories almost caused me to lose in life. My confusion about who I was almost made me miss Ashton back in college when I discovered my sexuality. It could have caused me to never have conceived and met Bobby. I think about all the people I have around me today who give me a new name, title, and sense of worth.

And suddenly, the sadness of having learned of Paul's death dissipates.

The tears recede and a flutter courses my belly. "You make me so happy."

Ashton sits up, then leans over to kiss me. "C'mon. We've gotta do this before the troops head out."

I'm still smiling behind him as he leaves our California king mattress he was insistent on getting when we finally furnished the place almost a year ago. "Okay."

"Middle school's so hard!" Maggie pouts over the kitchen table.

She's in an *Ellis Academy* where the curriculum challenges young minds but never leaves one behind, per their motto.

"Even if what you're saying is true, you're tougher than what you perceive to be so hard." Pouring my morning protein shake into a glass, I inspect her with hard eyes. "What did I tell you about school?"

"That my brain is built for it," she murmurs.

"That's right. Come on." I make my way to the door. "Dad's been waiting for us in the family room."

From the main hall of the first floor, I hear my baby's chatter. His voice melts my heart every morning. It means I have another day with him. Before his first birthday last month, I'd been counting down the days to where SIDS was no longer a possibility. As omen as it sounds, I've gotten so much better with the anxiety of it. I spoke to Bishop Carmichael several times and his take on it is my need of increasing my faith. My fear tells me I'm helpless to circumstances I can't control. Faith tells me not to fear when God's in control. Each day had been less of a battle, but one nonetheless.

"Here I come, Robbie!" Maggie cuts past me, skipping down the hall, even performing a cool cartwheel on the way.

Maggie may still be adjusting to being in a new home with me at the helm with her father, but she loves her brother. She resisted him for only a week after we brought him home to Ashton's place, something we struggled with. He wanted me as comfortable as possible, and the best place for that would have been my place until the house was done about two months later. But I had to remember Maurie and Maggie. The baby was their brother and they needed to bond with him ASAP. My insistence paid off. Of course, Maurie adored him the moment she laid eyes on him, but Maggie was obsessed with the little guy. Me? She's still working on, but my son gives me a little leeway with her.

When I make it to the gargantuan family room where NeNe, who stayed the night, is curled up in the armchair, typing into her laptop, and the kids are crowding Ashton on the sofa, I see it's normal play in the Spencer household. Maurie's at his left knee, trying to get the baby's attention. Maggie's sitting next to the baby, who's standing up on the sofa. Ashton's eating his breakfast sandwich—*without a darn plate!*

Ashton Robert "Robbie" Spencer has his own agenda set as he stands on one chubby leg and reaches over to bite into his father's sandwich. "Mmmmm!" He rubs his belly.

Immediately after, Ashton takes an even bigger bite. Then Robbie comes in for another bite and laughs at his dad. "Mmmm!" he expresses again and the girls eat it up, amazed by everything the boy does.

We all are. He's beautiful, perfect like his big brother. I couldn't shake the name Robert from my son's legacy. I'd never met Mr. Robert Spencer but from what I'd learned about the man years ago, he was a victor through tragedy. I imagined he was misunderstood by his parents all his life and was certainly not fully accepted by them as an adult. The man wasn't even understood or fully accepted by his son. Still, he shouldered through his rocky foundation and created a legacy by way of a fast food chain restaurant that would extend to the fruit of my loins; a nobody tomboy from a trailer park in a little-known town. Robert Spencer's life embodied the American dream and had inspired me.

"Okay!" Ashton announces, still chewing. "Before you guys leave for school this morning, it's about that time for our holiday planning and we have a few announcements to make."

NeNe looks up from her computer. "You're coming out of retirement?"

My face wrinkles and I shake my head. I've been enjoying retirement life. At most, I've missed the regularity of high endurance training. I resumed as much as I could two months after having Robbie, but the demands of parenting three children and running my other businesses made it challenging. I've mostly been working out in the gym here at the house.

"What's the first announcement, Daddy?" Maggie asks.

Ashton's eyes bear into me. "The first is, Tori and I are opening a new restaurant."

"When?" Maurie asks.

"Where?" NeNe follows up with.

I answer, "We're hoping for a soft opening next fall. We spotted a location about twenty-five miles from here, closer to metropolitan cities."

"But the purpose of it is having a low key location, mellow atmosphere, and with a running menu that'll be created by us."

"It'll be our touch on fine foods, even if it's a burger," I add.

"You guys will be working there?" Maggie gasps.

Ashton shares, "We'll have trained chefs who'll be led by us as we rotate the menu."

"That's dope. Me and my friends will have a place to come up and hang out at."

My head starts to shake before she's done. "This'll be an exclusive menu and environment. It will specifically repel a certain clientele. It's for everyday people with a specific palate. Not overly expensive—"

"But not your *TGI Fridays* or *Applebee's* either," Ashton qualifies.

I'm excited simply at the thought of it.

"What're you gonna name it?" Maggie asks.

Ashton looks to me again and I can't help my gushing. "*Bobby's.*"

"Like your foundation." NeNe shakes her head. "Cool."

"Who's Bobby?" Maurie asks and the girls laugh.

That made Robbie laugh before he went for another bite of his father's sandwich.

"Okay," Ashton moves along. "Christmas. Where are we going to spend it?"

"Here at home!" Maggie quickly offers before play-biting the side of her brother's back.

Ashton's face wrinkles. "Really?"

"Yeah," Maurie agrees, wiping her nose. "Let's do it here."

"Not in Colorado?" Ashton's stunned, and honestly, so am I.

"This is our new place, Daddy," Maggie explains. "And Christmas will actually be fun with Robbie this year. We got this brand new place. We can have everyone here."

"Yeah," Maurie seconds the notice.

"What about your grandparents, aunt, and cousins?" Ashton asks.

Maurie shrugs. "We can invite them."

"We have enough room," Maggie agrees. "This place is huge! Sherell doesn't believe me when I try to tell her." It bothers me that the girls don't refer to Aivery's sister with "aunt" as the prefix. It's something Treesha has them doing with her and Renata, which, in my opinion, was optional. Even June and Tabitha had them give them that title in their names. But for their real aunt, it was weird to me they didn't. She was the only biological one the girls had. Ashton told me it wasn't something the Coopers did, so I dropped it. "Wait till she sees the pool!"

"Yeah, and our playroom!" Maurie beams.

In disbelief, Ashton peers over at me again. I nod, feeling the girls have spoken. Would I have Aivery's family in my home? Regretfully, yes. It was still my karma. I simply wouldn't allow them to disrespect me or my family. And they'd have to stay in a hotel. That was my concession. But I know they'll likely decline. The Coopers, particularly Aivery's mother and sister, are still having a hard time accepting Ashton and me. And I simply don't care.

"Girls!" the new nanny, Ms. Kim, calls, entering the family room beside me. "It's time for us to go! The car's warming up." She smiles affectionately. "Robbie, I'll be right back for your sensory play!" she speaks so sweetly to him.

"Wait!" Maggie's hands pump in the air. "What about the rest of the announcements, Daddy?"

Once again, Ashton's eyes meet mine. This time, I'm gushing like mad. I've had my struggles in life and worked hard to overcome as best as I could. People like Paul may have disrupted my innocence and development, but I still have the life women like NormaJean would have killed for. I have the love that even Aivery Cooper attempted but never had in Ashton. Again, he's expanded me beyond my wildest dreams. Never again will I struggle with the loneliness I was once plagued with.

His eyes beam with so much pride and desire when he shares, "We're having another baby." Ashton points to me.

"Where?" NeNe asks in shock. "I don't see no bump?"

"She's still in her first trimester. With her athletic body, we probably won't see the bump for a couple of months, like with Robbie." He couldn't stop grinning and neither could I.

I mouth to him, *happy human*. Ashton tosses me a wink.

Another baby. I can't believe it myself, but I've been wanting it. I want even more babies—maybe two more. Thankfully, now I have the means to care for children, unlike when I was a kid myself wanting them. And I have the best partner to assist me with the task.

"Oh, no!" Maggie stood. "Not again! Another baby?"

"Congratulations, Tori!" Maurie smiles tightly, twisting my heart. She's everything.

"Thank you, baby girl!" I murmur and blow her a kiss.

"This is ridiculous," Maggie claims. "I'm calling Glammom!"

"What's wrong with another baby, Maggie?" NeNe asks.

"Yeah," Ashton agrees. "You love Robbie."

Maggie turns back to them. "Yeah, I do, but Tori needs a break, and so do we. Babies are a lot of work!" She turns to me before storming out. "We're perfect just as we are. This is starting to be as hard as middle school. God!"

And she takes off trailing fumes behind, leaving all the adults in the room with puzzled expressions. Everyone except me. I'm elated.

I slap my hands together. "Okay! That was productive!" I laugh. "You guys are off to school, and NeNe and I are off to work out! No angry humans here!"

And with that, I spiritedly leave out, too, dancing while sipping on my shake.

My karma...

###

The End

#PenningWithoutParameters
#ImGonnaMakeYouLoveMe

ASHTON AND TORI

www.LoveBelvin.com
See visuals from the series here on my website – https://www.
lovebelvin.com/projects/mutedhoplessness

~LOVE ACKNOWLEDGES

***Visuals:* 365 Photography** – Brooklyn! I worked your nerves for this one, and I can't promise I won't for the next, but what I do know is that our art does a beautiful dance together. Thanks so much for lending your creativity to bring my vision to life! **Fierce Faces** – Kaydene, you kicked me to the curb this time, but it was needed! BK knows all of my colors by now. I'm so fortunate to have your awesome talent to collaborate with. Thanks for your artistry and patience (I didn't get cussed out this time). DJ & Corrye, thanks so much for serving as visuals for our Ashton and Tori. Thanks for allowing me to be a part of your successful journeys. My best to you in all your endeavors!

Researcher: Shumethia S. — Thanks for your availability and wonderful energy. You're an amazing human.

Beta Reader: — Yorubia, words cannot express my appreciation for you. One day. Soon come.

LBTR — Afi, Angela J.J., Artemysia, Ashley, Ayanna, Bonita, Brittany, Courtney, Danielle, Denise, DeVona, Diva Dee, Doris, Ericka M., Gail, Grace, Heather, Heidi, Hyacinth, Jasmine, Kamashia, Karmen, Katrina, Kendra, Kerry, Keyma, Kim, Kimmiko, Kita, Korei, Lafay, LaSonde, Linda R., Linda W., Malaika, Marshall,

Michelle R.O., Michelle T., Mocha, Monique H., Monique N., Natoya, Nena, Nikki, Rakia, Quan, Regina, Richell, Rose, Roslyn, Samona, Sharon L., Sharon F.W., Shaun, Sophia, Stacey, Tanisha, Tara, Teresa, Terri G., Tesha, Tiffany, Tineka, Tonya, Tralaina, Vivian, Wendi, Yolanda P., Yolanda U., and Yorubia, I love you guys for being my home base. Many of you provide feedback, whether it's good or bad, and always with love and a sense of commitment to me. It's very rare in this game. Thanks for being that core of support.

Jemeka & ***Rita***: Countless have come and gone. Thanks so much for staying and having my back. Love you!

LB Universe Librarians – Roslyn & Tina, I have NO idea how to write a book without your references anymore. Yes, it's made me lazy, but more efficient, too. Thank you so much!

Christina C. Jones aka CCJ — You've been a wonderful ride companion in my career. Love you.

Interior Artist: Cedeara Ardell — Thanks, baby girl, for the imagery you've designed for my books! Love you always!

Proof Reader: Tina V. Young — Once again, you killed my self-diagnosed dyslexia. I appreciate your dedication to keeping me together. And thanks for all the college and pro football knowledge, per usual, making me look smart to the world!

Editors: Zakiya Walden of *I've Got Something to Say!* — You were less bossy to me this time, but ever so hard on Ashton and Dre. LOL!!!

Santisha Taylor of *AccuProse Editing Services* — I failed again. Again I failed. But you're learning my voice more and more. Thanks so much for your patience and much needed knowledge.

MDT: I may not publish when you wanna, but I'm "write" on time.

Master, my *Jireh*, my *Rohi*, Psalms 139:16 (NIV) "Your eyes saw my unformed body; all the days ordained for me were written in your book before one of them came to be." *Thank you, Father.*